Sammy Rambles
and the
Floating Circus

To Freddie,

Validus Aereus Draco

J T SCOTT

Praise for the Sammy Rambles series:

"The JK Rowling of the South West" - Brad Burton,
The UK's #1 Motivational Business Speaker

"A tale of finding yourself and achieving great things, the Sammy Rambles series of books keep readers of any age hooked through the myriad of adventures. JT Scott is the modern-day fantasy author whose stories are being brought to life by youngsters in the sports hall and playgrounds around the world." - Caroline Bramwell, Author of 'Loo Rolls to Lycra' and Inspirational Speaker

"Two hours to do the school run tonight. Sammy Rambles to the rescue, I turned on my Sammy Rambles and the Floating Circus audio book and kept everyone happy." - Francis, Plymouth.

"I loved it, only problem was I couldn't put it down. It's the first time in ages I have spent the entire day ignoring work and reading it from cover to cover." - L. Watts

"Great to hear about these fantastic books!" - Councillor Terri Beer (Cabinet Member for Children and Young People).

"It's a fantastic read, Lily is totally engrossed in the story, as am I! It's a huge hit here! We're looking forward to reading the rest of the Sammy Rambles books." – Jayne W.

"I've read all of the books and I'm starting to read them again. I think they're really good. They have a good story to them and they have a meaning behind them as well about the bullying and it can encourage other people to stand up for themselves." – Natasha, Dragonball Player

"A great read. Jenny has a very vivid imagination. Her descriptive writing style makes it easy to create your own picture in your mind. Looking forward to reading the rest of the series." – Peter Clarke

"If you've read the Floating Circus you'll know how captivating the story is! It draws you in on every page. A book for all ages. Great on every level." – G. Singh

"Sammy Rambles and the Floating Circus is a beautifully written and well-crafted story. It's pacy and a 'page turner' with unexpected twists and turns. Gentle writing and great fun!" – Amazon reader.

"I bought this book on a Friday. By Sunday I'd finished reading it. OK, so I'm not a child any more (a grandfather now, actually) but as a fan of Tolkein & Lewis, this appealed to me and I was not disappointed." – Amazon reader.

"I bought as a present for my grandson who loves dragons. It's been a fun bedtime story for us both." – Amazon reader.

Sammy Rambles and the Floating Circus

Sammy Rambles Dragon Talks

If you love the Sammy Rambles books, ask your school, library or club if you can have a Dragon Talk and learn about the Sammy Rambles journey.

Find out how the Sammy Rambles books were created from pen and paper to published. Learn about the origins of the character names and the inspiration for the places in the Dragon World. Plus, create your own Dragon Story and win prizes! Find more details at the back of this book.

Dragonball

Dragonball is the sport Sammy Rambles and his friends play in the books, but it's now a real-life all-inclusive sport anyone can play!

For more information or to book a game, please visit www.dragonball.uk.com.

Dragon Shop

You'll find lots of exciting things in the Sammy Rambles Dragon Shop, including soft toy dragons, colour-changing mugs, t-shirts, keyrings, badges, magnets and much more at www.sammyrambles.com.

J T SCOTT

J T Scott lives in Cornwall with Ari and Sam surrounded by open countryside, sandy beaches, lots of historical castles, pens, paper and a very vivid imagination.

Also available in the Sammy Rambles series:

Sammy Rambles and the Floating Circus
Sammy Rambles and the Land of the Pharaohs
Sammy Rambles and the Angel of 'El Horidore
Sammy Rambles and the Fires of Karmandor
Sammy Rambles and the Knights of the Stone Cross

Find out more about Sammy, Dixie and Darius and their adventures on the Sammy Rambles website.

www.sammyrambles.com

Sammy Rambles and the Floating Circus

Chapter List:

For Ari & Sam

CHAPTER 1

THE RAT CATCHERS

It was a warm sunny July afternoon outside Ratisbury School for seven to eleven year olds. In the Music Hall, there was the sound of the school choir practicing for a concert on Saturday and the rustle of papers in the fifth-year classrooms as the older pupils turned over their end of year exam papers. Birds sang in the trees outside and there was the faint sound of the school gardener mowing the sports field beyond the Gymnasium. Outside, it was a very peaceful afternoon.

Inside the Science building however, things were very different. A group of boys and girls from the top year were exercising their out-of-class privileges and were chasing a small blond haired boy wearing some torn white shirt and mud stained trousers along the long corridor on the ground floor.

When they were caught later, they would accuse the boy of breaking the rules and running away. The teachers knew they had a problem with Ratisbury's out-of-class privileges getting out of hand. They knew these students called themselves the "Rat Catchers" empowering themselves to police the school. They also knew that the Rat Catchers terrified the younger students into giving them lunch money, homework answers, anything the Rat Catchers fancied.

In turn, the Rat Catchers knew that on the last day of term, the teachers could do absolutely nothing about it.

At the end of the corridor, the boy ran faster down the narrow hallway. Notices flew off the notice board as he brushed past them. A group of the youngest pupils in the school leapt aside as he ran past.

'Get him!' yelled one of the Rat Catchers. 'Don't let him get away!'

The boy dragged the glass door open and ran, puffing, out of the Science building. The Rat Catchers were about twenty paces behind him, shouting about how they would take his school bag, his money, even his shoes and socks. The boy ran faster than ever, the school gates in sight.

A large green Range Rover was parked on the kerb next to other cars where mothers and fathers were waiting for their sons and daughters.

The boy jumped the three steps down to the gate and heaved open the passenger door.

'Hello Sammy,' said the woman in the driver's seat.

'We have to go Mum,' said the boy with dirty blond hair. 'Please.'

The woman gave her son the same concerned look that she had given him the day before. She pulled the gear stick out of "park" and swung the car off the kerb. The suspension creaked as they joined the road.

The boy looked back in the mirror. The Rat Catchers were at the school gates shaking their fists. One of them was holding a hockey stick to the throat of another boy, someone from his class. Another Rat Catcher held up a school bag, the contents scattering on to the floor.

'I have to leave that school Mum,' said the blond haired boy, 'I have to go.'

'I know Sammy,' said the woman, 'I know.'

CHAPTER 2

A NEW SCHOOL

Later that night, Sammy was tucked tightly into bed. His parents had said goodnight at ten o'clock. His mother had kissed a bruise on his forehead. They had both returned an hour later to check on him but Sammy found that he still couldn't sleep. He couldn't stop thinking about why the Rat Catchers picked on him.

'It's not fair,' Sammy whispered to a large stuffed dragon he had been given by his uncle on his last birthday. 'Just because my Mum works in the bank, they think I've got money.'

He squeezed the dragon's front paws, staring into its coal black eyes. 'I can't go back,' he told the dragon. 'No. I *won't* go back.'

Downstairs, he could hear his parents watching television. It was nearly eleven o'clock and he knew his mother would be catching up with the soaps she had recorded earlier in the evening. His father would be pouring a glass of brandy whilst they discussed what to do about Ratisbury.

It happened almost every night. Sammy knew this because he had often sat at the top of the stairs looking into the lounge. His parents went over the same things about how he kept coming home with torn clothes and bruises. They discussed the school, the teachers, even the school governors who only showed up once a year at prize giving.

His parents had agreed that the school was no good, but they hadn't yet done anything about it.

Sammy heard the television switch off and knew that they would be coming up to bed. He pulled the toy dragon close to his cheek and closed his eyes.

Sammy woke to the sound of his parents shouting downstairs. From the snippets he caught as he lay shaking in bed, they were still arguing about schools. His parents were always torn between wanting him to stand up for himself and wanting to take him to another school.

'You don't know it will be any better,' Sammy heard his father shouting. 'It might be worse!'

'Nothing's worse than Ratisbury. Just look in the papers!' his mother screamed. 'No son of mine should be bullied like that. He has to go to another school.'

'Fine, Julia!' yelled Sammy's father. 'I'll make some calls.'

There was a slam of a door and it suddenly went quiet.

Sammy took as long as possible to get dressed. Even though he would miss his favourite Saturday cartoons, it was worth it to avoid his parents arguing.

About half an hour later, he crept downstairs into the kitchen. His mother was outside hanging the remains of his school uniform on the washing line to dry. His father was in the lounge talking on the telephone.

'Hello Mrs Hubar...Yes, it's Charles Rambles. I'm looking for a new school, yes, Sam...mm...you do? Well, as soon as possible…that's good…thank you. We'll visit this afternoon.'

Sammy filled a bowl with Sugarcorn Flakes. Amongst the flakes, a plastic toy fell out of the box. Sammy took it out of its wrapper and set it on the worktop. It was part of the set he was collecting; a tiny blue-green dragon.

He took his cereal and the dragon into the lounge and curled up on the settee opposite his father. He took two mouthfuls before he noticed that he had forgotten to add any milk.

His father put down the telephone. 'Sam?'

Sammy looked up. 'What?'

'Your mother and I have decided that you should change schools.' His father looked uncomfortable. 'These Rat-thingys. I think you should stand up for yourself, but we have agreed to try another school…'

Sammy took a deep breath.

'On the condition,' his father continued, 'that you will stick with this school. Even if it is ten times worse. You have to learn to stand up for yourself.' Sammy's father looked across at him and smiled. 'Can you do that Sam?'

Behind his bowl of cereal Sammy grinned. 'When do I start?'

His father frowned. 'I have made some calls and there are three schools that may be suitable, although I should warn you, two are boarding schools. You would live away from home.'

Sammy stared. 'Boarding school?'

'Yes. I enjoyed it very much when I was your age. Gave me my confidence and you'll find you'll have friends in the evenings and at weekends as well.'

'Boarding school?' repeated Sammy, wondering if Ratisbury was that bad after all.

'It has been decided.' Sammy's father put down his paper and frowned. 'Fetch your mother and we'll leave when you've finished eating.' Sammy's father frowned harder when he looked at the cereal. 'You're allowed milk, you know.'

Twenty minutes later, Sammy found himself sitting in the back of his parents Range Rover. His mother was driving, his father barking instructions, eyes glued to the map.

'Next left Julia,' said Sammy's father, 'and we should be…'

Sammy looked up from his magazine. His mother brought the Range Rover to an emergency stop.

'My son is not going there!' she screeched.

Sammy looked out of the window. They had stopped outside a set of tall iron gates with razor wire wrapped from top to bottom. The gates were joined on iron hinges to a red brick wall that stretched high above the Range Rover. Multi-coloured graffiti obscenities peppered the wall as far as the eye could see.

'Is that to keep people out?' whispered Sammy.

'Speak up Samuel,' said Sammy's father. 'Don't mumble.'

'Leave him Charles. Sammy's right. This school is most certainly not suitable.'

'Fine,' snapped Sammy's father, 'drive on.'

Sammy peered over his father's shoulder. He had put a large black cross next to "St. Stephen's School for Boys." Underneath with a question mark was "Adrian Smythers School for Nature and Nurture."

Sammy's mother started the car and pulled a three-point turn.

'Through town, then left at the traffic lights.' Sammy's father unrolled his newspaper and started reading.

Sammy put down his magazine hoping that the Adrian Smythers school wouldn't be any good either. He didn't like the sound of "Nature and Nurture". The only nature he liked was watching documentaries on television at school.

As they went through town, Sammy waved to one of his Ratisbury classmates shopping with his mother. After an incident with the Rat Catchers, Philip Humphreys had a neck brace and his right arm in a sling.

The Range Rover came to a stop at the traffic lights.

'Right, wasn't it Charles?'

Sammy's father didn't look up from the paper.

'It was left Mum.'

Sammy's mother changed lanes. 'Thanks honey.'

About two miles later, they were out into the countryside. Sammy's father rolled up his newspaper. 'Left at the traffic lights.'

Sammy's mother clicked her tongue. 'Where next?'

Sammy's father rustled with the map. 'It was back there on the left.'

'There was no school there.'

Sammy shook his head, 'I didn't see anything Dad.'

'Too busy with that magazine of yours I expect.'

'You drive honey,' soothed Sammy's mother, 'I'm sure you'll find it.'

They switched places and Charles Rambles pulled the car away from the hedge. They stopped five minutes later next to another set of gates with a tiny plaque that read "Adrian Smythers school for Nature and Nurture. Closed until further notice."

'Oh,' said Sammy's mother, 'that can't be right.' She got out of the car and pushed open the gate.

Sammy pressed the button to open his window. It stopped at half way and he leaned out to see if he could find out what had happened to the school. His mother was talking to a woman dressed from head to toe in a black robe. He leaned out further.

'Sit back Samuel. It's rude to stare.' Sammy's father sniffed loudly and took out his black pen. Sammy knew the Adrian Smythers School for Nature and Nurture was about to be crossed off the list.

Sammy's father started the car as his mother got back into the Range Rover.

'It's no good Charles. They closed six weeks ago due to lack of interest. She said that we were the third set of parents from Ratisbury calling in today…'

'Mm.'

'…and they need twenty-five students to qualify for subsidised running costs.'

Sammy's father snorted. 'Let's try the last one then.'

'After lunch Charles. I'm sure Sammy's getting hungry.'

Sammy nodded hoping his parents would stop for burgers and chips.

'If the next one's no good, he'll have to go back to Ratisbury.'

Sammy shuddered. 'I'm not going back.'

'You'll do what you're told,' his father's voice came from the driver's seat.

Sammy was glad to stop for lunch at the Draconian Arms, an old inn run by a woman called Anne Witherton, who had gone to school with his mother, and her husband Ronan. Sammy thought Ronan Witherton had a dragonish face, the smokiest clothes and the worst breath that he had ever smelt.

As usual, Anne and Ronan came out to meet them from the gravel car park. Sammy followed behind as his father and Ronan. Although they didn't really get on, they talked about the weather and whether it was a good time of year to go fishing. His mother had already linked arms with Anne and was half walking, half skipping up the stone steps into the restaurant.

Anne and Ronan showed Sammy and his parents to their usual table, away from the main tables in a quiet alcove. A young blonde waitress brought them menus written in Gothic script that was almost impossible to read.

'Can I get you any drinks?' she asked with a lisp.

'No thankths,' said Charles, highlighting her lisp and making the waitress blush. 'I'll have the sthteak,' he continued, 'and my wife will have…'

'The chicken, thank you honey,' said Julia, 'and burger and chips for our son.'

Sammy grinned. 'May I have a cola as well…please,' he added feeling his father's frosty glare. "With good manners," he had been told on many occasions, "you can get almost anything you want." He sat back in the comfy chair and wished he had brought his magazine from the car.

An hour later, his father was sipping a large brandy counting out twenty pound notes to cover the bill for the meal. He scattered a handful of coins on the plate and helped Sammy's mother back into her fur coat.

Minutes later they were waving goodbye to Anne and Ronan. Sammy sniffed his jumper sleeve. As usual it stank of tobacco. He screwed up his nose and opened his magazine.

Charles unfolded the map. 'St. Elderberries High School is about three hours away. Anyone need the toilet?'

Sammy shook his head. Sammy's mother started the car.

It was almost dark when they arrived at the gates of St. Elderberries High School. An elderly looking man with a short grey beard was talking to a small woman wearing a long black tunic with matching wide brimmed hat and silk scarf.

They moved aside as Sammy's mother pulled the Range Rover onto the kerb, dangerously close to their ankles.

Sammy's father leapt out of the car almost before it had stopped. 'Mrs Hubar? Good evening. My name is Charles Rambles. I telephoned earlier about a place at St. Elderberries for my son.'

The woman peered into the back of the car and chuckled. 'Oh dear,' she said, shaking her head. 'When you said "Sam," I assumed you meant Samantha. This is a school for girls.'

'Do you mean to tell me,' demanded Charles Rambles, clicking his tongue violently, 'that we have driven all day to find this place and now you tell me it isn't suitable!'

'My friend here might be able to help you though,' interrupted Mrs Hubar. 'He's the headmaster of a mixed school, not far from here.'

From inside the car Sammy couldn't quite see his father's face, but he could imagine he wasn't best pleased. He hated anything not going to plan. Sammy craned his neck to hear the conversation.

'My name is Sir Lok Ragnarok,' said the man. 'As Mrs Hubar says, I am headmaster of a mixed boarding school. I would be happy to take on your son's education. There are always places for talented students.'

Charles Rambles paused for a second. 'Very well then, it's settled.'

Sammy saw the bearded man give his father a business card.

'Directions are on the back,' he said and to Sammy's amazement, as his father turned to pass the business card to his mother through the open window, both the woman and the man shimmered in a gold haze and disappeared.

'The 6th of September?' Sammy's father turned around. 'Hey! Where have you gone?'

'They just disappeared,' said Sammy helpfully.

'I can see that.'

'Perhaps we should go back home and try again tomorrow, dear?'

'No.' said Charles Rambles firmly. 'Samuel is going to that school if it's the last thing he does. I'm sick of traipsing around on a wild goose chase. This place, this…' he peered at the business card, 'this Dragamas, will be just fine. My son is talented and he's going there.'

Julia Rambles started the car and they drove home almost in silence. The only sounds above the engine were the swish of Sammy turning the pages in his magazine, even though he was too excited to read, and the clicking as his father tapped and twisted Sir Lok Ragnarok's business card for Dragamas.

CHAPTER 3

SIX WEEKS LATER

'Morning Sammy!'

Sammy rubbed his eyes. He was in bed having just slept his last night at home before setting off to his new school. In the corner of his bedroom was a large grey suitcase with his initials "S.R.R." sewn in large green stitches in the top right hand corner.

Inside the suitcase were five new white shirts, two pairs of new black trousers, ten pairs of new black socks and a selection of his own clothes: jeans, t-shirts, jumpers and a baseball cap.

The items carefully followed a list on the back of the business card his father had been given six weeks ago, at the start of the summer holiday, even down to the contents of the wash bag that lay on top of the suitcase ready for their last use in the family bathroom.

'Are you awake honey?'

Sammy couldn't ignore his mother for long. She had promised him a special breakfast of sausages, bacon, hash browns and fried bread before setting off for Dragamas. By the delicious smell wafting up from the kitchen, it was nearly ready.

'Coming!' he shouted. He grabbed the wash kit and headed for the bathroom.

'Slow down Sam.' Charles Rambles' voice was muffled through the bathroom door and drowned by the buzz of his electric razor. 'I'll be out in a minute. Make sure you wash properly this morning. Create a good impression.'

Behind the door, Sammy grinned and squashed his fingers against his thumb. 'A good impression,' he said, waiting patiently for the door to open.

Following his father's advice, Sammy arrived downstairs looking perfect. Charles Rambles nodded approvingly from behind his paper. 'Looking good Sam. Just keep your breakfast away from your shirt, eh?'

Sammy grinned. He had swarms of butterflies in his stomach that he decided were both nerves and excitement. He found that between checking each mouthful to make sure none spilled and checking the time, he could hardly eat anything.

'Are you all right Sammy?'

'I'm fine Mum.'

'Nerves I expect.'

'I'm ok, honestly.'

Sammy felt his mother staring at him. He looked up and saw that she was holding a piece of A4 paper with the shadow of a gold seal shining through.

'What's that?'

His mother looked awkwardly at him. 'It's nothing honey. Nothing to worry about.'

His father looked up from the paper. 'You might as well tell him Julia. It affects him as much as it affects us both.'

Sammy felt a new swarm of butterflies hit the walls of his stomach. 'What is it? What's wrong? Can I still go to Dragamas?'

His mother laughed nervously. 'Of course it's still all right to go to Dragamas. It's just that, well, your father and I…'

'Your mother is trying to tell you about her promotion,' said Charles Rambles. 'She's got a new job…'

'Oh,' said Sammy, 'that sounds good.'

'…in Switzerland.'

'Oh.'

'It's ok honey, you'll be away at school and you can come out to Switzerland with us if Dragamas doesn't work out.'

Charles clicked his tongue. 'Of course Dragamas will work out. That was the deal, Ratisbury or Dragamas.'

'They have schools in Switzerland,' said Julia Rambles, ruffling her hand through her hair like she did when things weren't going her way. 'Very good schools.'

Sammy nodded and passed his plate to his mother. 'I'll go upstairs and get my things.'

Unnoticed, Sammy slipped out of his chair and went to pack the last things into his suitcase. He picked up the toy dragon and looked into its eyes. 'I'm going to Dragamas,' he said firmly. 'I'm going to Dragamas and my parents are going to Switzerland.'

CHAPTER 4

ARE YOU GOING TO THE DRAGON SCHOOL?

The journey passed in a blur of motorways, roundabouts and town roads. Having accidentally packed his watch, Sammy had no idea how long or how far they had been travelling. His father was driving, following his mother's directions.

They had stopped twice, once for something to eat and once when Sammy had thought he was going to be sick. For the last few minutes, they had been climbing a steep hill at a snail's pace behind a huge orange tractor, pulling a trailer of golden hay bales.

'Come on, come on!' Sammy's father roared out of the open window. 'We haven't got all day.'

'We have actually,' said Sammy. 'It says on the card to arrive at any time.'

To keep the peace, Julia Rambles quickly handed around a large jar of mint toffees. 'Won't be long now Sammy. Keep an eye out and you might be able to see it soon. On the card, it says that your school is a converted castle.'

'I know,' said Sammy. He knew the words on the business card so well that he could recite them from memory. 'It was built more than four centuries ago.'

'It'll take more than four centuries to find it at this rate,' said Charles Rambles. 'Finally!'

Sammy looked out of the window. The tractor had turned off down a narrow country lane.

'Charles…'

'What!'

'We need to take that turn.'

Sammy gripped his seat belt as his father grasped the steering wheel and the Range Rover doubled back on itself. Luckily the tractor had turned off into a field and didn't hold them up any further.

A few minutes later, Charles Rambles slowed down. 'Should be just here on the right.'

Sammy looked up and felt his mouth swing open. Out of his father's window he could see a tall, towering castle complete with battlements, turrets and towers with flags flying from the top of the coned rooftops.

'Stop,' he whispered. 'This is it. We're here.'

'We're somewhere all right,' Charles Rambles snorted. 'Just look at those ruins.'

'Ruins?' said Sammy. 'It's a castle. It's amazing!'

Julia leaned around the passenger seat. 'Are you feeling all right Sammy?'

'I'm fine Mum. Drive in.'

'We're in the wrong place,' snapped Charles Rambles. 'Look, the sign says "Old Samagard Farm". It's the wrong place.' He slammed the gear stick into reverse.

'We'll keep searching honey. It'll be around here somewhere.'

'Can't you see it?' shouted Sammy. 'Look! The castle, the towers, you must see it!'

In the rear-view mirror, Sammy saw his parents exchange looks.

'It's there!' shrieked Sammy. 'Can't you see it?'

'No,' said Charles Rambles after a long pause. 'We do not.'

Close to tears Sammy slumped back in his seat. His father was reversing down the lane, taking them away from the castle. He rubbed his eyes, if his parents were right and the castle wasn't there, he was worried in case he was going mad.

'Must be over excitement.'

'Hopefully the new school will knock some sense into...whoa there!'

Charles Rambles slammed on the brakes. Sammy leaned over the back seat to see why they had stopped. An old blue Land Rover was blocking the middle of the road.

'Move!' shouted Charles Rambles. 'There's a turning space just back there.'

Sammy heard a car door open and looked up. A woman was getting out of the car. She came up to the passenger door. Sammy stared clapping his hand to his mouth torn between a gasp and a giggle. The woman, although she was dressed normally in a denim skirt and striped blouse, had dark green hair.

'Good morning, good morning,' said the woman in a cheerful sing-song voice.

'Good morning,' snapped Charles Rambles. 'Would you move your vehicle so that we can pass.'

'Oh of course,' said the woman with green hair. 'But aren't you going to drop off your son first?'

Charles Rambles shuffled uncomfortably in his seat. 'What do you know about my son?'

The woman tapped the side window. 'You have a suitcase in the boot and there's no hotels, no houses, no airport for miles. He's going to Dragamas isn't he?'

'If we can find the dratted place.'

The woman chuckled. 'Can't you see it?'

Sammy's mother shook her head. 'Our son says he saw it a moment ago, but all we could see were old ruins.'

The woman paused looking first from Sammy then to his mother and then to his father. 'Oh,' she said knowingly, 'of course you might not, might you.'

'If you know the way, please enlighten us,' snapped Charles Rambles. 'If not, move so we can find it ourselves.'

At this, the woman burst into tinkling laughter. 'If you don't listen to your son, you'll drive all day and might never find it. Leave him with me and I'll make sure he gets there. I'm dropping my daughter off for her first day. Perhaps they could go in together.'

'Perhaps,' snapped Charles Rambles. 'It is a mixed school, isn't it?'

'Of course,' said the woman. 'My sons go there and both my husband and I have been there in our time. It's the only school like it for miles around.'

'You can say that again.'

There was a rumbling and two more cars joined the queue behind the Land Rover. From the opposite direction, a minibus trundled towards them. Charles Rambles pulled the Range Rover up close to the hedge and got out.

Sammy followed his father, a little bit scared of the woman with green hair. He walked along beside the prickly hedgerow and stood on a stone jutting out of the bank.

From the stone, Sammy could see the grey castle towering on the horizon. Outside the car, it seemed much bigger and looked as though it was surrounded in a golden mist that looked very similar to the haze that Sir Lok Ragnarok and Mrs Hubar had disappeared into outside St. Elderberries High School.

Sammy heard a cough behind him and turned around. A small girl wearing black trousers and a spotless white shirt under a black blazer with a golden 'D' motif was standing beside him. If her smart uniform had got his attention, it was nothing compared with her head. An obvious relation of the woman they had just met, this girl had bright green hair.

Sammy knew that he had never been very good at talking to girls and especially not girls with bright green hair. He stood on the stone embedded in the hedgerow unable to do anything but stare.

'Are you going to the Dragon School?' asked the girl with bright green hair.

Sammy stared, sure that she had said "Dragon School."

'Er yeah,' he replied, 'Dragamas.' He checked behind him, his parents were deep in conversation with the woman with green hair and a larger man who had got out of the minibus.

'Or at least I was...'

'It'll be ok,' the girl reassured him. 'I'm Dixie. You've already met my Mum. My brothers are in the third year at Dragamas, they've told me all about it. It's going to be great!'

'Great,' Sammy repeated, trying to catch some of his parents' conversation edging a little closer along the embankment.

'Well, is he going?' asked the burly man looking anxiously at the children in the minibus who were rocking the bus from side to side. 'Stop it you lot!' He turned back to Sammy's parents. 'Are you going to let him go, or not?' He coughed importantly. 'Because if not, please would you move out of my way. I'm supposed to be meeting the new first years in twenty minutes and I can't be late this year.'

'Oh, are you a teacher here?' asked Julia Rambles. 'Is this Dragamas?'

'Yes and yes,' replied the man a little impatiently. 'However, I don't have all day so please choose - is Sammy going to the Dragon School or to Switzerland with you?'

'To Switzerland?' exclaimed Julia. 'How did you know?'

The burly man laughed and pointed. The book Sammy knew his mother had been reading, "Living and Working in Switzerland for the First Time" was clasped in her right hand.

'How did that...'

The burly man laughed. 'I'll give you my word that Sammy will be in good hands and will receive a good, if not better education than any of those other schools.'

Julia Rambles gasped. 'You read my mind.'

'It's settled,' said Charles Rambles firmly. 'Fetch your suitcase Samuel. It's time to go.'

Sammy followed Dixie back to his parents' car and picked up his suitcase. The green haired woman had brought Dixie's suitcase from her car and was giving her daughter a huge goodbye hug.

'Bye Mum,' whispered Sammy. 'See you Dad.'

'Bye honey, be good.'

'Work hard Samuel, make us proud.'

His parents got back into their Range Rover, leaving Sammy and Dixie with the burly man and his minibus. The green haired woman was already turning her Land Rover in the lay-by opposite the school gates. She sped away leaving a large cloud of dust in her wake.

The burly man consulted a lever arch file and held out his hand. 'Hello Sammy, hello Dixie, welcome to Dragamas. My name is Professor John Burlay.'

Sammy held out his hand in silence, in awe of the solid man in front of him. Professor Burlay was head and shoulders taller than him, dressed in a grey pinstripe suit with a white shirt and pale green tie. He had light brown hair swept back over his forehead and a thick beard that ran from ear to ear with a bushy moustache that almost covered his lips. His dark brown eyes twinkled kindly and Sammy felt safe in his presence.

'What do you think so far Sammy?' asked Professor Burlay as he helped Sammy then Dixie into the minibus. 'Take a seat anywhere, and keep it down the rest of you. You're giving me a headache!'

Still speechless, Sammy nodded and held tightly to his suitcase as they lurched through the gates over a cattle grid, up the long, tree studded driveway to the castle entrance. He counted the number of faces in the seats next to him. There were twelve people on the minibus including himself and Dixie, all first years no older than him, all looking anxiously up at the castle to find out what lay in wait.

Professor Burlay parked in a gravel courtyard that ran as far as Sammy could see around the castle walls. Up close, the castle was much larger than it had seemed at the gate and more frightening. The walls were made from large grey flagstones joined with cement and dotted with narrow slit windows at irregular intervals. The towers caught Sammy's eye the most. He had counted nine coned turrets, each flying a jet-black flag with a golden 'D' matching the design on Dixie's blazer. A large iron-bound oak door stood between them and the inside of the castle.

As he watched, the door opened and a small man wearing grey overalls appeared.

'Hullo Professor,' said the man, 'these the last of the first years?'

Professor Burlay nodded, 'I've got twelve here, that makes it thirty-nine, doesn't it?'

'Forty Professor, we had another one come while you were collecting these.'

'Good,' Professor Burlay smiled at the caretaker. 'Would you help them with their cases?'

The man nodded and started heaving the grey suitcase belonging to a blonde-haired girl sitting at the front of the minibus.

'Everyone ready?' Professor Burlay opened the minibus door and beckoned with his free hand for them to come out.

Sammy followed Dixie and two boys with jet black hair out of the minibus. He struggled under the weight of his suitcase but stayed silent since no one else mentioned that their suitcase was too heavy.

'Leave your bags here please,' said Professor Burlay. 'They'll be taken to your rooms by our caretaker, Tom Sweep.'

Sammy looked at Tom Sweep. The caretaker reminded him of his grandfather with a similar weather-wrinkled face and straggly grey hair tucked under a grey peaked cap.

'Thank you,' said Sammy as the caretaker took his suitcase.

Tom Sweep touched his cap. 'All part of the service young sir.'

Sammy felt a nudge in his elbow. Dixie, the girl with green hair was grinning at him.

'It's quiet, isn't it?'

Sammy nodded. 'A bit.'

'That's because they aren't back until tomorrow.'

Sammy looked blankly at her.

'The rest of the school silly. Then it gets sealed up so *they* can't get in.'

'Who's *they*?' whispered Sammy feeling sure that it couldn't be worse than the Rat Catchers at his old school.

Dixie leaned uncomfortably close. 'The Shape,' she whispered inches from his nose sending shivers down his spine.

He followed Dixie through the arched oak door. It was pitch black and there was a cool breeze chasing them inside. Sammy pulled his jumper down over his hands.

'Brr,' grumbled one of the dark haired boys. 'It's cold in here.'

'T'will get a lot colder yet boys and girls.'

Sammy looked up into the darkness to see who had spoken. His eyes made out a dark grey silhouette of a woman wearing a hooded cloak. She carried a glowing candle that cast soft shadows dancing around the room.

'Welcome to Dragamas,' said the cloaked woman, pointing her candle towards a long wooden table. 'Pick up your name, your house has chosen you already.'

'That must be Mrs Grock,' whispered Dixie at Sammy's side. 'My brothers told me about her.'

Sammy followed Dixie over to the table. There were a number of coloured envelopes, red, blue, green and yellow, each with names on. Sammy rummaged on the table top and found his name handwritten on a green envelope. The dark haired boys and Dixie picked up green envelopes as well.

'North,' said Dixie clutching her green envelope. 'Cool!'

'North, follow me,' Professor Burlay called from the back of the room.

Sammy looked up. Professor Burlay was standing in a line of four adults sandwiched between two women, one tall with closely cropped raven black hair and one no taller than himself. On the raven haired woman's left stood a tall sandy haired man wearing a grey jumper and jeans with a large black belt studded with three silver stars. The man nodded to Dixie and called: 'South, follow me.'

'East, follow me,' said the tall raven haired woman. A group of boys in front of Sammy shuffled towards the woman.

'West, follow me,' said the shorter woman. Another group of boys and three girls went up to the woman who checked their names against a piece of paper she was holding. Sammy stopped listening after she read "Peter Grayling" and "Samantha Trout" and leaned over towards Professor Burlay waiting for his name to be called.

'Melissa Brooks, Holly Banks, Dixie Deane...'

Dixie shuffled forward with two girls that Sammy guessed were Melissa Brooks and Holly Banks.

'Naomi Fairweather, Amos Leech, Helena Marchant, Darius Murphy, Samuel Rambles,' Professor Burlay paused for breath and ticked the names on his sheet of paper, 'and Gavin and Toby Reed.'

The dark haired boys pushed past the girls to be at the front of the crocodile line as Professor Burlay led them out of the room with the envelopes and into a candlelit corridor with grey stone walls and a grey stone floor.

They twisted around passage corners and up two flights of steep stairs until Professor Burlay stopped suddenly, causing Sammy and Dixie to bump into Gavin and Toby at the front of the line.

Sammy looked over one of the boys' shoulders not knowing whether it was Gavin's or Toby's. He could see a large wooden door, similar in shape to the door that they had come into the castle through. It looked very old and had dark iron studs from top to bottom holding iron reinforcement bars in place. In the middle of the door was a tarnished plaque with Gothic swirl writing that Sammy could just make out as "North."

Professor Burlay pushed the door open and it creaked eerily on its hinges. Sammy shivered as he walked through the doorway.

'Let's get some light in here shall we?' Professor Burlay raised his right hand and the room lightened into a warm glow.

As Sammy's eyes grew used to the light, he could see that they were inside a large circular room with bookshelves, tables, chairs, sofas and a large grandfather clock.

'Welcome to your common room,' said Professor Burlay. 'This will be a place for you to relax and to study.'

Sammy stared around the homely room, noticing two archways leading to two separate staircases. He stared for a moment longer before he realised that Professor Burlay was separating the boys from the girls. He moved away from Dixie and stood with Gavin and Toby, a boy with dark hair and dark skin and a fourth boy who was smaller with mouse brown hair, not knowing which was Darius and which was Amos.

'Boys, please wait here while I show the girls to their tower.'

Sammy nodded and settled into a green velvet armchair and picked up a car magazine. The dark-skinned boy came and sat next to him.

'Hi, I'm Darius.'

'I'm Sammy,' said Sammy, annoyed to find he was nervous now his parents had left. They would be halfway home by now.

Professor Burlay returned alone a few minutes later.

'Are you ready boys?'

Sammy put down the magazine and followed Darius, Amos, Gavin and Toby through the other archway, up the opposite staircase.

Like the rest of the castle, the stairs were grey stone, set at a short walking pace apart spiralling round and round, higher and higher. They passed four doors on the way up, before coming to the top of the staircase and a solid wooden door. On the door was plaque that read "First Years" written in the same Gothic scrawl as the plaque on the door to the common room. Above the door was an old-fashioned gold bell.

Professor Burlay held the door open for the boys to duck under his arm into the tower room.

Sammy was last to enter the room and he gasped as he did so. The room, although it was smaller than the common room, was equally circular, about double the size of his parent's bedroom at home.

There were five green quilted beds spaced evenly around the room. To the right of each bed was a curved wooden chest of drawers standing underneath a narrow slit window filled with clear glass. Running in a loop around the bed and chest of drawers was a curtain rail with thick green velvet curtains pinned to the wall. They looked as though they could be drawn around the length of the bed and drawers for privacy.

'Welcome to your tower room,' said Professor Burlay, smiling at them. 'Look to the end of the beds for your names and that's where you'll sleep.'

Professor Burlay backed away from the tower door and closed it behind him. 'Goodnight boys, see you tomorrow.'

Inside the tower room, Sammy bent down to look at the silver plaques with more Gothic writing. He was standing beside a bed with the name "Darius Murphy" written in black on the silver plaque.

'This is yours Darius,' said Sammy.

'Great!' Darius heaved his suitcase onto the bed.

'Samuel R. Rambles,' said one of the dark haired boys pointing at Sammy, 'is that you?'

'Yeah, I'm Sammy.'

'Great,' said the dark haired boy holding out his right hand, 'I'm Toby, this is my brother Gavin.' Toby waved his hand towards Gavin who was pulling clothes haphazardly out of his suitcase and stuffing them into the chest of drawers beside his bed.

Gavin waved. 'Hi Sammy.'

'Hi,' said Sammy shaking Toby's hand. He turned to the last boy in the room, 'you must be Amos.'

The boy shrugged and whipped the green curtain around his bed taking both himself and his belongings out of sight.

'Oooer,' Darius giggled. 'What's up with him?'

'Dunno,' said Gavin pulling his curtain between his and Toby's beds. 'See you tomorrow.'

'Night,' said Sammy pulling his own curtain. He dragged his suitcase onto his bed and pulled out his pyjamas and wash bag ready for the morning. As he rested the wash bag on top of the chest of drawers he noticed that a number of items had appeared on top of the chest that he was sure hadn't been there when he'd arrived.

There was the green envelope he had picked up downstairs that he had thought he'd put into his back pocket. Next to the envelope was a black stone that he recognised as onyx from staying with his uncle, a geologist who ran a jewellery sale and repair shop. There was a steaming mug of what looked like hot chocolate, a green school tie and a large mottle green, football sized egg.

Sammy stared at the mottle green egg for a whole minute before changing into his pyjamas. He picked up the drink, which turned out to be a sweet hot chocolate, and the green envelope. He opened the envelope single handed and pulled out a piece of crisp white paper with the golden 'D' Dragamas logo at the top.

"Dear Mr Rambles," he read from the letter. "You are now in the room where you will conduct your first year at Dragamas, the school for Dragon Charming…"

'What!' Sammy burped, choking on his hot chocolate.

"…Events in your life have paved the way for you to be here. It is not only your right to be here, but it is also your destiny. You have been chosen, and here you will raise your dragon, Kyrillan, to the best of your ability. You will learn skills that you never dreamed possible and will be offered the chance to do great things outside of the world of man…"

'Whoa there,' said Sammy staring at the letter, daring himself to read on. The letter went on for another three paragraphs signed at the bottom by Dragamas headmaster, Sir Lok Ragnarok. Sammy read and re-read the paragraphs until somewhere a clock chimed midnight. He put the letter into the top drawer of his chest of drawers and fell into a deep sleep almost as soon as his head touched the pillow.

He dreamed of his parents, merged with the words in the letter, merged with the egg Kyrillan sitting on his chest of drawers until at last he woke in the dimly lit room.

CHAPTER 5

THE SCHOOL TOUR

'I'm at Dragamas,' Sammy whispered to himself. He leaned over and picked up his new possessions. He picked up the egg last, half expecting something terrible to happen. What if he dropped it, he thought, not that he was careless, just curious, like most boys his age.

'Kyrillan huh,' Sammy said to the egg, thinking that the others probably had normal coloured eggs with normal names and, he thought, who gave eggs names anyway.

He stroked the surface of the green egg. It wasn't quite rough and wasn't quite smooth, a bit like used sandpaper he decided.

'Keye-rillan, Kiri-lan, Ky-rill-aaan,' the name was growing on him.

'Ky-rill-an,' said Sammy, trying out the name for the fifth time, and then it happened. The egg stirred in his lap. A large crack split down the left hand side.

'Oh no,' whispered Sammy. 'Just what I need on my first day.'

He pressed his fingers against the egg to try and stop the crack from widening. To his horror, it had the opposite effect and a piece of the egg came away in his hand. A dark green liquid oozed from inside the egg.

Sammy stared. He had absolutely no idea what to do. Through a chink in his curtain, he could see that the other curtains were drawn. A faint snore came from Darius's direction and he was fairly sure that everyone was asleep.

Resigned to the fact that the egg was going to hatch anyway, Sammy poked the green goo.

'Come on then, open sesame,' he muttered pulling at the eggshell to let more of the goo out.

As the second piece of shell came away, the egg let out a high pitched scream and burst open. Pieces of slime and shell flew up and hit Sammy in the face.

'Euggh!' Sammy wiped the slime with his arm and stared at the sheer amount of green goo in his lap. He got his second shock that morning when the goo wriggled and a pair of large black beaded eyes swung around and stared straight back at him.

Sammy screwed up his nose. As well as covering him in a green slime, the egg stank. He guessed it was a deterrent to predators. Sammy looked up and saw four wide eyed, open mouthed faces peering at him.

'That's amazing,' said Darius.

'How come mine hasn't hatched,' said one of the dark haired boys that Sammy thought was probably Gavin.

'Awesome,' said Toby.

'Amazing? Awesome? It's my first day, I'll be in trouble, get sent home or something,' said Sammy, staring at the green slime.

The boys burst out laughing.

'It's really rare,' said Darius. 'You must have bonded straight away. Most eggs don't hatch for at least a week and that's only with lots of petting and stroking.' Darius leaned closer to look at the goo, 'he must really like you.'

'Kyrillan,' said Toby. 'That's an awesome name.'

Sammy smiled, wishing he knew what he had done and what Kyrillan meant. The boys were obviously impressed. He put the Kyrillan goo on top of his chest of drawers and swung back his curtain.

'Hey, you've got five years too,' said Gavin pointing to the plaque at the bottom of Sammy's bed.

Sammy looked down, where his plaque had read "Samuel R. Rambles" it now read:

North House

Samuel R. Rambles

5 years

'Five years?' asked Sammy. 'What does that mean?'

'It's your year plaque,' explained Darius. 'It says how long you'll be at the school.'

'Oh,' said Sammy looking at the other plaques. Both Gavin and Toby's plaques read five years, Amos's read one year and Darius's read forty-five.

'I'm going to teach here,' said Darius. 'It says so in my letter.'

Sammy looked at Amos.

'I don't know what it means,' said Amos as if some dark shadow of shame hung over him.

'Perhaps it's a mistake,' suggested Sammy.

Amos shrugged. 'Who knows,' he muttered and left the room.

'Don't worry Sammy,' said Toby. 'It's pretty much the worst thing that can happen, to be chucked out.'

'Perhaps he'll die here,' said Gavin ominously. 'Like that other one...'

'Oh,' said Sammy looking closely at Gavin. 'Are you twins?'

'No,' said Gavin, giggling at him.

'Oh,' Sammy screwed up his nose. 'You look alike.'

'Don't worry about it,' said Gavin. 'We get it all the time.'

'But...' said Sammy looking first at Gavin then Toby.

'We are really,' said Toby ruffling Gavin's hair. 'It's a joke, we do it to everyone.'

'Bunch of freaks,' said Amos who had come back in.

'Are you sure they didn't get your plaque right?' snapped Gavin, giving Amos a dark look.

Ignoring Gavin, Amos turned towards Sammy and Darius. 'I met Professor Burlay on the stairs. He said breakfast is in the Main Hall in ten minutes.'

Darius, Gavin and Toby huddled around muttering about Amos. Sammy left them to it remembering the Rat Catchers at his old school. He had learnt quickly to wait before choosing friends, "be slow in choosing and slower in changing" his father had told him. Just thinking about his parents gave him a jolt in his stomach. They would probably be in Switzerland by now. He grinned, if they could see him with his green gunk – a dragon charmer – that's what he was going to be, if he had read the letter right.

'So, what's your family like?'

Sammy looked up, 'I'm, um...' He paused, the more he tried to remember the harder it was. 'My parents and me, we met Sir Ragnarok and he said I could come.'

'Wow!' said Darius. 'You've met Sir Ragnarok?'

Sammy nodded. 'Then we came here...'

'Cool! That's...' started Toby.

But they didn't get a chance to hear what Toby was about to say as a loud bell rang from outside the tower room door.

'Breakfast!' shouted Gavin. 'Any idea where to go?'

'Follow me,' snapped Amos.

'Do I take this?' asked Sammy pointing to the green goo.

'Leave him,' said Toby. 'Ours might hatch too. He won't be lonely.'

Sammy stared at the green goo as he left the room, not quite ready to treat Kyrillan as a pet.

'Come on,' shouted Gavin. 'I'm hungry!'

Professor Burlay met Sammy, Darius, Gavin, Toby and Amos in the common room and led them to the Main Hall. The other first years were already there with the other professors that had met them last night.

'Right,' said Professor Burlay, counting heads. 'Thirty-nine and forty.'

'Five boys and five girls in each house,' said Sammy, staring at the high ceilinged rectangular room.

'In each year too and only by invitation,' said Professor Burlay as he led the North students to one of four long wooden tables aligned vertically down the room. The tables were covered in thick tablecloths with different colours for the different houses.

Each side of the tables was a row of high backed wooden chairs with the Dragamas 'D' carefully carved into the wooden backs. In front of each chair was a place laid at the table with a shiny silver plate rimmed in gold and bordered by shiny silver cutlery; five pronged forks and knives that finished in the shape of a crescent moon.

'Be seated,' said Professor Burlay waving his arm towards the green clothed table.

Sammy shuffled forward. Toby and Gavin were already sitting down. Dixie was sitting next to a girl with platinum blonde hair.

'Hi,' he said nervously.

'Hi Sammy!' said Dixie enthusiastically. 'You're here, next to Milly.'

Sammy took a closer look at Milly recognising her from the night before. She was wafer thin with a small pointed face, the brightest of blue eyes and a scattering of freckles on her nose. She had a light dusting of glitter in her hair and to Sammy, she looked like some kind of an angel.

Milly was deep in conversation with the girl on her right. When she paused for breath, she grinned mischievously at Sammy.

'Come on Sammy, she won't bite,' Dixie grinned at him. 'Sit here.'

Sammy pulled out the chair nervously and sat down next to Milly, opposite Darius. He picked up his knife and fork getting his second shock that morning as the plate glowed a translucent green.

He watched in horror as food began to materialise on the plate giving a loud "popping" sound as sausages, bacon, eggs, fried bread, a full English breakfast exploded in front of him.

'You're supposed to wait for the professors,' Darius hissed across the table.

'Not to worry.' Milly giggled and picked up her own five-pronged fork and crescent shaped knife. 'Let's start!'

Dixie, Gavin and Toby picked up their knives and forks. Toby nudged Darius who, with a frown, picked up his own knife and fork, screwing up his eyes as the "popping" got louder and louder.

Amos stayed still, a small smile on his thin lips as the raven haired professor strode up to the North table.

'Von star from Rambles, Reed, Reed, Deane, Brooks and Murphy,' barked the woman, pulling a wooden stick from the sleeve of her teaching robes.

Sammy watched, his eyes glued open, as six black clouds of star shaped smoke flew from the tip of the stick and clung to a large noticeboard at the back of the Main Hall behind a central table that faced the four house tables lengthways.

'Simone, is that fair? It's their first day,' said Professor Burlay, his voice fading under a ferocious stare that the woman trained on him.

'Professor Burlay,' snapped the woman. 'May I remind you of two things. One, that gold and silver stars are awarded for good behaviour and classroom achievements, taken away with the black stars when the rules are broken.'

Professor Burlay lowered his head.

'And two, my name is Professor Sanchez in front of the students.'

Sammy caught, 'if you know what's good for you,' muttered under Professor Sanchez's breath as she flounced towards the central table and sat down next to the two professors from the South and West houses.

Professor Burlay followed Professor Sanchez to the teachers' table. He sat next to an empty chair leaving as much space between himself and Professor Sanchez as possible.

The room hushed as Sir Ragnarok, Dragamas headmaster, entered the room. The four professors stood up as Sir Ragnarok walked behind them and pulled out the empty chair.

Sir Ragnarok was dressed in the same dusty black robes Sammy had seen him wearing outside St. Elderberries High School. He lifted his head, sniffed the air and consulted a gold disc he pulled out of a pocket inside his robe.

From the North table, Sammy had the bizarre sensation that he was being watched. He looked down at his plate at the fried breakfast then back to the teachers' table.

'Good morning,' said Sir Ragnarok, putting away the gold disc. 'I see you have already started our feast. Let us enjoy the food while it is hot and then I shall introduce you to Dragamas. Not in the usual way of course, but today it seems, is a most unusual day.'

Sir Ragnarok sat down and picked up a gold five-pronged fork and gold crescent shaped knife.

Sammy jumped at the explosion on the table at the front. Sir Ragnarok's plate glowed not green, nor red, nor blue nor yellow, but a unique blend of all colours that turned his plate into a rainbow, filling itself with a tower of sausages, fried bread, bacon and eggs, but no mushrooms or tomatoes Sammy noticed pushing his to the side of his plate.

Sammy had eaten probably more than he should have when Sir Ragnarok put down his knife and fork and stood up.

'First years,' said Sir Ragnarok, his voice filling the hall. 'Welcome to Dragamas.' He looked around the room, making sure he had the attention of every student. A sea of forty faces looked up at him, listening with bated breath.

'You are each here today because you have been chosen.' Sir Ragnarok paused to let this sink in. 'You are here to learn and master skills that others will never dream possible. Some of you will do well...' Sammy felt Sir Ragnarok look him straight in the eyes.

'...and some of you will not. Enjoy your time here as you choose. Study hard and you will be rewarded with your skills, practice often to perfect your technique and play hard to keep the balance.' Sir Ragnarok smiled at them. 'This is your first official day to collect your books and learn your way around. Tomorrow the rest of the school will return from their field trip and term will begin.'

The professors stood up clapping as Sir Ragnarok nodded and walked out of the room.

'Work hard, play hard,' said Darius. 'That sounds fair.'

'Play hard sounds better,' said Gavin.

'Wonder what sports they have here,' said Toby.

Professor Burlay came over to the North table, casting nervous glances at Professor Sanchez as she stood at the top of the East table.

'Your timetables are under your plates,' whispered Professor Burlay. 'Pick them up and follow me.'

Sammy lifted his plate. Sure enough there was a withered sheet of yellow parchment with charcoal grey handwriting on one side accompanied by short lines separating the days of the week.

'Alchemistry, Astronomics,' said Sammy, wondering when Maths and English lessons would take place, or even if they would take place at all.

'Saturday lessons,' he grumbled looking at the sixth column on the paper. 'We won't be able to look forward to Friday afternoons.'

Professor Burlay led the ten North students back to their common room, pointing for them to sit down in a circle on beanbags and giant cushions.

'Any questions?' he asked looking around the circle.

Dixie put up her hand, whisking past Sammy's ear.

'Yes Dixie?'

'Will we be able to go to the Floating Circus when it comes?' asked Dixie, her eyes shining.

Sammy turned to her and stared. He had only been to the circus once and it certainly hadn't been a floating one. As he half expected, Professor Burlay was hesitant in answering. Sammy had the impression that he got pushed around by the students and picked on by the teachers. He looked again at his timetable and seeing the name next to the Astronomics lessons, decided that Professor Burlay must be very good at it to stay at the school.

'The Floating Circus Dixie, it may be possible…no promises. Sir Ragnarok will decide when the time comes.'

Sammy desperately wanted to know more and raised his hand. Professor Burlay waved for Sammy to put his hand down, apparently he'd had enough of answering questions and instead, he chose to explain more about the school.

'Dragamas,' began Professor Burlay as if reading from a history book, 'was founded in 1605, when some of the greatest wizards and sorcerers of the time had the money and the resources to build an educational establishment, a school, that would teach and train young men to perform various things that at the time were considered to be magical and witchcraft.'

Dixie threw up her hand. 'Did the school take women?'

'Not initially,' said Professor Burlay. 'However, there was pressure, considerable pressure on both sides, from both sexes, equally arguing why and why not men and women could and could not train together. It's quite a modern concept and Dragamas has only taken female students since the end of the 18th century. A terrible waste, if you ask me. We might have had more Morgana Montehues or Mercedes Menzies, fine female sorcerers.'

Sammy raised his hand again, hundreds of questions burning in his throat. He didn't know which to ask first.

'Yes Sammy?' Professor Burlay sounded annoyed to be stopped mid-flow.

'Please could you explain a bit about our lessons and show us how to get to the classrooms?'

Professor Burlay nodded. 'The classrooms of course, they may be moved this time next year, but for now look on the back of your timetables.'

Following the other students, Sammy turned over his timetable. Thin black lines criss-crossed the paper, showing the classrooms. Each room had a label and a doorway. Some of them had secret passageways. It looked really exciting.

'The lessons, I'm afraid, will have to be explained in more detail when you get there. However, I can tell you that this, your first year, will be your best year,' said Professor Burlay. 'This is the time to make friends that you will keep for life, the time to learn without pressure to get things right and the time to enjoy learning new skills.'

It sounded to Sammy like a summary of Sir Ragnarok's speech. 'What about our books?' he interrupted. 'Sir Ragnarok mentioned books.'

'All taken care of,' said Professor Burlay infuriatingly quashing Sammy's question without a proper reply. 'Let's move on and have some morning tea.'

Professor Burlay reached inside his suit sleeve and pulled out a wooden stick, longer than Professor Sanchez's, about three feet in length. He tapped the staff on the ground and eleven mugs of steaming hot chocolate appeared from nowhere. He tapped the staff again and produced a plate of golden biscuits that he passed around.

Copying Gavin, Sammy took four, not to be greedy, just that he couldn't tell from the timetable when they would stop for lunch.

As more students asked questions, Sammy quickly learnt that he had a lot to learn. He was the only North boy not to know anything about dragons. Even Amos, who still hadn't said more than two words to anyone, apparently had parents who rode fully grown dragons to work. Only Helena and Naomi were finding things as strange as he was.

He learnt more about the strange dragon egg that had hatched in his tower room and how he would learn various incantations and use crystals to solve everyday problems. Professor Burlay also explained more about the wooden staffs that the professors carried and the different spells that they could be used for.

'You'll find out for yourself soon enough,' Professor Burlay reassured them. 'Now I have some business to attend to and will be back shortly. Lunch will be in a few hours, beforehand I believe you will be shown the grounds.' He stood up and, using his staff, generated a golden mist that when it dispersed, Professor Burlay was nowhere to be seen.

'What do we do now?' asked Sammy.

'I've got some Dragon Dice,' said Milly. 'Anyone want to play?'

'That's a girl's game,' scoffed Gavin. 'A handful of dice can't predict the future.'

'They can,' said Milly.

'Shall we play Dragonball?' asked Toby, 'I brought my Excelsior Sports Draconis Plus set.'

'You've got a Draconis Plus set?' asked Amos suddenly interested.

'So?'

'Well, they're the best, aren't they?' said Amos. 'Really expensive.'

'Will someone tell me what's going on?' asked Sammy a little louder than he had intended suddenly aware that everyone was looking at him.

There was a hushed silence that Dixie broke. 'You really don't know, do you?' she whispered.

'Know what?'

'Just the greatest game in the world, well it will be once we have full grown dragons to play with.'

'Someone, please tell me what it is!'

'Dragonball,' said Milly a little irately. 'It's a thug's game. A set of coloured balls that get blasted out of the sky by fire breathing dragons. It's not just dangerous to play, there's always people getting hit miles away from the game.'

'Wow,' said Sammy trying to picture it in his mind. 'Tell me more!'

'Well,' said Gavin ignoring Milly's tutting. 'You start with anywhere up to fifty players...'

'But they don't all finish the game,' added Toby. 'One time, forty-eight players got injured and nobody won.'

'The keepers can't score,' said Dixie, who seemed to be very knowledgeable on the subject. Sammy had the feeling she was a bit of a tomboy, the exact opposite of Milly.

'So, can we play it indoors?'

'Kind of,' said Toby. 'It should really be played outside and without our own dragons, we'll have to play on the ground.'

'Ok, so are we going to play?' demanded Gavin.

'I'll get my set,' said Toby. 'Back in a minute.'

Toby returned in under a minute, without the Dragonball set. 'Hey Sammy guess what!' he shouted. 'Mine has hatched too.'

'Cool,' said Gavin enviously. 'Let's have a look.'

They raced up the stairs to the boys' tower. Designed for five, the tower room was cramped with ten people packed inside.

'It's just like our tower,' said Dixie sitting down in the middle of Sammy's bed. 'Yours has hatched right out Sammy,' she said poking the green jelly like creature.

'Hey! Don't touch it,' said Sammy, trying to work out if he was more annoyed that she was sitting on his bed and touching his dragon, or with himself for forgetting about Kyrillan in the excitement of breakfast.

'It won't hurt it,' said Dixie. 'Mine hatched this morning too.'

'Really?' said Sammy. 'That's supposed to be really rare, isn't it?'

Dixie looked at him with respect. 'Yes, it is. His name's Kiridor,' she added proudly.

They stood up and took a closer look at Toby's dragon goo.

'Sammy, meet Puttee,' said Toby picking up the goo in both hands. 'It's hard to believe that one day, this will be bigger than me and will be able to fly.'

Toby put the grey-green goo back on to his chest of drawers. It squelched into a semi-circle, almost motionless, its jelly like body rising and falling with tiny dragon breaths.

'Now can we play Dragonball?' asked Gavin impatiently.

Toby pulled a silver briefcase with a gold dragon motif from under his bed. Sammy made a mental note to ask for one for Christmas, not that he thought his parents would have any idea where to find Excelsior Sports, let alone identify the Draconis Plus set.

Sammy soon discovered why Milly had described Dragonball as a "thugs game." Far from being organised like football or basketball, he found himself barged this way and that, trying to catch and kick the black leather balls.

Gavin, Toby and Dixie seemed to be very good at it and he found himself wondering where and how often they played.

He ducked as Dixie shunted one of the balls over his head towards Toby. The ball knocked Toby over backwards and landed straight into the back of the makeshift goal they had put together using beanbags.

'Three all,' shouted Dixie, offering Toby a hand to help him up.

'It is not,' spluttered Gavin. 'That was too rough for indoors, are you ok Toby?'

'Yeah, let her have it,' said Toby taking Dixie's hand.

'No way,' said Dixie, 'I'm not having you saying later that you would have won. We'll play, fair and square.'

Dixie seemed to take the matter personally and wove in and out of the players. She put two more goals past Toby and one past Gavin.

Sammy found once he got the hang of the game, he was actually quite good at it. He put two goals past Milly, who despite herself, had put aside the Dragon Dice and joined in.

Darius played the best shot, wildly kicking two balls at once, whizzing them over Dixie's head and into the goal with a thump as they struck the common room wall. As they celebrated the goal Professor Burlay returned, wearing a thick winter coat and gloves.

'Great shot Darius,' said Professor Burlay clapping his hands.

Sammy froze, sure that there were rules about not playing Dragonball indoors. To his relief, Professor Burlay was smiling.

'I'm sure you'll make a fine Dragonball player one day Darius,' said Professor Burlay. 'Now, if you could fetch your coats, we will be joining the other first years to take a tour of the school. It should take no longer than three to four hours and some of you...' Professor Burlay looked in particular at Milly, 'may wish to bring a hat, scarf or some gloves. It's a little brisk out,' he nodded to himself.

Sammy thundered back up the tower stairs helping Toby carry the Dragonball set. He returned dressed in his bulky winter coat, his hands tucked firmly into his pockets.

In the main entrance, they met the first years from the other houses dressed as warmly as they were.

'Right,' said Professor Sanchez. 'We shall go for our tour of the school. The whole school,' she added ominously. Sammy wondered if her students knew the tour might be up to four hours long.

She marched through the door out into the castle courtyard. 'We shall go around anticlockwise, widdershins they call it. Keep up at the back.'

Sammy kept close to Gavin and Toby as they walked down the gravel road towards the school gate. As they got closer to the cattle grid separating the school from the road, Sammy could see the edges of the gold mist he had seen with his parents. It seemed to be a large pearlescent bubble covering the whole school.

They didn't cross the cattle grid into the outside world, but stopped for a second as a farmer drove two or three dozen sheep down the narrow country lane, blissfully unaware that through the bubble, he was being watched by forty-four pairs of eyes.

True to her word, Professor Sanchez led them anticlockwise away from the gate, then through a thicket of trees and tall bushes.

'This is the teachers' garden,' announced Professor Sanchez, pointing towards a carefully tended garden with picnic tables scattered amongst flowerbeds brimming with flowers of every size, colour and shape. A shoulder high stone wall protected the garden and there was an atmosphere of absolute stillness and calm as they walked between two pillars into the garden.

'Other than this tour, no student may enter the garden, unless they are in mortal danger,' said Professor Sanchez. 'It is protected by a password.'

Sammy stared at Dixie. 'Mortal danger?'

Dixie grinned at him. 'Wonder what really goes on in there. Did you see the grill? I bet they have the same kind of bubble that goes over the school.'

Sammy stared harder, making a mental note to be very careful where he stepped.

Sure enough, as they left the garden, they stepped over a second grill. Sammy looked back and although he could see the garden, it was empty apart from the flowers and the picnic benches. As he watched, students filed between the pillars and came back into view.

'They can see out, but we can't see in,' whispered Dixie.

'Invisibility,' said Sammy, his head spinning uncomfortably.

'Merely an illusion,' said a voice behind them.

Sammy looked around. The tall, sandy haired professor of the South house was behind him.

'Trust me, you will be able to do this and much more when I've finished with you,' he said, smiling warmly at them.

Professor Sanchez slowed down as she led them back towards the castle, carving a giant V as she swung up to the courtyard and back down towards some buildings at the end of the path.

'The Gymnasium and changing rooms,' said Professor Sanchez, loudly enough to be heard by the stragglers at the back. 'State of the art. It is a fine place to keep fit and to practice the games.'

'Dragonball,' Toby whispered into Sammy's ear. 'Look!'

Sammy followed Toby's outstretched hand. Beyond the Gymnasium was a large playing field, about the size of four football pitches, with a gold Dragonball crest in the centre matching the gold motif on Toby's briefcase. A stadium of wooden benches semi-circled the pitch and floodlights on tall metal poles towered above them.

Professor Sanchez's tour took them diagonally across the Dragonball pitch. Sammy stopped for a second by the golden dragon lying flat on the grass. He was sure the coal black eyes blinked and a faint wisp of smoke trickled from its mouth. After the things he had seen in the last twenty-four hours, he was sure that nothing could surprise him.

By walking almost to the far edge of the school grounds and back to the castle, Sammy guessed that they were walking in a star shape. He wondered if it was Professor Burlay's idea since he seemed to know about stars. "Astro," Sammy knew for a fact was to do with the sky and the night stars.

He was right as Professor Burlay took over from Professor Sanchez and led the students away from the castle and towards the most peculiar house that Sammy had seen in his entire life.

As they got closer, Sammy saw that it was an old fashioned bungalow with ivy trailing between two windows either side of a green front door. A further two windows peeked out from under the thatched roof and it looked like something out of a fairy tale, a gingerbread house or somewhere for Snow White or the three bears to live. Sammy spotted a letterbox on the front door and had trouble believing a postman would consider delivering mail inside a school with fire breathing dragons, even if he could see the house through the bubble.

What really caught his eye was the well in the corner of the cottage garden. The round wall was half covered with moss and ivy that ran up the wooden supports to a slate tiled roof designed to keep out the worst of the weather. The students gathered around the well taking it in turns to be at the front.

'Make a wish children,' a voice cackled behind them.

They spun around and saw the strangest looking woman coming out of the cottage. She wore a long velvet robe in patchwork colours of blues and oranges, reds and purples. She had a kind face, weathered with age and had strands of greying hair peeking from under a purple velvet bonnet. She was as tall as Sammy and was dwarfed by the professors.

'Meet Mrs Grock,' said Professor Burlay, resting a hand on the woman's shoulder, 'our school secretary and nurse. She can cure any ailment in the world,' he added proudly.

'Providing you live long enough to reach her,' said Professor Sanchez, scowling darkly at them.

'Ooch, go on with you John,' Mrs Grock giggled. 'You don't want to frighten the little children, and I canna cure any illness, just the ones medicine canna fix. Here,' she pulled a handful of shiny coins from her pocket, 'make a wish in my well.'

'Your well?' asked Sammy wishing he hadn't spoken out loud as Mrs Grock sidled up to him, her breath in need of some peppermints.

'Ahh yes,' she muttered, standing too close for Sammy's liking. 'What have we here? A young Dragon Knight perhaps?'

Sammy stepped back, aware that everyone was looking at him.

Mrs Grock pressed a coin into his hand. 'Make a wish child and it will come true.'

Under pressure to make the first wish, Sammy stepped up to the well, the coin burning in his hand, 'I wish…'

'Hush child,' interrupted Mrs Grock, 'hush, or it will not be so.'

'Uh,' said Sammy, wishing he could have gone second or third. He wasn't worried about making a wish; he'd done it often enough with his parents at posh restaurants. None of his wishes had ever come true.

'Put wrongs to right,' he said inside his head, letting go of the coin, 'and a Dragonball set.'

Sammy counted to twenty-seven before the coin splashed into the water. As he waited, he found himself wondering what would happen when the well was full of coins.

'Pure in spirit,' sighed Mrs Grock. She turned to Dixie and jumped slightly as she noticed Dixie's green hair. Mrs Grock gave Dixie a coin and moved on to hand out one coin per student.

Sammy backed away to let Dixie take her wish. He bumped into Professor Sanchez who looked keenly at him.

'A good wish Sammy,' said Professor Sanchez. 'Twenty-seven seconds to fall means twenty-seven minutes. Then it will be time to see what you have unleashed.' Professor Sanchez backed away to watch her students drop their coins.

'What did she mean?' asked Sammy, glad to be surrounded by Dixie, Darius and Milly.

'She's lost it,' said Dixie.

'My parents say wishing wells are cheap entertainment,' said Milly.

'Don't be too sure,' said Darius holding up a large bar of chocolate. 'You should be careful what you wish for.'

Milly looked at the chocolate and laughed, 'I just wished to be...'

'Shh,' said Dixie. 'Unless it wasn't what you wanted, don't tell us.'

'She said it would be twenty-seven minutes.' Sammy looked at his watch.

'Well as long as you didn't wish for snow, I'll be happy,' said Darius. 'It's getting cold, isn't it?'

'Twenty-seven minutes,' Sammy muttered to no one in particular.

The professor from the South house took the lead from Professor Burlay and walked them away from Mrs Grock's cottage towards a wooded area filled with birch and beech trees, covered from top to bottom in fiery yellow and orange autumn leaves. Although it was only the middle of the afternoon, dense clouds were drawing in overhead and it was starting to get dark.

'Just what did you wish for, eh Sammy?' asked Professor Burlay. 'Not an early Christmas I hope.'

'No sir,' said Sammy, not daring to say more. He could feel the staring eyes of the other students bearing into his back, desperate to know what he had wished for.

They followed a narrow soil path, surrounded each side with long, prickly grasses, through the trees into a clearing. The professor from the South house stopped to mutter to Professor Burlay.

'What did he wish for?' Sammy caught as they huddled together. 'Is it safe to go on? The weather has changed. Things are not as they should be.'

Professor Burlay looked up at the sky. 'I see no sign.'

'Gentlemen,' said Professor Sanchez, 'may we continue the tour of the school? Commander Altair, I believe you have their wands to prepare?'

The professor from the South house glared at Professor Sanchez, his blue eyes blazing. 'Witches have wands,' he snapped, 'Dragon Knights have staffs,' he turned to the huddle of students, 'and don't let anyone tell you any different.'

They walked on in silence, the wood closing in behind them. Sammy felt a pang of fear. Supposing they couldn't get out, got lost, or worse. He had noticed tracks here and there showing signs of recent activity, but the forest was quiet except for the rhythmic step-crunch, step-crunch of their feet on the fallen autumn leaves.

Commander Altair, professor of the South house, led them in the growing dusk for another ten minutes by Sammy's watch, through to another clearing where he stopped and beckoned for the forty students to gather round.

He took a solid wooden cane from inside his coat. It was the size of a walking stick but three times thicker. At the top was a perfectly formed quartz crystal ball shining like a diamond in the dim light.

He held the middle of the staff and pointed the crystal to the ground and shouted 'Fire!'

Sammy leapt backwards as a red spark burst from the crystal. As the spark touched the ground it turned into a bright orange flame that shot ten feet into the air. He watched open mouthed as the flame shrunk into a small fire that crackled merrily at the Commander Altair's feet. It was so unreal, so completely different from his old school.

'I have brought you here to choose your staff,' said Commander Altair. 'Do not wander far from the fire. There are plenty of young trees to choose a staff that feels right, not too heavy and not too light.'

The students scattered amongst the trees just beyond the clearing. Sammy stayed close to Dixie and Darius going up to the trees and trying branches for size.

'The staff should be between two feet, six inches and six feet in length. How you treat it will determine its performance,' said Commander Altair. 'Staffs are used to complement spells and charms. It must not,' he thundered, 'be used in anger against any fellow student. Not in my class, nor in any other.'

As Darius helped Dixie to reach a branch in an old oak tree, Sammy spotted a branch, perfect in shape and size, on the ground behind a tree stump. From nature lessons at Ratisbury, Sammy knew it was a branch from a horse chestnut tree and looked as though it came from what looked like the oldest tree in the forest. The branch was perfectly shaped with a bulge at one end ready to support a crystal.

Sammy tiptoed over to the branch, aware that he was out of sight of the fire. He picked up the branch and it felt alive in his hands, even though it could have fallen days, weeks or even years ago. It was perfect, the perfect height, the perfect weight and he desperately wanted to try it out.

'Fire,' whispered Sammy as he pointed the bulging end to the ground. 'Fire!' he said a little louder and then it happened. A huge bolt of red flame shot from the branch and set fire to the tree stump. In the light, Sammy saw something that made his blood freeze. He screamed. Out of the darkness he saw a circle of hooded figures surrounding him, chanting, drawing closer with every step.

Within seconds, Dixie and Darius were with him. Dixie seemed to run through the hooded figures and they melted away into the darkness. She put her arm around him.

'What happened?'

'Ssshapes,' stuttered Sammy. 'Hooded figures.'

'I can't see anything,' said Darius. 'Are you sure you're not imagining things?' Darius walked around the fire, tapping trees with his branch.

'I believe you,' whispered Dixie. 'I saw them too. The Shape, my brothers told me to stay close to the group on my first day. Now I know why.'

'Is that why you're good at Dragonball?' whispered Sammy staring at Dixie's green hair.

'Yeah,' said Dixie her cheeks turning crimson. 'Serberon, Jason and Mikhael. They taught me things most girls don't know. Milly's the daughter my parents wanted.'

Sammy looked again at Dixie's hair.

'Genetic,' muttered Dixie. 'Jason's got a ponytail like mine.'

'I like it,' Sammy grinned at her. 'So, how come you saw the figures? It looked like you jumped right through them.'

'It's the only way,' said Dixie, as if she was repeating something she had learnt by heart. 'Show no fear and they dissolve.'

'At that moment, Dixie cared more for your life than for her own.'

Sammy jumped, Commander Altair was behind them.

'I told you to stay close to the...fire.' Commander Altair stopped mid-sentence and looked at the fire on the tree stump. 'How did...'

'It was me,' said Sammy, 'my staff...' he tailed into silence as he saw the outline of Professor Sanchez looking more terrifying than she had at breakfast.

'My, my,' she whispered. 'We are full of surprises.'

She pointed her staff at the fire and without a word the fire fizzled out, spitting and crackling until it disappeared from sight.

Professor Sanchez took Sammy's shoulder in an iron grip. 'Let us get back to the group,' she hissed, pushing him on to the path.

Dixie and Darius followed with Commander Altair close behind them, back to Professor Burlay and the rest of the first years.

In the clearing, Professor Burlay was staring at the sky, pointing with his staff at clusters of stars. Two girls were collecting leftovers from lunch that Sammy realised he, Dixie and Darius had missed.

They started walking deeper into the woodland. Sammy moved closer to thank Dixie.

'Who knows what would have happened if you hadn't,' he whispered.

'It's ok, really,' said Dixie. 'Does it make us friends?'

'Of course,' said Sammy without thinking. 'Best friends.'

'Sammy's got a girlfriend!' Gavin chanted as they bunched up.

'Better watch it Gavin,' said Dixie. 'Sammy's staff can do fire like the Commander's.'

'You need crystals for that,' said Gavin.

'It does,' said Darius.

'Show us,' said Toby.

'Not now,' said Sammy. 'I've got into enough trouble already today.'

Professor Sanchez took the lead and led a quick march through the forest.

Professor Burlay caught up with Sammy's group. 'This is the Forgotten Forest,' he said, dramatically.

'Why is it called that?' asked Sammy.

'I can't remember!' laughed Professor Burlay, shrinking as Professor Sanchez glared at him.

'It is called the Forgotten Forest,' snapped Professor Sanchez, 'because people were put here to be forgotten. The lost souls of the men and women who wandered in, they got lost and never found their way out.'

Sammy thought back to the hooded figures he had seen. They had seemed real enough, until they vanished when Dixie ran through them. But if she said she had seen them too, they had to be real.

'It was named the Forgotten Forest of Karmandor after the King of the Dark Ages, King Serberon's dragon, Karmandor, who was lured in by a wicked witch,' added Professor Sanchez.

'Karmandor,' said Sammy thoughtfully. 'That sounds a bit like my dragon Kyrillan.'

'They could be related,' said Professor Sanchez. 'Some students have said their dragons have come from a historic past, a famous family tree. You may find out more in your Dragon Studies lessons.'

'Cool,' said Sammy, checking his watch. In the excitement of creating fire and seeing the hooded figures, he had almost forgotten his wish at Mrs Grock's.

'Five minutes...' Professor Sanchez whispered so quietly Sammy thought he had imagined it.

As the light disappeared completely, Commander Altair produced three storm lanterns lit by orange candles and passed them round. Sammy knew he hadn't been watching closely, but even so, it looked as though the lanterns had been created from rocks by the side of the path.

Sammy stayed close to Commander Altair and his lantern as they climbed down some ragged steps into a place where the trees where thinly scattered and a rock face towered above them. In the warm orange light Sammy could see milk white stones peeking through layer upon layer of fallen leaves at his feet.

Commander Altair tapped his staff against his lantern and it grew brighter, lighting up the clearing.

As the light flashed around, Sammy gasped. Straight ahead and nearly ten feet up, was a huge opening in the rock face, like a giant mouth, large enough to swallow Professor Burlay's minibus.

Roughly hewn rock steps led from where they were standing to a wide ledge and into the darkness. Along the ledge ran a row of pointed stones in the same milk white stone that was scattered on the ground.

'The Dragon's Lair,' said Commander Altair, 'guarded by the Dragon's Teeth.'

'The walkway to the stars,' said Dixie pointing at a mist swirling above the lair. 'I thought my brothers made it up.'

Split between listening to Commander Altair and looking at the mist, Sammy looked up to where Dixie was pointing. The night sky was pitch black with a sprinkling of stars dancing in a pearlescent column of mist.

Commander Altair stood on the bottom step resting against his staff, the lantern swinging in his free hand.

'This lair belonged to Karmandor.'

Sammy leaned forward, his attention piqued having learnt that his dragon, Kyrillan, might be a distant relation to Karmandor.

'Dragon of King Serberon,' continued Commander Altair, 'King of the Dark Ages who lived in our castle, long before it became a school.' He climbed to the top of the steps. 'They say his dragon still lives in this cave. That Karmandor is a prisoner, enchanted by an evil witch who lured the dragon into the forest then put curses on the trees, moving them, changing their shape, so it would never find its way out.

Sammy stared at the cave, the home of Karmandor the dragon if he had heard correctly.

'Tell them about the wicked witch of the west,' a voice came from the back of the group. Sammy spun around to see the professor of the West house waving her staff.

Professor Sanchez towered next to her, glaring first at the woman then at her staff.

'I know what you think Professor Sanchez, that nothing good comes from the sea but fish.'

'Fish, sea?' said Sammy. 'What's that about?'

'The West house,' whispered Dixie, 'is associated with water. That's why they wear blue.'

'Oh,' said Sammy, touching his green tie and looking at the blue, yellow and red worn by his new classmates. 'Green for trees, red for fire,' he said thinking out loud.

Dixie stared at him and burst out laughing. 'Green for trees, wait until I tell my brothers. They'll love that!'

'Oh,' said Sammy a little embarrassed.

'Green for the earth,' said Dixie, still giggling. 'Trees as well.'

'What's Professor Sanchez's house?'

'The East house is yellow and belongs to the air, the power of thought,' said Professor Sanchez kindly.

'That figures,' said Sammy, looking at the students with yellow on their uniform. 'How does she do that, keep coming up behind me whenever I have a question about her.'

'The tricks of the trade,' said Professor Sanchez tossing her dark hair back as she laughed. 'I see we shall get along, yes?'

Sammy nodded and was glad when Professor Sanchez whisked herself to the front of the group.

'Well done Sammy,' said Darius. 'You just made friends with the wicked witch of the East.'

Sammy grinned and took one last look at the dark hole in the rock as they left the clearing. The professor from the West house was leading them back to the castle. Sammy overheard Professor Burlay tell Gavin and Toby that she was Dr Margarite Lithoman, their Gemology professor, who would teach them more about the onyx stone they had been given as well as many other stones and crystals.

There was a rumbling behind them. Sammy stopped and looked back. The pearlescent tube was swaying from side to side, shimmering and vibrating, creating an electric humming sound overhead. The humming grew louder and louder. Sammy pressed his hands against his ears to block the noise.

'They come,' said Professor Sanchez, pointing at the tube.

'Early,' said Commander Altair.

Sammy noticed the four professors had taken out their staffs. They were holding them at arm's length, all pointing towards the Dragon's Lair.

Over Gavin's shoulder, Sammy saw silvery shapes rocket down the pearlescent tube and disappear inside the hilltop. As the shapes fell into the rock, the humming stopped and the tube stopped swaying. The four professors climbed to the top of the steps, poised, ready to fire on anything, or anyone, coming out of the darkness.

In the lantern light, a tuft of green hair appeared at the mouth of the Dragon's Lair. Dr Lithoman shot a bolt of red lightning from her staff. It hit the cave wall, shattering the rock and lighting up the inside of the Dragon's Lair. Sammy couldn't see clearly but he thought that he had seen the faces of two green haired boys in the shadows.

Beside him, Dixie was shrieking, even with his hands over his ears he could hear her. 'It's Serberon and Mikhael! The rest of the school are returning!'

Inside the Dragon's Lair came a scream of pain. It sounded like one of the boys had been hit.

As quickly as they had drawn their staffs, the professors put them away. Commander Altair and Professor Burlay ran forward.

Dixie ran up the steps after them. 'Serb, are you hurt?' she screamed.

Commander Altair held Dixie back as more faces appeared at the entrance to the Dragon's Lair. Boys and girls of all ages, shapes and sizes spilled out of the cave and ran down the steps. Sammy counted three green haired boys, 'Jason, Mikhael and Serberon,' he whispered to himself.

'Dr Lithoman,' Commander Altair shouted above the noise the students were making, 'take the students back to the castle.'

'Take him to Mrs Grock's,' Professor Sanchez said to Professor Burlay, pointing at the green haired boy.

'Let me go too,' said Dixie. 'He's my brother.'

Sammy looked at Serberon. The green haired boy had a line of blood dribbling from a gash in his cheek. He was dragging his left leg behind him and Sammy could see a dark stain running from Serberon's knee to his ankle.

'Very well,' said Professor Sanchez. 'You and you,' she pointed to Sammy and Dixie, 'may go with him.'

Sammy helped Professor Burlay to carry Dixie's brother back along the narrow path. Dixie walked ahead, holding the lantern and pulling up her coat collar to keep out the cold.

Serberon wriggled in Sammy's hands. 'You'll miss the welcome feast,' he croaked.

Sammy stared at Serberon's green hair.

'Genetic,' said Serberon.

Dixie turned around and grinned at them. 'He knows.'

'Come on kids, if you keep up the pace we might make dessert,' said Professor Burlay, puffing slightly.

Sammy's stomach grumbled. He'd had nothing but biscuits since breakfast and he was getting hungry.

'Don't know what Sir Ragnarok will make of it, you lot coming back early,' Professor Burlay said to Serberon.

Serberon didn't reply and Sammy shook him gently. His eyes stayed closed. 'Unconscious,' muttered Professor Burlay. 'Hope we're not too late.'

CHAPTER 6

MRS GROCK'S AGAIN

Sammy was glad when the path ended and Mrs Grock's house appeared in the lantern light. The cottage was in complete darkness, silhouetted against the sky.

Professor Burlay kicked the gate open gently and they walked up garden path, past the wishing well to the front door. Professor Burlay released Serberon's legs and knocked on the front door.

It creaked open spookily and Sammy shuffled forward, carrying Serberon's weight in his arms. They were in a large rectangular lounge lit by soft candlelight. There were three doors on the far wall, leading into the house. One of the doors was slightly open and through the narrow crack, Sammy could see what looked like a store room with large wooden barrels and sacks with white labels. From the doorway, he couldn't read the labels, but he hoped there would be something in one of the barrels to help Serberon.

Professor Burlay took Serberon's shoulders from Sammy and guided him into the room. Sammy followed

Dixie, taking in the musky smell of scented candles and the cosiness of Mrs Grock's front room.

Stretching the width of the house, the front room looked much bigger inside than it had appeared from the outside. On the left was a large wooden table with patchwork cushions resting on the seats of six wooden chairs. Behind the table ran row upon row of books stacked high on rickety shelves from the floor to the ceiling.

Sammy knew that, apart from Ratisbury library, he had never seen so many books in one place. He strained his eyes to read the titles. They seemed to be about illnesses, medicines and cures.

To his right there was a purple three-seat settee, facing an alcove where a stone fireplace was set deep into the outer wall. Yellow-orange flames licked the underside of logs crackling in the grate sending sparks on to the stone hearth.

'Take a seat kids, she won't be long.' Professor Burlay laid Serberon on to the settee and drew up three beanbags from next to the fireplace.

Sammy wandered over to the bookshelves. He took the stub of a candle from the wooden dining table and held it up to the spines to read the titles.

'Midnight Magic,' he muttered, '1001 Instant Cures, Third Century Illnesses, The Angel, A Generation in Magic, How to Fix Almost Anything, Cuts, Bruises and Broken Bones.' He paused as one book caught his attention, "The Mystery of the Wishing Well". Sammy reached out to touch the book and jumped as a shadow loomed on the wall in front of him.

'Ooch there's magic in that one all right.'

Sammy spun around. Mrs Grock was standing in the doorway. She whisked past him to pick "Cuts, Bruises and

Broken Bones" from the bookshelf and waved for him to sit down by the fire.

'I fancy we could do with a cuppa,' Mrs Grock said to Dixie. 'Do you know where it is?'

Dixie nodded and headed for the central door. Sammy stared as she walked into a modern kitchen that looked out of place next to the ancient feel of the lounge.

'Now then young Dragon Knight.' Sammy jumped as he realised Mrs Grock was speaking to him. She had put a pair of horn rimmed glasses on her short nose and was reading from the leather bound book.

'I will need three eggs, a turnip and a bottle of amberoid.'

Sammy laughed. He had almost believed her, until she had asked for the amberoid.

'Young Knight,' said Mrs Grock reprovingly. 'The eggs can be found outside with the hens, the turnip from my allotment and the amberoid from the bottle on the top shelf in my store, through the door on the left.'

Sammy nodded, thinking he would worry about finding eggs and turnips in the dark first.

Once outside, Sammy could see the wire frame of the hen house silhouetted in the cloudy moonlight and he stumbled into it, cracking his knee against one of the solid support poles.

'Good thing I'm not afraid of the dark,' he grumbled, scratching his hand on the sharp wire separating the sleeping hens. He picked out five eggs and a handful of straw and feathers. 'Turnips next,' Sammy whispered, putting the eggs into his coat pocket for safekeeping. He stumbled back on to the path, searching in the darkness for anything that looked remotely like an allotment.

Halfway along, Sammy tripped on an uneven bump and went flying, face first, across the path on to some squishy muddy ground.

'Uurrgh,' said Sammy, hearing the eggs crush together. As the moon reappeared from behind a cloud, he could see neat lines of vegetables and the outline of a family of rabbits feasting on a large lettuce. Sammy heaved himself up, brushing a round object away from his arm.

'Turnip!' Sammy exclaimed, picking up the turnip. He checked the eggs; just one had broken in his fall. He made his way carefully back to the house, reaching for the door handle as the moon disappeared behind another cloud.

A noise behind him made him turn around and his blood ran cold as he stared straight into the red eyes of one of the hooded figures from earlier in the afternoon. He rattled the door handle and leapt inside, away from the figure.

'Here!' Sammy thrust the sticky eggs and turnip into Mrs Grock's hands.

'Ooch!' squealed Mrs Grock. 'You'd best get cleaned up.' She pointed to the right hand door. 'You'll find my room that way, on the right again is the bathroom.'

Sammy headed for the door and stopped just in time as Dixie came out of the kitchen holding a tray of steaming tea.

'Watch it,' said Dixie, steadying herself.

Sammy waggled his sticky hands at her and squeezed past into Mrs Grock's low ceilinged bedroom.

The bedroom was about a third of the size of the living room with a large four poster bed draped in purple on the far wall. More bookshelves lined the remaining walls, the largest towering over a tiny writing desk with silver lamp and a half written letter.

Sammy knew he should head straight for the bathroom, but his curiosity nagged him to peek.

'Dear Sir Ragnarok,' he read. 'It is with regret that I must hand in my notice as school secretary and nurse...' Sammy stared, knowing that he shouldn't be reading the letter but desperate to find out why Mrs Grock might be leaving.

'...I fear for my safety as the Shape draws ever closer, lurking outside my house. It will not be long before they are strong again. A dragon has fallen in the forest and the stars are aligning in the formation that has not risen in the sky since the fall of the King of the Dark Ages...'

Remembering that he had come into Mrs Grock's room to clean himself up, Sammy tore his eyes away from the letter and over to the door on the right. His fingers closed around the door handle, a brass dragon tail set deep in an oak door that could easily have come out of the Dark Ages itself.

Thinking hard about the hooded figures in the clearing and at the garden gate, he rubbed the mud and soil from his face and rinsed his hands using a dragon shaped soap and the red and blue dragon head taps overlooking the deep ceramic basin.

Sammy dried his hands on a cream towel embossed in gold stitching with yet another dragon. As he turned to leave he noticed a half empty bottle of sleeping tablets on Mrs Grock's bedside table.

In the lounge, Dixie had handed around cups of steaming tea and was sitting on one of the purple beanbags gently brushing Serberon's green hair out of his eyes. Professor Burlay and Mrs Grock were nowhere to be seen.

Sammy grinned as he remembered the amberoid and headed for the store room. The door was now shut and he could hear muffled voices inside.

'...and I followed the tracks...gate to the forest...'

'The Shape?' said Professor Burlay.

'Aye.'

He knocked on the door, reaching for the dragon tail handle.

'One moment Sammy, we'll bring the amberoid.'

Sammy went back over to the fire and flopped on one of the beanbags.

'Eavesdropping?' asked Dixie.

Sammy didn't reply, his head churning with the conversation he had overheard.

'Fine,' snapped Dixie, tossing her hair. She ignored him completely until Professor Burlay and Mrs Grock came out of the store room armed with two brown glass bottles and a silver basin no bigger than a cake tin.

Mrs Grock knelt on the floor beside Serberon and took a sheathed kitchen knife from her front pocket. She sliced the turnip into eight equal slices and balanced them on the basin rim.

After re-sheathing the knife, Mrs Grock smashed the eggs together with a crunch, dripping the orange and white liquid into the bowl and throwing the shells into the fire.

Sammy watched as she unscrewed the two bottles of amberoid and poured a lumpy brown, gravy-like, liquid one drop at a time on top of the egg mixture. He screwed up his nose as wafts of the liquid evaporated around them. It smelt like a mix of used sports socks and soggy rice pudding. Professor Burlay and Mrs Grock carried on as normal, probably used to it, he thought.

'There you go,' said Mrs Grock whisking a slice of turnip through the mix with a flourish. 'The potion to fix cuts and bruises.' She looked at Sammy. 'Would my young Dragon Knight like to go first?'

'Um…' Sammy couldn't make up his mind which was worse, the pain in his leg or the vile smell of the healing potion.

'Serberon first,' said Dixie firmly. She reached for the bowl of frothy liquid.

'Ooch ok,' said Mrs Grock. 'Take some turnip and rub it on the wound. That's it. Keep it away from the eyes and mouth.'

'Ok,' said Dixie, clearly not expecting to be allowed to go first. She took the turnip as instructed, swirled it through the brown liquid and rubbed it on to Serberon's forehead.

Sammy gasped. Where the liquid had rubbed over the blood and cuts on Serberon's face, they had healed and he looked as good as new.

'Thanks sis,' said Serberon, touching his forehead.

Dixie beamed. 'That's ok.'

'Now for the young Dragon Knight,' said Mrs Grock. 'The left leg and the right hand.'

Sammy stared; how could she possibly know where he had cut himself.

Mrs Grock hitched her skirt up to her knee. 'I've done it myself many-a-time,' she chuckled, 'John keeps telling me to be more careful, especially in these days.'

Sammy didn't stop to wonder what she meant by "in these days" and took the turnip, gratefully stroking the liquid across his knee whilst holding his nose with his free hand. He took a deep breath and used his left hand to cover the scratches on his right hand.

The scratches vanished under the turnip mixture as quickly as the cuts had vanished from Serberon. As he ran out of breath, Sammy spluttered, glad to find the smell had gone.

Mrs Grock laughed. 'You get used to it in the end.' She threw the remaining slices into the fire and yawned. 'Time for me to get some kip.'

Professor Burlay nodded. 'It's time we were back at the castle and it's a little walk yet.'

'They could use the passage,' said Mrs Grock, hiding a second yawn behind her hand.

'Not tonight,' said Professor Burlay, starting to yawn himself. 'They've had more excitement today than any first years I can remember. It'll only cause trouble.'

'Your canna remember the way,' Mrs Grock laughed. 'Besides, it may be safer with the Shape in the woods.'

Sammy looked at Dixie. 'Secret passages!'

'Underground! Please Professor Burlay, can we use it?' begged Dixie.

'I don't know…' started Professor Burlay, every bit the pushover Sammy had suspected.

Mrs Grock was already on her feet holding out her hand to help Serberon up. She gathered their cups onto the tray, passed Dixie the lantern from the hearth and led them into the store room.

'In there, under the white grain sacks, you'll find a trapdoor opening inwards,' said Mrs Grock. 'Go down the steps and you're into the passage.'

Sammy grinned, not only were they going to be allowed to use the passage, but she was giving them an easy way to return to the cottage without being seen.

'You're sure the Shape don't know about these passages?' asked Professor Burlay.

'Ooch that's right John, but hurry or the little ones will be in trouble.'

Back on his feet, Serberon seemed to be at full strength. He heaved the heavy sack away from the trapdoor and kicked the metal handle. The trapdoor fell open, revealing the stone steps and dark passage exactly as Mrs Grock had said.

Serberon led the way. He took the lantern from Dixie who followed him, clutching his coat, down the steps into the passage. Sammy followed Dixie, using his staff to keep his balance. He looked back as Mrs Grock pushed something shiny into Professor Burlay's hand.

'Draconite,' whispered Mrs Grock, catching Sammy's eye, 'for Margarite.'

Sammy guessed that she meant Gemology professor, Dr Margarite Lithoman of the West house and he made a mental note to read up on what draconite was. At the very least, he would ask questions in her lessons.

They stumbled through the dark passage, barely inches from each other. It was cold and damp with a musty smell lingering in the air. Sammy half wished they had taken their chances above ground.

'Must be a leak somewhere,' said Professor Burlay, splashing through a puddle to take the lead in the narrow passageway.

Sammy tapped the walls with his staff. 'It's all stone,' he said. 'Maybe there's a crack somewhere.'

Professor Burlay looked worriedly at them. 'There's no cracks here, young Sammy.'

Sammy frowned. There was nothing worse than being called young, especially when he had tried to make a sensible suggestion.

Professor Burlay stopped again, making everyone bump together. Sammy leaned around Professor Burlay's shoulder to see why they had stopped. In the glow of Serberon's lantern, the passage seemed to split in two.

'Which way?' asked Sammy.

'I think…' said Professor Burlay nervously, 'I think we should go left.'

'Right,' said Serberon, swinging the lantern from side to side. 'We should go right.'

Professor Burlay started walking down the left hand passageway.

'Left would take us to the Dragon's Lair,' called Serberon. 'Right should lead us back to the castle.'

Professor Burlay walked back to the fork. 'A vote perhaps?' he said darkly.

Dixie huddled close to Serberon and pointed down the right hand passage.

'We should stay together,' said Sammy torn between Professor Burlay's authority and his gut feeling to trust Serberon.

'Yes we should Sammy,' said Professor Burlay, 'and we should go left. May I have the lantern please Serberon?'

Serberon stood still. Dixie looked up at him. 'Come on Serb, let's go left. We can always come back if it's wrong.'

'We should go right,' said Serberon, reluctantly handing over the lantern.

Dixie whispered in Sammy's ear.

'I can't,' said Sammy. 'It was a one off.'

'Just try it,' said Dixie.

Sammy coughed and held his staff tightly, the bulging end facing the ground.

'Fire!' he commanded.

Exactly as it had happened in the forest, red sparks burst from the end of the staff giving him a surge of confidence, power and adrenalin. A small fire formed in the passage at their feet.

Serberon stared. 'First years can't do that.'

Professor Burlay stepped close to Sammy. 'There's strong magic in that stick Sammy. Go easy with it eh?'

'Ok,' said Sammy, unable to take his eyes away from the flames.

Professor Burlay took out his own staff and pointed it towards the fire. As if invisible strings were in control, the fire lifted from the ground. 'Magic,' said Professor Burlay, taking the flames towards the left hand passageway.

'Hey look!' shouted Sammy, catching sight of some shapes on the passage ceiling. 'Directions!'

They craned their heads to see the faint chalk drawings.

'A dragon and a castle,' said Serberon smugly. 'Now can we go right?'

'Very well,' conceded Professor Burlay, taking them in silence down the right hand passage back to the castle.

As they climbed up a second set of steps, Sammy was intrigued to see that the passage extended into a lantern lit tunnel, stretching as far as his eyes could see.

'That's the Shute,' said Dixie. 'It goes from the school gates to the front door. We'd have used it yesterday if Professor Burlay hadn't given us that lift.'

'Humph,' said Serberon. Sammy guessed that he had walked on his first day.

The steps continued upwards at a painfully steep angle, at least the height of two storeys in a department store. Sammy's feet ached from the distance that they had already walked that day and he was glad to reach the top and breathe the fresh night air again.

Professor Burlay consulted his pocket watch and led them through the castle door. 'Dixie, you and Serberon may go up to your tower rooms. Sammy, please follow me.'

Sammy exchanged a worried look with Dixie and Serberon before they separated at the main stairwell. Dixie and Serberon headed for the North tower and Sammy followed Professor Burlay along a corridor to another staircase. They climbed higher and higher in spirals until Sammy thought they would surely reach the castle roof.

The spiral staircase ended with a solid door in the same way the North tower staircase ended with the door to the first year dormitory.

'Right Sammy,' said Professor Burlay. 'My orders are to leave you here to see Sir Ragnarok. We'll meet again tomorrow morning. You have an introduction to the science of Astronomics, starting at nine thirty sharp.'

Sammy stared. This was easily the worst moment of his entire life. He flinched as Professor Burlay slapped his shoulder and tapped under Sammy's chin.

'Keep it up,' said Professor Burlay, trying overly hard to be reassuring.

Sammy waited until Professor Burlay was out of sight before he knocked on the wooden door and stepped back, waiting for it to open.

CHAPTER 7

THE DIRECTOMETER

Sammy waited ten seconds, then thirty. He checked his watch, one minute had passed. He held tightly to the banister shivering with cold and tiredness. It was a long, long way down and he wasn't sure that he could remember the way. As he turned to go, the door creaked on its hinges and swung open.

Sammy spun around and came face to face with Sir Ragnarok. They stared eye to eye for a second before Sir Ragnarok nodded and beckoned for Sammy to follow him into his office.

Sammy followed the headmaster up seven steps, thinking how high up they must be. The stairs were lit by two red candles held in antique holsters and clipped to the walls with metal brackets. They walked through a second door opening into a small circular room.

Sammy stopped and stared at the wall in front of him. Ahead, in a giant curved screen stretching from floor to ceiling was an exact replica of himself, walking up the steps through the door. He rubbed his nose, watching as the boy opposite did exactly the same.

'Surprised?' Sir Ragnarok raised his bushy grey eyebrows.

'Yeah,' said Sammy, finding his voice. He was unnerved to see the boy in the screen open and close his mouth in perfect synchronisation.

'One of my toys,' said Sir Ragnarok, as if the screen was as common as a television. He waved his hand and the screen went blank.

Sammy looked around the rest of the room. On his left, there was a solid wooden desk and chair facing the screen. A photograph on the desk showed Sir Ragnarok laughing with a plump man with a twirling moustache and black bow-tie. Behind the desk was a picture framed aerial map of the school. Sammy recognised the places they had visited on the tour. On his right, a smoke grey cat lay on a curved couch covered in the same purple velvet as Mrs Grock's long settee.

Next to the couch was a curved table holding a decanter of red liquid, two crystal glasses and a ceramic bowl of rainbow coloured sweets. A metal spiral staircase with a pair of purple slippers on the bottom step led upwards, Sammy guessed, to Sir Ragnarok's bedroom.

The floor was covered in a thick green carpet so dark that it looked almost black. Emblazoned on a wool rug in the centre of the room were the four house logos arranged as a compass with the tailed 'D' stretching out to the four points.

'You like?' asked Sir Ragnarok, sitting at his desk.

'Yeah,' said Sammy.

Sir Ragnarok smiled. 'Is that a "yes"?'

'Yes,' said Sammy, clearly pronouncing the "s" as he repeated it.

'Then sit.'

Sammy sat down next to the cat and placed his staff gently on the floor.

'Lariston,' said Sir Ragnarok, 'he's nearly a hundred years old and full of life, during the day,' he added with a smile.

The cat purred.

'He approves of you,' said Sir Ragnarok. 'Cats are a fine judge of character.'

Sammy nodded politely.

'So how was your first day here Sammy?'

'I think I'm going to like it here.'

'Better than your old school?'

'Definitely,' said Sammy, 'I'm going to work hard and play hard.'

'Good,' said Sir Ragnarok. 'Now, to business. You know a little about the Shape?' Sir Ragnarok raised his right eyebrow.

Sammy nodded.

'Speak up boy.'

'Yes,' said Sammy. 'Dixie told me about them.'

'Dixie?'

'Dixie Deane. She's in my house.'

'Green hair?' asked Sir Ragnarok.

Sammy nodded. 'Yes Sir.'

'Yes,' said Sir Ragnarok. 'A little knowledge can be a dangerous thing.' He waved his right hand towards the screen.

Sammy leaned forward, he recognised himself at the front of the group of students. They were in the clearing where they had spread out to choose their staffs.

Sir Ragnarok stood up. 'It is better that you know enough to protect yourself but not enough to get involved.

You are young yet, although Mrs Grock seems to have other ideas.'

Sammy felt his cheeks burn. 'She said I could be a Dragon Knight.'

'And that you may...indeed you may.' Sir Ragnarok sighed and pointed to the bowl of sweets. 'I'll have a purple if there is one.'

Sammy reached across Lariston's warm body to the sweets and passed Sir Ragnarok a purple candy.

'Thank you. You may help yourself, but please watch the screen with me. It is important.'

Sammy helped himself to a green candy that turned out to be a banana flavoured toffee that gripped his teeth like cement.

Sir Ragnarok used his hand to move the screens forward to the part when Sammy had wandered off alone towards the tree stump.

'Watch closely.'

Sitting on the sofa, Sammy drew his breath sharply and almost swallowed the toffee. On the screen, hooded figures were following him. He looked over his shoulder, grateful to see the solid wall behind him.

He watched as his earlier self picked up the branch that he had chosen to be his staff and tapped it on the tree stump. Although he couldn't hear the words, he knew that on the screen, he would be shouting "fire." The staff quivered and projected the red sparks, casting the flames on to the tree stump.

Sir Ragnarok paused the screen. 'Very impressive. I haven't seen a first year, particularly one from an unconnected family, to be able to perform such an action.'

'Thank you,' said Sammy.

'I believe you did the same this morning,' Sir Ragnarok shuffled some papers on his desk, 'with…Kyrillan. Most unusual.' He waved for the scene to continue.

Sammy remembered only too well what came next. Himself jumping as he saw the circle of shadowy figures. His relief as Dixie broke into the ring, dissolving the shadows, Commander Altair and Professor Sanchez coming after him.

He stared at the screen as Commander Altair and Professor Sanchez not only came up behind him, but fired orange sparks and black powder at the figures who had reappeared amongst the trees.

'So they hadn't gone?' whispered Sammy.

'No,' said Sir Ragnarok. 'They dissolve and reappear. It's what makes them so dangerous. They will surround their target and dissolve if fired upon, only to reappear somewhere else seconds later.'

Sammy stared shaking his head.

'Your friend Dixie is a true friend,' Sir Ragnarok smiled. 'She has a soft spot for you, sees you as a fourth brother perhaps.'

Sammy nodded, 'Commander Altair said…'

'…She cared more for saving your life at that moment than protecting her own.'

'Will I get the chance…'

'…To repay your debt?' interrupted Sir Ragnarok. 'Quite possibly, these are difficult days and I have a sad announcement for tomorrow.'

'About Mrs Grock?' asked Sammy, surprising himself at being so forward.

'Big day tomorrow.' Sir Ragnarok gave nothing away. 'Now, can you find your way to the North tower?' he asked kindly, his blue eyes twinkling.

'I don't know,' said Sammy truthfully.

'Then take this,' said Sir Ragnarok handing Sammy his pocket watch. 'It's a Directometer made for me by Professor Burlay as a birthday present. Red and you're going the wrong way, green keep on going.'

'Ok,' said Sammy, taking the pocket watch.

Sir Ragnarok leaned over and tapped the dial. The clock face disappeared, replaced with an oily grey. 'North tower,' he commanded.

A red dot appeared in the centre of the dial. Sir Ragnarok guided Sammy's hands towards the door. The dot changed to a deep emerald green.

'I'll have it back at breakfast tomorrow please,' said Sir Ragnarok. 'It is not a toy.'

'Ok,' said Sammy waving the Directometer from left to right to get the hang of it. He stepped up from the couch and followed the green light to the first of Sir Ragnarok's office doors.

'One moment,' called Sir Ragnarok tapping his hand on his desk. A bulging bag and a folded grey rug appeared next to the pens and papers.

'Your first day wouldn't be complete without a midnight feast, would it?'

Sammy grinned, he had felt his stomach rumble while he sat in the office and he was glad that it hadn't escaped Sir Ragnarok that he hadn't eaten since breakfast. From the weight of the bag, it felt as though there would be plenty to share with all of the first years.

He wrapped the rug around his shoulders and picked up his staff, the bag and the Directometer.

'Good night Sir,' said Sammy, making his way slowly down the spiral staircase.

'Good night Sammy, I'll see you in the morning. Don't stay up too late, I understand that you have a lesson in predicting the patterns of the stars first thing.

Astronomics,' Sir Ragnarok explained, 'is a fine science from a fine teacher.'

The Directometer went red as Sammy reached the bottom of the staircase. He pushed past a large tapestry of a knight hanging on the wall of the Main Hall. The empty house tables stretched from one end of the vast room to the other. He swung the dial towards the arched doorway and the green dot appeared.

Sammy walked out into the corridor, following the green dot past tall and narrow purple curtained windows, past silver suits of armour each holding battle shields and lances. He followed the Directometer past paintings stretched from floor to ceiling of strangers in the same silver armour, fighting on huge dragons with fire blowing from behind their forked tongues.

He paused to take a closer look as one painting caught his eye. It was a portrait of five faceless figures standing at the school entrance with the caption "Shaping the Future of Dragons" written underneath.

He stared at the painting, trying to make sense of it when he heard footsteps and a muffled cough behind him.

A rough hand grabbed his shoulder, swinging him round. Sammy panicked, his staff and bag falling to the ground with a clatter.

'Get off me!'

'Relax,' said a gruff voice. 'It's just me, Tom Sweep, Dragamas caretaker. Sir Ragnarok said I might bump into a Sammy Rambles. Is that you?'

'Oh,' said Sammy, rubbing his shoulder and looking at the thin wild-eyed man dressed in a grey caretaker coat. At some point, Sammy thought the man must have jumped out of his skin in fright and only half of him had got back in, he had so many sagging wrinkles. He carried a swinging lantern, almost the only light in the darkened corridor.

'I'm Sammy.'

'With that rug, you look like one of them,' Tom Sweep nodded towards the picture.

'The Shape?' whispered Sammy picking up his staff and bag.

'Aye,' said Tom Sweep, covering a hacking cough with a weathered hand. 'Course no one knows who they really are. They're the ones who want to get rid of all the dragons, taking their stones.'

'Draconite?' said Sammy thinking back to Mrs Grock's.

'Aye, draconite if you will,' said Tom Sweep. 'Without it, the dragon will die.'

'Is that what Sir Ragnarok's going to announce tomorrow?'

'Aye Sammy, you're bright, and not too far off the mark either.' Tom Sweep held his lantern to the painting and stomped back down the corridor.

As the swinging lantern light faded away, Sammy felt a pang of fear now he was alone in the dimly lit corridor. He checked the Directometer. It was still green.

'Chin up, keep going,' he muttered, grateful to turn the corner and see the arched door with the "North" Gothic written plaque in front of him.

Sammy pushed the door open and walked into the warm common room. Huddled beside the open fire, three faces belonging to Dixie, Darius and Serberon looked up at him. He pocketed the Directometer and waved the bulging bag at them. 'Midnight feast!'

'Nice one Sammy!'

'Cool! What's in it?'

'Don't know, but it's been really heavy to carry!'

Dixie and Darius moved up to make room for Sammy to be nearest to the fire. They listened whilst munching sandwiches crammed full to bursting with turkey and lettuce, cheese and onion, chicken and cucumber as Sammy told them about his visit to Sir Ragnarok's office.

As he reached further into the bag, Sammy saw why the bag had been so heavy to carry. There were two bottles of fizzy drink, cherryade and limeade and four plastic cups. They mixed the two together calling it "lerryade" and "chimeade," but couldn't decide which was better.

At the very bottom, Sammy found a collection of Sir Ragnarok's brightly coloured sweets. Dixie took a red one which she said was a strawberry cream. Darius and Serberon both took a green banana-toffee and Sammy took a purple sweet. It turned out to be a cycling combination of all flavours.

'It's raspberry,' he said to Dixie, 'no orange, no banana, lime, blueberry!'

The sweet cycled three times before fizzing into a bitter sherbet. He washed it down with the last of the "lerryade" and rubbed his eyes.

'Come on,' Serberon said at last. 'Time for bed.'

Sammy, Darius and Serberon went up the boys' staircase. Serberon gave Dixie a quick hug before she went up the staircase into the girls' tower.

Serberon stopped at the entrance to the third floor tower room. 'Night then,' he said, entering a room identical to the first year dormitory, without the cone-roof ceiling.

Sammy followed Darius up the last fifty steps, wishing the tower had been designed with a lift. He pushed open the door to find their room splashed with beams of moonlight casting a natural light into the dormitory. One moonbeam was spotlighted on his pillow.

'I'll never sleep with that there,' groaned Sammy, resting his new staff up against the side of his bed.

Darius giggled and pointed to Toby who was sleeping with his mouth slightly open snoring gently.

Amos had his curtain pulled tightly around his bed. Sammy hoped he hadn't fallen out with Gavin and Toby again. He thought the curtain rustled as he crossed the room to his own bed, but he couldn't be sure.

Moonlight or no moonlight, Sammy found that despite trying to keep his eyes open to make his first day last as long as possible, he couldn't and he sank into a dreamless sleep almost as soon as his head touched the pillow.

CHAPTER 8

SIR RAGNAROK'S ANNOUNCEMENT

Despite the exhausting events of the day before, Sammy was first to wake up. He reached out to check he really was at Dragamas and touched Kyrillan's slimy skin. A pair of black, beady eyes rolled towards him.

Sammy pulled back the green quilt and swung his legs over the side of the bed. The stone floor was cold but he braved it and stood up. He nodded to Amos who was watching him, and swung the green velvet curtain around his bed to get dressed in private.

Seconds later he was wearing black trousers and a white long sleeve shirt with a t-shirt underneath to keep warm. It took three goes until he was happy with his tie, then he sat at the end of the bed to put on black socks and new black leather shoes; a present from his grandmother when she learnt he was changing schools. Sammy hadn't mentioned it at the time, but he was worried they would squeak on the stone floor.

Sammy stood up and tested walking in the new shoes. They were a little tight, but quiet. He picked up the onyx and Directometer from the chest of drawers, slipped them into his trouser pocket and looked out of the tower window beside his bed.

It was sunny outside and he could just see the outline of Mrs Grock's house tucked between the trees and a tiny blob that he knew would be the wishing well. He wondered about the underground passages. How many more were they and where did they go?

What interested him most was the end-to-end view of the Dragonball pitch. Sammy could see everything from his bedside window. Some fifty or so students were already out practising whilst riding on large dragons. He thought he caught a glimpse of green hair and wondered if it was one of Dixie's brothers.

Just as he was making up his mind, the bell above the door rang four times.

'Four,' Sammy said out loud.

'Breakfast,' said Amos.

The bell had woken Gavin, Toby and Darius, who exchanged "Good mornings" with him.

In almost no time at all, they were dressed and in the common room and met Professor Burlay at the bottom of the stairs.

'Morning boys,' said Professor Burlay, looking relieved. 'I'm glad you're ready, I should really have come up sooner. Breakfast is in the Main Hall and then I'll meet you in room thirty-seven for your first Astronomics lesson.' Professor Burlay ran to the stairs to the girls' tower and returned moments later with the five North first year girls.

'Morning Sammy,' said Dixie, grinning at him.

'Morn-ugh-ing,' said Sammy, holding his side where Gavin had elbowed him.

'Sammy's got a girlfriend,' Gavin whispered in his ear.

'Shut it,' Sammy whispered back.

When they arrived in the Main Hall, Sammy decided he'd never seen so many people in one room in his life. The hall was laid out just the same as it had been the day before; the four wooden house tables side by side and the teachers' table horizontally at the front. Today, it was filled with hundreds of students, sitting at the tables, talking and shouting amongst themselves.

Sammy looked nervously at Gavin who, for once, was silent.

Toby took the lead. 'I think we're over here,' he pointed to the green table clothed table nearest to them.

Even without the tablecloth, Dixie's brothers gave away which was the North table with their bright green hair. Serberon seemed to have fully recovered. Jason and Mikhael sat either side of him.

'You can sit with us if you like,' Serberon said to Dixie, pointing to an empty chair opposite him.

'It's ok, I'll sit with the rest of my year,' said Dixie.

'And Sammy?' Serberon grinned.

Dixie blushed and smacked Serberon's arm. 'Shut it,' she said, already on her way to sit with the girls from her tower room, her green ponytail swishing behind her.

Sammy noticed Dixie wouldn't quite look at him at breakfast; looking when she thought he wouldn't notice. Either side of him, Toby and Darius were discussing Dragonball and another sport that seemed to be called Firesticks.

From what Sammy could gather from their conversation about spells and staffs, Firesticks sounded even more dangerous than playing Dragonball, which he'd decided was a mix of rugby and football on the back of a flying dragon.

This time, Sammy knew to wait for Sir Ragnarok to arrive before picking up his silver cutlery. After nearly ten minutes, Sir Ragnarok appeared looking tired with large dark circles underneath his blue eyes.

With a scraping of chairs on the stone floor, the whole school got to their feet. Sir Ragnarok waved his hand and the chairs creaked as they sat back down.

'Students of Dragamas,' said Sir Ragnarok, 'I have some bad news, yes very bad news indeed,' Sir Ragnarok paused, surveying the school. 'As some of you will already know through your families, the Shape is on the move.'

Although Sammy hadn't heard of the Shape before he had arrived at Dragamas, he felt a cold shiver run up his spine and he gasped with every student in the hall.

'Dragamas is being held to ransom for a great sum of money,' said Sir Ragnarok.

Another gasp circled the room. Sammy's spine shuddered again. It must be a lot of money, more perhaps than the largest account in his mother's bank in Switzerland.

'We do not give in,' said Sir Ragnarok. 'I do not give in. Dragamas will not pay, even if it means closing the school. We have been given until the end of the summer term to make the funds available, which I am very much afraid will not happen, the sum is too great.'

Sammy felt his jaw drop, the bottom falling out of his world. His room with the view of the Dragonball pitch, his new friends, Darius, Gavin, Toby and Dixie.

'But I've only just got here,' whispered Sammy. 'They can't close the school.'

'They can and they will,' said Milly, tears shining in her pale blue eyes.

'We've only been here for one day,' said Dixie. 'One day!'

'One day,' said Sammy, thoughtfully. 'One day and eight months to fix it.'

'Fix it!' Gavin laughed. 'How do you plan to do that?'

Aware that he had the full attention of his table, Sammy faltered. 'I…I don't know.'

Dixie came to his rescue. 'Obviously,' she said, with an air of self-confidence, 'the money must be raised.'

Sammy looked at her gratefully. 'Yeah, er, yes, we must raise the money.'

'But how much, by when?' asked Gavin.

'By the end of the summer term,' said Sammy, hoping Gavin wouldn't notice he hadn't said how much.

'It's not fair,' said Dixie, after they'd talked about it for a few minutes. 'My brothers never had anything like this when they started.'

Sammy looked up at the third year table. The green haired boys were holding a similar council. In fact, now he came to think about it, the whole school was talking, voices rising with each student speaking louder to make him or herself heard.

'Enough!' shouted Sir Ragnarok and the room fell silent. 'School will go on. Term events will go on and exams will go on. I insist that one black star shall be given to any student caught being pessimistic.' Sir Ragnarok smiled. 'This may turn out to be a normal year with our usual visit to the Floating Circus…until the summer, when the situation with the Shape will be reviewed.'

'And the school closed,' finished Sammy.

'Do not give up hope,' said Sir Ragnarok, sitting on his throne-like chair and mopping his forehead with a plain white handkerchief. He tucked the handkerchief into his collar and picked up his crescent shaped knife and five-pronged fork. The room erupted with the familiar "popping" and wafts of fresh smelling bacon, sausages and fried bread swirled down the room. 'You may start!' said Sir Ragnarok.

Sammy picked up his knife and fork along with the rest of the school. The noise seemed hollow, empty, as if Sir Ragnarok's announcement had threatened more than just the closure of the school. He found he wasn't hungry any more, and by the look of the full plates and tiny mouthfuls people were taking around him, no one else was hungry either.

As Sammy pushed a piece of fried bread for the third time around his plate, he remembered Mrs Grock. Perhaps Sir Ragnarok didn't know she was leaving, or maybe he had thought with school closing it didn't matter, or that he had given out enough bad news for one morning.

'Put wrongs to right, that was my wish,' thought Sammy. If only he was to be given the chance. After all the end of the summer term was eight months away.

They finished breakfast, still talking about Sir Ragnarok's announcement and the visit to the Floating Circus as they filed out to start their lessons.

'Where do we go for Astronomics?' asked Sammy.

'It says room thirty-seven,' said Milly waving her timetable. 'Wherever that is.'

'Room seven, floor three,' said Amos, shoving past Sammy.

'Hey!' said Sammy, rubbing his shoulder where Amos had deliberately knocked into him.

'Leave it Sammy, he's just trying to get you into trouble,' said Darius.

Toby nodded. 'Let's follow him.'

They gave Amos a head start and followed him up the stone staircase, past the first floor where the grey corridor stretched out as far as the eye could see. At the second floor, Sammy found he was out of breath and stopped to look out of one of the windows. They were a long way up. He scrambled up the remaining stairs two at a time to catch up with Gavin, Toby, Milly, Dixie and Darius. He was pleased to see they were also out of breath as they reached the third floor.

As they leant on the banister to recover, Sammy looked up. The staircase twisted higher still, stretching up to the castle roof. He caught a glimpse of Amos and a handful of girls disappearing into one of the classrooms at the end of the corridor.

Sammy pointed to the door. 'It's this way.'

They marched down the corridor and through the doorway into a large, high-ceilinged rectangular room with two semi-circles of desks and chairs arranged in a horseshoe shape with a central gangway. The desks faced a tall blackboard with the words "First Year Astronomics with Professor Burlay" scrawled in emerald green chalk.

As if they were expecting Professor Burlay, the first years turned around when Sammy's group came in, then went back to talk amongst themselves. Without instructions to do so, the seating seemed to be divided neatly into the four houses.

Sammy pulled Darius towards Amos, who was sitting alone at the end of the "North" row. Amos shuffled up and ignored them as they crowded into the remaining seats.

Just as Darius was explaining more about their dragon eggs, Professor Burlay hurried into the room, adjusting his tie and pulling his suit jacket straight. He waved for the class to sit down.

'Good morning everyone,' said Professor Burlay, smiling at them.

'Good morning,' chorused the first years.

'I know what you're thinking,' said Professor Burlay. 'Why bother learning Astronomics when most of you will be going back to normal schools at the end of the summer term.'

Sammy noticed out of the students nodding, most were from the watery West house.

'Astronomics is a core science,' said Professor Burlay. 'Once mastered, it can be applied to anything, anywhere.'

Sammy felt a speech coming and was glad when one of the girls from the South house put up her hand.

'Yes, er...' Professor Burlay scanned papers on his desk. 'Rachel Burns from South what's your question?'

'What is Astronomics?' asked Rachel Burns.

Sammy groaned as Professor Burlay launched into an enthusiastic ten-minute monologue about how Astronomics was, as Sammy already knew, "the science of predicting star positions."

'But first,' said Professor Burlay, 'you must know the stars. Can anyone name a star or constellation for me?'

Nearly half the class raised their hands. Sammy put his hand up thinking of Orion and The Plough.

Professor Burlay chose a small skinny boy with dark hair from the East house. He looked down at his sheets again. Sammy guessed they were identity cards with a photo, student name and Dragamas house.

'Simon Sanchez from East,' said Professor Burlay, breathing heavily, 'your constellation is?'

'Orion Sir, or the Plough.'

Sammy recognised the name, the accent, the bony face and jet black hair. Simon Sanchez must be the son of raven haired Professor Sanchez. As for mind control, he knew the possibility of Simon coming out with word for word, the exact combination of stars he had chosen was pretty much non-existent. Simon Sanchez had stolen his idea. Sammy put his hand down, but it was too late.

'Don't be shy Sammy, what's your star?'

'I, er…' the words dried up in Sammy's mouth.

Professor Burlay waited an agonising five seconds while Sammy felt more stupid than he had in his entire life. His head was empty of all words, let alone the names of stars and constellations.

'Gemini,' whispered Dixie. 'It's a star sign.'

'Sagittarius,' said Sammy a little louder than he intended, grateful to remember his own sign. He didn't really know much about Astrology, but he remembered his mother chatting on the telephone, "November, yes he's a Sagittarius." Just because his birthday was November the 30th, still if it helped in Professor Burlay's lesson, it couldn't be that bad.

Out of the corner of his eye, he caught a furious glare from Dixie and he guessed she was surprised he knew about star signs and angry he hadn't chosen hers.

'Very good Sammy,' said Professor Burlay writing "Sagittarius" in green chalk on the blackboard. 'Anyone else?'

Within minutes, every hand was raised and every zodiac sign was written on the blackboard.

'Right then,' said Professor Burlay, looking pleased the lesson was going well. 'Shall we go outside on to the balcony and look at some of these stars? Ten groups of four please.'

Sammy formed a four with Dixie, Darius and Milly and headed for the far side of the classroom where twin PVC doors led out on to a stone balcony overlooking the Dragonball pitch.

'There are ten telescopes here,' said Professor Burlay. 'Share them in your groups and rotate so you all have the chance to see the stars.'

'But Professor,' said one of the boys in the group next to Sammy's, 'the sky's too bright. We can't see any stars.'

Professor Burlay looked through the telescope and nodded. 'It is a little light for this. It's not usual practice, but I think we can do something about it.' He reached for his staff and pointed it at the sky.

Sammy felt his jaw drop as a shimmer rippled across the sky, taking the daylight away like water down a plughole. The sky dimmed to dusk, then to pitch black with a thousand stars glittering next to a hunter's moon.

Angry shouts carried from the Dragonball pitch. Sammy found himself half frightened and half in awe that the game was still playing with students riding dragons the size of horses, passing a glowing ball from player to player. Several riders swooped close to the Astronomics balcony and Professor Burlay hurriedly waved his staff to restore the daylight.

Sammy took a step back, accidentally squashing Milly's toes. He had never seen anything like it in his life. He offered Milly an apology and craned his neck to take a look through the telescope. In the daylight, only dim white specks were visible.

'Perhaps this should be left for a night class,' said Professor Burlay, clearly disappointed.

They spent a few minutes discussing the few stars they had been able to see. Despite trying really hard, Sammy found having seen real people riding real dragons, he couldn't concentrate on anything Professor Burlay was saying.

Back in the classroom, Professor Burlay handed everyone a thin, brightly coloured text book "My First Astronomics Book" by American author Iseat Starz.

'A bit young for you I know,' Professor Burlay apologised. 'But we'll get to this,' he lugged a heavy volume from under his desk and held it up to show the class, 'after Christmas.'

Sammy groaned. As childish as "My First Astronomics Book" looked, it was probably more fun. He flicked through the pages and found there were more pictures than writing.

Professor Burlay looked at the clock. 'We may just have time to read the first pages. I would like you to read the rest in the evenings this week. We'll have a small test next Monday.'

'Homework?' grumbled Sammy.

'But not at home,' said Darius, grinning.

Professor Burlay made a second sweep of the class, handing out an A4 sheet with maps of the Northern and Southern hemispheres. 'You may find these are of assistance,' he winked at the class. 'Now, shall we read? Sammy, would you read the first paragraph out loud?'

Sammy coughed nervously and began to read. 'Astronomics is the science of predicting star positions used by day and by night in Britain and abroad.'

'Very good, Darius you're next, then move on clockwise so that everyone gets a turn.

It was only when Sammy stopped reading that he noticed that he was now sitting on the end of the row and that Amos had moved to sit next to Simon Sanchez. He couldn't quite place it, but he had a bad feeling about their new friendship and made a mental note to try to patch things up in the North tower as soon as possible.

CHAPTER 9

DRACONITE AND DRAGONBALL

As a girl from the East house read her paragraph at the start of the fourth chapter, the bell above the classroom door rang to end the lesson.

Sammy picked up his Astronomics textbook using the A4 sheet as a bookmark and made his way out into the corridor behind Gavin and Toby. His timetable marked the next lesson as "Gemology with Dr Lithoman," the "Wicked Witch of the West" as she had described herself.

'Where do we go now?' asked Sammy, turning his timetable upside down and back again, trying to make sense of the map on the back of the lesson plans. 'It says room seven, is that on the ground floor?'

'Probably,' said Gavin. 'Race you, Toby!'

Gavin tore down the corridor with Toby close behind him. With fresh memories of being chased by the Rat Catchers, Sammy preferred to walk down the corridor with Dixie, Darius and Milly beside him.

'I don't know,' said Sammy as they reached the stairs. 'If we're on the third floor, the second floor is below us, then the floor below should be one-something, like room seventeen...' he trailed off.

'I get it Sammy,' said Darius. 'If Gemology's not on the first floor, do you reckon it's underground?'

'That'd make sense,' said Dixie, her green eyes gleaming at the prospect. 'Gems, dwarves, mining, underground passages!'

'It makes no sense at all,' grumbled Milly, climbing painfully slowly down the stairs in her pair of unsuitably high, high-heeled shoes.

'Come on Milly! We'll be late,' groaned Darius.

'Better arrive late...' said Sammy. 'A great start this'll be.'

'Everyone got their stone?' asked Dixie.

They nodded, pulling black rocks from trouser and skirt pockets.

'Yours is bigger than mine,' Darius said to Dixie as they compared sizes.

Dixie shrugged. 'It shouldn't make any difference. It's what you do with it that counts. That's what Commander Altair said when we were finding our staffs.'

'Do we put the stones in our staffs?' asked Sammy.

'Where else would it go?' asked Dixie looking at him in disbelief.

'Come on, it starts in five minutes and we still don't know where to go,' said Darius.

'Everyone else has gone,' said Milly. 'Look.'

But there was nothing to "look" at. Both the ground floor corridor and ascending staircase were completely deserted.

'Ok, room seven should be somewhere along here,' said Sammy, surveying the corridor. He recognised the tall windows and formidable portraits from his journey from Sir Ragnarok's office. 'Room five,' he said, pointing to a large oak door. 'Let's keep going.'

'Room six,' said Milly, pointing to a smaller door with strange symbols carved into the gnarled wooden panels.

'Room eight,' said Dixie flatly as they walked on.

'Eight? Are you sure?' asked Sammy.

With one hand on her hip, Dixie stood aside and pointed defiantly at the double loops of a silver number eight shimmering in the corridor candlelight.

'It must be somewhere in the middle,' said Darius.

'You reckon?' snapped Dixie.

'Hey, let's not argue,' said Sammy, casting his eyes back and forth in the empty space between the two doors. Only a large curtained window stood between them.

Sammy used his staff to tap against the stone wall. It was solid, with hardly a sound bouncing back. The long purple curtain got closer and closer, and in a moment of inspiration, Sammy yanked it aside. He gasped as the heavy velvet curtain revealed a diamond studded door with the number seven embossed in a rich gold.

'Wow, look at that,' said Dixie.

'It's so pretty,' said Milly, touching a matching glittering diamond slide in her hair.

'Yeah, come on.' Darius pushed open the shining door.

Instead of opening into a classroom like room thirty-seven, the door led into a curved stone passageway sloping downwards. The passage was lit with pale blue candles that reflected small sparkling stones set into the limestone walls.

Looking down at the floor, Sammy noticed a groove about ten centimetres deep exactly in the middle of the passage. He could hear strange clicking noises and a hollow rumbling coming out of the darkness.

Darius closed the door behind them. 'Come on, it must be this way.'

'Like there's a choice,' said Milly, rubbing her high heeled feet.

Sammy ignored her. 'Let's go,' he said grabbing Dixie's arm.

As they turned the corner, the passage opened out into a perfectly round room with the same sparkling walls. Four large tables filled the bulk of the room, with ten small chairs, each with purple velvet cushions, tucked neatly underneath each table.

A pair of stilts stood next to a curved blackboard that ran halfway around the room, covered from top to bottom with notes about strange sounding items and pictures of stones coloured in red, pink, orange, green and blue chalk. The floor was grey stone with streaks of the same glitter shimmering under the fluorescent lighting, a stark contrast to the dim candlelit passages in the castle above.

The ten centimetre groove curved snugly around the edge of the room disappearing into a gaping hole to the right of the blackboard. Apart from the four of them, the room was completely empty.

'Where is everyone?' asked Darius at last.

Dixie found her voice first. 'We could follow the track,' she said, pointing towards the groove.

'Er, ok,' said Sammy, not really wanting to go anywhere near the strange black hole.

The rumbling grew louder as they moved closer to the hole, merging with a "squeak, squeak, squeak" as the most peculiar sight came towards them.

Sammy leapt back as he was nearly mown down by a large silver wheelbarrow loaded with dirt, its thin black tyre carefully following the groove in the ground.

Sammy stared at the man pushing the wheelbarrow. He was short, no taller than Sammy's waist, wearing navy dungarees over a grubby white shirt with a red spotted handkerchief and matching flat cap. Tough black leather boots protected the man's tiny feet, buckled by four shiny silver clasps that seemed to be coated in the same glitter they had seen on the walls of the classroom.

The man looked Sammy straight in the eyes and touched his cap. 'Captain Duke Stronghammer gentle sirs, and ladies,' he growled in a deep husky voice that didn't seem to suit his short posture. 'The rest of them are that way, mucking up my workers.' He tapped his watch-less wrist, 'and yer late,' he tutted, picking up the wheelbarrow handles and marching past the desks back up towards the castle overhead.

'Ok,' said Sammy, sure that whatever they encountered through the black hole, nothing would surprise him.

He felt Dixie grip his jumper as they stepped into the passage, the rumbling was getting louder and louder the further they went in. The deeper they got, the more the walls shimmered brighter, gleaming with diamonds and coloured jewels.

Ahead, they could see the rest of the first years and slipped unnoticed into the back row next to Gavin and Toby.

'And so the diamonds will be mined to raise money for the school,' said Dr Lithoman. 'We'll go back to the classroom and discuss what we have seen and let the miners carry on with their work.'

Sammy peered over Gavin's shoulder. About twenty short men, wearing the same blue dungarees and shirts in varying stages of whiteness, were feverishly swinging pickaxes at the walls, chiselling glittering shards from the rock face. Another dwarf with a red neckerchief was sifting through the findings, separating the jewels, rock and earth into separate wheelbarrows.

Having been the last to arrive, Sammy found that he, Dixie, Darius and Milly were now at the front of the class.

With her bright green hair, Dixie stood out and caught the Gemology professor's attention.

Dr Lithoman scurried to the front, her high pitched voice more of a squeak now that she was much lower to the ground.

Sammy remembered the stilts and her slow pace on their school tour. It figured, their Gemology professor might not mine the gemstones herself, but she was of the same dwarven race, just without the beard.

'Another greenhair!' shrieked Dr Lithoman. 'Back, back! All of you!'

Dixie lurched into Sammy's side as Dr Lithoman barged hawk-eyed through the first years, reaching out a pudgy hand to touch the fine green strands of Dixie's hair.

'A girl of the North,' said Dr Lithoman, pointing to the green stripe and North symbol on Dixie's shirt pocket. 'Children of the North sit here,' she waved to the table closest to the blackboard, 'so I can keep these on you,' she added, thrusting a chubby arm wrapped in silk and lace up to her coal black eyes.

Dr Lithoman turned to the other first years who were staring at the North table. 'Children of the East sit here,' she waved to the table closest to the mine entrance. Amos slunk from Simon Sanchez's side to sit at the North table.

'Children of the South sit here.'

More students shuffled to their house table, creaking out the small chairs and fluffing up the cushions.

'And my fishies of the West, please sit here,' said Dr Lithoman, her eyes glistening as five boys and five girls with blue pocket stripes and blue ties sat at the best table in the room. Sammy noticed the West house was out of the way of the wheelbarrow route and in clear view of the blackboard.

'Are you comfortable my fishies? Good, good, now let us begin,' said Dr Lithoman, holding up a large slab of black rock from her desk. 'Does everyone have the black stones I set beside your beds?'

Everyone nodded.

'Excellent,' said Dr Lithoman. 'This stone is onyx.'

Sammy nodded. He recognised the stone from his geologist uncle's jewellery shop.

'Onyx is found in the depths of the darkest caverns. It is rare and semi-precious and since both the stone and cave are black as midnight, they are not easy to come by.'

'But they can rustle up forty every year for the first years, huh?' said Dixie, clearly not impressed by Dr Lithoman.

'Shh,' hissed Darius. 'This is really cool.'

'The stone is placed on the end of your staff. Hmm yes,' said Dr Lithoman, smiling approvingly at the length and texture of the staff belonging to a mousey haired boy on the West table. 'Peter Grayling has chosen oak,' she said, picking up the staff. 'Solid and true. A good choice indeed.'

Peter Grayling beamed as Dr Lithoman beckoned for him to come to the front of the class. She took his hand, still clutching the staff and reached for his onyx.

'Like this!' said Dr Lithoman. She connected the black rock with the wide end at the top of the branch with a flourish. The staff hissed and a cloud of steam puffed out from under the stone. Peter Grayling stood up and held his staff in both hands above his head.

'Your turn,' said Dr Lithoman.

'It's easy,' said Peter Grayling.

'She did it for him,' said Gavin. 'Which end does it go?'

Just as Sammy slid his stone into the ready-made groove at the tip of his staff, Captain Stronghammer returned to the classroom, his silver wheelbarrow empty. He touched his cap to Dr Lithoman apologetically. 'Sorry m'am, it's the extra loads we're running for Sir Ragnarok. Some barrows will have to run through your class.'

Dr Lithoman's scowl faded. 'Of course they will,' she replied sugar sweetly.

Sammy couldn't help wondering if she was more worried than she let on. He raised his hand.

'Yes Sammy?'

He was surprised that she knew his name; Professor Burlay had needed notes.

'Um, what extra loads are they running?'

'Well,' said Dr Lithoman begrudgingly and as slowly as if talking to a three year old, 'the extra loads are to mine precious stones to sell and raise the money for the Shape's ransom. Sir Ragnarok has dedicated his life to this school and despite saying he does not want to pay, he will protect the school at all costs.'

Sammy gripped his staff, knowing he had to do more. He pressed his stone hard into the wide end of his staff, as if strength alone would force it into place. He needn't have bothered as the stone fused with the wood as easily as a jigsaw piece slotting into place, sending up a wisp of grey smoke as he connected the pieces.

Sammy looked up. Darius was on his feet, waving his staff from right to left. It looked a bit big for him, Sammy thought, as a wide sweep tapped Gavin on the head.

'Oi!' Gavin stood up, Toby at his side. 'Come on then!'

'Enough boys,' said Dr Lithoman, arriving swiftly at the North table. 'Sit down everyone. Your staffs are not toys. Let me teach you about the stone and its protection and healing properties.'

This promise alone was enough to settle the class. Darius was especially keen to learn about the healing properties which, he explained, was because his parents were Healers and spent every day tending to sick dragons.

Another rumble came from the tunnel and Captain Stronghammer re-appeared with his wheelbarrow, followed by two smaller dwarves, both with bushy ginger beards, pushing a large barrow between them. Both barrows were full to the brim with rock and earth with not a single diamond in sight. Captain Stronghammer touched his cap and Dr Lithoman waved them through whilst helping Milly with her stone.

'Onyx,' Dr Lithoman paused to make sure she had the attention of the whole class, 'is the only black stone you will be given at Dragamas. There are others, but none so powerful an aid to begin learning the wonders of the Dark Ages. A dark stone, from a dark past.'

Dr Lithoman looked at Darius, 'I taught your parents the same basics I shall be teaching you and all of you,' she beamed, holding her arms outstretched. 'First, I need three volunteers.'

'She's going to show us Firesticks,' Dixie whispered in Sammy's ear, tickling him.

'What's Firesticks?' asked Sammy, equally quietly, not wanting to look stupid again.

'Watch,' said Dixie, holding her hand high above her head.

'You, you and you,' said Dr Lithoman, pointing at Dixie, 'will find books, pens and pencils in the third drawer under the blackboard. Pass them amongst your classmates and we will draw some stones.'

Sammy grinned at Dixie's disappointed face.

'Pens,' grumbled Dixie slamming back on her chair and bumping into Simon Sanchez. 'Sorry,' she stammered.

'No problem,' Simon gave Dixie a creepy stare and dropped a folded note into Amos's lap.

Dr Lithoman called Simon, Dixie and Peter Grayling to the front and beckoned for the books from the cupboard under the blackboard. She took ten from the top of the pile and gave them to Peter with a selection of bright blue pens and a pile of cream paper. 'For my fishes,' she said, chuckling to herself.

Dixie returned to the North table armed with books, paper and pens. She adjusted her cushion and sat down. 'Anyone else think there are favourites?'

Sammy nodded and took his Gemology textbook called "Simply Gems" by Ron Pirate. 'It's not fair.'

'Have all my fishies got paper and pens?'

Dixie rolled her eyes at Sammy.

'Then draw,' said Dr Lithoman, turning to the blackboard where with one hand, she used a board rubber to erase the notes from a previous class and with the other she began to draw in bright blue chalk.

Sammy craned his neck to see the collection of scratches, which were building up into a larger than life drawing of a staff with onyx at the top. He ducked as Dr Lithoman suddenly picked up her skirt and weaved in between the four tables. She paused beside Darius.

'No, no, no,' said Dr Lithoman. 'Not like that. It's in the mind, not in the pen. See it and you shall draw it. Focus and you shall see.'

Sammy looked over at Darius's drawing. It didn't look bad, better than his, he thought, shielding his own drawing as Dr Lithoman swept past. It worked and she brushed past him without a second glance.

He looked up to see her tap a circular dial above the mine entrance. It looked like a clock, except that the hands stayed still and strange numbers floated backwards and forwards never quite completing a circle.

'We have time for a few questions,' said Dr Lithoman, looking expectantly at the West table.

Peter Grayling raised his hand. 'Will the stone on our staff help us cast spells?'

'Why yes Peter, it will,' said Dr Lithoman. 'Anyone else? Sammy, what's your question?'

Sammy took a deep breath. 'What's draconite?' he asked in a hurry to get the words out, surprising himself for having the confidence to ask the question in their first lesson.

Dr Lithoman's smile disappeared and she let out a faint gasp, as if the air was being sucked out of her body like a drink through a straw. The class fell silent and Sammy wished he had never asked the question, he had never felt so stupid. Some questions should be asked when alone, he thought.

Dr Lithoman forced a smile. 'Does anyone else have a question?'

Everyone shook their heads and Sammy was grateful when the end of lesson bell rang. Dr Lithoman waved for the class to leave, one table at a time.

Sammy noticed that despite being the second closest to the door, the North table was going to be the last to leave.

'Come on, let's go,' said Gavin.

And then she said it.

'Sammy, would you wait a moment please.'

Sammy felt his heart lurch; it wasn't really a question. 'Ok.'

'We'll wait outside,' whispered Dixie, nudging Darius who nodded a little begrudgingly.

'Thanks,' whispered Sammy.

Dr Lithoman waited agonisingly until the last swish of Dixie's green ponytail had disappeared around the classroom door, then she sat at her desk, a blue pen poised between her chubby fingers.

'What do you know of the evil stone?' she whispered, her voice echoing in the empty classroom.

'I, er...' started Sammy. He had expected to be told not to ask questions. What could she mean by "the evil stone".

'Speak boy.'

'Er...Mrs Grock, draconite, the Shape,' Sammy stuttered trying to focus as Dr Lithoman's eyes grew rounder and rounder.

'Mrs Grock has draconite?' she asked suspiciously.

'Yes, er, no, er, she did,' said Sammy, at a loss for words. 'Professor Burlay's got it now.'

'Professor Burlay has got it, has he.' Dr Lithoman sucked the top of her pen. 'No doubt he will bring it to me in his own time.'

'No doubt,' said Sammy, unconsciously copying Dr Lithoman's habit of repeating his sentences.

Dr Lithoman looked strangely at him. 'No doubt indeed. Do you know what draconite is?'

'No.' Sammy shook his head, looking at the tunnel entrance, where Captain Stronghammer had collected yet another barrow load of soil from the underground tunnel.

'Then come,' said Dr Lithoman, beckoning him to follow her out of the classroom into the tunnel. The dark passage sloped down past the dwarves who each touched their caps as they walked past.

'Are those real di-'

'Yes,' said Dr Lithoman without letting Sammy finish. 'All real diamonds, worth millions, all under the castle and no one outside suspects a thing!'

'How do-'

'How does the school negotiate the delivery and the sales?'

Sammy nodded, frustrated that she kept answering before he had a chance to finish his questions.

'It's so simple, yet so effective. The school, or should I say, us dwarves, we distribute them to a shop in the nearest village where they are valued, sold and sent to an anonymous Swiss bank account,' Dr Lithoman chuckled. 'The only trouble is we can't send them all at once, else the mine would be discovered, and, well, surely you can imagine the problems?'

Sammy nodded, aware that his mind was spinning and his mouth had fallen open.

'Yes, and this would be a real problem for Sir Ragnarok. Especially now he needs that money.' Dr Lithoman laughed, sending a cold shiver down Sammy's spine.

'Is it much further?'

'No, not far, then you shall see real draconite!'

A few paces further, the tunnel branched out into a large circular room with dozens of small doors sprouting into hidden rooms. Dr Lithoman pulled a bunch of shiny keys out of her skirt pocket and unlocked the first door on the right hand side.

Close behind her, Sammy followed Dr Lithoman into a small cell-like room lit by three blue candles and filled with basic wooden furniture; bed, drawers, desk and bookshelves with thicker, heavier books than he had seen in Mrs Grock's house.

Instead of medicines, these books seemed to be about rocks and minerals - where to find them and how to use them. There were only two that Sammy could make out with the word "draconite" – a "Where To Find" series book and a book half off the shelf, as if it hadn't been put back properly, called "Discovering Draconite - Inside a Dragon's Brain", which sounded particularly gruesome.

Sammy looked up. Dr Lithoman was by her bedside table pointing to a glass half filled with a peculiar green-yellow jelly with a dark rock-like lump at the bottom.

'Hands,' said Dr Lithoman.

Sammy obediently held out his hands and allowed Dr Lithoman to dribble the jelly and rock into his cupped palms.

'There,' Dr Lithoman smiled at him. 'Now you are holding draconite, the precious stone taken from the brain of a living dragon.'

Sammy felt his stomach turn over, pieces of sick building uncomfortably in his throat. Kyrillan would have a stone like this. A dragon somewhere had lost its stone.

Dr Lithoman picked up the draconite and held it up to the nearest candle. She rubbed away some of the jelly and the stone glittered and sparkled, dancing coloured rainbows around her bedroom.

'Oh yes,' Dr Lithoman replied to Sammy's unspoken thoughts, 'the dragon is most certainly dead. Without his stone, he cannot perform spells, cannot fly, cannot breathe fire, in fact, he cannot breathe at all. In our world, this is a very serious crime indeed.'

Sammy wiped his hands on the towel he was offered, unable to shake the image of Kyrillan from his mind.

'Can we go now?'

'Of course,' said Dr Lithoman. 'Forgive me, you are young. Perhaps this should not have been shown to you until you were older.'

'No, I'm ok,' said Sammy. 'It's just my friends, they're waiting for me.'

Dr Lithoman put the draconite stone back into the glass and picked up a fur coat, wrapping it around her shoulders. 'Very well, we will go back now.'

It took almost no time at all to walk back up the passage and into the classroom. Sammy picked up his Astronomics book and the new Gemology book, paper and pens. As he turned to go, Dr Lithoman stared straight at him. 'I hope that answers your question.'

Sammy nodded, stepping aside as Captain Stronghammer and three dwarves ploughed past him with empty wheelbarrows.

'You took your time,' said Dixie out in the castle corridor. 'We were getting worried about you.'

Darius nodded checking his watch. 'You've been gone ages. What happened?'

'Let's go to lunch,' said Sammy. 'I've got loads to tell you.'

By the time they reached, the Main Hall, Dixie and Darius were open mouthed and angry at the draconite Dr Lithoman had in her room.

'Do you think she's part of the Shape?' asked Sammy.

'Don't know,' said Dixie, 'but I think we should tell Sir Ragnarok.'

'Yeah, even if they are mining diamonds for the ransom, I think he should be told,' said Darius.

'Perhaps he already knows.'

Dixie stopped in her tracks. 'What? No way Sammy, he wouldn't know that.'

'It would make sense, wouldn't it?' said Sammy. 'It would explain why she's allowed to be down there, to live, I mean, no one would know.'

'I think we should tell Sir Ragnarok after lunch,' said Darius.

'How? We don't know where he lives, his office, it could be anywhere.'

'I think I can get us there,' said Sammy, touching the Directometer in his trouser pocket.

'How?' demanded Dixie. 'I know the school inside out through my brothers. How do you know where his office is? Even they don't know, they would have told me if they did.'

Sammy couldn't help agreeing with Dixie, if there was something to be had from her older brothers he could imagine her manipulating them like plasticine to get what she wanted. 'I just know.'

'But your family's not connected to Dragamas, how come you know all of a sudden?' asked Darius.

Keeping quiet about his suspicions about his uncle, Sammy held out the gold pocket watch with the blank screen.

'You've stolen a Directometer,' whispered Dixie.

'Cool,' said Darius, peering closely at the screen.

'No,' said Sammy hastily. 'Last night, after you left me, I went with Professor Burlay to Sir Ragnarok's office. He lent me this so I could find my way back to the North tower.'

'Oh,' said Dixie. 'That makes sense. You'd never find your way without it.'

'Serberon said we should try to find you,' said Darius, nodding his head towards Dixie.

Dixie cringed, 'I-didn't-want-to-go-in-the-corridor-at-night,' she explained in one breath, running the words together. 'I don't like the dark.'

'It's ok,' said Sammy. 'Sir Ragnarok asked me to give it back at breakfast, but when he said about the school closing, there wasn't the chance to, well actually I forgot about it until now.'

'Then it's settled,' said Dixie. 'We'll go tonight.'

'No,' said Sammy, pointing to himself and Darius. 'We'll go tonight.'

'I want to come,' said Dixie in a "you're not going without me" voice Sammy could almost hear her using on her brothers to get what she wanted.

'But you just said you were afraid of the corridors at night. You've got a thing about the dark!'

'That's different, you'll be there,' Dixie pointed at Sammy.

'Oh ho,' said Darius, a wicked gleam in his eyes. 'Wait until Gavin hears about this!'

'No!' shrieked Dixie. 'You're not telling him!'

'It's ok, he won't,' said Sammy, nudging Darius. 'So is that it then, the three of us, tonight at ten o'clock?'

'Can we make it eleven?' asked Dixie. 'Milly likes to read late.'

'Perhaps we should go alone,' said Sammy. 'We'll never be up in the morning.'

'Ten o'clock is fine,' said Dixie hastily.

'Right, let's find the others,' said Darius. 'They should be at lunch by now.'

Lunch turned out to be a surprisingly good school dinner of chicken in a mild pepper sauce, with potatoes and a variety of other vegetables; peas, carrots, sweetcorn and green beans, strategically arranged in the shape of a castle, with the vegetables forming the walls and the pepper sauce as the moat. Whether the chefs had intended it Sammy didn't care. It was the nicest school lunch he could ever remember having.

The best part, Sammy decided, was having the choice of orange, lime or cherryade, or a combination of all three that turned the liquid a dull brown but tasted really good. It was much better than the jugs of plain water at his old school in Ratisbury.

Professor Burlay arrived as they were finishing a Swiss roll in custard dessert. He was carrying ten black rucksacks with the North symbol (a diamond with a circle on the top point) stamped on the outside flap.

'Should have got these to you earlier,' apologised Professor Burlay. 'They're for your books, pens, paper, anything you get given. They've all got your names on, so let's see who's first, ah, Melissa Brooks.' Professor Burlay handed the first rucksack to Milly.

'Dixie Deane, Naomi Fairweather, Amos Leech, Helena Marchant, Darius Murphy, Samuel Rambles, Gavin Reed, Toby Reed. Everyone got one? Good.' Professor Burlay rustled with a yellow parchment timetable. 'Right, you're expected on the Dragonball pitch in fifteen minutes for a whole afternoon of sport. Rather you than me,' he shuddered. 'If any of you want sick notes for sport, come to me any time.'

Milly raised her hand, touching her perfectly aligned hair with the other, but Professor Burlay had moved up to the third year table.

'Grrr,' said Milly putting down her hand. 'I'll have to write home for some extra strong hairspray.'

'And some flats,' said Sammy, suddenly aware that everyone on his table was looking strangely at him.

'Flats?' asked Gavin. 'What?'

'Flats,' repeated Sammy. 'Shoes with no heels, my Mum wears them so she can go shopping for longer than in high heels. Milly's feet were hurting earlier, maybe flats would help.'

'Oh.' Gavin looked relieved, 'I thought you meant some sky rise apartments, like people live in.'

'My feet were not hurting,' said Milly.

'Yes they were,' said Darius unkindly. 'You were the reason we were late to Astronomics and Gemology.'

'Yeah, about Gemology,' started Sammy.

'Ask for the apartments or whatever,' said Darius.

'No, I have to learn to walk in these, Mummy says…'

'Mummy says,' spluttered Gavin. 'Hope you're not on my team this afternoon.'

'Or mine,' added Toby. 'Darius, you'll be on my team yeah? You played really well yesterday.'

'Ok,' said Darius. 'I think we play in our houses anyway.'

'Ugh,' grumbled Gavin, 'that's all we need.'

If it was possible, Amos looked less pleased than Milly at the thought of playing alongside the twins.

Sammy held up his parchment timetable. 'It says here to go to the Gym. Is that where Professor Sanchez took us yesterday?'

Toby nodded leaning over Sammy's shoulder. 'Don't know how we're going to play without full size dragons.'

'We'll find out when we get there,' said Darius. 'Who does it say is going to teach us?'

'It doesn't,' said Sammy flatly.

'What do you mean?'

Sammy held up the timetable. 'It just says "Sports."'

'Let's go anyway, look everyone else is leaving.'

Sammy looked around, the whole school was leaving the hall, hustling and bustling to get to their afternoon lessons.

It was raining heavily outside and the castle courtyard was splattered with deep puddles that had to be jumped. Even the muddy path that led to the Gymnasium was waterlogged. They had to really watch where they were going to avoid splashing mud on their trousers or tights.

Gavin arrived first and barged through the glass double doors which slammed back against the wall with a crunch.

Inside, the Gymnasium was as modern as the outside was ancient. It reminded Sammy of a plush hotel foyer, with two sets of staircases at opposite ends of the room. Straight ahead was a marble reception desk complete with filing trays, paperwork and a colour television. A small Indian man stood behind the desk holding an orange clipboard.

'Good morning first years,' the man beamed at them. 'My name is Mr Ockay. I will take the register and then you may change for your lesson. Mr Cross will be here in a moment to teach you the basics of dragon flying.'

'Changed into what?' demanded Gavin as Sammy mouthed "dragon flying?" at Darius.

Mr Ockay rattled through the forty names on his register in almost no time, simultaneously waggling his hand in frustration at the students from the West house who had discovered food and drinks vending machines hidden in the corner.

'Everyone listen to me please, yes to me and not your friends. Your sportswear is laid out in the changing rooms with name tags, one per person. Use the lockers and hand in your keys and any watches, rings or other valuables so that I can give them back to you at the end of your lesson.

Sammy took off his silver and black sports wristwatch and handed it to Mr Ockay.

'Name?'

'Sammy Rambles,' said Sammy, a little afraid of Mr Ockay's efficiency.

'Thank you Sammy Rambles,' said Mr Ockay, tying a label firmly around the strap and tossing it into an empty biscuit tin on his desk. 'Don't forget to collect it at the end of the lesson.'

'I won't,' said Sammy. 'My uncle gave…'

Mr Ockay wasn't interested. 'Next!' he shouted and collected three rings and a charm bracelet from Milly. 'Very pretty,' he said, tying her name tag through the items. 'Any more? No, very well, you may go up and get changed.'

Sammy followed Darius up the boys' staircase, through another set of double doors into a long rectangular room with rows of wooden benches laid horizontally across the room. Three-storey metal lockers lined the walls, each with shiny keys dangling from the closed doors.

On each wooden bench, there was a neat pile of clothes; a white polo shirt with the Dragamas "D" in gold stitching on the chest pocket and a pair of dark navy shorts with matching navy socks folded over a pair of gleaming white trainers.

'How do they know our sizes?' asked Sammy, pulling a perfectly fitting t-shirt over his head.

'They don't,' said Gavin. 'Mine's at least two sizes too small.'

Sammy looked at Gavin and laughed. 'You should swap with Amos. His is two sizes too big!'

Gavin frowned, as if this was the worst idea in the whole world, and prised the tiny shirt back over his head. He exchanged t-shirts begrudgingly with Amos. Luckily the shorts fit first time and they could go down to the foyer.

The girls were already waiting for them, flocking around a tall sandy haired man wearing the same white polo shirt under a navy tracksuit. The man scowled at Mr Ockay and glared towards the first years. 'Are these them?'

Mr Ockay nodded. 'Children, I would like you to introduce you to Lance Anderson Cross, ex-Dragonball captain for the Southampton Seals. He will be teaching you the basics of flying on your dragons.'

'Starting on the ground and you may call me "Mr Cross,"' said Lance Anderson Cross firmly. He frowned at a group of girls from the East house who were giggling together.

'Lunch, break times and elsewhere are the times and places to lark about.'

'Bet no one mucks around in Sports,' Sammy whispered to Darius.

Mr Cross spun around pointing a staff he assembled from his tracksuit pocket at Sammy's nose. 'That's right. Now since your dragons are still in their eggs or at best a lump of bedside gunk, we'll just run through some exercises to get your fitness up, then we'll watch the third years play their first game of the season. Observe closely please, you'll need to memorise the moves. Watch for any weaknesses, you'll soon be working as one big team and you may even get the opportunity to play against them at the end of the year.'

'Just before the school closes,' muttered Dixie.

'One star from North,' snapped Mr Cross. 'No one in my class says anything like that.' He spun his staff in a circle above his head, drawing a large black star that hissed and spat sparks at them. Mr Cross tapped the star and it flew out of the Gymnasium and headed purposefully towards the castle.

'Oops,' said Dixie.

'Never mind,' Sammy tried to reassure her. 'Everyone's thinking it.'

'Another star from North,' said Mr Cross, collecting a netted bag of black leather footballs from Mr Ockay. 'Come on please. Follow me out on to the pitch.'

It was still drizzling when they reached the centre of the Dragonball pitch. The gold dragon crest sparkled underfoot, its black eyes glistening a little too realistically for Sammy's liking and he stepped away from its front paws.

'Right,' said Mr Cross. 'Stretches first. Arms up and round and back. Turn to face your left, face right, up to the sky and down to your toes. Put one leg forward, bend your back knee. No, your back knee Milly. Change to your other leg, shake your ankles and turn them clockwise, and anti-clockwise.'

'Backwards,' said Dixie.

'Good. Now, there are four corners of the Dragonball pitch, run to one of them. The last person to get there must do five star jumps. Go!'

Sammy raced with the rest of the North house to the top left corner. Thanks to after school football practice at Ratisbury, he arrived comfortably at the front. They clustered together under the unlit floodlight.

'Milly Brooks of North,' shouted Mr Cross. 'You were last, five star jumps please!'

'How could he see me?' wailed Milly, taking minuscule steps off the ground, her arms flapping and her hair spilling out of the neat plaits. 'One, two, three, four, five,' she puffed.

'Five,' said Mr Cross. 'Now run to the corner on your right.'

They changed corners twice more, then ran back to the centre where Mr Cross had un-netted the black footballs. He tapped one of the balls with his staff and it started bouncing by itself. He tapped another and said "Milly". Sammy stared as the ball obediently rolled to Milly's feet.

'Two lines please, facing each other,' said Mr Cross. 'Chest passes to each other in a line, then overarm back to Milly to start again. Anyone who drops a ball must sit out. Go!'

Milly picked up the ball and pushed it to Sammy. He caught it and pushed it to Dixie who pushed it to Darius.

'Keep going to the end of the line. Faster! Mr Cross tapped a second ball to Milly. 'Same again!'

Mr Cross sent a third and a fourth ball along the line as the first ball reached Simon Sanchez standing at the other end.

'Overarm pass Simon, back to Milly.'

The passes got faster and faster and people started dropping out. Caught by surprise, Sammy had to punch one ball to Dixie as he received one back from Simon at the same time. The next pass back from Simon was short and it scraped his fingernails before falling to the ground.

'You're out Sammy,' shouted Mr Cross.

Sammy sat on the grass next to Darius and Toby. Only Dixie, Gavin, Simon Sanchez and two boys from the South house were remaining.

Gavin thumped a rough pass to Dixie that she caught and threw high above the head of one of the South boys. He raised his hand sportingly and trotted over to sit with them on the grass.

'Bit high?' asked Sammy.

'Yeah, wish my sister could catch like that though.'

'Wish I had a sister,' Sammy thought, then out loud he said, 'yeah.'

'She's only seven,' said the boy, 'I'm Tristan by the way, eldest son of Howard Markham, the village vicar' he finished proudly, though Sammy was none the wiser.

'Village idiot,' sneered Simon Sanchez, joining them with the other boy from the South house after dropping a tricky pass from Gavin. 'Who do you think will win?'

'Dixie,' said Tristan. 'She looks better.'

'Can't have a girl win, can we?' said Simon, nudging Amos.

Amos sniggered and shouted, 'hey Dixie!'

At the sound of her name, Dixie looked around and was smacked in the elbow by Gavin's pass.

'I win!' yelled Gavin.

Mr Cross laughed. 'Not so, the winner in cheating circumstances must fetch the orange juice from Mr Ockay. Dixie, you go as well, joint first eh?'

Sammy heard Dixie grumble "why is it always me" as she and Gavin marched to the Gymnasium entrance.

They returned with two silver trays stacked with white plastic cups filled with fresh orange juice and plates of corn cracker biscuits in the shape of suns and half moons.

Sammy slurped his orange down in one gulp and stood up, straightening his shirt.

Mr Cross helped himself to a biscuit. 'We'll watch from the benches at the top end of the pitch. I have taught the third years from day one and it should be a good match. North and South versus East and West. Dixie, your brothers will be playing.'

They sat on the wooden benches beside the white lines marking the boundary of the pitch and on the grassy bank leading up to the castle courtyard.

After nearly ten minutes of waiting and watching, Mr Cross pointed to a set of double doors half hidden behind some bushes growing against the castle walls.

A large group of older boys and girls bustled out of the doors. At the back, three boys with green hair were leading a procession of what looked like horses, but as Sammy stood up to get a better look, he saw that they were dragons covered from head to toe in bright shining scales of many different colours.

There were red dragons and green dragons. Dragons with purple scales and dragons with orange scales, big ones, small ones, spiky ones and smooth ones, all following the green haired boys from somewhere beneath the castle.

One that particularly caught his eye that was blue-green, shimmering in the same colour as the draconite stone he had seen in Dr Lithoman's lesson.

'Look!' shouted Dixie. 'It's Serberon, Jason and Mikhael!'

The three green-haired boys waved to Dixie and disappeared with their class into the Gymnasium changing rooms, emerging moments later fully changed into sparkling white t-shirts and navy trousers with leather patches on the inner thighs.

A group of teachers came to sit with Mr Cross on the top benches. Sammy recognised the four house heads and waved back as Professor Burlay nodded to the North students. He noticed Amos had moved again to sit with Simon Sanchez and the East students but didn't have time to mention it as Darius sat next to him, bringing a second round of orange juice.

Sammy watched as the third year students put on house-coloured bibs and mounted their dragons. Some took careful steps up their dragon's spiky tails and others swung their leg over the dragon's back and hoisted themselves up. Some had leather saddles and harnesses and other students appeared to be riding bareback. A tall girl with long silver blonde hair mounted the blue-green dragon Sammy had seen.

Mr Cross jogged to the centre of the pitch and blew his whistle. He threw seven of the black leather balls towards the golden dragon crest and backed away.

At once there was a flurry of activity and the dragons lurched forward, their riders confidently drawing them towards one or other of the leather balls, picking them up and hurling them at each other in the direction of the two goals.

It was tricky at first to remember which house was which colour as they mingled together in a complicated marking scheme. Mr Cross shouted instructions and waved his staff at the scoreboard each time a goal was scored.

Dixie's brother, Serberon, picked up one of the balls. Although Sammy hadn't been looking properly, it seemed to have vanished from the goal and re-appeared from the golden dragon's mouth.

'Jason – catch!' yelled Serberon, hurling the ball at his brother.

Jason caught the ball, just dodging a boy from the East house on a maroon and gold scaled dragon.

'Kayleigh – to you!' shouted Jason. He pushed a chest pass to a small girl with mousey brown hair who was dwarfed by the size of her large green dragon.

Sammy leant forward as Kayleigh kicked the flanks of her dragon. With a "hurrumph" the green dragon arched his back and lifted her high up into the air to catch the ball single-handed.

On the ground there was a ripple of applause and Mr Cross scribbled in his notebook.

'Good catch Kayleigh! Send it over,' shouted a girl from the other end of the pitch. Sammy saw that it was the blonde haired girl who was riding the blue-green dragon he had liked. He couldn't tell if she was North or South because she was ten feet up in the air!

Kayleigh hurled the ball in an arc and the girl on the blue-green dragon surged towards the ball. As she flew, her dragon's blue-green scales were shimmering, casting a shadow of rainbows on to the pitch.

All Sammy could say was "wow". He was glad he wasn't the only one who was impressed. Tristan had taken his eyes off Dixie and was staring skyward with Sammy, Darius, Gavin and Toby. In fact, all of the boys and most of the girls watched open mouthed as the girl swooped low on her dragon, caught the ball, and rose neatly between two boys, who swapped a look that said: "Did she just fly between us?"

The girl pulled the reins around her dragon's neck, urging him gently into a climb. She flew faster, curving slightly so she was turning in a forward somersault over another player and dropping the ball neatly into Serberon's outstretched arms.

Serberon kicked the ball confidently over the keeper and into the back of the net.

In the crowd, Sammy stood up, cheering and whooping with his classmates. He had never seen anything like it in his life. Even Mr Cross looked pleased, making furious notes in his book. He checked his watch and blew his whistle, for what Sammy guessed was half time.

One after another the riders came into land, some with graceful landings and others with wobbly steps their riders tried to cover up by jumping down before they were thrown off.

Mr Ockay brought more orange juice and Sammy drank it gratefully. He had shouted himself almost hoarse after each goal and especially at the end. He felt he couldn't wait for Kyrillan to grow so he could learn to fly and pass as well as the third years.

The second half started and was much rougher than the first half. The scoreboard showed that North and South were five goals ahead of East and West. More third years took to the skies, performing front flips, somersaults, backward rolls, every move imaginable.

Sammy craned his neck as two students flew high above the match chasing after a wildly thrown ball. One was the girl rider on her blue-green dragon and the other was a boy riding a jet black dragon with the East house compass point logo painted in gold on his dragon's scales.

Even with six other balls in play, Sammy found he was drawn to watching the girl on the blue-green dragon chasing after the runaway ball. The boy on the black dragon was close behind, rising higher and higher. They were level with the Gymnasium roof, at least thirty feet above the ground.

Sammy could hear the "hurrumphing" of the dragons and smell the wispy smoke pouring from their nostrils. He shielded his eyes from the rain as the dragon's tails entwined, pulling them closer together.

The two dragons crashed against each other with a jagged clash of leather and scales. Sammy felt his heart skip a beat and he held his breath. The East boy swung his arm out for the ball. The girl seemed to be off balance, falling in slow motion. She had leant too far and couldn't recover. She was slipping, half on half off her dragon.

The East boy seemed to realise she was in danger and threw the ball down to a team mate, hauling on the blue-green dragon's reins. Sammy gasped as the girl fell from about ten feet. She landed in a crumpled heap almost in front of him, her leg twisted awkwardly underneath her.

Mr Cross blew his whistle and ran to the girl who had landed right in front of the first years.

'Back please all of you,' said Mr Cross. 'Give Mary-Beth some space. Mary-Beth, can you hear me? Are you ok?'

Mary-Beth stayed still, her face scrunched up in pain.

'Mary-Beth, talk to me.' Mr Cross sounded worried. 'Open your eyes.'

Sammy watched, relieved, as the girl half opened a pair of green eyes. 'My leg,' she gasped.

'Thank goodness,' said Mr Cross. He offered Mary-Beth a silk handkerchief to dry her eyes. 'You'll need to visit Mrs Grock. You'll be better in no time.'

'But the match,' protested Mary-Beth.

'I have just the tonic,' Mr Cross smiled at her. 'Milly!'

Milly jerked to attention, shaking her re-plaited bunches from side to side. 'I can't do that, no, no, please no.'

'Yes,' said Mr Cross. 'It will be good practice.'

'No!' shrieked Milly. 'Sammy, save me, you do it!'

'What?' asked Sammy.

'The dragon of course,' said Mr Cross.

Mary-Beth nodded. 'She's gentle. It's just like riding a horse.'

'G-gentle?' gasped Sammy.

'Go on,' said Gavin looking extremely envious. 'If you don't, I will.'

'Yeah, and me,' added Toby.

Mary-Beth shook her head, taking off her green and red bib. 'Let this, Sammy, ride her if he wants, but will someone please take me to Mrs Grock's.'

Professor Burlay came forward and stood next to Mr Cross. 'She's in my house. I'll take responsibility for this. Sammy, you try riding the dragon, Kelsepe, isn't it?

Mary-Beth nodded, her eyes closed and her hands clutched around her left ankle.

'Kelsepe,' repeated Sammy. 'But I don't know anything about dragons…'

'Come on, let's go' said one of the green-haired boys. From his ponytail, Sammy guessed it was Jason.

'Hey look, it's Sammy!'

Sammy turned around. Serberon was sitting astride a large green dragon who was puffing grey smoke rings from its large nostrils. The grass sizzled and caught light.

Serberon kicked his dragon's flanks and it stepped forward and put out the fire.

Sammy felt his knees go weak. Up close, the dragons seemed much scarier than horses.

'Hi Serberon,' said Sammy. 'Feeling better?'

'Yeah, come on, we'll show you some moves,' Serberon grinned, yanking the harness reins. His green dragon belched a cloud of grey smoke and took off in a vertical roll, up, over Sammy's head and then back to where he started.

Sammy felt his jaw drop. 'Are you sure…'

'Yes, you can do it Sammy. Focus on the ball and remember what we practised earlier,' said Mr Cross. 'Perhaps don't take off until you feel a bit more confident.'

'Go on Sammy,' Professor Burlay forced a smile. 'It isn't that difficult.'

'Ok.' Sammy threw on the coloured bib and hooked his right foot on to the back leg that Kelsepe had bent obligingly to his height and hoisted his left leg awkwardly over the arch of the dragon's back. Mary-Beth was right, it was almost like mounting a horse, except that there were no stirrups, no saddle and only a set of loose leather reins tied to a harness strapped over the dragon's head and back under its front legs.

Just as he was wondering how to steer, Mr Cross blew his whistle to start the second half. Sammy gently tapped his heels into Kelsepe's blue-green scales and whispered, "let's go".

Kelsepe put her front right foot forward and plodded heavily towards the golden dragon. It wasn't the dramatic start that Sammy had hoped for, but he was grateful that he hadn't done anything embarrassing, like falling off in front of everyone.

Up close, the golden dragon seemed to be where balls that had been kicked or thrown into the netted goal posts ended up. It reminded him of a bowling alley where the balls were returned after each throw.

Kelsepe seemed to have a good idea of the rules, if there were any, other than to score and hold on tight. She positioned him in the perfect position to catch a newly spawned ball from a goal scored at the Gymnasium end.

Smoke poured out of the golden dragon's mouth and a black ball shot high up in the air with a "phut".

Sammy let go of the reins and reached out with both hands.

'We've got it,' he yelled at Kelsepe. 'We've got the ball!'

The crowd cheered and he heard someone shout, "Go Sammy!"

Sammy looked around. More students had appeared from inside the castle and were perched on the benches watching the game. He just made out the first years using Dixie's distinctive green hair as a marker.

Sammy jolted forward as Kelsepe seemed to have decided that she was bored of waiting for him. He held tightly to the reins as she trotted towards the goal.

Serberon hovered above him. 'Hey Sammy, pass it here!'

Sammy passed the ball hearing a cheer as another goal was scored.

'Hey Sammy!' Serberon circled Kelsepe from about ten feet in the air.

'What?' shouted Sammy.

'Make her fly! Dig your heels in, she wants you to!'

'What!'

'You won't get another chance until your dragon is big enough,' shouted Serberon. 'That could be anywhere between the end of your first year to the start of your second year!'

Sammy stared, clutching the reins as Kelsepe kicked her feet. Despite the pressure, he didn't want to miss anything, especially if the school closed and he didn't get the chance.

He dug his heels in, a little harder than he had intended and with a "hurrumph" Kelsepe plunged forward, faster and faster. From an invisible body seam between her front and back legs, two enormous blue-green webbed wings extended. Sammy held his breath and pulled the reins like Mary-Beth had.

Kelsepe cantered forward and then, with a final thrusting step, she pushed away from the ground and they were flying, not very high as Kelsepe seemed to understand his nerves and inexperience.

After ten wing beats, Sammy loosened the reins and looked up. 'I'm flying! Serberon look! I'm flying!'

Serberon clapped, gave him the thumbs up and took off after a stray ball.

Sammy loved it, from feeling the wind and rain rush through his hair to the rhythmic beat of Kelsepe's blue-green wings spread beneath him.

He spotted a wide pass between two boys from the opposite team and pulled Kelsepe across to intercept the ball.

'Got it,' he muttered as the ball fell into his hands.

'Oi!' shouted one of the boys.

'It's that squirt from the first year on Mary-Beth's dragon!'

'Get him!'

'Uh-oh,' muttered Sammy clutching the reins. 'Come on Kelsepe, higher.'

Obligingly, Kelsepe took him higher, sailing through a swarm of students passing ferociously between each other. Sammy wasn't looking where he was going and lurched forward as Kelsepe came to an abrupt halt next to a dark green dragon.

'What are you doing up here?'

Sammy rubbed rain out of his eyes, it looked like Serberon. 'You said I should fly.'

'No I didn't,' said the green haired boy.

'Oh,' Sammy realised this must be Mikhael, Dixie's third brother, as Serberon flew over to meet them.

'Mik – meet Sammy,' shouted Serberon. 'He's in Dixie's class.'

'Hi Sammy,' said Mikhael. 'You'd better go down, it's dangerous up here.'

'Let him be,' said Serberon, grinning. 'You're jealous no one like Mary-Beth fell off in our first year.'

'Bet his egg hasn't even hatched,' said Mikhael.

'It has!' Sammy joined in despite himself.

'Has not.'

'It has, and Dixie's too.'

'Dixie's?' shouted Serberon flying away slightly. 'She never said!'

'Ha,' shouted Sammy, pleased he was standing up for himself. He kicked his heels and led Kelsepe and his prized ball up towards a group of East and West third years defending their goal from airborne attacks.

They didn't seem to notice him, as a first year, smaller both in age and in size, he posed no threat. They didn't see the ball he held tightly to his chest as he flew around them. Sammy pretended to investigate the pitch boundary, moving closer to the goalkeeper who was so laden with pads and body armour, Sammy couldn't tell if it was a boy or a girl.

The keeper saw him coming and shouted to the overhead defenders. Sammy lunged forward, positioning himself to score. Behind him, Mikhael plunged towards the goal pursued by most of the opposition. Sammy was deafened by the beating of wings and yells from the older students.

'Shoot!' yelled Mikhael.

Sammy threw his ball into the left corner as Mikhael threw his into the right corner of the goal. The keeper froze in mid-decision and both balls hit the back of the net. The crowd of students supporting the North-South team erupted in a giant cheer and the East-West crowd booed.

'Good shot Sammy!' shouted Mikhael doing a loop the loop to celebrate.

Mr Cross ran to the centre of the pitch blowing hard on his whistle. 'Time! North-South win by twenty-seven goals to nineteen.'

Kelsepe followed Mikhael's large green dragon, taking Sammy down to the golden dragon in the middle of the pitch.

'Good game everyone?'

The third years shouted, "Yes Sir" and Sammy felt excluded from Mr Cross' talk. He felt a pang of envy as the first years disappeared into the Gymnasium to change. He was still listening to Mr Cross review everyone's performance some fifteen minutes later when the first years were led back to the castle by Professor Sanchez and Dr Lithoman.

'So,' Mr Cross concluded. 'Do you have any questions?'

'No,' Sammy muttered under his breath as several students raised their hands.

Interesting as it was to hear about the manoeuvres and practices of Dragonball, Sammy just wanted to catch up with his friends and hear their opinions of his flying rather than be a hanger-on with the third years. With three years of practice, plus the benefit of using their own dragons, it wasn't surprising that they were good, world class some of them, according to Mr Cross. Although no one said anything about him still being there, he felt out very of place.

Serberon shuffled close to him. 'Come on, we're going while the showers are hot and there's space to get changed.'

'But,' started Sammy, 'Mr Cross hasn't said we can go yet.'

'Hah,' Serberon whispered. 'He'll still be here in twenty minutes, this always happens.'

'Ok,' Sammy rubbed his chaffed inner thighs, feeling he was being led astray.

Jason and Mikhael set off for the changing rooms.

'Come on,' hissed Serberon. 'Let's go.'

Sammy pulled Kelsepe's reins and trotted after Serberon, Jason and Mikhael.

'Hey,' shouted Mr Cross. 'I haven't finished boys! Come back!'

Sammy gripped the reins as Kelsepe took off to catch up with the green haired boys and their dragons. Mr Cross let them go. Kelsepe bucked against him, as if she disapproved of leaving early. Sammy guessed Mary-Beth usually stayed until the end. For a horrible moment, Sammy imagined flying into the girls' changing room window.

He needn't have worried as Kelsepe came to an abrupt halt at the foyer entrance and arched her back. Sammy lost his balance and slid most backwards down her prickly tail. He stood up to a round of applause and rubbed the back of his shorts.

'She's annoyed with you Sammy,' Serberon grinned at him.

'What?'

'Wait until Mary-Beth hears about this, she'll laugh like anything,' added Mikhael.

'Humph,' muttered Sammy, not impressed with his undignified landing.

'Hey, don't worry, your dragon will probably do it to you at first,' Serberon reassured him.

Cheered-up, Sammy followed the boys into the foyer.

Mr Ockay tapped his watch. 'Early again boys?' He looked at Sammy. 'Did you get lost?'

Sammy shook his head. 'I played in the match.'

'Unusual,' said Mr Ockay, handing Sammy his watch.

'He scored a goal,' said Mikhael. 'Cool huh?'

'Very,' said Mr Ockay, waving to the colour monitor on his desk. 'I saw the whole game, a most impressive finish.'

Sammy grinned. This was the closest he'd got to a "well done", not that he was looking for compliments, just reassurance that the game hadn't been a complete disaster.

Mr Ockay opened his desk drawer and gave them each a gold coin, just like the ones they had been given to use in Mrs Grock's wishing well.

'Thank you,' said Sammy. He copied Dixie's brothers and accepted the coin. He followed Serberon to the drinks machine and bought a can of cola.

Sammy finished his drink in three gulps and threw the can into the bin.

'Good shot,' said Serberon. 'Thirsty?'

'Yep,' said Sammy, wiping his mouth with the back of his hand.

'Would you like another?' Sammy turned around and saw Mr Ockay holding out another four shiny coins.

'Uh no, thanks,' said Sammy. 'I expect we'll have some with tea.'

Serberon picked up the four coins and thanked Mr Ockay. 'Don't turn them down Sammy,' said Serberon. 'You never know when they might come in handy.'

Sammy pocketed the coin, thanking Serberon and Mr Ockay. He followed Serberon, Mikhael and Jason upstairs to shower and change.

As Sammy tied his shoelaces, there was a noise like thunder on the stairs and a tidal wave of boys barged into the changing rooms, laughing and shouting, fighting for space to sit, chat and change into their uniforms.

Sammy had never been so intimidated. Most of the boys were getting on for six feet tall, all aged between thirteen and fourteen, some with broad shoulders and bulging muscles and others with stick thin arms and legs. All of the boys were talking at the tops of their voices about the match and the goals they had scored.

He was quickly forgotten as Jason, Mikhael and Serberon joined in and launched into a full scale re-run of the match.

Sammy ducked under the arm of a powerful looking boy from the East house and picked up his things. He slipped out of the changing room and walked down the stairs.

Mr Ockay was talking to Mr Cross in the foyer. They nodded to Sammy as he pushed open the Gymnasium glass double doors.

Outside, Sammy bumped into a short man wearing blue dungarees and a white shirt with a red neckerchief. The man was herding the dragons into two neat lines. Sammy recognised him from the Gemology mines.

'Hello Captain Stronghammer.'

Captain Stronghammer stopped in his tracks, apparently not used to being interrupted. Behind him, the dragons shuffled impatiently.

'Hullo.'

'Are you taking the dragons back?' asked Sammy, his curiosity getting the better of him.

'Aye,' said Captain Stronghammer eyeing him suspiciously. 'They live under the castle, under your North tower in fact.'

'Oh,' said Sammy. 'How do they get through the doors?'

Captain Stronghammer laughed heartily. 'They don't, they get led underneath. There are passages from the outside. I shouldn't be telling you this, next thing you'll be wanting to go and find them!'

Sammy nodded, the idea sticking firmly in his head.

'Of course, with someone after the dragons, it's my job to make sure they get there safely…and stay there safely,' he added ominously.

'Because of the draconite?' asked Sammy.

Captain Stronghammer shuddered. 'Don't let me hear that,' he whispered. 'That's my worst nightmare, the death of a dragon in my charge.'

'Sorry,' said Sammy. 'Do you really think…'

'I don't know,' Captain Stronghammer shrugged. 'No one does, not when they'll strike, nor whose dragon is next.'

'The Shape?'

Captain Stronghammer nodded.

'What do they do with the stones?' asked Sammy.

'That's for Sir Ragnarok to find out. My guess is they use the stones to enhance their powers, make themselves immortal perhaps.'

'Immortal,' breathed Sammy. 'Like the Greek Gods?'

'Worse, much worse. You get taken over to their side, beyond death, alive but not alive if you follow me.'

Sammy shook his head.

'They don't eat, don't sleep. Time and season means nothing to them. Those who murder dragons for their own gains have no souls, not in this life, nor the next.'

Sammy felt his jaw drop. 'Black cloaks and red eyes?'

'Aye, so I've heard,' said Captain Stronghammer. 'Don't want to scare you, but word is one of these is going to go.'

'No,' whispered Sammy, looking at Kelsepe nestled up to Serberon's green dragon.

'Aye,' said the dwarf. 'That's why I have to check each and every one. Make sure no harm comes to a scale on their backs.'

Sammy left Captain Stronghammer tending to the dragons and walked back towards the castle. He was glad the rain had stopped. Halfway back, the third years overtook him, thundering up the path. He ran with them, grateful to Serberon for waiting for him at the castle doors, his left side aching with a stitch.

Dinner was beef casserole and dumplings and Sammy sat wedged between Dixie and Gavin who were equally keen to hear about the match. He was exhausted by the time he got to the part about Captain Stronghammer and he dragged out every detail watching eagerly as he held everyone's attention.

'Wow,' whispered Darius. 'You think a dragon will die?'

Sammy nodded. 'That's what he said.'

'That's so terrible,' said Milly.

'Yeah,' said Dixie. 'Did he say whose dragon?'

Sammy shook his head, wishing he'd asked Captain Stronghammer when he'd had the chance.

'Well,' said Gavin matter of factly, 'at least it won't be mine. He hasn't hatched yet.'

'What about my egg?' asked Sammy. 'My dragon, Kyrillan, he's hatched.'

'They only kill big dragons,' said Amos.

'How do you know?'

'Yeah Amos, how do you know?'

Amos puffed back his shoulders importantly. 'It's the draconite, it's only found in fully grown dragons. It says so in our Gemology book.'

'Swot,' muttered Gavin.

Thinking about Gemology made Sammy feel sick, draconite wasn't the thing he wanted to talk about at dinner.

'These potato-thingys look like draconite,' said Gavin prodding a dumpling with his fork. 'If they were blue.'

'Serberon lets me ride his dragon sometimes,' said Dixie, changing the subject.

'That's really cool, wish I had an older brother like that,' said Gavin.

Toby looked put out. 'What do you think I am?'

Gavin grinned. 'Only by five minutes.'

'Wish I had brothers and sisters,' said Sammy.

'You have in term time,' said Milly unexpectedly. 'Can't say I like Dragonball, but you're all okay.'

'Cool,' said Sammy. 'Have you got brothers and sisters?'

Milly shook her head. 'No, it's just me, Mummy and Daddy at home.'

'They saw you and didn't want any more!' Gavin laughed.

'Humph,' said Milly, 'I suppose your parents didn't have a choice!'

Sammy grinned, enjoying the banter. He nudged Dixie who was nearest. 'So was I flying really high?'

Dixie's green eyes opened wide. 'Really high, and that goal with Mikhael at the end, that was awesome!'

'Yeah,' said Sammy. 'That was good.'

'It's not fair,' said Darius. 'I wish more people had fallen off.'

'Our dragons will be hatched in no time,' said Dixie. 'Mine hatched this morning. He's called Kiridor.'

'That's unusual,' said Milly.

'What?'

'A girl having a boy dragon.'

'What are you trying to say?' Dixie glared at Milly.

'Yeah Dixie, is that normal?'

'Shut up Gavin, you might get a girl dragon, how about that?'

Gavin shut up, clearly worried at the prospect.

As they finished more Swiss roll and custard dessert, Professor Burlay came up from the teacher's table.

'Time for the common room,' he said helping himself to the last slice of Swiss roll. 'You'll need a good night's sleep tonight, Professor Sanchez will be helping with your eggs tomorrow. Take whatever you've got with you. It doesn't matter if it's shell or jelly and don't forget your Astronomics test next week. If I was you, I'd forget all about Dragonball for the rest of the year,' he added.

'Rest of our lives if the school closes,' said Dixie.

'Dixie.'

Dixie looked up. 'Yes Professor?'

Professor Burlay weakened. 'That should be a star. Go on, I'll be up at ten o'clock to make sure you're all asleep.'

Sammy waited until Professor Burlay was back at the teachers' table talking to Commander Altair, before he whispered to Dixie and Darius to make it half past ten.

Amos overheard. 'What's that Sammy? Sneaking around?'

'It's nothing,' said Sammy doing his best to look innocent.

'Secrets,' muttered Amos, brushing roughly past as they got up to go back to the common room at the base of the North tower.

Amos sat alone reading the Gemology and Astronomics text books while most of the North house played a furious game of indoor Dragonball. On the sofa facing the makeshift pitch, Milly kept giving Dixie reproving stares, making no secret that she thought Dixie should be playing Dragon Dice with her, Holly and Naomi.

Most of the fourth and fifth years went upstairs at nine o'clock. Serberon explained that the fourth years had private study desks and the fifth year dormitory had a television, cooking facilities and a pool table.

At half past nine, the room was nearly empty. After a rough tackle, Darius was sitting on the sofa where Milly had played Dragon Dice and Dixie was helping him bandage the cut.

Sammy kicked a ball to Serberon and flopped on the sofa. 'Come on,' he whispered. 'If we go up now and come down in an hour, everyone will be in bed.'

'Cool, meet here at ten thirty,' whispered Darius.

'Night all,' said Sammy, feeling guilty as Serberon clapped him on the back and said "sweet dreams". He didn't want Serberon upset with him if Dixie got into trouble.

CHAPTER 10

RETURNING THE DIRECTOMETER

'Perhaps you'd better not come,' Sammy whispered to Dixie at twenty-five to eleven.

'Hah!' said Dixie. 'If you don't let me come, I'll tell everyone you went out.'

'She'll tell everyone,' said Darius, bursting in to giggles.

Sammy gave in. 'Ok, but we have to go now…quietly.'

'Shh!' said Darius, stopping laughing as Dixie glared at him.

'Which way Sammy?' asked Dixie when they reached the main stairwell.

Sammy hesitated.

'Don't say you don't know.'

'I…'

'Use it,' whispered Dixie. 'Use the Directometer.'

'Yeah,' said Darius. 'It'll take us straight to him.'

'Ok,' said Sammy, reaching into his trouser pocket. He opened the gold case and looked at the screen. 'Sir Ragnarok,' he whispered holding the device up towards the stairs. To his relief, a green dot appeared in the centre of the dial.

'Cool,' said Dixie, peering over his shoulder.

Sammy held the Directometer in front of him and they climbed up past the Main Hall, higher and higher up the stone stairs.

'Are you sure this is right?' whispered Dixie. 'If we keep going up, we'll be in the Astronomics classroom.'

Sammy didn't let on that he was worried. When Sir Ragnarok had programmed the device, it had looked easy enough, but in the dark corridor he had a bad feeling in his stomach. He turned around on the step and the Directometer turned red if he pointed it anywhere other than up.

'Up again,' said Darius. 'Maybe his office is on the roof!'

'Maybe we should go back,' said Dixie.

Sammy stopped in his tracks. 'I can't do that. I promised I'd give it back today.'

'Ugh,' grumbled Dixie. 'You're worse than Serberon.'

'Go back if you want,' said Darius.

'No,' said Sammy firmly. 'We're here together. Let's keep going, it can't be much further.'

At each bend in the stairs, Sammy looked nervously out of the tall windows. There was nothing but darkness above and below. He counted seven windows, before the Directometer led them away from the stairwell and down a candlelit passage. They stopped outside a thick windowless door with a silver plate that read "Room 79, Alchemistry" in thick black Gothic lettering.

'Alchemistry,' whispered Sammy. 'Isn't that first thing tomorrow?'

'Maybe we should stay here,' Dixie laughed nervously. 'Hey, what's happened to the Directometer?'

Sammy looked down. The green light had turned red. He jerked his hand back towards the staircase and the green light reappeared.

'He's moving,' groaned Dixie. 'What a waste of time.'

Sammy felt sick. 'We should have said Sir Ragnarok's office. He must be around here somewhere.'

'Where?' asked Dixie. 'The corridor's empty.'

'No it's not!' Darius pounced forward. 'Look!'

Sammy spun round. Amos and Simon Sanchez were crouching beside a large chest. 'What are you doing here?' he demanded.

Amos shrugged. 'Just out for a walk.'

'Liar!' said Dixie. 'That's what that note was for in Gemology.'

'Don't know what you're talking about,' said Simon. 'What are you doing here?'

'Nothing to do with you,' snapped Dixie. 'Come on, let's go.'

Sammy ran with Dixie and Darius down the stairs, holding the green Directometer out in front. Amos and Simon bumped against him as he stopped in front of the tapestry in the Main Hall. He shoved the knight aside and scrambled up the spiral stairs, Dixie and Darius ahead, Simon and Amos behind.

Sammy was out of breath as he knocked twice on Sir Ragnarok's door at the top of the stairs.

The door creaked back on its hinges and Sir Ragnarok was there, dressed in a long navy gown that covered him from head to toe. He didn't seem surprised to see them and Sammy remembered the vertical screens, Sir Ragnarok had probably seen their whole journey.

'You're here now, come in, come in,' said Sir Ragnarok warmly. 'Welcome to my office.'

Sammy walked up the seven steps, stopping as he saw that the room was crowded with teachers, including Professor Burlay, Commander Altair, Mr Cross and several others he didn't recognise. They looked up as the five students stepped into Sir Ragnarok's office.

'Where is my mother?' asked Simon.

'I'm expecting her shortly,' said Sir Ragnarok, moving Lariston from his chair.

'Is that what you were doing, looking for her?'

'Yes Simon,' said Sir Ragnarok patiently. 'I'm sure she will be here in a moment.'

'How did you get here without us seeing you?' asked Sammy holding out the Directometer. 'All of a sudden it went red and then you were behind us.'

'You were in her classroom,' Simon accused Sir Ragnarok. 'Where is she? What have you done to her?'

'Wait patiently,' said Sir Ragnarok, taking the Directometer from Sammy's hand. 'She will be here.'

'No!' shouted Simon, pushing past Darius towards the door, straight into a shadowy shape that grunted as he barged forward.

'What's this, what's this?'

'Mum,' shouted Simon. 'You're ok.'

'Simon? What are you doing here?' said Professor Sanchez. 'In fact, what are all of you doing here?'

'We followed Sammy,' said Simon.

Professor Sanchez looked darkly at Sammy. 'Is this true?'

'Sammy kindly returned my property,' interrupted Sir Ragnarok, 'although I seem to remember asking for it to be returned discretely at breakfast, eh Sammy?'

Sammy stared at his feet. He was tired and nervous in front of the teachers. He worried what Professor Burlay would think of him and wondered how many stars it was possible to lose in one go.

Sir Ragnarok seemed to understand. 'Very well. Professor Burlay, would you be so kind as to escort our explorers back to their tower rooms. Four to North and one to East if I'm not mistaken.'

Professor Burlay nodded and, without complaining that the towers were opposite ends of the castle, he marched briskly to drop Simon off at the East tower, then back to the North common room.

'Can you manage from here?'

Dixie nodded, hiding a yawn in the back of her hand.

'Good,' said Professor Burlay. 'Sleep well and rest assured that if I catch any of you out of bed again tonight, I will make sure Sir Ragnarok sends you straight home in disgrace.'

'What on earth was that about?' whispered Sammy. 'That meeting with all those teachers up there.'

'No idea,' said Dixie, yawning again. 'Can we talk about it tomorrow?'

'Today you mean,' said Darius pointing to the grandfather clock which was showing ten past twelve.

'Yeah,' said Dixie pulling up the collar of her shirt. 'Good night!'

'Night Dixie,' said Sammy.

'See you today!'

Up in the topmost tower room and for the first time since he had arrived at Dragamas, Sammy felt homesick. Not just "I want my mum" homesick, but really bad. Worse, he let on to Darius, than scout camp in Blackpool last year.

He was grateful as Darius listened to him talk about his Mum and Dad, the new job in Switzerland and his old school with the Rat Catchers. Apparently, Darius felt the same when he stayed with his grandparents when his parents were called abroad to heal dragons. Sammy felt his own worries were pale in comparison.

'How do you manage?' he asked, but Darius had fallen asleep. Sammy yawned and pulled the duvet up to his chin. He could just see Kyrillan's black eyes as he tickled the green goo on his bedside chest.

'Hope you turn out the colour of Kelsepe,' whispered Sammy. 'A nice blue-green.'

Kyrillan just blinked and closed his eyes.

Sammy closed his eyes too. He dreamt about a future Dragonball match where he was riding a larger Kyrillan, higher and higher, blue-green scales glittering in the sunlight. In the dream, he heard a shot and he was falling with his dragon down, down on to the ground.

Sammy snapped his eyes open. Everything was quiet in the tower room, with gentle sounds of breathing and the occasional snore. He stood up and checked the stairs. No one was down there. He checked his bedside window and though he couldn't be sure, it looked as though there were dark shadows running from under his window towards the forest.

'The dragons,' he whispered, remembering Captain Stronghammer telling him that they lived under the North tower. 'Must tell Sir Ragnarok.' But it was no use, he was too tired and he knew he didn't know the corridors well enough to get back to the tapestry in the Main Hall, nor did he want to run the risk of meeting Professor Burlay for a second time in the same night.

Sammy woke to the frantic ringing of the gold bell above the door. Everyone else seemed to be up, Darius had probably told them not to wake him after feeling homesick. As he threw on his uniform, Sammy hoped he hadn't said anything stupid to Darius. He checked Kyrillan and ran downstairs into the common room where another indoor Dragonball match was taking place.

'Hey Sammy!' shouted Dixie. 'Are you ok?'

Sammy nodded, wondering if Darius had said anything.

'Come on, we're all playing!' Dixie threw a ball across to him just as the common room door opened and Professor Burlay stepped in.

'Were playing,' said Professor Burlay grouchily. 'Follow me to the Main Hall please. Sir Ragnarok has some bad news this morning.'

Sammy's dream flooded back. 'What news Professor?'

'Bad, bad news Sammy. Sir Ragnarok will explain at breakfast. Don't forget your bags and books, you have a lesson at half past nine. Check your timetables for the lesson and the room.'

'We've got Alchemistry,' said Dixie. 'You were right Sammy.'

'Right at the top,' said Sammy. 'We should have stayed there.'

'Should be fun,' said Serberon looking over Sammy's shoulder, 'Professor Sanchez takes Alchemistry. It's all pots and potions.'

'Pots and potions,' echoed Sammy. 'That doesn't sound too hard.'

Serberon laughed, 'I wouldn't swap as we've got a nice easy Astronomics lesson.'

'Oh yeah,' said Sammy, remembering their Astronomics lesson. 'We've got that test on Monday.'

Sammy followed Professor Burlay and the first years to the Main Hall, a little jealous of the way the older students seemed so confident marching ahead, knowing exactly where they were going.

Sir Ragnarok was waiting for them, standing alone at the teachers' table. He waited until the last first year had arrived and raised his staff. The door slammed shut and the sea of students fell silent.

'Following my announcement yesterday morning,' said Sir Ragnarok. 'I'm afraid I have more bad news.'

The students at each of the four house tables gasped. Wide-eyed, Sammy knew before Sir Ragnarok opened his mouth, exactly what the news would be.

'The bad news,' continued Sir Ragnarok, 'is...'

'Mrs Grock,' whispered Sammy.

'...is that Mrs Grock, school secretary and nurse, will be leaving us for personal reasons at the end of the week. She will be replaced shortly with someone equally as...'

Sammy looked to the double entrance doors. Mrs Grock was bustling forward, her bonnet bobbing up and down.

'Sir Ragnarok, am I too late to take it back? I canna be more use to you here.'

Sir Ragnarok wiped his forehead and handed Mrs Grock some papers. 'Of course,' he smiled, 'Dragamas will be the better for it.' He turned to face the school. 'That's one less piece of bad news. Mrs Grock is staying!'

Even though he'd only known Mrs Grock for a few days, Sammy cheered as loudly as the fifth years who were raising the roof with shouting and foot stamping.

Sir Ragnarok waved for silence. 'The terrible, devastating news I have to give you, will probably most affect the third years since it relates to Mary-Beth Howeson...'

'Kelsepe, no,' whispered Sammy, a lump as hard as draconite in his throat.

'...her dragon in fact.' Sir Ragnarok cleared his throat. 'Mary-Beth herself is fine, recovering from yesterday afternoon in Mrs Grock's capable hands, however,' Sir Ragnarok took a deep breath, 'during the night, a terrible, terrible thing has happened to her dragon Kelsepe who was taken to the North tower along with the other dragons from the game yesterday...'

The hall was silent, everyone focussed on Sir Ragnarok.

'...her dragon is dead.'

Sammy shuddered as Sir Ragnarok told him what he had guessed. A cold, damp feeling chilled his bones as he remembered the blue-green dragon he had flown.

'We believe this to be the work of the Shape,' continued Sir Ragnarok. 'We know that they would see this school closed and all dragons banished from the land.'

The hall was silent as each student took in the unpalatable truth that the Shape was very bad. Sammy had known this from Dixie mentioning them and his own encounter with them in the forest, but how could they do something so evil.

'Did you know?' Dixie interrupted his thoughts. 'You said both things before they happened, before Sir Ragnarok said.'

Sammy whispered in Dixie's ear without anyone noticing about Mrs Grock's letter he had seen.

'That was the day we helped Serberon?'

'Yeah, sorry I couldn't tell you at the time.'

'Tell me next time yeah?'

Sammy nodded, pleased that breakfast was "choose your own". He chose a small bowl of cereal and a glass of orange juice, upset that around him everyone else seemed to have got over Kelsepe's death and piled their plates high with sausages, bacon, eggs, hash browns, beans tomatoes and mushrooms as if nothing bad had happened.

Professor Burlay came over as they finished, rustling with the first year timetable.

'You have Alchemistry first, top floor, room...'

'Nine,' said Sammy without thinking.

'Yes Sammy, room nine,' Professor Burlay looked strangely at him. 'Don't forget your dragon eggs.'

'Mine will be easy to carry,' said Gavin.

'So long as you don't drop it,' said Toby.

'What are you going to do, carry it in one of these glasses?' Gavin held up Sammy's glass still full of the orange juice.

'Ugh,' Sammy groaned, leaving the table clutching his stomach.

'What's up with him?' asked Gavin. 'It's only orange juice.'

'Never you mind,' snapped Dixie. 'Remember he was last to ride that dragon.'

'Oh,' said Gavin. 'Oops.'

'What's orange juice got to do with Kelsepe?' asked Darius.

'Doesn't matter,' said Dixie. 'Ask Sammy another day.'

'Why?'

'Leave it Darius.'

'No, I want to know.'

'Know what?' asked Sammy as they paused in the corridor to let the rest of the first years go up the stairs.

'Er, nothing,' said Darius. 'Did it upset you?'

'Yeah,' snapped Sammy, 'it did all right.'

'It would have happened anyway,' said Darius.

'What?'

'It would have happened anyway,' repeated Darius.

'He heard you, what do you mean?' asked Dixie, impatiently.

'Well look at it this way,' said Darius. 'That girl Mary-Beth, she was the only one to get injured and it's her dragon that's dead.'

'So?' Sammy and Dixie asked together.

'Well what if someone was watching, saw that she wouldn't be near her dragon for a few days...'

'...and took their chance,' finished Sammy.

'No, that's terrible, that means...'

'It means,' whispered Sammy, 'that someone at the school is part of the Shape. Someone who was there that day.'

'Just the whole school,' said Darius. 'That'll be easy!'

'We need to find out how, then who,' said Sammy.

'Well we can rule out our year,' said Darius. 'We haven't been taught anything about dragons, let alone how to kill one.'

'Who knew where they lived?' asked Dixie.

'Yeah, where do they live?' asked Darius

Dixie shrugged. 'No idea.'

'They live under our North tower,' said Sammy. 'Captain Stronghammer told me. He said he leads them into a hidden passage on the outside wall. They live under the castle.'

'That's so cool, our tower is above the dragon entrance!'

'That should limit the number of people,' said Darius.

'Why?' asked Dixie.

'Well if you don't know, that means your brothers don't know, and if they don't know nobody knows!'

'Humph,' said Dixie. 'You don't know they don't know.'

'No, but I bet they would've said.'

'Do you think it was Captain Stronghammer?' asked Dixie.

'He's guarding the dragons,' said Sammy. 'But he would know which dragon to take.'

'Maybe it doesn't matter,' said Darius. 'He could've killed any dragon.'

'No,' Sammy thought out loud. 'There's got to be more to it.'

'Sir Ragnarok will sort it out,' said Darius.

'As well as raise money for the Shape?' asked Dixie.

'How much do you reckon draconite's worth?' asked Sammy. 'Dr Lithoman said the diamonds in the mines will be used to raise the money, but they can't get rid of them quickly enough without people getting suspicious.'

'They can't pay the ransom with draconite,' said Dixie. 'Sir Ragnarok's trying to save dragons not kill them!'

'Dr Lithoman had draconite in a glass in her room,' said Sammy.

'You've been in her room!'

'Is that why you got upset?' asked Darius as they reached the North tower common room.

'I was not upset,' spluttered Sammy. 'The orange juice just reminded me of the stone in its yellow brain-juice.'

'Ugh!' Dixie clutched her stomach. 'Let's get our dragons. What are you carrying yours in Sammy?'

'Probably my towel, or a box if I can find one.'

'Mine's still in its egg,' said Darius. 'As long as it doesn't hatch along the way, it should be really easy!'

'See you in a minute,' said Dixie.

Sammy ran with Darius up the long spiral staircase to the first year dormitory. As they walked in, Toby, Gavin and Amos fell silent.

Darius saw it first. 'What's going on? Who did that?'

Sammy followed Darius' hand and gasped. Darius's egg had fallen from his bedside chest and was in pieces on the floor, blue dragon goo covered in broken shell and dust.

'Who did this?' shouted Darius. 'It wasn't like that this morning.'

'It was like it when we came in,' said Gavin quietly, 'on the floor, in pieces, no one's touched it.'

Darius glared around the room. 'Were you here first?'

'No,' said Gavin. 'Amos was here when me and Toby got here.'

Darius turned to Amos. 'Was it you? Couldn't you get your own egg to hatch so you tried mine?'

'Amos?' asked Sammy. 'Did you do it?'

Amos turned away. 'I would've liked to, but no, when I got here, the stupid thing was already on the floor.'

'We've all got dragons,' said Sammy. 'They'll all hatch soon, Gavin's hasn't hatched either.'

'Yes it has.' Gavin held up a blob of pink and grey goo. 'It hatched just now.'

Sammy looked at the goo and grinned, 'Dixie was right!'

'Shut up Sammy, it might not be a girl dragon!'

'What about my egg?' Darius was close to tears. 'I can't take this to the lesson. I'll be expelled for not taking care of it.'

'You can't be expelled if Amos dropped your egg,' said Sammy, wrapping his towel carefully around Kyrillan.

'He says it wasn't him Sammy,' said Toby. 'I believe him.'

'Me too,' said Gavin. 'Where is he anyway?'

Sammy pulled back the curtain, Amos, his egg and rucksack had gone.

'Wait until I see him,' said Darius, angrily scooping his navy goo from the floor on to his towel. 'Hey!'

'What?' asked Sammy.

'He's only got one eye!'

'What!' Toby knelt down next to Darius.

'Look, one eye, the other must've got lost.' Darius scrabbled under his bed and beside his chest of drawers.

'You'll have to leave it,' said Gavin looking at his watch. 'We've got five floors to climb down and seven flights of stairs to climb up!'

'No!' wailed Darius. 'I'm not taking a dirty dragon with one eye!'

'I'll stay and help you look,' said Sammy.

'Yeah, us too,' Toby nudged Gavin. 'It can't have gone far.'

'Thanks.' Darius sniffed. 'You don't have to do this.'

'Yeah we do,' said Sammy. 'Hey, isn't that another eye, a blue one, under that piece of shell?'

'Yes!' shouted Darius. 'Thanks Sammy. He's got two eyes, one black and one blue.'

Toby leaned over Darius' shoulder. 'You don't reckon he's blind in one eye, like dogs?'

'Don't say that,' hissed Sammy.

'Look he's called Nelson as well!' Gavin pointed at Darius's letter and laughed.

Darius scooped up his towel full of dragon goo and glared. 'This is all Amos's fault. Come on we're late for Alchemistry.'

By Sammy's watch, they were nearly ten minutes late as they ran with bundles of dragons in their arms, up to room seventy-nine, high in the castle roof.

'Well we are late,' said Professor Sanchez as they came in, heads bowed meekly. 'Ah Sammy,' she smiled at him. 'Welcome Sammy and friends to Alchemistry. Take your seats. We were just about to start.'

Sammy sat on the wooden bench in the second row between Dixie and Darius. He set his towel gently on the desktop, turning Kyrillan around to face him. Kyrillan's black bead eyes obstinately turned to face the front, as he was waiting for something to happen.

'As most of you will know,' said Professor Sanchez, 'Alchemistry does not cover the looking after of the dragons.'

'So why did we bring them?' asked Darius poking Nelson's blue eye gently.

'However, in the light of the recent events, Sir Ragnarok has asked me to help you hatch your eggs and you will learn more this afternoon in your Study of the Dragon lessons. Please put up your hand if your dragon has not hatched yet.'

Across the room, sitting next to Simon Sanchez, Amos put his hand up. Most of the West house and roughly half of the South and East houses put up their hands. As well as Amos, only Milly, Helena and Holly from North put up their hands.

Dixie whispered that the last North girl, Naomi, had tapped her egg open with a spoon she'd borrowed from breakfast.

Sammy was relieved to see that Dixie had pulled off the shell pieces. She had a blue-green dragon just like Kyrillan. Looking around, it was easily the best colour amongst shades of green, red, orange and blue and Simon Sanchez who had a jet black lump of goo in front of him.

'Very well,' said Professor Sanchez. 'We will begin by calling their names. Amos you may go first. Everyone else, please watch.'

Amos stood up, leaning over his mottled purple flecked egg and said "Morg".

'Louder!' barked Professor Sanchez. 'He will not hear you inside the shell.'

'Morg,' said Amos, loud enough for the whole class to hear.

'Morg!' Darius laughed. 'What kind of a name is that?'

At Darius's laugh, Amos's egg suddenly gave an ear piercing screech and exploded. Bits of shell flew high up to the classroom ceiling and fell scattering amongst the East house. Sammy peered over. Amos had a grey dragon with two black eyes swivelling round and around.

'He has hatched!' Professor Sanchez clapped her hands. 'You Darius, you called him and he hatched. Are you and Amos close friends?'

'What! No! Never! He smashed my egg open just this morning.'

Everyone turned to stare at Amos.

Amos turned a light shade of grey. 'It's not true. It was like it when I got there.'

'Simon?' Professor Sanchez turned to her son. 'What do you think?'

Next to Amos, Simon went crimson. 'You promised you would let me get on with school and not pick on me.'

'Very well,' said Professor Sanchez over the class laughter. 'If that is how it happened. Darius do not discuss the birth of your dragon again.'

'What?' demanded Darius. 'Why not?'

'She might be right,' whispered Sammy. 'We weren't there. We have to believe him.'

'No,' said Darius. 'You do what you want.'

'Peter, you're next,' said Professor Sanchez.

Peter Grayling from the West house stood up with his orange egg. It took five goes with everyone joining in before his dragon, Netta, emerged with a shriek covering the class in soggy shell.

'We must hurry,' said Professor Sanchez, checking her watch. 'Anyone whose dragon is still in its shell, try together now.'

Soon only Milly and Holly were left, their dragons refusing to come out of their shells. Professor Sanchez bustled into the third row and helped tap the eggs with her staff several times before the eggs split open and the last two dragons hatched.

'Very good,' Professor Sanchez seemed pleased with the results. 'We will move on to Alchemistry. Please put your dragons to one side, I have enough boxes for one each.'

'Great,' said Sammy, lifting Kyrillan into his shoebox. 'I'll have to get this towel washed before tomorrow.'

Professor Sanchez spent the rest of the lesson explaining about the things they would learn in Alchemistry, about creating potions and changing one thing into something else.

Sammy was interested to learn about the strange amberoid liquid Mrs Grock had used in her healing potion. It turned out that it was created from the excretions of a number of animals, including the greater horseshoe bat commonly found in the murky caves beneath the castle.

Professor Sanchez had just asked everyone to write up notes from the lesson when the bell rang. They left the classroom with a rucksack slung over one shoulder, each student carrying his or her cardboard box gently in outstretched arms.

Sammy followed the first years down a flight of steps into a narrow corridor that apparently led into the east wing, where their Dragon Studies lesson was to take place in room fifty-five.

Instead of the deep pile carpet and interesting décor found in the rest of the castle, the east wing was bare. There were no paintings on the walls or ornaments on the windowsills. Underfoot, the uneven flagstones were scorched with burn marks and were broken in places.

Inside room fifty-five there were four rows of desks with a central gangway dividing the room into eight segments, each with five wooden desks and five wooden chairs. At the front was a large teacher's desk with a blackboard in behind. Apart from four arched windows opposite the door, the stone walls were bare. The two radiators in the room were small and tucked one each side of the teacher's desk and did very little to warm the cold room.

Sammy sat next to one of the four tall windowless windows overlooking the Gymnasium. He found that his chair had a wobbly leg that squeaked whenever he moved.

As Sammy was about to mention the chair to Darius, the classroom door opened and a gaunt and ghostly man wearing a suit and carrying a briefcase walked in, closing the door behind him.

'Good afternoon class, my name is Dr Shivers,' said the ghostly man. 'Shivers by name and shivery by nature,' he laughed sending a shiver up Sammy's spine.

'They say he uses voodoo dolls,' whispered Darius.

'Ooh,' said Milly.

Not knowing much about voodoo dolls, Sammy wasn't sure if this was a good thing or not. One thing he was sure of was that he needed to wear an extra t-shirt for the next Dragon Studies lesson.

'Brr,' said Dixie. 'It's cold in here.'

'Did everyone manage to hatch their dragons?' asked Dr Shivers.

The class nodded.

'Professor Sanchez helped us,' said Peter Grayling.

'Good,' said Dr Shivers, taking a small bottle of blue liquid out of his jacket pocket and resting it beside his briefcase on the front desk. 'In your first Dragon Studies lesson, I will demonstrate the life cycle of a dragon.'

Dr Shivers opened his briefcase and pulled out a large grey egg. 'Bit of luck this one hatching this morning,' he said, turning the egg to show a crack in the grey shell. 'Are you ready?'

The class nodded, shuffling forward to get a closer view.

With one hand, Dr Shivers held the egg and with his other, he poured the blue liquid one drop at a time on to the crown of the egg.

There was a loud crack and the eggshell exploded leaving an orange jellylike blob in Dr Shivers's left hand.

'A rare species indeed,' said Dr Shivers. 'Can anyone tell me where golden dragons originated?'

Sammy shook his head. He had no idea where any dragons came from, let alone rare golden ones. He made up his mind to ask Dr Shivers where blue-green dragons like Kyrillan and Kiridor came from.

'Not to worry, it's a little advanced for first years perhaps,' said Dr Shivers, making no attempt to answer the question. 'It may come up in your end of year exams,' he added, scrambling inside his desk and pulling out a reddish brown stick with coloured crystals on the end.

The staff was the size of a hockey stick and looked several times as heavy. Dr Shivers swayed it uncertainly in mid-air and brought it down on the desk with a thump. 'Grow!' he commanded.

Sure enough, two eyes swung forward to face the class and a forked tongue poked out, hissing angrily at the class.

Dr Shivers poured more drops of the blue liquid on to the dragon. 'Largo Oil,' he explained. 'It's your mother's recipe,' he waved the bottle towards Simon Sanchez.

'Bet he couldn't make it,' whispered Sammy watching open mouthed as the dragon sprouted four short legs, the eyes floating up a newly formed neck.

What looked like a fifth leg grew from under the back legs, but with another drop of Largo Oil, it turned into a golden tail armed with short sharp looking spikes. As soon as the head was formed, the dragon looked complete, if only the size of a poodle. It puffed a wisp of smoke out of its nostrils and a small flame flew from its mouth.

As the flame died away, Sammy saw that the dragon had two rows of pointed teeth.

'Ouch!' Dr Shivers dropped the dragon on to his desk and rubbed his hand. He poured another two drops of Largo Oil on to the dragon's back and it grew to the size of an Alsatian. Two drops later it was the size of a miniature pony, some five feet tall and eight feet long.

Dr Shivers took a step back. 'This dragon is now somewhere between one and two years old,' he informed them.

They watched as the golden dragon blew a ring of fire above their heads scorching the wall behind them. Sammy was surprised Sir Ragnarok allowed wooden furniture in the Dragon Studies classroom.

'More?' asked Dr Shivers.

Without waiting for a reply, and looking as though he was thoroughly enjoying himself, he poured the remainder of the bottle on to the head of the golden dragon. 'Three years old and that's enough for indoors,' said Dr Shivers, chuckling to himself.

With a thunderous roar, the dragon grew again and looked big enough to win a fight with a small car. It stamped its front foot shaking their desks and making their dragon goo quiver with fear. It stamped again, this time cracking the teacher's desk in two and sending papers flying. Dr Shivers was laughing as hard as his face would stretch, tears pouring from his eyes. He looked ten, maybe twenty years younger than when he had arrived.

'Enough,' said Dr Shivers, still giggling. He pulled some green pellets from his other jacket pocket and threw them at the huge golden dragon.

The dragon snorted three of the pellets, each the size of a small bar of chocolate, through its wide mouth and curled into a ball at Dr Shivers's feet.

'Good as gold,' said Dr Shivers with a hint of relief. 'I haven't had this much fun since I bred my first dragon some forty years ago.' He looked directly at Sammy, 'I was in North as a boy, being a teacher means I must show a little responsibility these days.' He laughed again. 'Very well Goldie, must set you free I suppose.'

'Dr Shivers wait,' said Sammy an idea for the dragon coming to him. 'Could Goldie be given to Mary-Beth, it was her dragon that was…' he couldn't bring himself to say it.

'Was murdered?' finished Dr Shivers. 'That's a lovely idea, a most unfortunate affair. I'll speak to Sir Ragnarok tonight, and to Tom Sweep,' he added, surveying his broken desk. 'Write this up please and hand in your essays at the beginning of our next lesson.'

'Including Goldie breaking the desk,' said Darius. 'Did you see how big she got?'

'Three years' worth,' said Sammy. 'Wish I could get hold of some of that Largo Oil.'

'Me too,' said Gavin.

'Me three,' Dixie and Darius said together.

'Ugh,' grumbled Milly, 'I don't want to ride those things, there's too much slime and too many scales.'

The Dragon Studies lesson ended with Milly still telling the other North girls how she would write to her parents asking to be let off raising and riding a fire breathing, smoke blowing dragon.

Sammy was glad he had Dixie and Darius either side of him at lunch so they could talk non-stop about their dragons, which were now safely back in their tower rooms.

'What's next?' asked Sammy, pleasantly full of their sandwich and cake lunch.

Sir Ragnarok had ensured that there was quantity and variety to go around and Sammy had tried almost every combination of the half-slice triangular sandwiches; cheese and onion, cheese and crisps, cucumber and lettuce, chicken, ham and cheese. The only ones he hadn't tried were the egg and mushroom sandwiches that Gavin said were very good.

'Armoury,' said Dixie holding up her timetable.

In almost no time at all, they were sitting in a cramped classroom facing a large fireplace and a large blackboard, waiting for their Armoury teacher to arrive.

'This is stupid,' grumbled Dixie. 'He can't be late.'

'Shall we get a teacher from the staff room?' asked Milly.

'If you can find it,' said Darius, laughing at her.

'He'll be here,' said Dixie.

'He is already here,' said a quiet mysterious voice from the front of the class.

Milly screamed and everyone else gasped.

'Welcome to Armoury,' said the voice. 'Here you will learn skills you never dreamed possible.'

They gasped again as with a loud crack and a puff of smoke a man appeared at the front of the classroom, accompanied by a large and sleeping golden dragon that looked suspiciously like Goldie from Dragon Studies.

The class stared at the man emerging from the smoke. At nearly six and a half feet tall, he towered over them sitting at their desks. He was as thin as Dr Shivers but without the lifeless appearance. His hair was sandy coloured and shiny, slicked back from his face. His eyes were bright as he took in the students, a smile on his suntanned face. He would have been in his mid-twenties, a picture of power, a war lord, a commander.

'Wow,' said Dixie, totally transfixed.

Sammy recognised him from their tour of the grounds. It had been Commander Altair and Professor Sanchez that had saved him, Dixie and Darius from the Shape. This close, he seemed taller and more powerful than before. Sammy almost wished he was in South to have a Dragon Commander as his house master.

'Shall we begin?' said Commander Altair, although it was more of a statement than a question. He stood by the classroom door surveying the class.

'I sense a strong presence amongst you. There are several people here who will go on to do great things, Dragon Knights certainly and maybe a commander or two here as well.'

Dixie nudged Sammy's elbow. 'Remember Mrs Grock's?'

Sammy nodded, his eyes glued in tunnel vision to Commander Altair as the professor took his wooden staff from beside the blackboard.

'Do you have your staffs?'

They nodded, apart from a girl from the West house who was sent red-faced to fetch her staff from her tower room dormitory.

She returned as Commander Altair cast his staff towards the classroom floor and said "Fire". A red shoot burst out of the crystals, creating a fire that shot flames three feet into the air with a burning heat that reached even the students at the back, then retracted into a warm glow.

'Good,' Commander Altair smiled at the fire crackling at his feet. 'I see that Dr Lithoman has helped you assemble your crystals. Soon you will be able to do this.' Commander Altair lifted the flames with his staff and paraded the fire over the class.

Sammy could hear the fire crackling and feel its heat pouring down. He was glad when Commander Altair threw the flames into the fireplace below the blackboard.

'A bit advanced for your first lesson,' said Commander Altair, carefully avoiding Sammy's gaze. 'By the end of the year, you will be able to do this standing on your head.'

Sammy grinned and made up his mind up to try it again, perhaps in his tower room where, if it went wrong, only Darius, Gavin, Toby and Amos would see.

With the fire crackling merrily behind him, Commander Altair spent the rest of the lesson reading pages from a thick leather bound book about the work that they were going to achieve during their first year of learning Armoury.

Sammy listened as hard as he could, not just because he was in the back row, but because he desperately wanted to learn the practical side of Armoury. From what Commander Altair was saying, this would involve woodwork and metal skills, designing tools and weapons in their final year and practising self-defence manoeuvres that would be helpful both on the Dragonball pitch as well as helping to fight the Shape.

Sammy felt his heart sink as he remembered Sir Ragnarok's warning to close the school if they failed to find the money or defeat the Shape. He cheered up when Commander Altair didn't give them any work to complete before the next lesson, though he did warn them against setting fire to things.

'Practice if you will, but only outside or in a fireplace, I don't want reports from Sir Ragnarok of any of you in any trouble.'

The South students groaned loudest. Sammy noticed that some of them already had plasters and bandages. Dixie had said they'd been fencing with their staffs during the lunch break.

'That will be all,' said Commander Altair as the bell rang.

As they filed out of the classroom looking forward to dinner, Commander Altair held Sammy back and pointed to the dragon sleeping beside his feet.

'Sir Ragnarok likes your idea Sammy. Goldie will be given to Mary-Beth on her return from Mrs Grock's.'

Sammy grinned and caught up with Dixie and Darius. At least something good had come out of the lessons. He hoped Mary-Beth would be pleased.

CHAPTER 11

THE FLOATING CIRCUS

After several weeks at Dragamas, Sammy felt he'd got the hang of the boarding school routines, the new teachers, the new classes. He hardly missed his parents and certainly didn't miss the Rat Catchers at his old school in Ratisbury.

The Astronomics test had come and gone. Sammy had nearly fallen off his chair when Professor Burlay told him he'd scored a nearly perfect mark of ninety-eight percent. It was ten percent higher than the nearest mark, scored by Rachel Burns from South whose father was a Lantern Lighter and had apparently taught her star positions before she could read or write.

Sammy was firm friends with Dixie and Darius. They saved each other seats and worked together in the common room after classes. Even Gavin and Amos had put their differences to one side and often studied together, opposite Sammy, Dixie and Darius at one of the long common room study tables.

Sammy was about to ask Darius what the difference was between onyx and jet for part of their Gemology homework when Professor Burlay burst into the common room clutching his staff.

'Guess what,' said Professor Burlay, throwing the door back on its hinges. 'You're all going to the Floating Circus this weekend!' He left as soon as he had arrived, leaving a tidal wave of manic hysteria behind him.

'The Floating Circus! Wow!' shouted Dixie. She leapt up, sending the Gemology papers flying and scrambled up the girls' tower, returning seconds later with Milly, who was recovering from a stomach ache, and a tatty sheet of pink paper covered in pictures and tiny writing.

'Look Sammy,' Dixie shouted, waving the pink paper at him.

'What?' asked Sammy, his concentration on gemstones broken.

'The Floating Circus, it's all here!'

'Let's have a look,' said Gavin, shoving the textbooks aside. 'Does it have everything?'

'Yes,' said Dixie. 'Everything from acrobats to aardvarks, ice cream, hot dogs, loads of animals.'

'Have you been before?' asked Sammy.

'Well no,' Dixie paused, 'but Serberon brought this back for me when he went.'

Sammy laughed and pointed to the second paragraph next to a picture of a lion. 'It says here the acrobats can feed tamed lions as they jump through hoops of fire!'

'Wow.' Gavin looked very impressed.

'No way,' said Darius. 'No one can do that. Let me look.'

With the visit to the Floating Circus planned, the rest of the week passed agonisingly slowly for Sammy. Everyone in the castle was excited, from Milly who was the youngest in school (by two days as she was quick to remind anyone who mentioned it) to a burly sixteen year old boy from the

West house called Nathan who, since he was leaving Dragamas in the summer, couldn't care less about floating circuses or the school closing. When Sammy bumped into him going to Alchemistry, Nathan said he'd had enough excitement to last three dozen lifetimes.

With just eighteen hours to go, Sammy and the rest of the first years were having trouble concentrating in Armoury, their last class before the weekend.

Commander Altair finally lost his patience. 'Enough!' he shouted above the crackling of the fire they were trying to produce, some with more success than others.

'I said enough!' he bellowed, sweeping back his hair and revealing bulging veins on the side of his forehead. 'Hasn't Professor Sanchez taught you how to put fire out with your minds?' He relaxed as the room became fire-free, his face looking less purple and more like normal.

'No Commander Altair,' said Milly. 'She said that we could try mind control next week.'

'Next week?' Commander Altair sighed. 'That may be too late.'

'Too late for what?' asked Dixie, trying overly hard to look innocent and sweet to get her answer.

Commander Altair laughed. 'Those big, round eyes might work on Professor Burlay, Dixie, but not on me. You'll all find out soon enough.'

Dixie sat down to laughter from the class, a mischievous grin spread across her face.

'No,' said Commander Altair resolutely. 'You are not to ask Professor Burlay about this.'

Behind Commander Altair's back, Dixie gave him a "try and stop me" look whilst nudging Sammy's elbow. 'He didn't say you couldn't ask.'

Sammy grinned at Dixie, thinking he'd never been happier. He fitted in perfectly at Dragamas and was glad his parents had allowed him to come.

Despite Commander Altair's protests, they started to leave two minutes before the bell went, talking and shouting about the things they would see and what they would do at the circus.

'No homework this weekend,' Commander Altair shouted above the racket. 'Not that you care. Come on, the Floating Circus isn't that good, you could all do with some Armoury practice instead!'

His advice fell on deaf ears. Sammy was just about to leave when a hand grabbed his shoulder.

'Ugh,' he groaned, tired of being held back at the end of classes. 'You go on,' Sammy muttered to Dixie and Darius, 'I'll catch you up.'

Commander Altair waited until everyone apart from Simon Sanchez had gone before he asked, 'do you know why I've kept you back?'

Simon Sanchez nodded and so that he didn't look stupid, Sammy nodded as well.

'Good,' said Commander Altair. 'Out of the forty students and forty fires, yours were the only two to put it out without my assistance. Do you know what this means?'

'That we get A-grades?' asked Simon.

'No, it means you may be useful tomorrow.'

'To put out fires?' asked Sammy, annoyed Commander Altair might ruin the fun he was hoping to have. 'Surely there are enough teachers to do that?'

Commander Altair laughed. 'I was hoping you'd use your mind control.'

'What!' said Sammy, taken by surprise. 'I'm ten years old, nearly eleven, but I can't get a fire to go out let alone try mind control!'

'What did you do here?' Simon asked coldly.

'I...er...I...' Sammy faltered feeling both stupid and scared at the same time.

'Some students never manage to put fires out,' Commander Altair smiled at him. 'Casting spells and magic is easy but putting wrongs to right, that can only be done by true Dragon Knights.'

'My wish,' said Sammy. 'What have I done?'

'You should heed Milly, Sammy, wishing wells are a gimmick, cheap entertainment. Professor Sanchez and I arranged for the items to appear out of thin air, Darius's chocolate, your Dragonball set.'

'Oh,' said Sammy. 'I never got...'

Commander Altair laughed. 'Professor Sanchez I expect. We can't have people taking two wishes. She was probably put off by your first wish.'

'Did she...'

'Arrange for the school to return? No Sammy, apparently your wish did that. According to Sir Ragnarok it protected them from an attack by the Shape. The land they were visiting was blown out of the sky. It disintegrated into thousands of pieces.'

Sammy felt his jaw drop, 'am I a...'

'A Dragon Knight?' answered Commander Altair. 'No, not yet, but the professors here agree you have the makings to be one, both of you in fact. I assume Simone taught you Simon?'

'Yes,' said Simon, blushing slightly.

'Simon and Simone,' Sammy grinned. 'Cool!'

'Grr,' said Simon. 'May we go?'

Sammy woke bleary eyed and early on Saturday morning, remembering in an instant where he was and where he was going. He had squeezed every last detail about the Dragon's Lair and the pearlescent tube that led up to the lands above the school from anyone and everyone in the common room the night before.

He remembered stumbling upstairs with Darius at nearly two o'clock in the morning armed with gossip and pictures of lots of lands that had been visited.

Serberon had squashed any fears of it all being a joke by showing him souvenirs and giving him a toy lion from the circus that used to roar when you squeezed its front paws, but now only went "grrr" quietly and non-threateningly.

Sammy squeezed the lion's paws and it grrr'd at him. Hearing whispers from Gavin and Toby, he stuck his head out from behind his curtain. They were both dressed and looking through the pictures of the Floating Circus they had borrowed.

He ducked back into his own area to dress. Serberon had recommended jeans, t-shirt and school jumper, but with it being two weeks into October and not wanting to get cold, Sammy put a second t-shirt under his jumper just in case.

There was a knock on the door as he tied his shoelaces and Professor Burlay's head peeked around the corner.

'Are we ready?' asked Professor Burlay, who seemed unusually happy for this time of the morning.

'Yes Sir,' five voices shouted back at him.

When they reached the common room, Dr Shivers was leading the second, third, fourth and fifth years out into the corridor.

'First years go last,' explained Professor Burlay. 'I have to go through some basic rules. Don't look so worried, Gavin. It's nothing drastic, mostly safety. Wait here please, I'll fetch the girls and explain the rules to you on the way.'

Sammy had swarms of butterflies chasing each other in his stomach as Professor Burlay returned with the five girls.

They were dressed similarly with black jeans and the navy Dragamas jumper. Dixie had her sleeves rolled up and came over to stand next to him and Darius.

'Rule one,' said Professor Burlay checking his watch, 'is that if any professor says it's time to go, don't wait for me, follow them. Rule two, try not to talk to strangers. You get all kinds of folk up there sometimes and whilst most will have your best interests at heart, some do not. Thirdly, keep in groups of at least two or three and keep together. Finally,' Professor Burlay broke into a smile, 'rule four is to have fun!'

'That's easy,' said Gavin. 'Don't talk to strangers and do what the teacher says.'

'Yeah sure,' said Sammy, answering Dixie who had asked if she could go in a three with him and Darius.

'Milly and Holly and Naomi and Helena have paired up,' she added a little resentfully when they were outside.

Sammy was glad they were the last group to go to the Dragon's Lair. It was a longer walk than he remembered and even the trees seemed different in the daylight that penetrated through the thick leaves overhead. He followed Dixie and Darius into the clearing where the other first years were waiting and looked up at the dark entrance guarded by the sharp rows of milk white Dragon Teeth stones.

Professor Burlay led the North first years up the steps counting each student. He reached Milly who was last and stopped.

'Eight, nine...where's Amos?'

Sammy looked round, he was sure Amos had been behind him.

'Here Professor Burlay,' Amos shouted from the bottom of the steps. 'Is it ok if I join the East house for today?'

'Professor Sanchez?'

'This is fine,' said Professor Sanchez, looking straight at Sammy as if she expected him to join the East house for the day too. She barked instructions at her students to hurry up and Sammy thought she would have been happy to swap with Professor Burlay altogether.

'Very well,' said Professor Burlay, 'Sammy, you, Dixie and Darius take the lead, when you get inside, pull the red lever to activate the lift.'

It was cold and dark inside the Dragon's Lair and Sammy shivered, feeling as if he was walking into a real dragon's mouth. Several diamonds glistened in the walls and there was a familiar wheelbarrow groove in the floor that suggested the cave had once been mined.

'Light a fire Sammy,' whispered Dixie.

'I think it is ok,' said Sammy, nervous at what the light might reveal. He didn't like the musty cavern smell and wondered what animals might live inside it. He was sure he'd seen a pair of golden eyes looking at him.

'I've got a torch,' said Darius, fumbling in his jeans pocket. 'Got it!'

With the small beam, Sammy could see the red lever, but luckily no eyes. He pulled it hard to the right and stood back against the rocky wall.

The lift creaked and groaned as it crept down the tube. When it finally arrived, Darius opened the door and they crammed inside, jostled by the other first years who were just as keen to get in.

'Max ten persons,' Sammy read out loud from a notice on the lift wall.

'Must be small persons,' said Gavin. 'Press the button Sammy, you're nearest.'

'Ugh,' Sammy jumped as something jabbed him in the ribs.

'Move out of my way,' said a rough voice from somewhere around Sammy's waist. 'I do the lift around here.'

'Who's there?' demanded Gavin.

'It's just me, Captain Firebreath. I'll be making sure you get up and back in one piece. Are you ready?'

'Yes,' said Dixie, linking arms with Sammy and Darius.

Sammy took a step back as the man came under Darius' torchlight. He was short with a full head of ginger hair and ginger beard, a flame-haired twin of Captain Stronghammer, dressed in a similar white shirt and navy dungarees with a red and white spotted neckerchief.

'Not another greenhair,' said Captain Firebreath, looking at Dixie. 'Had your brothers here earlier, causing trouble.'

Dixie grinned. 'We're ready to see the Floating Circus!'

'Oh-kay, let's go!' shouted Captain Firebreath, slamming his fist against a grey button on the lift wall.

The doors rumbled shut and there was a lurch that brought the taste of their midnight feast to the top of Sammy's throat. He gulped, hoping he wouldn't be sick in front of everyone.

The lift jerked upwards, screeching occasionally as it touched the sides. Out of the small window in the lift doors, Sammy saw they were high above the school, which was now only a tiny blob somewhere far beneath them.

After several minutes, Captain Firebreath shuffled to the lift door and pressed the grey button. 'All right then' he said. 'We're here and it just took five minutes, you lot must be lighter than the last.'

'We're here,' echoed Sammy, wishing it wasn't so dark inside the lift.

'You're at the reception office where they check you in and out,' said Captain Firebreath, pulling open the doors. 'Like they need it up here.'

Sammy stepped out of the lift and into the middle of a large bustling room with a glass dome ceiling. Around the walls he saw counters similar to the ones he'd seen with his mother in the bank. Behind each counter there were men and women dressed smartly in identical striped shirts and navy suits. A large Dragamas banner was draped over one of the counters and he made his way across to the oldest looking man he'd ever seen.

'Over here for Dragamas,' said the man, his face creasing with wrinkles. 'Just the ten of you is it?'

Captain Firebreath shook his head. 'No such luck Rocky. There's thirty more and the professors as well. I'll be back and forth a hundred times before the day is out.'

The man laughed. 'Right-o Firey, bring them up. I'll sort these out.'

Captain Firebreath stepped backwards into the lift, mopping his forehead with his shirtsleeve. 'Enjoy your day boys and girls.'

The lift doors rumbled shut and there was a high pitched squealing as the grey cage slipped out of sight. Sammy was glad when a navy suited woman pushed a sliding grill across the gaping hole. It was a long, long way down.

'Right-o,' said the man called Rocky. 'This your first time? Be sure to visit the circus itself, won't you.'

They nodded and Sammy said, "Yes Sir."

'My brothers told us loads about it,' said Dixie.

Rocky looked solemnly at Dixie and the North girls. 'Your brothers should be told not to lead their sister astray. This ain't no place for ladies.'

'I'm not...' started Dixie.

'Yes you are Miss Greenhair,' retorted Rocky. 'Know your father well I do. He'd want to think you are.'

'But...'

'Yeh, I know he can't be with you as much as he'd like, what with being a...' Rocky didn't get the chance to finish as a white haired lady on his left coughed loudly.

'Ahem Sergeant Rockhammer,' said the white haired lady. 'Send the young ones this way if you're going to talk and talk. They want to be out in the sunshine enjoying themselves up here.'

'Pah,' snorted Rocky. 'They want to be down the mines. Can't think what Sir Ragnarok's thinking bringing them all up here when there's work to be done.'

'Don't listen to that old fool,' the white haired woman chuckled. 'I just need to take your names and give you your wristbands and then you can explore our land.'

Sammy held his right wrist forward feeling slightly weird. Out of the glass domed building, he had no idea what to expect. They were as high as the clouds and he was nervous about walking in case he fell back down to Dragamas. Next to him, Dixie seemed unsettled and kept looking back at Sergeant Rockhammer as if she hoped he would finish his sentence.

There wasn't any time to worry as the white haired lady snapped a fluorescent orange band around his wrist and wished him a good day. With more first years spilling into the reception office, Sammy was swept towards the door with his house mates, who seemed especially keen to get outside.

'Back at six o'clock,' said the white haired lady. 'Any later and Captain Firebreath lives up to his name!'

Looking back at flame haired Captain Firebreath, Sammy believed her and allowed himself to be hustled out of a large set of double doors with Dixie and Darius flanked either side of him.

He blinked in the bright sunshine, surprised to see that he was walking on what looked like grass. Trying to be discreet, he bent down and it felt like grass, real grass, growing in real earth, in the sky. He shook his head, half expecting to wake up, wondering if he'd find himself back in the North tower ready to get up for lessons as usual. Dixie and Darius didn't seem bothered and were laughing and jumping as if it was all normal.

Sammy scratched his head, he was sure he could hear the sound of cows mooing. If it was a trick, it was a good one. He took a step forward on to a paved path that led through some trees where the rest of his house mates were already disappearing out of sight. The path seemed real and took his weight as he took tiny steps forward, expecting it to cave in at any moment and send him plummeting down to Dragamas.

A few steps later, Sammy had convinced himself that the path wasn't going to disappear and they were in fact in another land at the top of the lift. As he was getting used to the idea, he walked past a large oak tree and stopped dead in his tracks.

Beyond the tree in every direction there were tents and small buildings, sideshows and stalls. In the distance, there was an enormous red and yellow tent with the words "Big Top" in black writing. Sammy was standing at the edge of a giant circus stretching as far as the eye could see.

'Come on slowcoach,' shouted Dixie. 'Where have you been?'

'Just, y'know, making sure we're here,' said Sammy.

Dixie gave him a strange look. 'Everyone else has gone,' she scolded. 'Gavin and Toby went that way.'

Sammy looked at the tent Dixie had pointed to. It was a shooting range that looked as though you could win prizes for hitting the targets.

'Yeah and everyone else went that way.' Darius pointed towards a large Ferris wheel that was spinning multi-coloured carriages in a vertical circle.

'Where do you want to go first?' asked Sammy. Fast overcoming his disbelief that it was even possible to be at the Floating Circus, he was spotting one thing after another that he fancied looking at. 'There's a caravan selling hot dogs, ice creams and candyfloss over there, or it looks like we can get to the Big Top that way.'

'Ice creams first,' said Darius patting his stomach. 'Anyone got any money?'

'Yeah, I'll get these,' said Dixie. 'You get my ticket into the Big Top.'

Sammy ran with Dixie and Darius over to the ice cream caravan. They stood in front of a ring of white plastic tables and chairs at the hollowed out window and read the blackboard of ice creams to choose from. Sammy was still deciding what to have, sure he could hear cows mooing, when a plump woman wearing a pink and white striped apron and an oversized straw bonnet appeared at the window.

'Welcome to Merry Megan's Icy Ices,' she said, beaming at them. 'What can I get for you three? Don't worry about the money. These are free to first years.'

'How do you know we're first years?' Dixie demanded, pocketing her five pound note.

'Orange wristbands,' explained the woman. 'First years' are always orange and orange means everything is free! What flavour would you like?'

Sammy looked back at the blackboard. There had to be at least a hundred different flavours each printed in tiny coloured chalk letters. 'Could I get a strawberry cone please.'

'Short cone, long cone, round, square or triangle?' the woman chuckled.

'Short, round,' said Sammy, 'no, triangle!'

'Coming right up.'

The woman disappeared and emerged seconds later with a beige triangular cone about thirty centimetres high crowned with a monstrous dollop of bright pink, strawberry smelling ice cream, complete with a ring of real strawberries perched perilously on top.

'Wow,' said Sammy reaching for the ice cream. 'I've never seen one that big!'

'How big is a big one?' asked Dixie, gawping at the ice cream mountain.

'I'm gonna find out,' said Darius. 'I'd like a large round cone with chocolate ice cream and marshmallows, and a flake please.'

The woman smiled. 'That's a good choice, my favourite actually,' she said, disappearing back inside the caravan.

Sammy was halfway through eating his ice cream when the woman returned out of the side entrance of the caravan carrying an enormous ice cream that looked the best part of a metre tall. If it had stood on the ground, it would have easily come up to his waist.

Darius took a step back as she thrust the ice cream into his hands. He needed them both just to steady the mountain of marshmallows towering above his head.

'Are you going to eat all that?' asked Sammy in disbelief.

Darius nodded. 'Gonna try.' He licked his lips and took a bite out of the side of the ice cream. 'Ooh, cold.'

'What are you going to have Dixie?' asked Sammy.

Dixie looked at him, transfixed by the enormity of Darius's ice cream. 'Strawberry and marshmallow I think.'

'Strawberry and marshmallow is it lovvie? There's lots to choose from you know. Banana, blackcurrant, blueberry, cherry, raspberry, strawberry, toffee, lime, they're all on the board there, or if you like, try a combination of all of them!'

'That sounds good,' said Dixie smiling at the ice cream lady. 'A bit of each then please.'

'Take a seat and I'll bring it over.'

Sammy, Dixie and Darius sat down at one of the white plastic garden tables. After nearly ten minutes, the woman returned with a round cone, the size of Sammy's topped with layer upon layer of dollops of all of the flavours on the blackboard. There were marshmallows and strawberries down one side and several flakes protruding amongst a shimmer of chocolate powder and fairy dust sprinkled amongst silver balls and hundreds and thousands.

'Wow,' said Dixie. 'That's amazing.'

'Mmm,' agreed Darius, his mouth full of flake.

They sat on the garden chairs talking and waving to classmates who were mingling with the circus folk in groups of twos and threes. Two young men walked past with monkeys on their shoulders followed by an old woman carrying a basket of flowers.

Sammy couldn't quite place an odd feeling he had about the people who walked past. They were definitely human, but they seemed more relaxed, almost carefree as they went about their business.

Several passers-by waved to the ice cream lady, although they didn't all come up and order. After a while, she came and joined them at their table bringing a tray of fizzy drinks with multi-coloured straws and umbrellas pinned into slices of orange and lemon.

'All right lovvies?' she asked. 'How's your ices?'

'Mm, really good,' said Sammy, crunching the last of his cone and rubbing his hands on his jeans.

'Yeah, really nice,' added Dixie who had also finished her ice cream. With the size of the cone he had chosen, it didn't look as though Darius had started.

'Are you Merry Megan?' asked Sammy, pointing to the sign above the caravan.

'Oh no lovvie,' the ice cream lady took off her straw bonnet with the "Merry Megan's" pink bow, 'I'm Molly, Merry Megan's me Mum. She's round the back of the caravan tending to the pumpkins if you look.'

Sammy turned around and couldn't believe he'd missed what had to be millions of pumpkins, some the size of cricket balls, some the size of Dragonballs, each being prodded by a frail old lady with milk white hair. She wore a long sleeved tunic in the same pink and white stripes that Molly wore and was surrounded by half a dozen Friesian cows that explained the mooing he thought he'd heard when they arrived.

'Is your Dad here too?' asked Dixie suddenly.

'Why no lovvie,' Molly stared at Dixie. 'He's, well he's with yours if you like, different sides perhaps, but the same cause.'

'My Dad's been gone for three years,' said Dixie, rubbing her left eye with the back of her hand.

'He'll be back soon enough,' said Molly. 'We have to believe it.' She stood up to serve a group of second years. 'Don't forget to see Mum before you go, she'll have a pumpkin each for you.'

'What did you have to say, mm, that for?' asked Darius. 'You upset her.'

'Don't talk with your mouth full,' snapped Dixie. 'Let's go see Merry Megan.'

'Ok,' said Sammy. 'Did you see the size of some of those pumpkins?'

They waited while Darius finished his ice cream, with Dixie muttering "pig" under her breath every other bite.

'Finished,' said Darius as he pushed the end of the cone into his mouth and burped loudly. 'That was awesome!'

Merry Megan and her cows had disappeared when Sammy, Dixie and Darius walked around the people sitting at the other tables and across to the pumpkin field at the back of the caravan.

'Oh,' said Dixie. 'I was hoping to talk to her.'

'Let's go to the Big Top,' suggested Sammy 'We can meet up with everyone, maybe we can see her on the way back.'

They walked between the brightly coloured stalls, each selling something different, up towards the Big Top with its bold red and yellow stripes. Gavin and Toby were already there, showing Milly and Holly a collection of prizes. Milly was clutching a pink soft toy rabbit and was telling anyone who would listen that Gavin had given it to her.

'Have you got tickets?' Dixie interrupted Milly.

'Not yet, we were waiting for Professor Burlay,' said Milly waving the pink rabbit in Dixie's face.

'Do we have to,' groaned Darius. 'I really need the...'

'Through there,' said Gavin.

Darius disappeared inside the tent, returning moments later with a big grin. 'It's all through here!'

They followed Darius into the entrance, showing their orange wristbands to a brightly dressed giggling clown who squirted water at them through a larger than life trick nose.

'Eugh!' shrieked Milly.

The clown giggled harder and pulled a bunch of flowers from his baggy sleeve. The flowers were followed by strings of coloured handkerchiefs, tied in knots. He swung the garland around Milly's neck and danced with her while they waited for the rest of the first years to turn up.

Commander Altair and Professor Sanchez arrived with the South and East students. Amos was sharing a pot of popcorn with Simon Sanchez.

'Where is Professor Burlay?' asked Professor Sanchez, frowning at them. 'He should not have left you by yourselves.'

'We've only just got here,' said Sammy. 'He'll be here soon.'

But it was Dr Lithoman and the West first years that arrived next, decked from head to toe with beads and garlands. Many of them had soft toys in one hand and bulging bags of candy floss in the other. There was still no sign of Professor Burlay.

'Very well,' snapped Professor Sanchez, checking her watch. 'North boys with me, girls with Commander Altair. We must go now or we shall miss the start of the show.'

Dixie looked back as she moved closer to Commander Altair with the girls from North. Tristan grabbed her arm and offered her some multi-coloured popcorn and she disappeared into the Big Top.

Professor Sanchez rounded up the East students, bumping into Sammy.

'Sammy, you have no popcorn,' she exclaimed.

'We got ice cream instead.' Sammy tried to explain, but Professor Sanchez wasn't listening.

'Simon, Sammy has no popcorn,' said Professor Sanchez.

If Sammy thought he was embarrassed, it was nothing compared with the bright shade of crimson that flushed Simon's cheeks.

'Have mine,' said Simon, holding out the half empty carton.

Sammy caught Amos looking darkly at him and he shook his head. 'Thanks anyway,' he said, pulling Darius away from a discussion about Dragonball and into the tent.

They followed the East first years up some scaffolding stairs into a long row of folding benches that towered over the circular ring in the centre of the Big Top.

Before long, every seat was filled, mostly with Dragamas students, but also with many other people visiting the circus. Sammy thought he could see the clown from the entrance throwing sweets from a bucket into the crowd. Then the lights dimmed until the only light in the Big Top came from a giant spotlight trained on the ring.

Sammy jumped as there was a huge explosion and coloured streamers and glitter fell from the tent roof. More spotlights danced around the crowd and people started running from behind a purple curtain into the ring. There were acrobats in purple and pink gym suits leapfrogging over each other, girls in flowing skirts dancing and holding coloured streamers, clowns, cowboys and men in Indian headdresses, all moving in perfect synchronisation, never bumping into each other as they performed their introduction routines.

Sammy watched as the circus people turned to stand in an outward facing ring, clapping as the lights dimmed. On one side, a man dressed as Tarzan beat a drum and everyone in the audience clapped and stamped their feet in time with the drum, getting faster and faster until he beat his drum three more times then stopped.

The applause died away and a single spotlight shone down from the ceiling on to a man emerging from the darkness. He was tall and slim, with jet black hair and a twirling moustache, dressed in a red ringmaster's jacket with black trousers, white ruffle shirt, black top hat and bow-tie. He carried a whip that he swished down into the sandy floor, spraying sand and glitter in the ring.

'Welcome!' shouted the man, taking off his top hat. 'I am Andradore and I welcome you to my Floating Circus!'

In the rows high above the ring, Sammy had almost forgotten they were suspended in mid-air above the school.

As if to explain, the man raised his voice louder and roared into the crowd, 'Andradore's Floating Circus floats from place to place, like a magic carpet. Ladies and gentlemen, boys and girls, we are now floating above Dragamas School for Dragon Charming, run by my personal friend, Sir Lok Ragnarok!'

The applause was deafening, people in the stands stood up and clapped and cheered. The Tarzan man beat a drum roll as Andradore strode around the ring cracking his whip in time with the drumming.

Sammy gasped as a ball of gold rolled through a gap in the purple curtain and stopped at Andradore's feet. It uncurled itself and stretched into a lion the size of a miniature pony. Its coat gleamed in the spotlight and the lion marched proudly around the edge of the ring, pausing every so often to stare at the boys and girls in the front row. It stopped in front of Andradore and rose on to its hind legs and opened its mouth wide.

Behind the rows of sparkling teeth, came a deep rumbling like thunder and the lion roared, long and loud, drowning out the drumming. Andradore cracked his whip in the sand and the lion dropped to all fours, rubbing his head against Andradore's side. It reminded Sammy of the toy Serberon had given him. When new, the toy lion had probably roared as loudly.

'Welcome one, welcome all,' shouted Andradore. 'Enjoy the performance!'

The lights went out and came back on. Andradore and the lion had gone, replaced by the line of acrobats vaulting through hoops and swaying on trapezes suspended from the roof. They disappeared to thunderous applause and were followed by tightrope walking clowns who threw sweets into the audience whilst playing tricks on each other. After the clowns, came a woman with three elephants who squirted water at each other.

Sammy nearly fell off his bench laughing as all three elephants turned on the woman and blew a torrent of water at her. Next were the cowboys and Indians staging a mock battle against each other with lots of running around, falling over and getting back up again. They were followed by two knights on horseback jousting with lances, each cheered on by the audience closest to them.

At the end, Andradore returned with his lion. Two acrobats held up a giant hoop that the lion jumped through twice, then twice more when the acrobats lit the outer edge of the hoop with a ring of fire.

Sammy had never laughed so loud or clapped so hard and he was disappointed when the whole circus crew, almost a hundred of them, came out into the ring for a final bow, then the circus lights dimmed and the main lights came on.

'That was awesome,' said Sammy, blinking in the sunlight as they got outside.

'Amazing,' said Gavin. 'Did you see that lion jump through those hoops?'

'Yeah, had to be ten feet tall, easy,' added Toby. 'It must be really tame.'

Just like the toy lion, Sammy thought to himself. He grinned as the North girls caught up with them, Tristan still hot on Dixie's heels, carrying his popcorn carton. Dixie didn't look impressed.

'Great show, wasn't it,' said Tristan, his mouth full of popcorn.

'Yeah,' said Darius.

'Did you enjoy it Dixie?' asked Sammy.

'Yeah, it was brilliant, awesome!' Dixie rolled her eyes towards Tristan. 'Wish I could've sat with you though.'

'Me too,' said Tristan over enthusiastically. 'Commander Altair's all right, but they say he can read your mind.'

'I think Professor Sanchez can too,' said Sammy.

'The happy couple,' said Dixie.

'Simon won't like that,' said Sammy.

'What would Mummy say?' Darius bent double in a fit of infectious laughter.

'Shh,' hissed Dixie. 'They're coming.'

Deep in conversation, Amos and Simon walked right past them and disappeared inside a fortune teller's tent.

It was baking hot outside the Big Top and it wasn't long before Dixie suggested getting another ice cream. In fact, they all agreed that it would be a good idea to go back to Merry Megan's for a second round of ice creams. At Darius' suggestion, they set off in the opposite direction, to loop around the whole circus so they wouldn't miss anything, ending up at the caravan with time for an ice cream before going back to Dragamas.

Gavin and Toby stopped to throw darts at a deck of cards pinned to a noticeboard. A rough looking man was running the stall and he didn't seem pleased to let them play for free when they waved their orange wristbands. Fortunately for everyone, Gavin and Toby left empty handed.

'Really wanted one of those crystal ball prizes,' said Gavin. 'Would've looked great in our tower. Glows in the dark as well.'

They stopped again as rows of glittering beads caught Dixie's eye.

'I want to get some of those,' she said, her eyes shining at the coloured glass beads, dragon scales, and pearlescent shells. She picked out four differently patterned dragon scales dangling from plaited black leather chains and handed some coins to the gypsy woman running the stall.

'For your friends, dearie?'

Dixie nodded.

'Here,' said the woman taking a fifth chain from her shirt pocket, 'take this one for yourself.'

'She gave me mine,' said Dixie when they were out of earshot.

'That was nice of her,' said Tristan.

'Yeah,' said Darius. 'They look really good.'

'Good? They're supposed to be pretty.'

'Uh yeah, really pretty,' said Darius. 'It'll take more than a necklace though.'

'Hey! There's Merry Megan,' interrupted Sammy. 'Look!'

Wizened Merry Megan in her marshmallow pink and white dress was hunched up in conversation with a man who from the back looked just like Professor Burlay.

As they got closer, Sammy realised it was Professor Burlay. He was holding the arm of the frail old lady, helping her back into the caravan. He spotted them and waved with his free hand. 'Come and see Mum.'

'Mum?' whispered Sammy. 'No way.'

'That means he'll know about my Dad,' said Dixie.

'Not again,' groaned Darius. 'Molly said he'll be back.'

'My Dad told me that too,' said Dixie her face white with anger. 'Three darn years ago.'

'Language!' Darius laughed. 'You'll never suit that necklace!'

Dixie stormed up to the caravan, arriving ten to twenty paces ahead of Sammy and the others.

When they got there, Professor Burlay had his arm around Molly and was surveying the pumpkin fields.

'Are they ready for picking yet Mum?' Professor Burlay called through the caravan window.

'Aye John, take as many as you need.'

'Great.' Professor Burlay turned to Sammy. 'Sorry I couldn't be with you earlier. You didn't miss anything, did you?'

'No,' said Darius, sitting on one of Molly's plastic chairs. 'Professor Sanchez took us into the circus.'

'I went with Tristan and the South house,' added Dixie.

Tristan grinned. 'Can I get you an ice cream Dixie?'

'We had one earlier, thanks.'

'You have one,' Sammy winked at Darius.

'Yeah, try a large one,' said Darius. 'The small ones are, y'know, too small.'

'Ok,' said Tristan. 'What flavour did you have Dixie?'

'Molly did a bit of everything,' said Dixie. 'Get a small one though.'

'No, I'll have a large one,' said Tristan firmly. 'Does anyone else want one?'

Sammy and Darius shook their heads.

'We've already eaten,' said Gavin.

'Just me then.' Tristan looked disappointed, but went to queue up behind Captain Firebreath and Sergeant Rockhammer.

'You shouldn't have done that,' said Dixie.

'Done what?' asked Darius, shovelling his jumper into his mouth to stop one of his giggles erupting.

'You know what.'

'Let's see if he does it.' Sammy nudged Darius and followed Tristan to the caravan. They sat at the closest plastic table, under a pink and white striped parasol, out of sight, but close enough to hear Tristan's order.

'Never you mind those dwarves,' they heard Molly talking to Tristan. 'Always want the big ones they do. Send me running round making huge ice creams, then they have the cheek not to finish them!'

'Aye she worries too much,' said Captain Firebreath.

'We pay for 'em,' added Sergeant Rockhammer. 'What do you care, Molly? It's good business for you. Better than all these free ones.'

Sergeant Rockhammer and Captain Firebreath shuffled past Sammy's table, each carrying an enormous pink and green ice cream with two flakes sticking out high above their heads like rabbit ears. They sat at the furthest table, munching noisily at the cones and laughing as the ice cream dripped in the afternoon sun.

'May I have a small chocolate and vanilla cone, please m'am,' said Tristan. 'I was going to have a large one but...'

'Not sure you can manage it?' Molly chuckled. 'Why don't you try a small one this time and a large one when we're back in the summer.'

'You're coming back?' asked Tristan. 'Cool.'

'They're coming back,' said Sammy, grinning at the growing group of first years gathered around his table.

'Oh yes, you'll probably see us in between,' Molly said to Tristan. 'Sir Ragnarok usually has us back for Bonfire Night. We do hot dogs, burgers and chips as well.'

'That's brilliant,' said Tristan. 'Are you sure these ice creams are free?'

'Oh yes lovvie, just don't say I told you about us coming back. I'm sure John will want to tell you himself.'

'Who's John?'

'My brother, oh, Professor Burlay to you I'm sure. You are in his house, aren't you?'

'No, I'm Tristan Markham. I'm in South.'

Molly laughed. 'Here's me thinking you've got your house badge on upside down! Well anyway, you can tell Commander Altair for me that he should visit more often. He and John were friends at school you know.'

'At Dragamas?'

'No lovvie, they went to Kings Astronomy College. That's how he knows almost as much about stars as John, though he was always more interested in weapons and war strategy for my liking. But that's me rambling. Enjoy your ice cream Tristan lovvie.'

'Thank you m'am, I certainly will.'

Tristan arrived at their table carrying his ice cream. 'Hey you'll never guess what!'

'We heard,' said Darius. 'I'm Tristan Markham, I'm in South.'

'Oh.'

'They're coming back,' said Dixie.

'That's right,' said Professor Burlay. 'Come and give me and Mum a hand with the pumpkins. Sir Ragnarok wants five hundred this year.'

With the help of the other first years who had just arrived, Sammy started pulling at the orange fruits, tugging them off their thick stalks and throwing them to Dixie and Darius who were packing them into netted bags.

Molly and Megan's caravan seemed to be the unofficial meeting point for Dragamas students after their day at the Floating Circus. In their twos, threes and sometimes fives and sixes, the school congregated at the white tables under the pink and white striped umbrellas.

Professor Sanchez arrived with a large group of East students. 'Ah, Professor Burlay, it was here you were hiding. Myself and Commander Altair, we were looking after your first years. They were well taken care of.'

'Thank you,' said Professor Burlay, throwing Professor Sanchez a large pumpkin.

'One for Simon, yes?' Professor Sanchez handed the pumpkin to Simon who had gone very red again.

When everyone had a pumpkin, Professor Burlay kissed Molly and Megan on the cheek and led the school back to the reception office. At Sergeant Rockhammer's request, Sammy and the other Dragamas students removed their orange wristbands and handed them in to the white haired lady.

Captain Firebreath organised the Dragamas students into five lines, one line per year. He led the first years to the lift. 'Little ones go first. It's supposed to cause less trouble,' he explained, separating a scuffle between two third years.

Sammy went in the first group of ten with Dixie, Darius and Tristan who squeezed between Toby and Gavin to come down with the North first years.

A woman in a navy suit pulled open the grill and opened the lift doors.

'Come on then,' said Captain Firebreath. 'Let's get you down to Dragamas.'

Sammy stood close to the lift door. In one hand, he held a sack of pumpkins and with the other, he clutched his stomach in the other as the lift lurched suddenly downwards.

In almost no time at all, Captain Firebreath pressed a large red button on the lift floor with his foot and the lift slowed down, creaking and screeching as it came to a halt.

It was as dark in the forest outside as it had been on the short walk through the cave from the lift. Sammy reached for his staff and created a small fire. Using his utmost concentration, he guided the flames at waist height towards the cave mouth, down the steps between the milk white tooth shaped stones and back up to the castle.

Sir Ragnarok had prepared a feast for their return, nothing, he promised, like the feast planned for Halloween. Sammy didn't care and wolfed down the sandwiches, miniature pizzas, crisps, pies and cakes as hungrily as everyone else. Sir Ragnarok also promised prizes for the best-cut pumpkin and scariest costume which would be awarded to two students per year.

CHAPTER 12

THE HALLOWEEN TREASURE HUNT

In the eight days between the visit to the Floating Circus and Halloween, Sammy spent as much of each lesson that he could get away with, scribbling pumpkin and costume designs on paper notes and passing them between himself, Dixie and Darius.

Darius suggested the North boys went as ghosts, made from their bedsheets coloured with red and black ink. Dixie suggested creating a coloured flame to go inside the pumpkins and having large round eyes and a fanged mouth. After a little persuasion, Gavin and Toby agreed to go as ghosts and Amos said he would think about it.

In Armoury, Commander Altair allowed them to shape the pumpkins using their staffs. After blasting a jagged mouth that bore no resemblance to the fangs he had intended, Sammy decided Commander Altair had been too optimistic telling them that guiding the sparks into the design you wanted would be easy.

Dr Shivers set them a task in Dragon Studies to see who had the longest dragon by the end of term. Dixie said the challenge was hopeless since hers was only ten inches long. Dr Shivers had laughed and said that in seven weeks anything could happen.

By the 31st of October, everyone in the school had carved their pumpkin; even the teachers. Sammy had a suspicious feeling their pumpkins would be far scarier.

He finally got in the party mood when Captain Stronghammer interrupted their Astronomics lesson with instructions from Sir Ragnarok.

Captain Stronghammer coughed importantly. 'Sir Ragnarok wishes me to inform you,' he coughed again, 'that you are to queue in an orderly fashion at the entrance to the Main Hall at seven o'clock tonight.'

Sammy drummed his hands on the desk with Gavin and Toby. Everyone was cheering.

'Sir Ragnarok requests that you bring your pumpkins and an empty stomach. We shall eat drink and be merry together. Thank you.' Captain Stronghammer gave a half bow and backed out of the classroom.

Sammy decided he wouldn't be surprised if Sir Ragnarok had slowed time to prepare for the feast. Lessons took longer than usual and there was no tea. Even the time he usually enjoyed in the common room was spent pacing up and down urging the grandfather clock to hurry up.

He envied the second and third years sitting calmly at the shared study desks, talking amongst themselves and occasionally throwing paper aeroplanes. Whilst retrieving a stray plane, Serberon had told him that the fourth years had their own private study desks in their rooms that he was looking forward to. The fifth years were nowhere to be seen.

At half past six, Professor Burlay arrived looking damp and a little windswept. He carried a candlelit pumpkin with two neatly cut square eyes and a wide toothless grin that let the light shine out into the common room. He handed out rope and candles and asked everyone to line up so he could light the candles himself.

Sammy was third in the line and quickly tied the rope twice around the pre-cut holes for safety.

'That's a scary pumpkin you've got there Sammy,' said Professor Burlay as he lit the tiny candle. 'If you go up now, you should be there first.'

'We'll get the best seats,' Dixie whispered in Sammy's ear.

Even Gavin, who had claimed he was too old for Halloween to try and impress Milly, joined in swinging his pumpkin lantern down the corridor as they walked up to the Main Hall.

Sammy noticed all the North first year girls were wearing the dragon scale necklaces Dixie had brought back from the Floating Circus. The necklaces, and being friends with the boys in the first year, had made her more popular. She was dressed as a witch, in a long black cape and pointed black hat. With her natural green hair, Sammy thought she looked very realistic.

As they stepped up to the entrance, Sammy threw his ghost costume over his head. He slotted his arms through the pre-prepared gaps they had stitched using Naomi's emergency sewing kit. Looking again at the red and black ink marks, he hoped Gavin was right that an overnight soak in the Banish powder his Mum had sent him would return them to normal.

'Woooh! Scary!' shouted Gavin swinging his lantern dangerously close to Sammy's sheet. 'Come on Amos, put yours on too!'

Amos nodded begrudgingly and put his sheet over his head until only his eyes could be seen. Sammy noticed that Amos had tied pillowcases around his ankles and was leaving a trail of talcum powder behind him.

At exactly seven o'clock, everyone in the school had arrived and Sir Ragnarok swung the double doors open, shouting "Happy Halloween!" as he welcomed them in.

'Happy Halloween,' Sammy replied, amazed that Sir Ragnarok had joined in. Although he was wearing his normal grey robes, he had dyed his hair so that it was as green as Dixie and her brothers' hair.

'Welcome to my Halloween feast. I must warn you, it's a little different this year.' Sir Ragnarok chuckled, holding the doors open with his staff.

Sammy followed Dixie into the Main Hall and gasped. The hall was darker than usual, with a dingy orange light and a fruity smell wafting into the corridor.

'It's a pumpkin!' shrieked Milly. 'He's turned it into a giant pumpkin!'

'It's real,' shouted Gavin, picking up his sheet and dancing round the edge of the room.

Sammy peered closely at the orange walls and decided they were right. Sometime between breakfast and seven o'clock, Sir Ragnarok had magicked a giant fleshy orange pumpkin inside the Main Hall.

Giant seeds, the size of shoe boxes, hung on thick silvery threads from the ceiling and eerie footsteps and whistling wind blared from a small music box on Sir Ragnarok's table. Underfoot, the ground squelched away from Sammy's feet and he jumped as a volley of bats swooped past him, grazing the top of his costume.

'Bats!' shrieked Milly, the wings on her angel costume bobbing up and down.

'Come on!' shouted Dixie.

Before he knew it, Dixie had grabbed his hand and was sweeping Sammy and Darius into the middle of the room where the four house tables had been pushed together into a giant rectangle piled high with all kinds of Halloween food.

Sammy put his pumpkin on the table with the carved face towards him so he could use the light to see what he was doing and read some of the labels.

On a plate nearest him there were piles of sandwiches that claimed to be everything from ham and egg, cheese and onion and chicken and cucumber. To his right there was a bowl towering with foil wrapped sweets and plates with umpteen slices of pies and cakes with cocktail sticks with labels with names like "Bread of the Dead", "Deadman's Pie", "Graveyard Gravelcake", "Tombstone Pie" and a plate of spaghetti with a label saying "Bran's Brains".

'Yuck,' said Dixie looking over his shoulder. 'That's worse than the Batwing Soup and Spider Cake next to me.'

'Spider Cake?' asked Sammy nervously. 'Those aren't real legs, are they?'

'Yeah,' said Gavin, grinning. 'Real liquorice!'

'Eugh! I hate liquorice,' said Milly looking distastefully at the black straggly cake.

Gavin spat his mouthful into an orange napkin. 'Me too.'

'Don't you have any table manners?' asked Milly. 'Mummy says…'

But there wasn't time to hear what pearl of wisdom Milly was about to relate from her mother's never-ending advice as Serberon and a group of boys from the third year stood up at Dixie's signal and shouted out the chant they had made up.

Sammy knew most of the words as they belted out:

Mummy says, Mummy says,
Tell us Milly what Mummy says.
Brush your hair, we don't care.
Don't stare, we don't care.
Be polite, it's not right.
Don't swear, we don't care!

The song ran for four verses, but they were cut short as Sir Ragnarok returned with Captain Stronghammer and the teachers, each carrying a medium sized barrel of what they claimed was pumpkin wine, but Sammy found was just orangeade.

To Sammy's relief, Milly's cheeks turned a light shade of pink and she laughed.

'I'm not that bad, am I?'

'Yes,' said Dixie.

'Please be seated and start,' said Sir Ragnarok. 'Eat everything.'

'Cool,' said Darius, cramming three sandwiches into his mouth at once.

'Hey Dixie, pass some Tombstone Pie,' shouted Serberon, 'and some sandwiches.'

'They're all gone,' said Dixie. 'Darius, you pig, no one else had any.'

Darius looked sheepish. 'There weren't that many. I'll swap some Bat Droppings for some Batwing Soup!'

'Yuck, what's Bat Droppings?' asked Sammy.

Darius passed over a bowl of brown blobs. 'Try one, it's just chocolate.'

Sammy took a handful. 'Mm, I like Bat Droppings!'

'Me too!'

When most of the plates were empty, Sir Ragnarok stood up. 'May I have your attention please?'

The room went quiet almost instantly with just the hollow footsteps crunching music in the background.

'As you may or may not know,' Sir Ragnarok continued, 'it is traditional to play games at our annual Halloween feast.'

'Yeah!' shouted some boys from the fourth year.

'The Professors, and Doctors,' Sir Ragnarok acknowledged a frosty glare from plump Dr Lithoman and a waggle of Dr Shivers's hand, 'yes, the Doctors and Professors of Dragamas have put together a treasure hunt which will finish on the stroke of midnight, followed by a midnight feast, then bed,' he added, suddenly drowned out by a loud roar from the students who were already organising teams of fours, fives and sixes.

'The first clue,' Sir Ragnarok shouted above the scraping of chairs and the murmur of voices, 'is to find something wet. The clue will be tied to it.'

'A tap!' shouted Dixie, loudly enough for the teams on both sides of the table to hear.

'Tell everyone why don't you Dixie,' groaned Gavin. 'Come on, Sammy, Milly, Darius, let's go!' Gavin waved to Toby, who had formed a group with Holly and Naomi, Tristan from South and two boys from the West house.

'See you at the finish!' shouted Toby as they split up at the hall entrance.

With Gavin, Dixie, Milly and Darius, Sammy ran to the nearest set of taps which they found in the fifth year boys' bathroom in the South tower. They burst into the tiny room where there were two cubicle toilets, two large washbasins with mirrors and a small cupboard shaped shower. Tiny yellow notes were tied with blue wool to each of the golden taps.

'Which one do we take?' asked Dixie.

'Any I suppose,' said Sammy unhooking the nearest note. 'They're probably all the same.'

'Hurry up,' said Gavin. 'Everyone's coming!'

Sammy looked up. There was a sea of faces at the door. It looked as though fifty people were trying to barge into the bathroom at once.

'Is the first clue in there?' asked a tall dark haired boy.

'Yeah,' said Dixie. 'They're on every tap.'

'Thanks!' shouted the boy. 'Come on everyone, the first years found it!'

Sammy squeezed out of the bathroom into a stretch of open corridor. He unfolded the note and read it in a whisper as they huddled together.

'It says, I may be small, I may be white, but with me you'll never fight. Out of doors, on the second of floors, find me quick or else be scorched.'

'That doesn't rhyme,' said Dixie.

'Or else be scorched?' said Sammy, ignoring Dixie complaining about the poor verse. 'Do you reckon it's...'

'What?' interrupted Gavin.

'The Dragon's Lair? That's kind of on the second floor?'

'I don't like the sound of that,' said Milly.

'Me neither,' Gavin added quickly. 'We'll wait here. Milly hasn't got the shoes for going outside anyway.'

'Ugh,' groaned Sammy, looking at Milly's silver high heels that matched her angel costume. 'You'll have to change them. We may need you if the next clue after this one is outside.'

'Useless,' muttered Dixie as Milly scuttled off. 'She's got a pair of boots that would have gone just as well, but Milly says look your best at all times because Mummy looks perfect wherever she goes.'

'With bells on her fingers and twinkly toes,' finished Darius with one of his giggles.

'Shut it,' snapped Gavin. 'She's back.'

'That was quick,' said Sammy.

Milly smiled and rolled her meringue skirt up to her knees to show them a pair of dark green pixie boots with silver buckles and a splattering of glitter that Sammy couldn't believe had been on them from new.

'You'll be able to run in those,' said Sammy, looking approvingly at the flat soles.

Milly took a handful of hair clips and smoothed her hair back using the candlelit window as a dark mirror.

'Come on,' groaned Darius. 'We'll be last at this rate. Half the schools gone past while you changed your shoes.'

'Well then,' Milly sniffed snootily, 'we'd better get going.'

Darius led the way out of the South entrance on to the lawn they used at break times. Rows of tiny lights were spaced out on the short grass.

'Look!' shouted Dixie. 'They've lit candles to guide us.'

'They're pretty,' said Milly.

'Which way do we go?' asked Sammy.

'They look like a star chart,' said Dixie tipping her head to one side, 'if you look at them funny.'

Commander Altair stepped out of the shadows, where Sammy was sure no one had been standing.

'Oooh!' shrieked Milly. 'Commander. Altair, you scared us.'

'Scared you Milly, not all of us,' snapped Dixie. 'Was I right? Is it a star chart?'

Commander Altair nodded, his eyes darting from left to right, as though he was expecting someone other than Dragamas students to come out of the South entrance.

'You're first actually,' said Commander Altair, staring at a rustle in the bushes behind him. 'Everyone else has gone to Mrs Grock's.'

'Oh,' said Sammy, disappointed.

205

'You're right to be here. The clues are supposed to be in different orders to keep you apart,' explained Commander Altair. 'The trouble is, everyone seems to be following your brother Dixie. Quite the ringleader I'm told.'

'Serberon?' asked Dixie.

Commander Altair nodded and pulled a Directometer out of his jacket pocket. 'All three of them actually. There they are,' he pointed to a series of green dots, 'and here we are,' he flicked the Directometer and it showed the South tower and six dots.

'You didn't need to say their names,' said Sammy suddenly. 'How did you make it do that?'

'I heard about your adventure with the Directometer Sammy. It's all in the mind, listen.'

From the other's blank looks, Sammy realised he was the only one who could hear Commander Altair inside his head.

'It's the plough,' said Sammy out loud.

Commander Altair nodded. 'Follow the North star.'

'How do you know?' demanded Dixie.

'Weird,' muttered Gavin.

Sammy turned to thank Commander Altair, but he had walked off into the darkness. He caught a faint mutter of, 'I told Sir Ragnarok, any night but tonight.'

'Weird,' said Sammy. 'Let's go.' He marched through the candles in the plough shaped pattern safely to the other side followed by Gavin, Milly and Darius.

Dixie stood behind, her face like thunder.

'Come on Dixie,' said Sammy. 'Follow the plough.'

Dixie stomped across. 'You said you'd say if you could do stuff.'

'Oh,' Sammy remembered their pact to be Dragon Knights. 'I didn't know I could do it until then. It's usually with things, not voices.'

'Are you sure?' Dixie asked suspiciously.

'Yes,' said Sammy. 'Try me.'

'Ok.'

'You counted,' said Sammy, 'one, two, three, four, five.'

'You heard that?'

'Yes.'

'Teach me,' begged Dixie.

'I can't, I don't know how I did it. Just concentrate on nothing, I'll say something now,' said Sammy thinking, "the next clue is in the Dragon's Lair".

Dixie frowned. 'The text drew is in the cavern bare?'

'Close,' Sammy laughed and said the real version out loud.

Dixie laughed. 'Not bad for my first try.'

'Let's muddle the lights up,' suggested Darius. 'It'll slow everyone else down.'

'Yeah,' said Gavin pulling at the candleholders. 'Ugh, they won't budge.'

Behind them, and Sammy thought he was the only one who could hear it, he heard Commander Altair laughing at them. They walked across the tarmac driveway and into the thicket of trees towards the Dragon's Lair.

'Sammy, can you do that fire thing Commander Altair showed us in Armoury?' asked Gavin.

'Sure,' said Sammy reaching for his staff. He pointed the end with the black onyx stone to the ground and said "fire" at the same time that Dixie and Darius did the same.

A huge roaring fire appeared in front of them, hissing and crackling, singeing the ground.

'Everyone will see it,' squealed Milly. 'Mummy says the best thing is to keep quiet so no one will see you.'

'Must be boring at your house,' said Darius. 'Mummy says this, Mummy says that.'

'Shut it Darius, she's getting better,' said Dixie. 'Sammy, how do we turn it down?'

'It's not an electric fire you know,' snapped Sammy, annoyed he wasn't sure how to do it. He focussed on the flames and, surprising himself, he was able to tone down the flames to a small picket fire that he could pick up and control with the black crystal end of his staff.

'Which way?' asked Dixie nervously. 'I can't see the castle any more.'

'Dunno,' said Sammy, swinging the fire from left to right about two feet above the ground. There was a faint crackle behind them.

'What was that?' asked Dixie. 'I don't like the dark.'

'Badger or maybe a fox,' said Gavin. 'My Dad's a farmer, he's got a gun. I wish he was here.'

'A gun,' muttered Milly.

'Yeah, he lets me and Toby clean it sometimes.'

'What does he shoot?' asked Sammy.

'All sorts,' said Gavin. 'Foxes mainly, sometimes rabbits. He nearly hit one of our sheep once.' Gavin looked sombre.

'Is that why you're good at shooting?' asked Milly. 'You won me that rabbit on the shooting range at the Floating Circus.'

'Uh, no,' said Gavin, sheepishly. 'I gave him a fiver.'

Sammy laughed. He could picture Milly's face, even though it was too dark to see anything. 'We must be nearly there.'

'Out of doors, on second floors,' said Dixie. 'It's got to be the ledge with the Dragon Teeth.'

'I bet it is,' said Sammy, brushing past some brambles into the clearing. 'Look, there's Professor Burlay.'

'Makes sense,' said Darius. 'He would have helped Commander Altair with the star charts.'

'Hi Professor Burlay!' shouted Dixie. 'Are we first?'

Professor Burlay turned around. He was still wearing his vampire Halloween costume, a black suit that made him invisible, apart from his flour white face and dripping blood fangs. He waved his staff at the entrance to the Dragon's Lair and it lit up with blue and green strobe lights forming a portcullis in lights over the mouth of the cave. A golden Dragamas twin tailed 'D' motif shone above the portcullis from a yellow light at Professor Burlay's feet.

'Come,' whispered Professor Burlay, shining a torch under his chin. 'Come into the Dragon's Lair.'

'Spooky,' whispered Dixie, clutching on to Sammy's arm and making him jump.

'Before you go in, I must warn you not to use the lift in any way shape or form,' said Professor Burlay in his normal voice. 'Doing so will disqualify you from the treasure hunt and may you lose house stars.'

'Ok,' said Gavin climbing the rough steps. 'What are we supposed to do?'

'Um,' started Sammy, unsure whether he should mention the eyes he had seen in the passageway.

'What?' demanded Gavin. 'It's just the lift in here.'

'No look,' said Dixie. 'Sammy, move the fire this way, further, it looks like it's a secret passage!'

'That's what I was going to say,' said Sammy.

'Yeah right,' scoffed Gavin. 'Well spotted Dixie, let's see where it goes.'

Gavin led the way with Milly and Dixie on either side of him. Sammy cast the fire ahead of them not liking the way it cast a reddish tinge on the passage walls. They looked like giant veins, bursting from time to time with sparkling diamond shards.

'I saw the eyes too,' whispered Darius. 'Maybe they were some lights put here for the treasure hunt, trying to scare us.'

'I think they belonged to a dragon,' whispered Sammy.

'What?' spluttered Darius.

Dixie stopped in her tracks. 'What?'

'Nothing,' said Sammy.

'What?' asked Gavin. 'Come on Sammy, tell us.'

Milly sniffed loudly. 'Mummy says it's rude to...'

'Shut up Milly,' said four voices.

'Fine,' said Milly walking on into the darkness alone.

'Where's she going?' said Sammy. 'We're supposed to stick together.'

'What was it Sammy?' demanded Dixie.

'Dragon eyes,' said Darius before Sammy had a chance to answer.

'What!'

'Dragon eyes,' repeated Sammy. 'I wondered if it was Karmandor, you know, the lost dragon of...'

'The King of the Dark Ages,' finished Dixie, her voice shaking.

'It's probably some lights they put up for the treasure hunt,' said Gavin.

'That's what I said,' said Darius.

Sammy stepped forward, shining the fire into the darkness. 'Come on. Let's find Milly and the next clue.'

'Milly!' shouted Dixie. 'Mi-ll-ee, where are you?'

'She must've been running,' said Sammy after a while.

'It was your idea for her to change shoes,' said Gavin. 'She wouldn't have got far in those high heels.'

'And we'd have heard her,' added Dixie.

'Perhaps she's been eaten,' suggested Darius with a giggle. 'No more Mummy says.'

'It's lights,' snapped Gavin. 'Just lights.'

With Milly nowhere in sight, Sammy couldn't help wondering if it was Karmandor, and if it was, what they would do if they ran into a fully grown dragon. He shook his head, telling himself it was just lights. Aloud he said, 'let's keep going.'

They turned a corner in the passage and Gavin stumbled over something.

'It moved!' shouted Gavin giving the floor in front of him a kick.

'Ow!' shrieked the something.

'It's alive!' shouted Gavin.

The something uncurled itself and it turned out to be Milly, dusty and with one of her angel wings bent out of shape.

'Well of course I am. Mummy says...'

'You're alive,' repeated Gavin.

'No thanks to you,' Milly sniffed. 'What do you think you were doing? Playing Dragonball?'

'Uh, sorry,' mumbled Gavin, giving Milly a hug that lasted a microsecond. 'What were you doing on the floor anyway?'

'Go and see for yourself,' said Milly. 'There's a huge dragon in there.'

Gavin nudged Sammy's shoulder. 'You've got the fire. You have a look.'

Sammy took a deep breath and followed the passage into the darkness. The passage opened up into a large circular room. On the far wall, half hidden in shadows was a monstrous purple dragon with piercing gold eyes staring straight at him.

'Woah,' muttered Sammy, having a bizarre thought that one day Kyrillan might get that big.

The dragon puffed a billow of purple smoke at him that settled on the fire, putting it out and plunging the room and the passage into pitch darkness.

Sammy stepped backwards, feeling his way back to the others by touching the rough passage walls.

'Watch it,' grumbled Dixie as Sammy bumped into her.

'Sorry. Uh, Milly, did you see any steps in that room?'

'I don't know,' Milly sniffed. 'All I saw were the gold eyes. What do you want to know about steps for?'

'To get out,' said Sammy. 'We're on the right track or Professor Burlay wouldn't have sent us in here.'

'Maybe we could get him,' said Dixie her voice sounding very small in the darkness. 'He'll get us past the dragon.'

'No,' said Sammy firmly. 'There have to be some steps in that room. We'll find them. Fire!'

A small group of flames appeared at the end of his staff, brightening the passage.

'Let's go then,' said Gavin, edging slowly forward.

Sammy held the fire as far forward as he dared, expecting the purple dragon to put it out at any second. They reached the circular room and Sammy stepped forward, ready to point out the giant animal.

He swung the fire from left to right, but there was nothing in the room but darkness. No sign of a dragon.

'Where's it gone?' asked Sammy. 'It was right here.'

'What?' shrieked Milly. 'It must be here! Smoke, gold eyes! Where's it gone?'

'Purple smoke,' added Sammy.

Gavin pushed past them. 'Well it's not here now. Look, there's your steps Sammy, we can get out.'

'Let's run for it,' said Dixie.

'On three,' said Darius preparing himself. 'One, two and run!'

Sammy reached the steps first and grabbed hold of an iron rail. 'Hey Dixie, isn't this the stairs to Mrs Grock's?'

'Could be,' said Dixie uncertainly. 'Are we going up?'

'Yeah. Has anyone seen the dragon?'

'No,' said Gavin. 'There's no other way out either.'

'What?' asked Sammy a shiver running down the back of his ghost costume. 'A dragon that size couldn't get up these stairs, or out of the passage without bumping into us.'

Gavin shrugged.

'Perhaps he's still here,' whispered Dixie, 'invisible like Commander Altair.'

'Ha!' snorted Gavin. 'There's no dragon here. Milly was seeing things.'

'Sammy saw it too,' said Milly, obstinately. 'You did, didn't you Sammy?'

'Could be an illusion,' said Sammy thoughtfully, 'like the lights over the cave entrance.'

'No!' shrieked Milly, almost in tears. 'You know it was real. Real eyes, real smoke. It put our fire out.'

'Let's get up the steps,' said Darius. 'Maybe the next clue is up there.'

'Maybe,' said Gavin pushing past Darius to go up the steps. 'Hey there's a trapdoor here.'

'Push it,' said Sammy. 'It should be under Mrs Grock's house.'

At the top of the steps, Gavin bent nearly double to shove his right shoulder up against the wooden trapdoor. 'Ugh, it won't budge. Can you send up the fire?'

Sammy concentrated on the black crystal at the end of his staff and split the flames into two bundles and guided the smaller of the two up to Gavin.'

'That's really cool,' said Dixie. 'How did you do it?'

'Dunno,' said Sammy, focussing on the fire. 'Just a little concentration.'

'Ow,' yelled Gavin from the top of the steps, 'concentrate harder, that hit my arm!'

'Sorry,' said Sammy. 'This isn't easy you know.'

'You're doing fine,' said Darius, craning his head up the steps. 'Gavin, does the trapdoor say anything? Is there a note?'

'Uh yeah,' said Gavin. 'It says pull here.'

'Go on then, pull,' said Dixie, 'and hurry.'

As Gavin reached for the trapdoor handle Sammy saw it give way above his head, sending him sprawling backwards into Darius, Dixie, Milly and then Sammy, pushing them into a heap on the floor.

Gavin giggled. 'It's open.'

'Gerrof me,' grumbled Dixie reaching out for Darius and Milly's hands to help them up.

Sammy got up last and dusted himself off. In the ceiling above them there was a square of light and he could see people queuing to come down.

'Gavin?' said a voice from the square of light.

'Yeah,' said Gavin, squinting upwards. 'Toby is that you?'

'Yeah,' said the voice. 'Move back, we're coming down.'

Gavin shuffled down the steps bumping into Dixie.

'Hey,' she grumbled. 'Look where you're...oh, hello Toby.'

'Hey Dixie,' said Toby, grinning at her. 'You're going backwards on the treasure hunt, you know.'

'Are not,' snapped Dixie. 'You are. Professor Burlay is at the entrance.'

'Oh,' said Toby. 'Come on everyone, Gavin's down here.'

There was a scurry of footsteps and Naomi, Helena, Holly from North and Tristan from South followed him down the steps.

'We've picked up two clues so far,' said Toby holding up some coloured paper tags. 'We think the prize is in Sir Ragnarok's office, wherever that is!'

'Why?' asked Sammy, wondering if there was an easy way to finish the hunt.

'He said he had some paperwork to do,' said Toby.

'We met him in the corridor after we left the North bathroom,' added Naomi.

'That doesn't mean anything,' said Gavin. 'Anyway, watch out for the dragon down there.'

'The dragon!' exclaimed Toby. 'Mrs Grock never said there was a dragon down...'

'Sammy,' interrupted Tristan, 'may we have some of your fire?'

'Please,' muttered Milly.

'Uh, please.' Tristan glared at Milly.

'Sure,' said Sammy re-joining the pieces of fire. They fused perfectly and he was   pleased with the results, still not quite taking it for granted that these things were now possible. 'Take the lot. We won't need it in Mrs Grock's.'

'Thanks Sammy, we owe you one.'

Sammy nodded. 'No problem.'

Tristan pointed his staff at the fire and picked it up, holding it a few paces in front of him. Toby and the boys from the West house followed him with Naomi and Helena giggling their way down the passage and out of sight behind them.

'What did you do that for?' asked Gavin. 'He's got fire now. You helped him.'

'I didn't,' said Sammy shuffling his feet. 'There's writing on the floor here.'

Gavin laughed. 'Cool. Can't have my brother beating me.'

'What does it say?' asked Darius.

Sammy knelt on the stone floor to wipe some mud from his shoes from the engraved letters. 'It says, up the stairs or out of the cave, whichever you choose you are brave. The cave leads to the stars…'

'Commander Altair's clue,' interrupted Dixie.

'The steps to Ma's,' finished Sammy.

'Mars?' asked Gavin. 'Surely that's a star too.'

'Planet,' said Dixie. 'Don't you know anything?'

'Hang on,' said Sammy. 'It says Ma's, not Mars.'

'Oh,' said Dixie, 'shall we go up?'

'Yeah, it must be Mrs Grock's,' said Darius.

At the front, Dixie climbed up the stone steps and out into the room above. 'It is Mrs Grock's,' she said, hoisting herself up.

From the bottom of the steps, Sammy heard Mrs Grock's familiar voice, welcoming them into her cottage.

Dixie leaned back down. 'Hey Sammy, this is the store room where she got the stuff for Serberon's potion, remember?'

'Yeah,' said Sammy, his muffled voice sending an echo around the room below.

'What?'

'He said "Yeah",' said Gavin, climbing up the steps. 'Come on, move up. It's bright up here.'

Dixie moved aside and Gavin went up, followed closely by Milly then Darius. Sammy looked back into the cave before he climbed the steps and let out a yelp in fright. Two yellow-gold eyes were staring at him. They blinked and he scuttled up into the store room. He closed the trapdoor with a bang and took a deep breath, trembling from head to toe.

'It was there all along,' said Sammy, his hands shaking. 'It was at the bottom of the steps.'

'Course it was,' scoffed Gavin.

'Really? Wish I'd seen it,' said Dixie.

'Mrs Grock?' Sammy called, stumbling past a sack of grain and just missing his head on a low a wooden shelf laden with potion bottles.

'Ooch, there's more of you.' Mrs Grock's voice floated through from the hallway. 'Come in, come in.'

They stepped over an assortment of wooden barrels and sacks with white labels that Sammy didn't have time to read and marched into Mrs Grock's front lounge area.

Sammy sat with Dixie on the same purple beanbags they had sat on nearly two months ago. Gavin, Darius and Milly sat in front of the fire on the purple velvet three seat sofa.

'Look at all these books,' said Milly.

'Ay, there's magic in those lassie,' said Mrs Grock, appearing from the kitchen with a tray of steaming hot chocolate. 'Ooch, it's my young Dragon Knight.'

Sammy felt his cheeks burn. 'Hello.'

'Why, it's been such a long time. John tells me you are doing very well.'

'Who's John?' asked Milly.

'Why he would be Professor Burlay to you dear. My great friend from my college days, John Burlay.' Mrs Grock's eyes glazed over. 'Ah, if things had been different.'

'What happened?' asked Dixie leaning forward and almost upsetting her hot chocolate.

'Dixie,' Milly gasped. 'You can't ask her that!'

'Aye lassie, she's all right. Well see, it happened when we were at Kings Astronomy College. Commander Altair was there too, though we never saw eye to eye. I still think it was him who stopped John going through with it.'

'With what?' asked Dixie, ignoring Milly's tutting.

'Why our wedding of course. I never really got over that. He listened more to his friend than to his heart. Still,' she pointed to a picture frame on the mantelpiece, 'Alfie

217

Grock who I did marry did me very well. He's serving with your father Dixie, but I expect you already knew that.'

'No.' Dixie lurched forward. 'Molly, Professor Burlay's sister, the ice cream lady at the Floating Circus, her Dad's supposed to be with mine too, but no one ever gets the chance to tell me where, or why,' she added darkly.

'Looks like today's no different.' Mrs Grock laughed as a group of older students burst into the lounge from the underground passageway. She stood up, hands on her hips, a frown burrowed into her weather worn face. 'You tell Molly when you see her I've got a bone to pick with her. She started courting John with her best friend the day after he called off the wedding. Thick as thieves, her, him and Commander Altair they were and thief they did, stealing John from me. Go on, all of you, the next clue is in the Dragon Chambers, or in the Gymnasium, or tied to a Dragonball goalpost, go on, go please.'

Sammy was upset to see her dab her eyes with the corner of her apron. He followed Darius out of the cottage and through the small garden out into the school grounds.

'Hope we didn't upset her,' said Dixie as they passed the wishing well.

'Well you kept on at her,' said Milly, her blue eyes unusually large. 'What about her and Professor Burlay.'

'Mm,' said Dixie, 'I bet that was big news at the time.'

'So where do you reckon your Dad is?' asked Sammy.

'Dunno. I'm going to find out though, if it's the last thing I do.'

'How,' asked Gavin. 'Every time you get close, there's never the chance.'

'I'll have to try harder.' Dixie rubbed her eye with the sleeve of her witch's cloak.

'You'll rub the make-up off,' said Milly, reprovingly.

'So,' said Sammy, 'which way?'

'Dragon Chamber,' said Dixie with a gleam in her eye. 'We can see Goldie.'

'What about the Gym,' protested Milly, 'or the Dragonball pitch? That must be where the goalposts are.'

Sammy didn't listen to Milly. At the mention of Goldie, he, Darius and Gavin were agreeing with Dixie that they would find the Dragon Chambers next.

'How do we get there?' asked Gavin.

'Under the North tower,' said Dixie. 'There's an entrance, isn't there Sammy.'

'Captain Stronghammer, the dwarf from...'

'Yeah we know,' said Gavin, impatiently.

'Well, he said the dragons live under our tower.'

'The North tower?' asked Milly.

'Yeah, deep underground,' said Dixie. 'Let's go!'

They ran to the main entrance, searching by moonlight for any signs of activity, but there was no one in sight. They marched alongside the castle wall, looking for trapdoors, tunnels, even pushing bricks.

About halfway between the North and West towers, they stopped. At ankle height, there was a dark semi-circle hole in the wall barred with tough iron railings.

'This could be it,' said Gavin, kneeling in the gravel courtyard. 'Look.'

Gavin moved aside and Sammy peered in with Darius breathing heavily by his shoulder. It was pitch black.

'Let me see,' said Dixie impatiently.

Sammy moved to let Dixie and Milly look through the bars.

'Eugh, it stinks in there,' said Milly.

'It must be the Dragon Chamber,' said Dixie pulling at the bars.

'Good,' said Milly. 'We can't get in. Let's find another clue.'

But Dixie had already rattled a loose bar free and had stuck her head through. 'It's dark in here,' she muttered, her voice echoing back, "dark in here, in here, here, here."

'Spooky,' said Gavin poking his head through. "Spooky, ooky," said the deep rumbling echo followed by a patter of thumping footsteps.

'Ooh,' said Dixie pulling her head back quickly. 'There's something in there.'

'Dragons hopefully,' said Sammy. 'Maybe we should look for Captain Stronghammer.'

'Or another clue,' suggested Milly.

'I've got my torch,' said Darius. 'It's only small, but you might see something.' He shone the torch inside, but it didn't show them anymore. The room was too big and the light couldn't penetrate the deep darkness. 'Are there any more loose bars?'

Dixie bent down and pulled at the other bars. 'This one, maybe,' she said, giving it a tug, but it didn't move.

'Let me have a go,' said Gavin. He bent down and yanked the bar which creaked, then sprung free leaving a gap big enough for a small person to crawl through. Gavin pulled hard at the other bars, but they stood firm. 'They won't move,' said Gavin. 'I can't get through. Sammy, you Milly and Dixie will have to get it.'

'What about me?' demanded Darius looking at the small gap. 'Oh. Won't any of the other bars budge? I'd love to see another fully grown dragon.'

'Take my place,' said Milly.

'Hah,' Darius snorted. 'My shoulders are too big.'

'Well, I'll just stay up here with you and Gavin,' said Milly.

'Just us,' said Dixie, grinning at Sammy. She took the torch from Darius. 'Ready?'

Sammy nodded. He took off his ghost sheet and sat facing the wall, his legs suspended through the gap in the castle wall. 'How far down do you reckon it is?'

'Not very,' said Dixie, 'course, it could be, uh Sammy?'

But Sammy had jumped.

He landed with a thud, scraping his knees on a stone floor. A thin slither of light came from high above his head, moonlight shining into the Dragon Chamber. 'It's not far,' he shouted up. He jumped as his voice echoed around him, mustn't shout, he thought to himself as the echo repeated, "not far, far, far".

With a thud, Dixie landed cat-footed beside him. 'It's dark in here,' she whispered, flicking on the small torch.

'Yeah,' said Sammy, as quietly as he could.

'Sammy,' Gavin called down. 'You won't be able to get out this way. We'll do up the bars and try to find another way in.'

'Ok,' said Sammy, a knot twisting in his stomach. He hoped there was another way out. 'Can I have the torch?' he whispered, 'I don't' want to light a fire in here.'

Dixie handed over the small light. 'Did you hear that?'

In the darkness, Sammy nodded. There was the sound of something shuffling, the smell of smoky breath and dragon scales purging towards them.

'This way,' whispered Sammy. He pulled Dixie's arm as the shadow of a dragon sidled close to them.

'That was close,' whispered Dixie, her voice shaking. 'They should be tame, shouldn't they? Not like the one under Mrs Grock's.'

'I suppose,' whispered Sammy. 'I think we should go this way.' He pointed the torch straight ahead and stared as the light bounced off a mountain of silver green scales that rose and fell from a sleeping dragon.

'That was really close,' whispered Dixie. 'Another inch and we'd have walked into her.'

'Her?'

'Well, her, him, whatever,' said Dixie. 'Can we just find Captain Stronghammer and get out of here?'

'But look at all these dragons,' Sammy shone the torch around. It picked up four sleeping dragons, all the size of minibuses, their scaly tails coiled around their long bodies. 'They're beautiful. We could explore the whole chamber.'

'But it's Halloween,' whispered Dixie. 'What better night for the Shape to attack and where are they going to look for dragons? Here, that's where.'

'That's why Sir Ragnarok organised the treasure hunt.'

'Why? So we can dress up, look stupid and end up in the Dragon Chambers?'

'No,' said Sammy. 'We're like police, a patrol, guarding the school. The Shape couldn't attack tonight. Not when they don't know where everyone is.'

'We don't know where everyone is,' whispered Dixie. 'Maybe they got Mary-Beth's dragon when we went inside after that match.'

'Yeah, and they took her Kelsepe because Mary-Beth was injured and she wouldn't see her dragon for a while.'

'So, we should be ok tonight?'

'Sir Ragnarok wanted the hunt to end at midnight.'

'The witching hour,' whispered Dixie, the echo picking up her fear.

'Yeah, all right,' said Sammy feeling the hairs on the back of his neck sticking up. He wished Darius and Gavin had squeezed into the Dragon Chamber as well.

'There's a light over there,' said Dixie. 'Might be a way out.'

They stepped cautiously between the sleeping dragons towards the light. As they got closer, Sammy recognised

Captain Stronghammer sitting on the floor outside a tiny office with a lantern on the desk. Another dwarf half hidden in darkness towered over him. They seemed to be arguing.

'Wait,' Sammy hissed in Dixie's ear. He pulled her in behind a tall pillar and turned off the torch.

'It's not my place to say it. You know I don't like to get involved in your doings,' said the larger of the two dwarves.

'Captain Firebreath,' whispered Sammy. 'What's he doing here?'

'What is it, hic-Fire-hic?' asked Captain Stronghammer.

'I believe you've had too much of that pumpkin rum of Sir Ragnarok's.'

'Hic, good 'tis,' replied Captain Stronghammer

'That may be, but you've had enough. Next you'll be telling the world about our secret.'

Sammy pricked up his ears, silently begging the dwarves to say more.

'It's not-hic-my fault Firey. You know it's not.'

'We have to keep it quiet, or else we'll be thrown out of the school. No more mining, a disgrace, that's what we'll be.'

'Firey-hic, I canna help what-hic-I said.' Captain Stronghammer sloshed back some more pumpkin rum and dropped the bottle on the floor. 'It was a-hic-accident, slipped-hic-out it did.'

'The damage is done,' growled Captain Firebreath. 'You told her that dragon wouldn't be needed for a while.'

'An-hic-experiment she said. Never hic-thought she'd be taking its stone.'

'She teaches them stones. Darn it Duke, didn't you think? No, you didn't think. I should have told Sir Ragnarok, but he'd have thought you did it on purpose. You're so stupid, and lay off that rum will you?'

Captain Stronghammer cracked open another bottle and stood up. 'Let's check-hic-the drag-hic dragons?'

'You can wait here. It'll be quicker for me to do it alone.'

Sammy and Dixie ducked into the shadows. Sammy's head spun. Who had Captain Stronghammer told about the dragon? Who would be capable of coming down to the chamber and killing a dragon to take its stone?

'We have to get out without being seen,' whispered Sammy.

They crouched under Dixie's witches cloak as Captain Firebreath marched past. He reeled out the names of the dragons, counting them. He reached thirty and moved away from them into another area of the chamber.

'Thirty-one, Maligna, thirty-two, Angore, thirty-three...' Captain Firebreath's voice faded as he got further and further away.

Sammy grabbed Dixie's hand and tiptoed to the entrance. Captain Stronghammer had collapsed with the rum bottle still in his hand.

'Bet that's strong stuff,' whispered Dixie.

Captain Stronghammer snored, completely oblivious to them.

'Come on,' whispered Sammy. 'We have to get out.'

In his haste to get out, Sammy accidentally kicked a small stone. Captain Stronghammer stirred. 'Whats-hic you doing here?'

'Uh,' said Sammy, his mind blank.

'The next clue,' said Dixie quickly. 'We're on the treasure hunt.'

'A-ha,' said Captain Stronghammer eyeing them suspiciously. 'The hic-clue is Sir Ragnarok, his-hic-office. Tell Sir Ragnarok.' Captain Stronghammer slumped down, asleep.

'Is that a clue or not?' asked Dixie.

'Don't think so,' said Sammy. 'Let's find the others.'

Leaving the dwarf snoring gently, they snuck past the office door and ran up a cobbled stone ramp out into the castle grounds.

Looking back, Sammy could see how they had missed the entrance earlier. The tunnel mouth and ramp entrance they had just climbed had disappeared behind some tall rhododendron bushes.

'That's how we never saw it before,' said Dixie.

'Wonder how many more secret passages there are,' said Sammy.

'Loads I bet. We'll have to find them all.'

'Where do you reckon everyone is?'

'Back to the Main Hall I guess,' said Dixie. She showed him the luminous hands on her watch. 'It's five to midnight.'

Sammy and Dixie found Gavin and Milly in the Main Hall. They were sitting with Toby and Tristan, tucking into the food that Sir Ragnarok had replenished for their midnight feast. There were as many sandwiches, pies and sweets as there had been at seven o'clock.

'...then they jumped in,' said Gavin. 'We haven't seen them since, probably eaten by the dragons.'

'Talking about us?' asked Dixie.

'Uh, Dixie, Sammy, I was just saying you'd be back.'

Tristan grinned at Dixie. 'Bit of an adventure?'

'Come on,' said Sammy. 'Let's find Darius.'

'He'll be back in a minute,' said Milly. 'He went to hand in our names. We found another two clues while you were gone. That makes six.'

'Did you count our clue from the chamber?' asked Sammy.

'No,' said Milly. 'It turns out you shouldn't have gone in there. Mrs Grock found us when we were on the Dragonball pitch and said it was a mistake.'

'Course we didn't let on you'd already gone in,' said Gavin, handing Sammy back his ghost costume sheet. 'Would've caused all kinds of trouble.'

'She said she'd forgotten that first years don't keep their dragons underground. We told her we'd split up and you were finding another clue.'

'Oh,' said Sammy, tucking into another helping of Tombstone Pie.

'Wish we had some of that pumpkin rum Captain Stronghammer was drinking,' said Dixie.

'Ladies don't drink rum,' said Milly, looking shocked at the very thought of it.

Dixie glared at her.

'What rum?' asked Tristan.

'Nothing,' snapped Dixie. 'What else does Mummy say, Milly? Anything about talking with your mouth full?'

'Mushurp,' said Milly, her mouth full of orangeade.

They laughed at her indignant face as Darius returned and helped himself to some more sandwiches.

'Sir Ragnarok's going to announce the winners,' said Darius, pointing to the teacher's table.

'Good evening everyone,' said Sir Ragnarok. 'Thank you for taking part in my treasure hunt. Those of you who successfully completed the quest should have ended up here to receive your prize bag with some Halloween treats.'

Sammy looked around. Some students were waving small pouches with toys and coloured sweets. Not everyone had one. It seemed that anyone who'd followed Dixie's brothers had a bag, anyone who hadn't, didn't.

'However,' continued Sir Ragnarok, 'it wouldn't be much fun, or fair for that matter, for those of you who equally helped patrol the school as best you could, did not end up with a token of my appreciation – prizes,' Sir Ragnarok explained. He held up more bags. 'Come forward if you haven't already received one, come and collect your goodie bags!'

Sammy leapt up with his team mates and pushed his way to Sir Ragnarok's table.

'Quite an adventure, eh?' Sir Ragnarok beamed and handed Sammy a lumpy grey pouch tied with a green ribbon.

'Yes sir,' said Sammy.

'Any time you want to tell me anything,' said Sir Ragnarok pointing to the pouch. 'Any time. You are closest.'

'Ok,' said Sammy, not entirely sure what Sir Ragnarok meant.

'Any time,' repeated Sir Ragnarok, staring at the bag.

Sammy shook the grey pouch. It was heavy and there seemed to be something metal inside. He opened it back at the empty food tables. Inside there were a number of chocolate gold coins, a keyring and a set of Dragon Dice. Underneath the dice, Sammy's fingers closed in on a metal object, shiny, smooth and heavy.

He thought he knew what it was, but it couldn't be. Sir Ragnarok had said it was a present from Professor Burlay. He'd never give it away, but it couldn't be anything else. Keeping the disc hidden in the grey bag was best for now. For whatever reason, Sir Ragnarok had given him, and just him, a Directometer. Did Sir Ragnarok know that he'd wanted one since the day he'd borrowed it, or, he wondered, did Sir Ragnarok have a use for it, and him, in mind.

'Mine's blue too,' said Dixie, pulling Sammy out of his thoughts. 'Hey Sammy, I said mine's blue.'

Sammy looked up. Dixie was waving her keyring at him. He looked in his hands, the keyring was there. It was the last thing he'd taken out of the bag before he felt the Directometer.

'Yeah, cool,' said Sammy, glad Dixie hadn't noticed why he hadn't been listening. He clipped the keyring to one of his jeans belt loops and threw his ghost costume back over his head. Under the sheet, it would be a lot easier to hide as much of the remains of the feast as he dared carry for their own midnight feast in the tower room that Gavin was busy organising.

CHAPTER 13

UNMASKING THE SHAPE

After the excitement of the treasure hunt, Sammy enjoyed sitting on the grassy bank watching a ferocious game of Dragonball between the second and fifth years.

It wasn't a fair match, but the second years on their smaller dragons put up a furious fight for fourteen out of the fifty goals scored. After a particularly dirty tackle by the fifth years, Mr Cross called the match a draw. He wouldn't budge even when the largest fifth year, a strapping boy of fifteen called Mark Banks towered over him and, threatened to set his dragon on him.

The only dampener on the afternoon was a message from Professor Burlay asking them to come one by one over the next week for a progress meeting to check that things were going well.

Up in the tower dormitory Sammy yawned. He was tired and stiff after watching the four hour game and nervous about the meeting with Professor Burlay. 'What's first tomorrow,' he asked Darius who was just back from the bathroom.

'My favourite,' said Darius, grinning. 'Double Gemology.'

Sammy groaned and pulled the green velvet curtain around his bed. Despite thinking he wouldn't, he slept right through the night and woke early to the sun streaming through a gap at the top of the curtain.

In the underground classroom, Sammy found it almost impossible to concentrate in Dr Lithoman's two and a half hour Gemology lesson. To his horror, she had planned to use the whole lesson covering the draconite stone and its magical properties.

Dr Lithoman was showing them a grisly slideshow with mountain researchers tracking dragons in the wild. Although the slides were from a study in Central America, Sammy couldn't help wondering if the same research took place in Britain.

'This,' said Dr Lithoman, pointing her staff at the slide with a flourish, 'is the deepest and darkest cavern ever found. Over five hundred dragons were found at this location.'

'But it's blank,' said Peter Grayling from West.

'Look closer,' said Dr Lithoman. 'Eyes, thousands of them, in the darkness. The people in these slides are very brave to enter an unknown cavern with wild dragons. Very brave indeed.'

'I can't see anything,' said Gavin, bumping Sammy's elbow as he stood up to get a better look.

'Come,' said Dr Lithoman. She beckoned for Gavin to come over to the overhead projector and pointed a stubby finger at minuscule specks that Sammy had thought were dirt on the slides.

Large sausage shaped lines appeared on the wall as Gavin made a rude sign when Dr Lithoman turned to face the class.

Dr Lithoman looked round to see what was funny and Gavin whipped his hand down and clasped them angelically together.

'I don't see what's funny,' said Dr Lithoman. 'You'll find better pictures of the study in your "Simply Gems" text books. You have all got your text books, haven't you?'

The class nodded. Those who hadn't already, shuffled to take their Gemology book from their rucksacks.

'Page forty-four if I remember rightly. Good friends of mine those explorers.'

'They top up her supplies,' muttered Sammy as he flipped straight to page forty-four. At the top of the page, a brightly dressed man and woman stared back at him. They were wearing full climbing gear and appeared to be at the top of a mountain.

"Mr and Mrs Gravenstone of Hampshire, England, have successfully located the last of the missing Dragon Chambers that were built on King Serberon's orders in the middle of the Dark Ages," Sammy read, staring at the woman in the picture. With her pointed nose, bright eyes and long, black, straggly hair, she looked a bit like a dragon herself. In fact, they both did, he thought. Very dragonish.

'I have telephoned Mr and Mrs Gravenstone,' said Dr Lithoman. 'They may be able to visit us this time next year. Can't make any promises, have to clear it with Sir Ragnarok, a treat for my fishies and first years. Sammy, are you listening?'

Sammy shut "Simply Gems" with a bang, un-hypnotising himself from the solid stares of the Gravenstones and realising he was still in the underground chamber, in Gemology.

'What are you doing?' spluttered Dr Lithoman. 'Double homework for you Mr Rambles and be sure to listen thoroughly from now on.'

Dr Lithoman flicked to the next slide and Sammy shook his head in despair.

'Double homework from double Gemology,' he muttered to no one in particular, disappointed because the North fifth years were doing a Dragonball training session after tea that he'd been looking forward to. Now with Professor Burlay's progress meeting at lunch and double Gemology homework, Sammy didn't think he'd be able to make it.

Twenty slides later, Captain Stronghammer and Captain Firebreath trundled through the classroom with heavily laden wheelbarrows. Captain Stronghammer's was filled with glittering diamonds and Captain Firebreath's carried dull stones and soil. Captain Stronghammer waved at the North table as he passed them, carefully guiding his barrow along the groove in the floor.

Dr Lithoman tapped her head as if she'd remembered something and marched down the tunnel. She returned with a leather bound presentation box and set it on her desk.

'Come close,' whispered Dr Lithoman. She opened the box, revealing two deep blue crystals coated in a sparkling diamond glitter crust. 'These are draconite stones. This one,' she pointed to the left hand stone, 'belonged to Mary-Beth Howeson in the third year, her dragon, Kelsepe.'

Sammy's stomach lurched. Beside him, Dixie covered her mouth with her hand.

'Whose is the other?' asked Sammy.

'Don't know,' said Dr Lithoman, 'and don't care. If you ask me, it was probably some stray. Mrs Grock gave it to me several weeks ago and I polished it this morning. It's come up nicely don't you think?'

'No!' shouted Sammy. 'You killed a dragon to get those stones.'

There was an uncomfortable silence that lasted nearly a minute. Sammy felt his cheeks burn. Dr Lithoman was staring at him, almost through him. She shook her head. 'Class dismissed. Go on all of you. Go to your next classes.'

Out in the corridor, Sammy was grateful for the chilly breeze cooling his cheeks. A boy from the West house patted him on the back. Sammy still couldn't remember his name, Brian or Graham, it didn't matter, Dr Lithoman favoured them all over students from the other houses.

'Yeah, no homework,' said Gavin walking out with Toby and Milly.

That cheered Sammy up. 'Double nothing,' he said, grinning at Dixie and Darius, 'must do it again sometime.'

'You've got your progress meeting with Professor Burlay next,' said Dixie.

'Hope he doesn't see Dr Lithoman first,' said Darius, giggling at him. 'Double homework for Mr Rambles, and that was before you accused her of being in the Shape!'

'Well,' said Sammy, a little uncomfortable with his outburst. 'You weren't down there. You didn't hear them.'

'"She teaches them stones," that's what he said,' added Dixie. 'Dr Lithoman said they'd come up nicely. Who else could it be?'

'All right, I'll tell you,' said Darius, looking unusually serious. 'My parents work with the Mr and Mrs Gravenstone. They're dragon healers, not murderers. If Dr Lithoman says they're her friends, then that's good enough for me.'

'Fine,' said Sammy. 'I still think she's in the Shape, and I'll prove it!'

'How?' asked Dixie.

'He can't,' snapped Darius, 'because she didn't do it.'

'She's part of the Shape,' said Sammy. 'A dragon killer. Your parents might be too.' Sammy ducked as Darius threw a wild punch at him.

'Never say that about my parents,' shouted Darius. 'You come to my house one day. They heal dragons I tell you, heal, not murder!'

Darius shoved some third years out of the way and stormed up the steps to the Main Hall for lunch.

It was a difficult meal with all of the North first years taking Darius's side, apart from Amos who was having his progress meeting with Professor Burlay.

Sammy was glad when they were allowed to leave the table and reached the Astronomics classroom early. He waited nearly ten minutes for Professor Burlay to arrive and when he did there was no apology or explanation.

'Hello Sammy,' said Professor Burlay picking up an orange clipboard and waving for Sammy to sit on a chair at the front of the classroom. 'Just had Amos in here, says he's getting on well, but his marks don't reflect as much. Anything you can tell me that might be causing it?'

Sammy shook his head, not in the right mood to tell Professor Burlay about Gavin and Toby's teasing about Amos's one-year bedroom plaque.

'Your marks however, I'm really pleased with. Perhaps you and Amos could study together,' suggested Professor Burlay. 'I've put the idea to him, he seemed a little unsure, but I think it will be fine, don't you?'

'Ok,' said Sammy, not wanting to in the least.

Professor Burlay ran his hand through his hair. 'It would mean a lot to me Sammy. Mrs Grock thinks you have the makings of a Dragon Knight. Your name crops up in the staff room more than most.'

Great, thought Sammy, wait until you hear about Gemology. Out loud, he said, 'ok, I'll do what I can.'

'Starting tonight please. Amos will meet you here at seven o'clock. I'd like to run through some star charts, oh, and bring your dragon eggs as well. I'd be interested to see how much they've grown.'

'Is there anything else?' asked Sammy, disappointed that after skipping homework from Dr Lithoman, he was being sentenced to a detention style study session with Amos of all people. Why couldn't he have kept his marks up? He would still miss the training session put on by the fifth years, a show of their dragon skills before they knuckled down to revise in preparation for their summer exams.

'That's it,' said Professor Burlay, checking his clipboard. 'It must be nice to have some of your family close to the school.'

'Family?' asked Sammy. 'My parents are in Switzerland.'

'Your uncle lives in the village. Thank him when you see him, he's doing the school a great service.'

'Ok,' said Sammy, privately thinking Professor Burlay had mixed up his notes.

'Oh, and don't forget Bonfire Night,' Professor Burlay called as Sammy reached the classroom door. 'At Dragamas, the teachers put on a fireworks display. You might find it a little boring, some students, well, they're old before they're young.'

'No,' said Sammy, wondering where this was going. 'I like fireworks.'

'Good, good,' said Professor Burlay. 'Your friend Milly thought she'd seen enough. Quite the little lady, still, perhaps you'll change her mind eh?'

First Amos, now Milly, thought Sammy. 'I'll see what I can do,' he muttered, almost bumping into Dixie who looked like she had been crying. 'Are you next?'

Dixie nodded and went into the classroom with an overly cheerful "hello Professor" that left Sammy alone and bemused in the dark corridor.

He walked back to the North tower to collect the tracksuit and t-shirt he would need for Sports.

Kyrillan rolled his eyes towards Sammy as he took the clothes from his bedside chest of drawers. Still no bigger than the toy lion Serberon had given him, Kyrillan was beginning to take shape with four tiny paws, a set of wings and a spiked tail.

Sammy felt the pair of black bead eyes staring at him as he sat on the end of his bed thinking about Sports and worrying about the evening to come.

Some twenty minutes later the other boys came back from lunch. Amos gave Sammy a darker look than Darius, before whipping his curtain around his bed.

Sammy was glad Gavin and Toby didn't seem to care about the argument. He ran with them to the Gymnasium changing rooms. The girls were already there, changed and eyeing Mr Cross with what Sammy could only describe as gooey eyes and silly smiles.

'We're doing a warm up first,' said Dixie, breaking herself away from the group. 'Then our first game of Dragonball!'

'Great!' said Sammy, looking forward to it. He ran upstairs with Gavin and Toby, followed by Amos and Darius.

They changed quickly into their white t-shirts and navy shorts. The boys from the other houses arrived just as they were going downstairs to hand in their watches to Mr Ockay.

'Any more to come?' asked Mr Cross as eventually the last three boys from the West house dragged their feet coming down the stairs.

'No Sir,' they chorused.

'Good,' said Mr Cross. 'Don't let me catch you being last again.' He turned to the class and held open the Gymnasium doors. 'Let's go!' he shouted, 'I want three laps of the Dragonball pitch, then get together in a group in the middle. Go!'

Some two hours later, Sammy wished he'd been quicker than Milly to ask to go in goal. He was exhausted and bent down to touch his toes to ease the pain of a stitch in his side he'd picked up running the entire length of the Dragonball pitch. He'd been flanked by three boys from the South and West houses, but had scored a goal.

Mr Cross didn't seem interested in the scores but by Sammy's count, the North East combined team was five goals ahead. He caught a wild pass from the golden dragon in the middle of the pitch. It was one of seven balls in play and had travelled underground from the goal at the end of the pitch, to the smoking mouth of the dragon statue in the middle.

Sammy dropped the ball when Mr Cross finally blew his whistle, one long blast followed by a short pip. He ran to join the rest of the first years at the bottom end of the pitch, nearest the Gymnasium.

'Great game everyone,' said Mr Cross, pointing his staff at the seven balls, reeling them in as if using invisible thread. 'Same teams next week. Keep practising your passes and some running if you can. I want to see you all do two laps of the pitch and then you can come in and get changed. I'll have a word with Mr Ockay, see if he'll organise something to drink. Yes, Milly?'

'Mr Cross, I think I've hurt my ankle,' said Milly, 'I fell over.'

Mr Cross inspected Milly's left ankle. 'Go on the rest of you, two laps. Milly come with me.'

'Mr Cross,' Darius mimicked Milly's whine, 'my ankle really hurts too! Can I come in with you as well?'

'No,' Mr Cross clicked his tongue. 'I suppose you're faking it are you?'

'No Sir,' said Milly, shifting her weight.

'It was your other foot a minute ago Milly. Two laps please. Gavin and Toby are almost back to start their second lap.'

Sammy saw Milly give Darius a black look.

'If it wasn't for you, I'd be inside drinking orange juice.'

Darius laughed and started jogging. 'Come on Sammy, he's gone in, we'll just do one lap!'

Milly giggled mischievously and pulled her ponytail tight. Her "bad leg" caused no problems as they caught up the rest of the class who were completing their second lap. Sammy snuck in behind Dixie, Gavin and Toby to collect his orange juice and corn cracker biscuits from Mr Ockay.

Mr Cross gave him a long stare but didn't say anything about the laps. He repeated his tips about practising and let them go up and get changed.

Even after Dragonball, Darius was still a little cool towards Sammy at dinner, where they ate leftovers of the Halloween feast. It wasn't the half-eaten sandwiches and soggy cake that Sammy had expected after overhearing students from the third year talking about it. There were pies, pastries, cakes, soup and literally thousands of fresh sandwiches. Sir Ragnarok promised that the Halloween food would continue through to Bonfire Night on Friday.

'This is really good,' said Sammy, helping himself to a cheese and cucumber sandwich.

'Mmm,' agreed Darius, jerking as he realised he wasn't really talking to Sammy.

'Have you heard about the fireworks they've got planned for Friday?' interrupted Dixie. 'Serberon says they're going to be huge.'

'Professor Burlay said a bit about them in my progress meeting,' said Gavin.

'Me too,' said Sammy, his mouth full of chicken and ham pie.

'What else did Professor Burlay say?' asked Dixie. 'He said I should try harder in Gemology, but I think Dr Lithoman is marking me down on purpose.'

'Did he say anything about earlier, when you said she killed that dragon?' asked Darius.

'No,' said Sammy. In the afternoon of Dragonball, he'd forgotten his outburst. 'He said I need to, uh, to do some extra study,' he finished, catching a begging look from Amos out of the corner of his eye.

'Great,' said Dixie brightly, 'we'll study together.'

'Ok,' said Sammy, thinking Amos probably wouldn't be too pleased.

CHAPTER 14

EXTRA STUDY

In fact, when seven o'clock came, Sammy found himself, Amos, Dixie and Darius, with whom Sammy had called a truce, sitting in the front row of the Astronomics classroom. They had each brought their dragons which were now the size of the shoe boxes but still sticky and jelly-like.

Professor Burlay turned up at five past seven carrying two scrolls. He paused in the doorway.

'Well, this is a surprise,' exclaimed Professor Burlay. 'Nice to see you're all so keen on Astronomics. I've only brought two star charts so I'm afraid you'll have to share.'

Sammy took the scroll handed to him and spread it out on the desk. Dixie leaned over his shoulder and pointed out a constellation she said was Orion.

Darius looked torn between sharing with Sammy who had insulted his parents and with Amos, who he had accused of blinding Nelson. After a long pause, Darius stayed in his seat and leaned over Dixie's shoulder.

Professor Burlay looked up from the books he was marking. 'Sammy, why don't you share with Amos, that was the original idea, for the two of you to study together.'

'O-ho!' said Darius, a big grin stretched across his face.

'I..er...' started Sammy, staring hard at Kyrillan's black bead eyes, focussing on the mottled blue-green scales.

'Come on Sammy,' said Amos, shuffling the scroll closer to Sammy's elbow. 'What's this star?'

Grateful for the distraction, Sammy identified the Plough.

'Good Sammy,' said Professor Burlay. 'I'll give North one star for that.' He drew a shiny silver star with his staff and tapped it to make it fly out of the classroom door. 'Follow the line of the Plough to find the North Star. Have you got it? Good. Now follow the line a short distance to the right and you'll see a cluster of smaller stars. We'll go outside in a second, see if we can see them in action.'

After a minute or two finding various stars Professor Burlay called at random whilst finishing his marking, he stood up and opened the twin doors that led out on to the Astronomics balcony.

'One each this evening,' said Professor Burlay pointing to the telescopes. 'It's a perfectly clear night,' he nodded approvingly at the stars twinkling in the jet black sky above them. 'There, you can see the Plough without using the telescopes.'

Sammy followed Professor Burlay's outstretched hand and easily picked out the seven star saucepan shaped formation.

'There's the North star,' said Professor Burlay. 'Look through the telescopes and tell me if you see the cluster we're looking for.' He went to a fifth telescope and put one hand to the fine tuning dial and the other crooked into the small of his back in a gentlemanly poise.

'Ah yes,' came Professor Burlay's muffled voice from under the telescope, 'the North Star.'

'Professor Burlay,' said Dixie, equally muffled, 'I can see it too.'

'Good Dixie. Boys can you see the North Star?'

'Professor Burlay,' called Amos, 'I think I can see that cluster of stars. There's one blue, one green, one yellow and one red. It looks like they're circling a white star.'

'The Dragamas constellation,' said Professor Burlay solemnly. 'Your house logos are based on these five stars; North, South, East, West and the central star represents the dragons that we protect.'

'Look,' exclaimed Dixie. 'They're circling faster and faster.'

'Let me look,' said Professor Burlay, almost barging her aside in his haste to see through her lens.

'Why are they circling?' asked Darius.

Professor Burlay sighed deeply. 'Could be bad news I'm afraid. The stars are protecting a dragon tonight.'

'Is it the Shape?' asked Sammy, half sure he already knew that it was.

'I fear so,' said Professor Burlay sombrely. 'We'll call it a day, or night, if you prefer. My presence will be required in Sir Ragnarok's office soon.

Professor Burlay cast a final look at the spinning stars and stepped through the balcony doors into the classroom.

'Hey!' shouted Professor Burlay. 'What are you doing?' In a split second, he was inside, standing by the desks where they had left the dragons.

Watching anxiously from the balcony, Sammy saw he had his hand around the neck of a small person. 'It's a dwarf,' he whispered, pushing open the balcony doors to hear their conversation.

'What are you doing here Margarite?' demanded Professor Burlay. 'This is an extra Astronomics lesson, nothing to do with Gemology.'

'Dearie me,' came Dr Lithoman's rasping reply. 'I must have the wrong room.'

'No,' said Professor Burlay. 'You were here for a purpose. On a night like tonight I'd be careful. The stars…'

Dr Lithoman laughed coldly. 'You pay too much attention to the stars, Professor. It's the stones,' she cast a long look at the dragons in their boxes, 'it's the stones that have the answers.'

'Get out,' snapped Professor Burlay. 'There aren't any stones here, just four students and their dragons catching up on extra study.'

'So I see,' said Dr Lithoman. 'Yet this one,' she pointed at Darius's dragon, 'he looks a little worse for wear.'

Sammy craned his neck over Amos's shoulder as Dr Lithoman tapped the side of the shoebox. An orange spark flew from the end of her staff and landed on the navy dragon.

'No!' shrieked Darius, running to the table pursued by Sammy, Dixie and Amos. 'You've killed him!'

Dr Lithoman laughed. 'You've been listening to that Rambles boy. Look, your dragon is alive and well. He can see with both eyes now.'

Sammy peered cautiously into the shoebox. He couldn't see any eyes, let alone two black ones. Darius prodded his dragon gently with his forefinger. Two black bead eyes rolled from under the navy belly and blinked.

'Nelson!' Darius gasped. 'You can see.'

In reply, Nelson stuck out a pale pink forked tongue and licked Darius's finger.

'Thank you, thank you, thank you,' said Darius, 'I mean it, thank you so much!'

'No need to thank me,' said Dr Lithoman coolly. 'I'm glad he's well.' She turned on her heels and marched out of the classroom.

'Ok everyone, the fun's over,' said Professor Burlay. 'Come back inside please.'

Sammy took one last look through the telescope. He had come out to check the stars while Darius thanked Dr Lithoman. Almost as he had expected, the stars in the Dragamas constellation were still, no longer circling the white star.

'Sammy?' Professor Burlay stuck his head through the open doorway. 'Come back inside please.'

'But they've stopped,' said Sammy, sure Professor Burlay would want to look.

Professor Burlay nodded. 'I know,' he whispered. 'Come back inside please.'

Sammy reluctantly left the telescope and sat down with the others. Kyrillan seemed to be staring at him and Sammy gently stroked his back, noticing the smoothness of the soft dragon skin.

Professor Burlay stood in front of Darius and frowned. 'What happened in Gemology? Dr Lithoman seems to think you have a conspiracy against her.'

Amos shrugged. 'I wasn't in Gemology. I had my progress meeting with you.'

'Darius?' What did Dr Lithoman mean when she thought you'd been listening to Sammy? And Sammy, what have you been saying?'

'Nothing,' said Sammy.

'It's not just Sammy,' interrupted Dixie. 'We all think it.'

'She favours the West house,' added Darius.

'And she kills dragons,' finished Sammy.

'Woah there, one at a time. That's quite an accusation Sammy. You know that anyone who takes a dragon's life for their own gain is punished severely.'

Sammy shook his head. 'She has draconite.'

'From reputable sources I may add. Mrs Grock and Sir Ragnarok,' said Professor Burlay. 'Surely you're not accusing them as well?'

'No Sir. Captain Stronghammer said she killed Kelsepe, Mary-Beth's dragon, from the Dragonball match at the beginning of term. He said so.'

'He did,' added Dixie, 'and Dr Lithoman showed Sammy the stones.'

'Draconite?' asked Professor Burlay.

'Yes,' whispered Sammy. 'In a drinking glass, it was in yellow jelly stuff and there was a blue-green stone at the bottom.'

'She showed us two stones in class today,' said Dixie.

Professor Burlay laughed. 'And you thought she'd killed the dragons to show you draconite?'

'She wants to be immortal,' said Sammy, feeling more and more stupid as the conversation went on.

Professor Burlay laughed harder. 'Really?' he wiped a tear from his eye. 'She'll need five stones to do that, not just two!'

'That's why she was here tonight - to take our dragon stones.' shouted Sammy, standing up, his hands gripping the desk. 'She's a murderer!

Professor Burlay frowned. 'You have quite an imagination Sammy.'

'It's true,' said Dixie. 'I was there too when Captain Stronghammer said about getting the information from him.'

'I see,' said Professor Burlay, 'and was she mentioned by name?'

Sammy looked down at his knuckles which were turning white. 'Not exactly, Captain Stronghammer said...'

'Regardless of what Captain Stronghammer said, I would encourage you not to heed his advice. Sir Ragnarok tells me he indulged somewhat in our pumpkin rum. His mind would perhaps not have been, hmm, focussed shall we say.'

'But Professor...'

'Enough Sammy,' snapped Professor Burlay. 'I don't want to hear of this again. The Shape is not something students are expected to deal with, much less first years who have been here less than a term! Bring me evidence and I will believe you,' he added, his grey-eyed stare softening. 'Perhaps we need all the eyes and ears available.'

Sammy nodded, hiding a yawn with the back of his hand. It was only nine o'clock, but he was tired from the long day and extra study.

'Right,' said Professor Burlay, folding up the maps. 'Do your dragons fly?'

'Fly?' asked Sammy, suddenly alert.

'Yes fly Sammy, you know, flap flap.' Professor Burlay waggled his arms comically and they laughed.

Darius let rip one of his famous giggles that sobered Professor Burlay in an instant.

'Yes, well.' Professor Burlay coughed. 'They look well formed. Reach under their bellies and lift them out of the boxes. Yes, like that Amos, that's good.'

Within seconds, the four dragons were out of the cardboard boxes and held by their owners. The only time Sammy remembered feeling this nervous was when he was seven, and he'd held his next door neighbour's baby rabbit, Flopsy, for the first time.

He looked down at Kyrillan's blue-green face, if you could call it a face, he thought to himself, looking at the tiny jaw with small breathing nostrils. He'd seen a puff of smoke come out of them yesterday before bed. Kyrillan's smooth scaly body reached into a tail that was already half the length of his body. Sammy shuffled Kyrillan from hand to hand to stop the four clawed paws digging into his palms.

'Good,' said Professor Burlay. 'Now thrust the dragon into the air, like this,' he scooped air through his hands, as if bailing water from a leaking boat without a bucket. 'Darius, you go first.'

Darius copied Professor Burlay's movement, throwing Nelson high into the air. Like lifting a dead weight, Nelson came crashing back into Darius's hands.

'Hmm,' said Professor Burlay. 'Perhaps he isn't ready. Sammy, you try please.'

'Here goes,' said Sammy, copying Darius's thrust. He released the curled ball of his dragon, shouting, 'Fly Kyrillan, fly!'

Sammy felt his eyes goggle as from underneath Kyrillan's belly, two large wings unfolded, showing a magnificent display of shimmering green and mottled blue.

Kyrillan swooped in a large circle over their heads and landed with the grace of a trained aeroplane pilot smoothly on the desk in front of them.

Open mouthed, Professor Burlay was first to speak. 'That was amazing Sammy, I never expected, well never mind, that is very, very unusual. You have bonded with your dragon. Tell me,' he added, ignoring the other students, 'have you been practising?'

'No,' said Sammy, half wishing Kyrillan had come crashing down like Nelson. 'I stroke him a lot, say goodnight and stuff, but I haven't practised, I haven't, honestly.'

'Hmm,' said Professor Burlay, 'can we see it again?'

Sammy didn't have to pick Kyrillan up. The tiny dragon seemed to know instinctively that he was expected to fly again. He puffed a dribble of grey smoke and took off almost before Sammy said, "fly".

'Very good,' said Professor Burlay as Kyrillan completed his second lap of the classroom. 'Bring him in Sammy. He'll get tired after flying for the first time.'

'Bring him in?' echoed Sammy.

'Why yes, you are controlling him, aren't you?' Professor Burlay tapped the side of his head. 'Use your head boy and bring him in.'

Not knowing what he was doing and terrified he might do something wrong, Sammy held out his hands, silently asking Kyrillan to land in them.

To his surprise, Kyrillan seemed to jerk in mid-air. With a swooping arc and a flap of blue-green wings, Kyrillan turned and nosedived. He landed a little unsteadily in Sammy's hands, wings folding in at the last possible second.

'Bravo!' said Professor Burlay clapping hard. 'Dixie, you're next.'

Dixie stared at Professor Burlay. 'I can't,' she whispered, 'I can't do that.'

'Try my dear, just try. That's all I ask of you. If you don't try, you have already failed.'

'Ok,' said Dixie picking up her mass of blue-green dragon. 'Kiridor, fly round the room!' She thrust her dragon high into the air, gasping as Kiridor took flight.

'Wow!' shrieked Dixie. 'He's flying, Kiridor's flying!'

Sammy could barely keep up watching the blue-green ball hurl itself from one end of the classroom to the other.

'Land!' shouted Dixie, holding her hands wide apart. Kiridor plunged into her hands so fast that she took a step back to steady herself. 'I did it Professor, look!'

Professor Burlay nodded, smiling broadly. 'Very good Dixie. I'm truly impressed. Amos, can you make it three in a row, then, yes Darius?'

'Can I have another go Professor?'

'Of course. Amos, Darius, both together.'

'Fly,' shouted Amos, throwing his dragon into the air. 'Go Morg, go!'

'Nelson, fly,' shouted Darius at the same time. 'Fly! Fly! Fly!'

The two dragons, navy blue Nelson and purple flecked Morg, seemed to pause in mid-air, as if thinking what to do. Then Morg spread purple and silver grey wings, hovered a second, then soared to the ceiling. Nelson copied him, extending dark sapphire blue wings that caught the air and he glided at waist level over Professor Burlay's desk.

After nearly a minute, both dragons landed on shaky legs on the desk in front of their owners.

Sammy saw Amos and Darius grinning at each other, their quarrel completely forgotten.

'That was awesome,' said Darius. 'Can we do it again?'

'No,' said Professor Burlay firmly. 'Look, your dragons are already sleeping.' He checked the clock over the blackboard and compared it with his wristwatch. 'It's ten o'clock. We're already later than I expected. You've got an early start with Professor Sanchez in Alchemistry tomorrow. I probably shouldn't say, but she's going to be working on the fireworks for Friday with you.'

'Wow,' said Dixie. 'That should be good.'

'Yes, it should.' Professor Burlay smiled. 'Now bed!' He ushered them out of the Astronomics classroom and escorted them back to the North tower.

There were only a handful of students in the common room, a girl studying at the large tables in the middle of the room and three others playing with Dragon Dice on the floor in front of the grandfather clock.

'Good night all,' said Professor Burlay, closing the heavy oak door behind him.

CHAPTER 15

BONFIRE NIGHT

In room seventy-nine at the top of the castle, Professor Sanchez's lesson disappeared at lightning speed. At the tables in groups of four, Sammy spent the lesson with Dixie, Darius and Amos filling cardboard tubes with coloured salt.

Professor Sanchez moved from one table to the next, checking the fireworks were safe and everyone was behaving.

Sammy counted over a hundred tubes that his table had filled with generous scoopfuls of salts that Professor Sanchez had labelled barium, sodium, strontium and copper. At the start of the lesson and in no uncertain terms, she had said that the wires used to ignite the fireworks would be added only by herself.

At her next round of checking, Professor Sanchez slotted the fireworks into pre-prepared carriers and stacked them behind her desk at the front of the classroom.

'This is good work,' she said, surveying the mountain of firework boxes. 'We will have a good time on Friday.'

Surveying his hands, red and sore from sealing the tubes, Sammy wasn't altogether disappointed when the bell rang.

In room fifty-five, Dr Shivers set the class two hours of note-taking as he explained in great detail the procedures involved in de-scaling dragons. He talked non-stop whilst simultaneously scribbling notes and diagrams on the blackboard.

'Very messy,' said Dr Shivers running his nails down the blackboard. 'But of course, you won't be de-scaling until your dragons are at least a year old. Their scales should be fully hardened by then.'

Dr Shivers picked up the chalk and scratched the number one on the blackboard. 'Consider it like teeth, once the baby teeth are out, your dragon will grow scales strong enough to withstand almost any form of attack. From then on, de-scaling is carried out once per year.'

'Where do we de-scale our dragons?' asked Dixie.

'At school,' said Dr Shivers. 'I will help and assist you while you are here. I suggest that it is done outside, some dragons have been known to object quite strongly to the process and the more room available the better.'

'My mother does hers outside,' said Simon Sanchez. 'Sometimes her dragon blows smoke and breathes fire.'

'Perhaps she would like to try this.' Dr Shivers pulled a box of matchbox sized green rectangular tablets from a drawer under his desk. 'Give one to the dragon before you start and he or she will fall fast asleep. Makes the process very easy indeed. Yes Sammy?'

'What happens if they aren't de-scaled?'

'Nothing really,' said Dr Shivers. 'Of course, they de-scale anyway, shedding their scales like a snake sheds skin. There's a new layer already growing underneath. There's no control, it can happen anywhere, for weeks on end. A terrible mess I'm told.'

'Dr Shivers, what happens to the scales?'

'A good question Milly. When carried out in a controlled de-scale, it's up to the owner of the dragon. Some people keep them, some use them in jewellery, like your necklace, and yours Dixie, oh, how sweet, you North girls all have one. A rare species if I'm not mistaken.'

Sitting next to him, Sammy saw Dixie blush. 'I got them from the Floating Circus,' she said, holding up the teardrop shaped scale.

'Ah yes, Helga Halfwhistle's stall. Did you know she collects scales from all breeds of dragon?'

'She gave me mine,' said Dixie.

'Very nice I'm sure,' said Dr Shivers dismissively. 'Anyhow, some people keep the scales for potions, firewood and so on. Others simply throw the scales away.'

'I could never do that,' Dixie whispered in Sammy's ear.

'Me neither,' replied Sammy. 'Potions sounds good.'

'Oh yes,' said Dr Shivers, his ashen face drawing into a frown. 'There are both light and dark potions to be made with the properties of different scales. Perhaps you could investigate this, research it as a project. Search around the castle, you may find the odd scale on the Dragonball pitch.'

Dr Shivers paused and surveyed the class through his narrow grey eyes. 'Yes, a project for Bonfire Night. As you look up to see your fireworks, look down for dragon scales. Perhaps I can find a prize for the group to collect the most between now and after Christmas.'

Everyone nodded, talking and shouting to arrange the groups. Sammy teamed up again with Dixie, Gavin, Milly and Darius.

'Bet we get the most,' Gavin challenged his brother.

'Bet you don't,' said Toby.

Used to their brotherly competition, Sammy agreed with Darius that it would be close.

'Right,' said Dr Shivers when he had finished making notes on who was in which group. 'Eight teams of five and a prize after Christmas for the team who collects the most. I'll see you all on Friday for the fireworks, then same time next week.'

As usual, Dr Shivers had timed his lesson, setting homework and his closing speech to coincide with the first chime of the end of lesson bell. Since there were no clocks in the classroom, other than on the students with wristwatches, Sammy always found this impressive.

Three days later, just after seven o'clock, Professor Burlay burst into the North common room armed with a bundle of unwrapped sparklers. He thrust handful after handful of sparklers into the outstretched hands of the first, second, third, fourth and fifth year students.

Everyone was wrapped warmly in outdoor clothes, thick woollen jumpers, school blazers, jeans and boots. Most people had hats, scarves and gloves too.

Tom Sweep passed them in the corridor. He muttered to Professor Burlay to be careful not to bring mud into the school. Sammy wondered about the groundsmen, he hadn't met any so far, but he was sure they would object to the entire school trampling on the neatly mown Dragonball pitch.

They walked out of the East entrance, the nearest to the Dragonball pitch, in neat crocodile lines. In their team, Sammy had volunteered to hold the bag, ready to collect the scales for Dr Shivers.

On the Dragonball pitch amongst the growing number of students scuffing mud between their boots, it looked as though it would be nearly impossible to collect any scales.

'Got one!' shouted Dixie, picking up a mother of pearl coloured scale the size of a seashell.

'That's pretty,' said Milly. 'Just like our necklaces.'

'Come on,' said Gavin. 'Put it in the bag and let's go round the edge where there are less people.'

'We could try by the Gym entrance,' suggested Sammy. 'That's where the dragons line up. There might be some there.'

Professor Burlay stopped them as they walked up to the goalposts. 'Not here, not here,' he said looking ruffled. 'I know about Dr Shivers's project, but please keep away from the goalposts. Most of the rockets will be launched from here.'

'Cool, can we light them?' asked Gavin.

'Absolutely not,' said Professor Sanchez appearing from behind a monstrous firework. 'None of the students may cross the goal lines. Back please, all of you.'

She stopped and Sammy felt Professor Sanchez stare at him 'Well, perhaps you could light one Sammy.'

'Ok,' said Sammy. 'Can I light that big one please?'

'Very well,' said Professor Sanchez, handing Sammy a large box of matches.

Professor Burlay frowned. 'Simone, are you sure?'

'Very sure, thank you,' replied Professor Sanchez.

'Well let him do it properly,' a voice came out of the darkness. Commander Altair appeared and made Professor Sanchez jump.

'Very well,' she agreed, putting the matches away.

Sammy stared at Commander Altair. 'Are you sure?'

Commander Altair looked keenly at him and nodded. 'Say the magic words.'

Sammy passed his sparklers to Darius and took his staff out from under his blazer. He pointed the onyx end towards the ground and whispered, 'fire.'

To his relief, a spark sprung from the onyx and ignited on the dry ground. Using his mind, he carried the flames to touch the tip of the taper wire on the huge rocket.

It caught first time. The fire travelled up the wire and fizzed as it connected with the base of the cardboard tube. With an almighty BANG, the firework took off, leaving a kite-tail of sparkles behind. High above the Gymnasium roof, the firework erupted in the gold, straight-edged circle shape of the Dragamas "D" logo

Everyone on the Dragonball pitch stopped and stared. The firework was busy spelling out the school name and motto in golden sparks that shone brightly in the starry night.

'D.R.A…Dragamas,' said Gavin, following the firework. 'Mighty is the…'

'Golden dragon,' finished Dixie, her eyes wide open, staring at the sparks. 'That's the best firework I've ever seen.'

In the darkness, Sammy thought he saw Professor Sanchez blush. 'That was wonderful, Sammy.'

Sammy had to admit that it was the best firework he'd ever seen too. 'Come on,' he said to the rest of his group as the firework finally fizzled to its end. 'We've got to find some scales.'

'Yeah,' said Gavin, looking longingly at the mountain of fireworks. 'It's not fair, Dad always lets me and Toby light them at home.'

They moved away as Professor Sanchez lit three Catherine wheels. One came loose and Professor Burlay tutted loudly as it sent sparks over their heads. They couldn't hear what Professor Burlay said, but could guess from the way Professor Sanchez threw the taper at him, that she had invited him to have a go instead.

With Bonfire Night well underway, people spread out and it was easier to spot the coloured scales on the grassy pitch. Sammy picked up four maroon scales with gold flecks.

From the distance, they saw the Professors and Commander Altair set off an impressive array of blue-green flames that danced their way around the white lined edges of the Dragonball pitch. The flames were followed by a series of orange and purple shooting stars that flew from both goal posts into the huge bonfire in the middle of the pitch.

Closer to the Gymnasium, they saw a familiar set of white plastic tables and chairs. Beyond the tables, Merry Megan and Molly Burlay were serving the same giant ice creams they had enjoyed at the Floating Circus. Easily identifiable by Dixie's green hair, Molly spotted them and came over.

'This is Molly,' said Dixie introduced the ice cream lady, 'and Milly and Gavin,' she pointed towards Milly and Gavin who were transfixed by the size of the ice cream Merry Megan was serving to a fourth year boy to share with a fair haired girl he was rumoured to be dating.

'Hi,' said Gavin, without taking his eyes off the monstrous cornet.

'Hello lovvies,' said Molly with a rosy cheeked smile. 'Would you like an ice cream or a hot dog?'

'Uh, no thanks,' said Gavin. 'We're working on a school project.'

'Ah yes,' said Molly, scratching the side of her nose. 'Your friend Tristan was here earlier. You're looking for used scales, aren't you?'

'That's right,' said Darius. 'Actually, I would like a hot dog, please.'

'Coming right up,' said Molly. 'That'll be one gold coin, please.'

Darius's face fell. 'I, uh...'

'Oh, you thought...' said Molly kindly. 'I would love to, but if I do one free for you, everyone will want one.'

'That's ok,' said Darius.

'Here,' said Sammy, remembering the coin Serberon had given him in the Gymnasium foyer on the first day. Despite several washes in the school laundry, the coin had stayed firmly put.

'I can't take your money,' said Darius. 'I'll go back and get some.'

'Go on. Please take it Molly.'

'If you're sure...'

'I am,' said Sammy firmly.

'Thanks Sammy, I'll pay you when we get back to the tower.'

'It's ok. It wasn't really my money anyway. Mr Ockay gave it to me to buy a drink after Dragonball. Hey!' Sammy spun round as someone tapped him sharply on the shoulder. 'Oh. Hi Serberon.'

'It's Mikhael,' said the green haired boy. 'Don't worry, you'll get us right eventually. Have you seen Serberon?'

'He's with Jason,' said Dixie. 'I saw them earlier by the trees.'

'Ok, see you later, and tell your friend not to give away all our secrets,' Mikhael said stiffly. Spotting some green hair in the crowd, he yelled for his brothers to come over.

'It's ok, he likes you really,' whispered Dixie. 'He's just a bit protective.'

'A bit?' said Sammy laughing.

'Hey Sammy!' Serberon clapped him hard on the back as he arrived with pony-tailed Jason. 'Having fun?'

'Yes, definitely,' said Sammy, happier in Serberon's company than Mikhael's.

'Hi Dixie,' Serberon ruffled his sister's hair.

Dixie smoothed her ponytail. 'What's up with Mik?'

'Nothing,' said Serberon, suspiciously quickly.

'Just a few duff marks,' added Jason.

'Oh,' said Dixie. 'Look at those fireworks.'

'Oooh,' said Milly, finding her voice, shy in front of Dixie's older brothers.

'Good, aren't they?' said Serberon, a little smugly. 'That was one of ours.'

They looked up as the firework spun round and round. There was a curious whine and the firework launched into a crescendo of sparks spelling out the initials "S, M, J". The letters flashed three times, then exploded in an earth shattering BOOM that Sammy was sure shook the ground they were standing on.

'Hot dog anyone?' asked Serberon passing a handful of coins to Jason. 'Get ten Jase, we'll all have one.'

Sammy counted quickly. There were only eight of them.

'Mary-Beth's coming in a minute,' explained Serberon, 'with her best mate.' He winked at Sammy. 'Here, open your pockets, quick.'

'What?'

'Your pockets.'

Sammy did as he was told and opened his coat pockets as wide as he could. Serberon leaned close and there was a "clink-clink" as dark objects poured in.

'We de-scaled last week,' explained Serberon in a hushed whisper. 'These should be enough to win, but not enough to look like you cheated. They're scales from my dragon and Mikhael's and Jason's.'

'Wow, thank you,' said Sammy.

'That's ok, have a hot dog as well,' said Serberon, grinning as Jason returned with hot dogs stacked up to his chin.

'Thank you,' repeated Sammy.

'Yeah, ok, you'll end up like Milly in a minute!'

Sammy looked round. Milly was deep in conversation with Mary-Beth and her best friend who looked a spitting image of a grown-up Milly, right down to the green pixie boots and glittering blonde hair trailing halfway down her back.

He saw why Serberon had winked as he watched Dixie's green haired, smooth talking brother wrap an arm around the shoulders of the two girls. He led them towards Jason who was handing a second hot dog to Darius and a first to Milly and Gavin.

Sammy pulled Dixie to one side. 'Are they, y'know…'

Dixie giggled. 'No, but Serberon wants to go out with Mary-Beth and Jason wants to go out with Miranda. She's the blonde one who looks like Milly.'

'He'll have to get his hair cut,' said Sammy. 'Otherwise his hair will be as long as hers.'

Dixie giggled louder and Jason gave her a frosty stare that said, "go away".

'Come on,' said Dixie. 'Let's go over to those trees. Should be a better view of the fireworks.'

'Ok,' said Sammy.

'Where are you going?' asked Darius, his mouth full of hot dog.

'To the trees,' said Sammy as quietly as he could.

'Oooer,' said Darius. 'Don't tell Gavin, you'll never live it down.'

'Not like that stupid,' said Dixie. 'We're going so we can see the fireworks better.'

'Just fireworks,' said Sammy firmly. 'There might be some more scales as well.'

'What about them?' Darius pointed to the others.

'Leave them,' said Dixie. 'Milly will talk for hours with Miranda about hair slides. She's a right one, my Mum loves her.'

'Really?' asked Sammy.

'Yeah, she's always round our house. Mum thinks she's the perfect daughter.'

'Daughter-in-law,' said Darius giggling.

'Ugh,' Dixie screwed up her nose. 'Can you imagine that?'

Under the tall horse chestnut trees surrounding the Gymnasium, Sammy found that they were completely hidden from the view of the Dragonball pitch.

'Look,' said Dixie excitedly. 'There's another of those mega-rockets, like the one you set off!'

'Must be the end of the show,' said Darius. 'We should have come here first. It's less crowded and there's even a seat.' Darius sat down on a chopped tree stump, the size of two of the classroom chairs put together.

'Woah!' Darius leapt up as if he'd been bitten. 'It's alive!'

The tree stump was visibly shuddering.

'Hide!' shouted Sammy, his voice drowned out by tumultuous applause from the Dragonball pitch.

They ran to a large knotted and gnarled tree and stood in its shadow, as still as statues.

'It's moving,' whispered Dixie. 'Look, there's something coming out!'

As if opening a box, the top of the tree stump flipped open. It reminded Sammy of the trapdoor at Mrs Grock's. The lid blocked their view, but they could hear muffled voices from somewhere within the tree stump.

'Is it clear?' came a cold, rasping voice that made Sammy shiver.

'Yes,' said a second voice that sounded vaguely familiar. 'I told you, after the last firework, they will return to the castle. The students will go to their towers and the professors to their chambers. The castle and the grounds will be clear.'

'Good,' said the rasping voice. 'You have researched this well.'

'Hopefully better than the last time,' came a third voice. 'That was too close for my liking.'

'And mine,' said the rasping voice with what Sammy took to be distorted laughter. 'I will go first.'

From behind the tree Sammy peered into the darkness, desperate to catch a glimpse of the people as they emerged from the hole under the tree stump.

They rose up like shadows dressed all in black with dark hoods concealing their faces.

'The Shape,' whispered Sammy, his heart pounding in his chest.

Dixie was holding his arm and Darius was kneeling against the tree with his back to the figures. There were five hooded figures, each as dark as the other, almost invisible against the dark night.

One figure stiffened, sniffing the air. 'Where is the boy?'

'He was at the hot dog stall gorging himself with his friends. He'll be there until Sir Ragnarok calls them to bed.'

'Are you sure?' asked the rasping voice. 'We cannot afford to make mistakes. I am told your cover is blown.'

'I assure you my friend it is not. I showed him the stones and he will not be searching for any more.'

'Lies,' snarled the rasping voice. 'I am told he accused you to your face.'

Behind the tree, Sammy was sure his heart skipped a beat. 'We have to get out of here,' he whispered to Dixie and Darius.

Darius stood up. He threw aside the shrubbery he had used to disguise himself. 'Run for your life!'

One of the hooded figures looked up and gave an angry shout. 'Get them!'

They gave chase as Sammy, Dixie and Darius ran flat out to the now empty Dragonball pitch.

'Everyone's gone!' shrieked Dixie. 'What can we do?'

'The Gymnasium,' yelled Darius, turning to his left.

The hooded figures were so close behind them that Sammy was sure their fingertips were clutching his coat collar. He dug some of the scales Serberon had given him out of his pocket and threw them at the Shape.

The hooded figures paused for a second.

'Just scales,' said the rasping voice. 'Get them!'

Darius leapt up to the foyer door and pounded on it. 'It's locked!'

'What?'

'It's locked! This way!'

'Wait,' shouted Sammy, reaching for his staff. 'Fire!'

On command, a ball of orange flames exploded from the onyx at the end of his staff. It cannonballed between the hooded figures and gave them a precious lead as the Shape regrouped.

'The teachers' garden,' said Dixie, panting as they paused behind a large rhododendron bush. 'You go on, I've got a stitch.'

'No way,' said Sammy. 'Your stitch can wait. We'll make it.' He took Dixie's hand and set off for the walled garden.

'No,' wailed Dixie, clutching her side.

Sammy was relieved she ran as quickly as Darius. He could hear the Shape the other side of the bush. They were still after them.

At the pillared entrance of the teachers' garden, Sammy saw the grill they needed to cross to become invisible. He stepped forward and bounced back, stopped by an invisible wall.

'Password,' said a bored bodiless voice from behind the entrance. 'Give me the password to enter the teachers' garden.'

'We don't have a password,' shouted Darius, kicking the pillar in frustration.

'Karmandor,' said Sammy without thinking.

'Correct,' said the voice behind the pillar. 'Enter at will.'

'That's amazing,' said Dixie. 'How did…'

'Get inside,' shouted Darius. 'Quick!'

They pushed through the narrow gatepost. Sammy saw a small dwarf scuttle behind one of the picnic benches. Even though he knew they couldn't be seen, Sammy crouched behind one of the pillars, huddled as close to the wall as he could.

Dixie and Darius crouched beside him, holding their breath as the Shape stepped closer.

'They are around here somewhere,' said the rasping voice. 'There is nowhere for them to go.'

'What about in there?'

'The teachers' garden? Impossible. It is guarded securely. No student may enter without the password.'

'To my knowledge no student has ever cracked the code.'

'Not even that boy?'

'He has the making of a Dragon Knight.'

'Hah,' said the rasping voice. 'We'll go this way. We have what we came for.'

'The third stone. Just two to go, then we can make your potion.'

'And become immortal, once and forever.'

'Our work will be done when the school closes,' said the rasping voice. 'Let us go back, retrace our steps. I would be happier with those three out of the way.'

When the hooded figures were out of sight and their footsteps had died away Sammy peered out between the pillars. 'They've gone,' he whispered.

They tiptoed out of the garden and didn't speak until they were safely in the North common room which was deserted, strewn with the remains of a midnight feast.

Sammy picked up a glass and poured himself some lemonade. 'That was close,' he whispered. 'Wonder what they wanted.'

'They were going to kill us,' said Dixie, her hands shaking as she picked up a plate of sandwiches.

'For what? Why?' asked Darius.

'Because we have the power to stop them,' said Sammy. 'We have the power. Don't ask me how, but I seem to be in all the right places, all the right times. Everything's happening because of me. My wish at Mrs Grock's, "put wrongs to right" that's what I wished for.'

'I wished to have friends like my brothers,' whispered Dixie, 'and look, I got you and Darius. You're the best friends I've ever had.'

Sammy looked from Dixie to Darius. 'What did you wish for?'

Darius looked sheepish. 'I wished for chocolate. A whole bar all to myself under my pillow, every day.' He laughed. 'It's getting a bit of a problem to hide it, but Nelson seems to like it so we share it.'

Sammy looked at Darius and burst out laughing. 'I thought he was growing quickly!'

Darius laughed and yawned loudly. 'Come on, there's a Dragonball match first thing tomorrow.'

'Or an extra lesson in the library to show us where to find the books,' added Dixie.

'Like that's difficult,' said Darius. 'I bet my grandparents' book room is bigger. If you can't find a book there, you won't find it anywhere. It's always in such a mess.'

'I'm going to take Kyrillan out and practice flying,' said Sammy, tidying up the plates and glasses.

'That sounds good,' said Dixie, trying to hide a yawn with the back of her hand. 'Let's do that.'

'We'll meet here tomorrow morning after breakfast. I'll see if Gavin, Toby and Amos want to come as well.'

'Ok. Shall I ask Milly and the others?'

Darius grinned broadly. 'Milly will come if Gavin does.'

News of the flying practice travelled fast and nearly everyone from the first year turned up in the North common room. Amos had invited Simon Sanchez at breakfast. Then Simon had invited the East first years and Tristan had overheard and invited the South and West students as well.

In the vast school grounds, there was room to spread out and in Sammy's opinion, it went really well. Outside, Kyrillan flew higher and for longer. No matter where they stood, Kyrillan would always land on Sammy's outstretched arm, then spread his wings and take off again.

To Sammy, it seemed as if the whole weekend disappeared in one long flying practice, coupled with races and competitions. Despite being new to a world with dragons, Sammy was pleased to win several races, beating even the students who had grown up with dragons in their families.

News of the flying practice travelled further and it became a regular weekend event with students further up the school often coming to watch. Before he realised, Sammy found he was firmly settled in boarding school life and it was nearly the end of November, the day before his eleventh birthday.

A large parcel had arrived that morning from his parents with strict instructions not to be opened before the 30th. Sammy had wanted to open it then and there, but Darius had persuaded him that he would appreciate it more opening it on his birthday.

Despite tapping, rattling and even kicking it lightly, Sammy had no idea what they might have sent. For his tenth birthday, he had asked for a skateboard and been given a mountain bike. He had written after Bonfire Night to ask for a Dragonball set although he knew his parents would be unlikely to know what it was, let alone where to buy one. Serberon had given him the name of a good sports shop, but Sammy was still sceptical.

At the crack of dawn on the 30th of November, Sammy awoke with a start. He remembered dreaming about flying on a larger version of Kyrillan, only to be woken by a sound like a gunshot at the start of a race.

Sammy sat bolt upright. He was sure the noise was in the room. The gunshot had been the click of the tower room door.

He pushed back the duvet and swung his legs over the side of the bed, ready to stand up. Next to him on the chest of drawers Kyrillan was already standing up, alert and ready to pounce. His scaled head was cocked towards a chink in the curtains, his bead eyes black and unblinking.

As quietly as he could, Sammy stood up and reached for his staff. His heart skipped a beat as a hand reached through the curtain. It was light skinned, gnarled with a blue-green stone set in a ring on the second finger.

'Draconite,' whispered Sammy. He gripped his staff and stepped forward.

In the bed next to him, Darius gave a loud snore. In an instant, the hand pulled back out of sight. By the time Sammy got to the curtain, the tower door had opened and shut. No matter how hard he pulled at it, the door wouldn't open.

Sammy pulled harder, wondering why it felt soft and squidgy. He snapped his eyes open. He was still in bed, the quilt pulled high over his head and his arms wrapped in the covers. He shuddered, the memory of the dream fresh in his mind.

Sammy pinched his arm to make sure he was now awake. On the chest of drawers, Kyrillan was asleep, his spiky tail curled around his feet. Sammy got up, shivering as his feet touched the stone floor and opened the curtains.

The tower door was shut and the curtains around the five beds were tightly drawn. To be absolutely certain, Sammy peeked through the edge of each curtain. Everyone was still asleep, Darius snoring gently. Sammy resisted the urge to wake him to say about the dream.

Sammy went back to the end of his bed and stroked Kyrillan who was still on edge. Just as he began to relax, there was an unmistakeable click of the tower room door. This time it was real. Sammy heard footsteps and saw a dark shadow at his curtain.

More bravely than he felt, he picked up his staff, marched to the curtain and slung it aside with a rattle of the overhead rails.

'Aaargh!' shouted Sammy, raising his staff.

Behind the curtain, Dixie screamed and dropped something that fell to the floor with a squelch.

'What are you doing?' shouted Dixie. 'Put that down!'

Sammy lowered his staff feeling very foolish. Darius and the others had woken up and were standing next to Dixie each holding a small present.

'Surprise,' said Darius in a fit of giggles. 'Dixie, you weren't supposed to drop the cake!'

'It wasn't on purpose,' snapped Dixie, kneeling down to scrape up the remains. 'Sammy jumped out at me. Look, it's ruined.'

'It'll be ok.' Sammy tried to reassure her, giggling as hard as Darius. 'Most of it landed on the plate.'

'It's ruined,' said Dixie, abandoning the remains. She scooped up some of the crumbs. 'Wait there.' She disappeared out of the tower room and clattered down the stone stairs.

The tower room filled quickly. All of the first year North girls arrived to wish Sammy a happy birthday. They broke off singing as Dixie returned with her brothers and an even larger cake.

"Wow" was the only thing everyone managed to say as they saw the size of the cake Serberon was helping Dixie to carry.

'That's awesome,' said Darius, his mouth full of cake he'd salvaged from the floor.

'You didn't have to go to so much trouble,' said Sammy, unable to take his eyes off the cake. He was sure it was growing.

'It's all right Sammy, she didn't,' said Serberon. 'We used some of Dr Shivers's Largo Oil.'

'The stuff he used to grow Goldie,' added Dixie. 'It's perfectly safe to eat. We won't turn into giants or anything.'

'Ok,' said Sammy, not entirely convinced.

Serberon laughed. 'Don't worry we've got some of his green pellets, just in case.'

Sammy didn't admit that he didn't like the sound of Serberon's "just in case" and tucked into the triple layer sponge cake.

It had already outgrown the plate that Dixie had used to carry it and although everyone in the room had taken a large slice, it continued to grow.

'How do we stop it growing?' asked Sammy, unwrapping a box of chocolates from Milly.

'Got to get rid of it entirely,' said Serberon. 'Feed it to the dragons, anything. If there's even a tiny crumb, it'll grow to this size in an hour.'

'Oh,' said Sammy having a brief vision of a giant cake squeezing them out of the tower windows.

'How do you know?' demanded Dixie. 'It hasn't stopped growing since we made it.'

Serberon simply tapped the side of his nose and winked at Jason and Mikhael. 'Our secret.'

'Tell me,' begged Dixie. 'Make him Sammy.'

Sammy laughed, knowing Mikhael would never agree. 'Help me open this parcel from my parents.'

Everyone crowded round as Sammy held the box still and Dixie pulled off the thick brown parcel tape.

Inside, there were several smaller parcels tightly packed with bubble wrap. Sammy opened a stuffed toy dragon that his parents had re-wrapped from his last birthday, a leather Meteor football, shin-pads, gloves and a large box of chocolates with "to share" handwritten on top. At the very bottom, his mother had packed several pairs of socks and some shoe polish.

'I get it,' said Serberon, howling with laughter. 'Dragon, ball, Dragonball!'

'Ugh,' groaned Sammy. 'I wish my parents understood about dragons.'

'Sometimes,' said Darius, 'I wish my parents knew nothing about them. Less pressure,' he explained with his mouth full, finishing the last of the cake.

Dixie was still asking how they knew how to stop Largo Oil in the middle of December when the castle was heavily decorated ready for Christmas. Sammy loved the long trails of holly and ivy that were growing naturally along the corridor walls. Red and green berries were intermingled with what looked like tiny fairies flying from branch to branch talking nineteen to the dozen about Christmas and presents and not caring who heard.

Sammy wanted to take one home so badly that he spent two hours one afternoon trying to entice them on to his hand. Annoyingly, the fairies danced inches from his fingers and laughed at him, daring him to catch them.

The Main Hall seemed to be where Sir Ragnarok had focussed his attention. It still had a faint smell of pumpkin from Halloween, but was now host to an indoor forest of fir trees on Sir Ragnarok's stage behind the teachers' tables.

One exceptionally tall tree had been singled out to hold a giant star on its uppermost branch. Tinsel streamed through the branches of all the trees and they were laden with lights and baubles. Underneath the tall tree with the star were many presents. Sir Ragnarok had promised that there was one small gift for every student. They would be given out at the end of term.

Despite the initial shock, Sammy found he was looking forward to spending Christmas at school as much as he had been when he had hoped to be going home. On the Wednesday before the end of term, he had been called to Professor Burlay's office to open an airmail letter from his parents.

Although brief, the letter explained that his mother was needed at work over the holiday and his father would be working unpredictable shifts. Without asking whether he wanted to go to Switzerland, they had given him the choice between staying at school and having Christmas with his grandparents. They had promised to send presents to whichever he chose.

Professor Burlay had been understanding and had let him have until the end of the day to decide. Sammy discussed the letter with Darius at lunch before they went to their last Sports lesson before Christmas.

'I'd go and stay with your grandparents,' said Darius. 'I do it all the time when my parents are away. They're a bit funny about having people around.'

'Why's that?' asked Gavin.

'Uh, no reason,' said Darius hastily. 'Just that when they're away a lot, they don't want to come home to, you know, to a mess.'

Sammy felt sure there was more to it and was about to ask when Gavin said loudly, 'well you can come and stay with me and Toby, both of you, and you Amos if you want, everyone can come and stay with us!'

Amos looked completely overwhelmed at Gavin's offer. 'It's ok, I've just been invited to have Christmas with Simon. My Mum said "yes" a few minutes ago.'

'Ok,' said Gavin, looking slightly relieved. 'Just the four of us. I'll check with my Mum later.'

'Make it three,' said Darius awkwardly. 'I, my family, we don't celebrate Christmas.' He pushed up from the table and disappeared quickly out of the Main Hall.

Professor Burlay was delighted when Sammy told him about Gavin's offer.

'That's wonderful news Sammy. With all the North students away for Christmas, I can go up there.' Professor Burlay pointed to the ceiling and Sammy understood. He would spend the two week holiday at the Floating Circus with his family.

Sammy ran back to the North tower and found it deserted. Everyone had gone to the Gymnasium to get ready for the last game of Dragonball.

Halfway through the bitterly cold lesson it began to snow. Mr Cross let them play on until a blizzard of snowflakes fell in every direction, making it almost impossible to see each other, let alone the seven Dragonballs. Mr Cross shouted across the pitch for them to come into the Gymnasium.

'Even my whistle has iced up,' complained Mr Cross, holding the foyer door open.

Sammy shivered, grateful when Mr Ockay handed round steaming mugs of hot chocolate and warm towels to huddle in.

Mr Cross used the small television on Mr Ockay's desk to show them a recorded Dragonball match. Sammy found it really distracting when he paused the match in the middle of a move to explain various rules and pointing out possible passes.

Finally, he held out the biscuit tin of jewellery and watches and sent them upstairs to get changed.

On the last day of the winter term, Sammy woke to find the school covered from top to bottom in crystallised white snowflakes. From the tower room, he could no longer see Mrs Grock's house or even make out the edge of the Dragonball pitch.

Following an enormous feast, Sir Ragnarok sent them armed with toys, books and games from their presents under the tree, to their tower rooms with instructions to pack ready to go home.

Having packed most of his possessions last night, Sammy just had to roll up his bedding and put it in the laundry bin that been placed at the top of the stairs. He fed Kyrillan small titbits be had smuggled from the feast.

Kyrillan licked his fingers and blew tiny smoke rings.

'I'm going to miss you,' whispered Sammy. 'Still, it's only for two weeks.'

He picked up his suitcase, checked that the five windows were securely closed and went down to the common room to find Gavin and Toby.

They were waiting for him by the fireplace, warming their hands in the dying flames.

'Come on!' shouted Gavin. 'Darius left ages ago. There's no school for two weeks!'

Sammy's suitcase bumped against his ankles as he ran with Gavin and Toby to meet their mother who had come to pick them up in their brand new Land Rover.

He liked the look of Mrs Reed as soon as he saw her. She reminded him of the weather women he had seen on television, bright, bubbly and friendly with the same jet black hair as Gavin and Toby.

'Come on all of you,' said Mrs Reed, or Anita as she quickly introduced herself. 'Put your cases in the boot, I made your father clean it specially. We'll be home in no time!'

Sammy watched the Dragamas castle turrets disappear in a sudden flurry of snowflakes and sat back in the comfy seats ready to enjoy his first Christmas away from both home and his parents.

CHAPTER 16

BACK TO SCHOOL

Christmas disappeared in a volley of decorations, meals, guests and parties, not to mention a most enormous Christmas tree.

Gavin and Toby's father, Graham Reed, had cut the tree himself from the small woodland that surrounded their country mansion, just a few miles from the school.

Sammy had spent most of the holiday upstairs in Gavin and Toby's room playing games whilst Anita and Graham entertained their friends from the village.

Overall, he hadn't missed his parents as much as he had expected. They had telephoned from Switzerland last thing on Christmas Eve and first thing on Christmas morning. He'd even had a stocking from Father Christmas.

After a New Year party that went on late into the following day and with the weather still bitterly cold, they had packed their suitcases and returned to Dragamas just as the light was fading. Although Sammy had enjoyed a wonderful Christmas with the Reeds, he was glad to get back to Dragamas to check on Kyrillan.

'Lessons tomorrow,' said Sammy, heaving his grey suitcase up the last of the tower stairs. 'Can't believe Christmas went so fast.'

'Me neither,' said Darius, looking enviously at the amount of presents Gavin and Toby were stuffing into their chests of drawers. 'It's nice to have the holiday, but it's hard seeing everyone else celebrate, open presents, big family meal.'

'You have other celebrations, don't you?' asked Gavin, kicking his suitcase under his bed. 'Maybe your parents will let you come and stay with us next year?'

'Maybe,' said Darius still looking gloomy, but helping himself to some Christmas tree shaped chocolates that Toby offered him.

'You'll all have to come to mine one year,' said Sammy lying down on his bed, pleased to see that Kyrillan came straight to him and licked the remains of a chocolate tree from his fingers. 'My parents should be home soon and my Mum does a great Christmas dinner, as good as your Mum's,' he added hastily to Gavin and Toby.

'Wonder how Sir Ragnarok's doing raising that money.'

Sammy sat up. It was the first time Amos had spoken since they'd been back and it hit him like a punch in the stomach. 'The money,' he whispered, annoyed amongst the celebrations he'd forgotten all about it.

'Professor Sanchez says he's raised half the money from selling diamonds from the school mines,' said Amos knowingly, 'but he can't produce the full amount without raising suspicion. Imagine if everyone knew there was a diamond mine under Dragamas!'

'Did she say how the rest will be raised?' asked Sammy, hoping Amos would have more to tell.

Whether he knew more or not, Amos wouldn't say. Infuriatingly, he tapped his nose and pulled an imaginary zip across his lips. 'That's for me to know and you to guess,' said Amos slinging his curtain around his bed for the night.

Darius pulled a face at Amos's closed curtain and Sammy shook his head. He wished Amos would make an effort to be friendly.

'Ask Professor Burlay,' said Toby. 'If you don't, I will.'

'A challenge,' said Gavin. 'See who gets the answer first.'

'Ok,' said Sammy. 'Starting now!'

'I'm going to bed,' said Toby, yawning. 'Let's start tomorrow.' Toby pulled his curtain around his bed. 'Night all.'

Sammy pulled his curtain shut and lay down on top of his quilt staring at the ceiling. Whether it was the change in routine from the holiday or the excitement of being back with his friends he didn't know, but he did know that he was finding it very, very hard to fall asleep.

Amos's words were ringing in his ears, "Sir Ragnarok has raised half the money". Sammy wondered how on earth he would raise the rest.

He reached out in the darkness and felt Kyrillan sleeping peacefully on his chest of drawers. Sammy ran his hand down Kyrillan's spiky tail and felt a cold metal object.

'The Directometer,' whispered Sammy, remembering the disc Sir Ragnarok had lent him last term.

He tickled Kyrillan's stomach until the little dragon awoke, blowing angry smoke rings at him. Sammy gripped the Directometer firmly. 'Are you thinking what I'm thinking?' he asked Kyrillan, in the Western accent he'd seen on a film over Christmas. Kyrillan blew some smoke at him and shuffled excitedly on the chest of drawers.

'Come on,' whispered Sammy getting dressed as quickly and quietly as he could.

Kyrillan lurched forward, extending and beating his wings to stay in the air. He landed perfectly at Sammy's feet.

'That's good,' whispered Sammy, pleased the practice they'd had before Christmas hadn't worn off. He held the tower door open and Kyrillan flew ahead. At the bottom of the candlelit spiral staircase, Kyrillan landed and looked at Sammy as if to say he'd done enough flying for one night.

'Come on Ky,' whispered Sammy pulling the Directometer out of his pocket. He flicked open the gold disc and spoke clearly to the screen as if it was a microphone.

'Sir Ragnarok's office, please,' said Sammy, holding the disc at arm's length.

It flashed green when he swung it towards the common room door.

'Well that's obvious,' muttered Sammy reaching for the iron handle.

The Directometer led him up a short flight of stairs hidden behind a curtain on the fourth floor and brought him out in a narrow empty corridor that Sammy was sure he'd never seen before.

At the end of the corridor, the Directometer flashed red until Sammy held it next to a large tapestry that looked similar to the one of the knight in the Main Hall. Sammy kicked himself. If he'd thought about it, he could have used the staircase behind the tapestry in the Main Hall but the Directometer seemed to have shown him a short cut.

Sammy swung the tapestry aside and saw, almost as he had expected, a large opening with steps leading up into the darkness. There was a small metal hook next to the hole and Sammy clipped the tapestry securely aside. It fitted exactly and seemed to be there for that very purpose. He jumped as Kyrillan blew an orange flame at a mouse that scuttled past them. After a moment to settle his nerves, Sammy lit a small fire himself and walked into the darkness.

The staircase was spiral and steep with no hand rail. Sammy crouched and touched each step to keep his balance. Seizing the opportunity, Kyrillan flew up to Sammy's shoulders and perched like a parrot as they wound slowly higher and higher.

Just as Sammy was about to admit defeat, he felt fabric instead of stone. Keeping the fire away as best he could, Sammy pushed against the material. It lifted against his fingers and Sammy crawled out into what looked like a second spiral staircase lit with red candles.

He put out the fire and checked the Directometer. As he expected, it went red when he held it down and green when he pointed it upwards. Sammy looked up. Through narrow gap between the stairs and the central column, he could see a door that he recognised.

He paused for just a second to catch his breath and let Kyrillan down, then he ran up the twenty or so steps to Sir Ragnarok's office door.

The door opened before Sammy could knock. Sir Ragnarok's smoky grey cat, Lariston, was there staring at him with large yellow eyes. Apparently satisfied, Lariston twisted round, tail erect and marched up the seven steps to Sir Ragnarok's office.

Sammy helped Kyrillan up the steps and followed Lariston into the circular office. The room was empty, but the Directometer indicated that Sir Ragnarok was somewhere up the spiral staircase next to the sofa. Sammy guessed it led to Sir Ragnarok's private bedroom and didn't like to follow it.

'Sir Ragnarok?' Sammy called hesitantly up the spiral stairs.

Lariston wound himself around Sammy's legs and gave Kyrillan a disapproving stare, as if to say that dragons were not permitted in his master's quarters.

'Be down in a second, Sammy.' Sir Ragnarok's disembodied voice came down the iron stairwell. 'Make yourself at home.'

'I..er..,' stuttered Sammy, wondering how on earth Sir Ragnarok could possibly know it was him and not any one of the other hundreds of people who taught, learned at, or serviced the school and its grounds.

Sammy sat on the purple three seat sofa. Kyrillan curled up at his feet and Lariston jumped up beside Sammy and settled in his lap, purring as Sammy smoothed his glossy coat.

From the comfortable sofa, Sammy looked at the monitoring screens. They were divided into several miniature screens, each with a different view of the castle. In the top left, he saw his North tower room with Gavin, Toby, Darius and Amos fast asleep. Next to Darius, Sammy saw his own bed, unmade and empty.

Sammy felt a little guilty about not being there. He wondered whether Professor Burlay would check the room and notice he wasn't there. Checking through the other screens while he waited, Sammy saw Mrs Grock's house in the school grounds.

He was relieved to see Professor Burlay and Mrs Grock sitting together on the sofa in front of her fireplace. They appeared to be reading from one of Mrs Grock's library of rare and mysterious books. Sammy half wished Sir Ragnarok's monitors had sound as well as pictures. He stood up, moving Lariston gently aside, and went to take a closer look.

'Ahem,' coughed a voice behind him.

Sammy turned round. Sir Ragnarok was at the bottom of his bedroom stairs dressed in a long purple and silver dressing gown.

'Perhaps there are some things that should not be seen by one so young.' With a wave of Sir Ragnarok's hand the screens went blank.

'I, er, I wasn't...'

'I know.' Sir Ragnarok smiled, wrinkling his lined forehead. 'I was the very same at your age, at these very windows too. My days at Dragamas are long ago, but the memories are as fresh as yesterday.'

Sir Ragnarok rolled back his sleeves revealing thin, weathered but muscular arms. 'So,' he asked kindly, 'what may I do for you this evening, Sammy? Do you have news for me, or do I have news for you?'

Unprepared for Sir Ragnarok's way of addressing his questions, Sammy was at a loss.

'I came to ask,' said Sammy, the idea of approaching Sir Ragnarok in the middle of the night felt much worse than when he had rehearsed it on his way up to the office. 'I, er, came to ask about the money – for the Shape – to save the school – Amos said Professor Sanchez...'

'Aha!' interrupted Sir Ragnarok, eyes blazing and his face like thunder. 'Professor Sanchez has revealed what exactly?'

He looked so fierce that Sammy stood there wishing he hadn't come. Lariston wound his warm body around Sammy's legs, both comforting and mesmerising him.

'Amos said you have only raised half of the money.'

'Sometimes Sammy,' said Sir Ragnarok, 'the naming of names is not so important. I shall speak with Professor Sanchez, ask her to show some discretion with regards to the school's private affairs.'

'So it's true?' asked Sammy, his voice shaking as much as his knees. 'Without the ransom, Dragamas will close.'

'Over my dead body!' spat Sir Ragnarok. 'She knows full well we have three quarters of the money saved already. However,' Sir Ragnarok thundered, 'I do not propose to pay the ransom!'

Sammy heard his knees clack together, his eyes wide open.

Sir Ragnarok noticed. 'Sit my friend. Eat some chocolate and calm your nerves. I should be more careful. I have frightened you.'

Sammy sank into the deep sofa and pulled Kyrillan on to his lap. Sir Ragnarok handed Sammy the bowl of coloured sweets taking a handful back to his desk where he perched and eyed Sammy with his keen blue eyes. Sammy took a green sweet from the ceramic bowl and unwrapped it slowly.

'Now,' said Sir Ragnarok, 'it is your turn. You didn't climb all this way in the middle of the night for nothing. What news do you have for me?' Sir Ragnarok cocked one of his bushy grey eyebrows in anticipation.

'Why,' asked Sammy, trying to clear the sticky sweet from where it had gripped his teeth, 'aren't you going to pay the ransom?'

Sir Ragnarok leaned back and twisted his hands. 'A good question, but I was hoping you would have the answers for me. If I can get to the Shape first, I will disable them so that they leave our dragons alone,' he explained. 'You do have some news, don't you, else why would you risk being caught out of bed by your housemaster?'

'It was Toby's idea,' said Sammy, remembering too late not to mention names. 'Amos wouldn't tell us if it was true that you didn't have enough money, so we set a challenge to see who could find out first.'

'And here you are,' finished Sir Ragnarok, his eyes creasing as he chuckled. 'Was the answer as you had hoped?'

'It's much better. You have three quarters of the money with half the year to go.'

'Alas,' Sir Ragnarok frowned, 'we cannot filter any more diamonds through the shop in the village. Captain Stronghammer had to answer some difficult questions over the holiday. It was only on my intervention he was able to return.'

'Oh,' said Sammy, thinking how else the money could be raised. 'What about the draconite?'

'Never,' said Sir Ragnarok firmly. 'Give the Shape what they want? Oh they would love to see me kill a large number of dragons to fund their ransom. It would be like doing their dirty work for them.'

'So they want the dragons dead?' whispered Sammy. 'They would like it better if you killed all the dragons, and then...'

'Paid them for me to do it! No thank you,' said Sir Ragnarok reaching behind him and taking a jug and two glasses from a hidden cupboard. 'Do you have any idea who may be involved with the Shape? I understand you have run into them on more than one occasion.'

'Well,' said Sammy, accepting a glass of blood red juice. He took a small sip. It was cold and very bitter. 'Eeugh, what's this?'

'Just a small concoction,' said Sir Ragnarok, staring at him. 'Professor Sanchez created it. It reacts with your blood and might come in handy.'

'For what?' asked Sammy, feeling groggy and light-headed. His eyes burned and he thought his head was going to explode. The room spun round and round and he passed out.

When he came to, Sammy found he was still in Sir Ragnarok's office and Kyrillan was still in his lap. The only difference was the clock. It showed that twenty minutes had passed.

'What was that?' asked Sammy sitting upright.

'In what?' Sir Ragnarok mildly, as though nothing had happened. 'Just juice. I take a glass sometimes before bed. Helps me sleep.'

Still groggy, Sammy remembered Sir Ragnarok asking him for news. It swum in his mind as he remembered Professor Burlay telling him to find evidence.

'Dr Lithoman,' said Sammy out loud. 'I'm sure she's involved.'

Captivating Sir Ragnarok's full attention, Sammy told his headmaster of the events in the classroom, at Halloween and Bonfire Night.

When he had finished, Sir Ragnarok stood up. 'Very well,' he said in a brisk, business-like manner, 'I will take this up first thing in the morning. Thank you Sammy. If you are right, this could be just the link I was looking for.'

'Please don't tell Professor Burlay I told you about Dr Lithoman,' said Sammy feeling suddenly anxious. 'He said I needed evidence before I told anyone, but she has draconite in her room under the West tower.'

'Aha!' said Sir Ragnarok. 'That's good, very good. Perhaps I shouldn't find out how you got there, but very good boy, very good.'

'But!' exclaimed Sammy, desperate to tell Sir Ragnarok that Dr Lithoman had insisted she show it to him. Sir Ragnarok seemed oblivious as he scribbled notes in a book on his desk.

'Sir, may I go back to the North tower?'

'Ah yes,' said Sir Ragnarok looking up. 'Thank you for your help.' He seemed to switch back to his headmaster voice. 'Back to bed indeed. I hope you enjoy this term as much as the last. We have another land coming soon. It should be a nice break for the fifth years after their preliminary exams.'

Sammy pricked up his ears and Sir Ragnarok seemed to notice. 'Oh I see, another piece of news for your friends. Very well, since you have given me the best news in a long while I will tell you. It will be the Land of the Pharaohs. I'll say no more, I don't want to spoil the surprise.'

Thinking Darius would love the sound of the Land of the Pharaohs, Sammy nodded, his eyes shining. 'That sounds awesome!'

'On another note,' said Sir Ragnarok frowning slightly. 'Perhaps I could have the Directometer back. I keep getting lost, you know how it is.'

'Ok.' Sammy reluctantly handed over the disc. 'How will I find my way back?' he asked, hoping Sir Ragnarok might change his mind.

'Trust your dragon,' said Sir Ragnarok, smiling at the blue-green dragon. 'He is wise and will guide you back safely.'

'Thank you,' said Sammy, standing up. Kyrillan uncurled himself and flew to the top of the stairs.

'Strong and wise,' said Sir Ragnarok thoughtfully, as though Sammy was no longer in his office. 'That's what Kyrillan means. Strong and wise.'

'Strong and wise,' muttered Sammy, some ten minutes later as he retraced his steps for the third time in the same corridor. 'We'll have to work on that!'

The next morning Sammy went down to the Gemology classroom with the rest of the class. Dr Lithoman was nowhere to be seen.

After nearly five minutes, everyone started looking around the room whispering and gossiping about where she could be.

Sammy had a nasty feeling that her disappearance was caused by his late night meeting with Sir Ragnarok. Dr Lithoman hadn't been at breakfast, nor had she woken the students in the West tower. In fact, no one seemed to have seen her since yesterday afternoon.

In notes passed under the table Sammy told Dixie and Darius about his visit to Sir Ragnarok's office. Sammy found his bad feeling intensified greatly when Dixie wrote back saying "uh oh" and Darius passed him a note saying Professor Burlay would probably take over.

Sure enough at seven minutes past nine, Professor Burlay walked into the classroom. He caught a paper plane deftly in one hand and screwed it into a ball.

'No games please,' said Professor Burlay pushing his hair out of his eyes. 'Take out your books and turn to page 400. You should see a table of gemstones and their supposed healing properties. Copy down the entire table and commit it to memory.'

Professor Burlay sat in Dr Lithoman's chair and took out a set of red, green and blue pens. 'As quietly as possible please, I have a headache this morning and a mountain of books to mark.'

'Can I share your book,' Darius whispered.

'Sure,' said Dixie on autopilot. Darius had forgotten his books from the Christmas holiday and was waiting for his parents to send them by post.

'The whole table?' groaned Sammy under his breath. 'There must be at least a thousand here.'

'She's got it in for you,' said Dixie. 'You'll probably get a low mark even if you get all the Gemology questions right.'

'Is this for a test?' asked Gavin leaning over.

'Who knows,' said Sammy. 'She may not even be coming back.'

'Why? What's she done?' asked Toby. Toby's eyes grew round as Dixie told the North table as quietly as possible. 'She never?'

Sammy nodded. 'Sir Ragnarok thinks so too.'

'Good,' said Gavin, snapping his Gemology book shut. 'If she's not coming back, we don't need to bother with this!'

'Then you have spoken too soon,' said a cold voice from the passage doorway. Dr Lithoman stepped into the classroom. 'You,' she pointed at Gavin, 'will start from a minus mark, minus five shall we say? Then we'll see how good you are.'

Professor Burlay packed his books away. 'That's a little harsh Margarite. They should all start equally.'

Dr Lithoman fingered the blue-green beads around her neck, her hands wrapped in flesh coloured bandages. 'This is my lesson,' she snapped. 'It makes no difference – my fishies will always come out on top. They understand the art of Gemology, not your ridiculous out-dated star rubbish. Tell me Professor Burlay, when did you last do any night navigation or predict a star pattern correctly?'

The class turned to Professor Burlay but he firmly ignored Dr Lithoman's bait. 'I'll be going now, Margarite. If they start unfairly, Sir Ragnarok will hear of it.'

Dr Lithoman stuck her tongue out at Professor Burlay's back as he left the underground classroom armed with his books and marking pens. 'Basement's the best place for her,' he muttered just out of Dr Lithoman's hearing.

Dr Lithoman waited for the click of the classroom door then she smiled and drew a chart on the blackboard.

'My fishies, you will start on twenty points,' announced Dr Lithoman. 'South and East on ten points and North shall start on minus five. Taking it in turns, write a gemstone on the board, spelling it correctly, and tell the class what you have learnt about the wonderful gemstones and their magnificent healing properties.'

Dr Lithoman paused for breath and handed out sticks of coloured chalk. 'Gemstones were used first by the ancients, then by the Dark Ages, then our generation and they will be used for many generations to come.'

Samantha Trowt, a large faced girl with twin mouse brown plaits and thick glasses, from the West house went first.

'Onyx,' said Samantha Trowt, 'is famous for its protection properties, especially when...'

Sammy didn't wait to hear what Onyx could do. At the first strike of the classroom bell, he, Dixie and Darius had packed up and were running out of the classroom hotly pursued by Gavin, Toby and Milly.

'No extra work!' shouted Gavin punching the air. 'I didn't know you could run that fast Milly!'

'Humph,' said Milly straightening her hairband. 'What's next?'

'Dragon Studies,' said Sammy grinning hard. It was his favourite lesson and Milly's worst. She frequently said she hated it as much as Dragonball.

'Ugh,' said Milly predictably. 'I suppose we have to get our dragons.'

CHAPTER 17

KYRILLAN GOES MISSING

In the North common room, they split up, the girls using their staircase to the girls' tower and the boys into theirs.

Sammy was last into the tower room, ready with a come-back for the usual comment that he was slow to climb the last flight of stairs between the fourth and fifth floors. It never came and Sammy peered around the tower room door to check they were still there.

Inside the four boys turned to look at him, each silent and ghostly white. Darius pointed and Sammy followed his hand, the words drying up in his mouth.

'What happened?' asked Sammy, his voice husky and unfamiliar. 'Who's trashed my stuff?'

He walked past Gavin and Darius surveying the room.

'No one else's stuff's been touched.' Sammy bit his lip, close to tears as he pulled the shredded curtain aside. 'No,' he whispered as he took in the full extent of the damage. His clothes had been pulled out of the drawers, his glass of bedtime water spilt on the top, soaking his Christmas photos and leftover sweets. The bedding was torn and there were nasty trails of red stretching from the pillows to the foot of the bed.

'Where's Kyrillan?' whispered Sammy, dragging the torn bedding into the middle of the room. 'They can trash my stuff, but not my dragon!' Sammy sank to the floor clutching his head in both hands. He pushed away Darius's handkerchief and the handful of sweets Toby tried to give him.

'I'll get Professor Burlay,' said Amos. 'Wait here. Don't touch anything. He needs to see this.'

'I'll come with you,' said Gavin, looking awkwardly at anything except Sammy.

'Ok,' said Amos disappearing out of the room. 'We'll be quick.'

They arrived within a few minutes with Professor Burlay two steps behind them.

'Oh my,' said Professor Burlay as he saw the room. 'What a terrible thing.' He scooped up the torn bedding and examined it closely. 'Not to worry Sammy,' he said overly cheerfully, 'we'll have this straightened up in no time. Dry your eyes Sammy, it's going to be fine.'

Sammy sniffed loudly and wiped his eyes on the back of his hand. 'Kyrillan's gone,' he said, his voice still not sounding normal. 'They've taken my dragon.'

Professor Burlay helped Sammy to his feet. 'I'm sure he's safe. The windows are open, he could easily be in the grounds. I'll ask Tom Sweep and Captain Stronghammer to keep an eye out.'

'But Professor…' started Gavin.

Professor Burlay held up his hand. 'Enough. I'll request for this to be cleaned up, wash all your clothes and bring you fresh bedding. It'll be back to normal in no time. What lesson do you have next?'

'Dragon Studies,' said Gavin quietly.

'Oh, uh, I see,' said Professor Burlay. 'Well, I don't think it's a good idea for you to go Sammy. Take an early lunch with one housemate. Darius, perhaps you would accompany Sammy. I'll explain to Dr Shivers what's happened.'

'Thank you,' said Sammy, really meaning it. Professor Burlay might not be the best of housemasters, but he had certainly come to the rescue.

At the end of the Dragon Studies lesson, Sammy and Darius were still sitting in the tower room when Gavin, Toby and Amos came back with their dragons and a big bag of sweets from Dr Shivers.

'We won,' said Gavin handing out the foil wrapped confectionery. 'We collected nearly ten thousand more scales than anyone else. You should have seen Amos's face. It turns out he was hoping Professor Sanchez would descale her dragons over Christmas, but she didn't!'

'You have mine,' said Sammy pushing the sweets to Toby and Amos. 'I know you weren't in our group, but I don't want anything to eat, ever.'

'You'll find him,' said Toby sitting on the freshly made bed with his dragon, Puttee, in his lap.

'I doubt it, the cleaning lady said it was blood,' said Sammy gloomily.

'She was spooky,' added Darius. 'A bit like Professor Sanchez, but five hundred years older!'

'Wow!' said Toby. 'I always wondered how they…uh, never mind. So, is she sure it's Kyrillan's blood? Was it from defending himself?'

Sammy shook his head. 'Don't know, but the window's been open all day. There's a chance he could've squeezed through.'

'Let's go outside and look!'

'Already done that,' said Darius. 'There's no sign of him anywhere.'

Toby was persistent. 'Come on, you might have missed something.' He stood up and marched to the tower door with Gavin and Darius.

'Is anything else missing?'

'Only my dragon,' Sammy snapped at Amos and regretted it. 'Sorry. No nothing else, just Kyrillan.'

'I'm sorry,' said Amos. 'Really.'

'Come on!' Toby's voice came up the stairs.

'One last look,' said Sammy heaving himself up. 'Just a second,' he shouted down to Toby.

Amos stayed with him as Sammy stuffed the clean clothes back into his chest of drawers and righted his photo frame. Under the photo, there was a soggy piece of paper with "where is it" and a sketch of a disc scratched in black pen.

'What's that?' asked Amos.

'Nothing,' said Sammy, the attack on his possessions making sense. Someone knew Sir Ragnarok had lent him the Directometer and they didn't like the thought that he could track them.

'Come on Sammy,' said Amos, a little impatiently. 'Tidy up later else we won't have time to look for Kyrillan before lunch.'

Sammy jerked around. 'I can't. I've got to go somewhere. Save me a seat!'

'Where? I'll come with you.'

'No, it's ok,' said Sammy sweeping his new curtains around the rail. 'I'll only be a minute and it may not be worth it.'

'If you insist.' Amos shrugged and gave Sammy a weak smile. 'Hope you find him.'

Sammy arrived in the Main Hall as the apple pie and chocolate sponge cake deserts were being passed along the lunch tables. He sat between Dixie and Darius and helped himself to a giant sized slice of chocolate sponge and poured a large dollop of custard from the jug nearest him.

'Where have you been?' asked Darius. 'Amos said to save you a seat. You missed the main course.'

'Chicken, broccoli and mushroom pie,' said Gavin screwing his face up, 'or vegetable bake.'

Sammy grinned. 'Guess what!'

Noticing his grin, Darius guessed. 'You found Kyrillan?'

'Yep,' said Sammy cramming a huge spoonful of cake into his mouth. 'Yow! Custard! Hot!' he explained opening his mouth to let the steam out. 'That's better.' Aware everyone at the table was waiting for him, Sammy poured a glass of cold water from the green ceramic jug and took a long sip. 'Remember I said Dr Lithoman killed those dragons?'

Dixie nodded. 'Yeah, Professor Burlay said not to mention that. He said you need to get evidence.'

'That's why she tried to get my Directometer,' said Sammy.

'Your what?' asked Milly.

Gavin nudged her, anxious to hear the story. 'Go on!'

'With the Directometer,' Sammy explained, 'I could say the name of anyone, anything or anywhere and it would take me there. Red for the wrong way, green for the right way.'

'Is that how you found Kyrillan?' asked Darius, a spoonful of apple pie paralysed halfway from the bowl to his mouth.

'No, I took it back last night.'

'What did you do that for?' asked Toby. 'We could've had fun with that.'

'I asked Sir Ragnarok about the money. He's actually got three quarters of it.'

Amos nodded, eager for Sammy to continue. 'So how did you find Kyrillan?'

'Well,' said Sammy taking a deep breath. 'I knew that I'd told Sir Ragnarok about Dr Lithoman, so I guessed he'd spoken to her this morning. She missed most of Gemology, remember. It makes sense she'd want to…'

'Teach you a lesson,' said Gavin gripping the table so hard his knuckles went white. 'She must've gone up to our tower straight after he spoke to her.'

'Wait,' said Milly in a shrill "you don't know for sure" voice, 'you don't have any proof.'

'I do.' Sammy took the note out of his pocket. 'It was taped to my photo.'

Milly peered distastefully at the soggy paper. 'That's not her writing, I should know, she keeps writing over my work.'

'So how did you know where to find Kyrillan?' asked Darius. 'You still haven't told us.'

'Yeah,' said Sammy, enjoying the storytelling. 'It figures that if she can't kill my dragon, he's too young to have proper draconite formed and Sir Ragnarok would find out, so, where do you hide a dragon?'

'With other dragons!' shrieked Dixie. 'Oh Sammy, was he there? Under our North tower all along!'

Sammy nodded. 'Captain Stronghammer let me in. He even said Dr Lithoman had taken a baby dragon in there this morning.'

'That's why she had bandages on her hands this morning, Kyrillan must've scratched her.'

'Good,' said Dixie firmly. 'Have you told Sir Ragnarok?'

'Uh, no,' said Sammy. 'I can't do that. What if Milly's right and it's not her?'

'But you said Captain Stronghammer said...'

'Tell Professor Burlay,' said Darius matter of factly. 'He'll know what to do.'

'Maybe,' considered Sammy. 'Perhaps it'll be enough of a shock when she goes to the dragon chambers and Kyrillan isn't there.'

Darius giggled and waved his arms like Dr Lithoman. He put on a high pitched mimic voice to impersonate their Gemology teacher.

'Oh my, oh my, where is the dragon! Dukey, Du...' but Darius couldn't carry on, he was giggling too hard, along with the rest of the North first years.

The laughter died away as Professor Burlay strode over and frowned at them.

'Keep it down will you? I'll take some stars if I have to come over again. Oh, and Sammy, I have some good news for you.'

Sammy looked up.

'Sir Ragnarok has traced your dragon. He's under the North tower would you believe?'

Sammy nodded. 'I know, I've got him back.'

Professor Burlay took a step back, his mouth slightly open. 'What, how? No don't tell me, I probably shouldn't know. I'm glad you have him back. Did they fix your room?'

'Yes,' said Sammy, grinning at Professor Burlay. 'I've got new curtains and won't have to do any laundry for a week!'

Professor Burlay laughed. 'That's good Sammy. It'll give you extra time to learn your Astronomics. Don't forget you have exams at the end of the year and some of you could do with putting in a little extra effort I fancy.'

Milly adjusted her hair clips as Professor Burlay left. 'He's always picking on me,' she groaned.

Gavin laughed. 'Not as much as Mr Cross!'

'Ugh,' groaned Milly, 'do we really have to go outside? It's still really cold, and windy.'

After lunch, the first years assembled in the centre of the Dragonball pitch, next to the golden dragon statue. In his navy shorts and short sleeved shirt, Sammy was freezing.

Mr Cross wore his usual navy tracksuit with the zip done right up to the neck. He refused to acknowledge the cold and insisted everyone would warm up in due course. He had brought with him a bundle of sticks that looked like firewood and a small wooden box. Several students stepped back as he tipped some bright pink tennis ball sized objects out of the wooden box.

Mr Cross kicked the pink balls aside and reached into the bundle of sticks. 'Firesticks,' he said, a little muffled as he bent over, 'is as popular as Dragonball, played the world over, just without the dragons.'

'Yay!' said Milly, receiving harsh looks from Gavin, Toby and Dixie.

'We'll do a quick warm up, some star jumps, then I'll hand out the firesticks.'

Sammy took a close look at the "firestick" that Mr Cross held outstretched. It looked like a hockey stick, except there were two curls at the end, like a "w" shape with the long stick handle coming out of the middle hump.

'More advanced players have been known to use their staffs as firesticks,' said Mr Cross. 'However, since one or two inevitably get broken along the way, I would prefer to keep in Commander Altair's good books and keep your staffs in tip top condition for your lessons. Three laps of the pitch please!'

Sammy was first back from the warm up, legs stinging and teeth chattering from the cold. Mr Cross handed him one of the wooden sticks. It was quite old and a little battered. Someone had carved their initials in the top but it had worn away and could have been "C.R." or "G.B", Sammy didn't know.

'Hold your firestick like this,' Mr Cross showed him the correct grip. 'One hand at the top for control, the other half way down for power.'

Sammy copied the grip and practised hitting imaginary balls while the others finished the warm up.

'One stick per player,' said Mr Cross when everyone was back. 'Four teams of ten. I have coloured bibs if you don't want to play in houses.' He threw a pile of coloured vests amongst the first years. Since they were blue, green, yellow and red, most students, including Sammy, picked their house colour.

Tristan swapped with Naomi to play on the green team and Amos swapped with Matthew Iris, a tall boy from East, to be on Simon Sanchez's team.

'Good,' said Mr Cross, taking notes of the teams. 'Choose a captain please. Captains, collect some pink balls. They're the easiest because they roll better.

'Ok, I'm captain,' said Gavin. Before Toby could argue, Gavin was back with a handful of pink balls.

'When you get better, we'll play with the purple ones,' continued Mr Cross. 'Maybe in the fifth year you'll be ready for these,' he held up a black ball that flashed in and out of sight. 'Ah yes, the Invisiball,' Mr Cross rubbed his chin, 'reminds me of my first real injury, a broken jaw. I might throw it in at the end if you get the hang of it.'

Sammy stared at the black ball. It appeared and vanished so fast, he couldn't see how it was possible to play with it.

'To the four corners please,' said Mr Cross. 'To score, the ball must land in the dragon's mouth. The balls will be fired back at random, so watch out!'

Mr Cross took a stopwatch out of his pocket and ran to the side of the pitch. He blew his ear piercing whistle to start the match.

Despite the cold, Sammy found Firesticks as much fun as Dragonball. He ran forward with one of the pink balls close to the end of his stick. He dodged past Amos and thumped the ball towards the dragon statue's mouth. The ball ricocheted away and he ran after it.

'Right!' yelled Mr Cross from the top corner. 'I'll start scoring now. Tackle each other and stop the other teams from getting points. One point per goal!'

The game got a little violent as Dixie was struck on the shoulder by a flying pass between two boys in red bibs.

'Oi!' yelled Dixie. Forgetting the game, she thumped the ball back at them.

'Five – Five – Four – Two!' shouted Mr Cross. 'Red, yellow, green, blue respectively.'

'Come on!' roared Gavin. 'We can't let Amos's team win.'

Sammy found he really got the hang of Firesticks and was disappointed when Mr Cross blew his whistle to call them back to the central dragon. He read the notes he'd made on each player in turn, picking Sammy up on a few bad passes.

Mr Cross finished the lesson showing the class the correct way to hold their firesticks and handed out leaflets for a local sports company called Excelsior Sports Supplies.

The leaflets had pictures and prices for a large range of sports equipment including pads for almost every part of the body. There were pictures of knee pads, elbow pads, shin guards, gum guards, helmets with optional visors and padded gloves.

On the back was a full colour picture of Excelsior's new firestick range of metal sticks that promised to be more powerful than wooden sticks and were better suited to the long range passes needed in outdoor play.

Back in the common room, Sammy poured over his leaflet, picking out his favourite gloves and gum guard.

'I've never heard of Firesticks,' he admitted to Dixie who was sitting closest to him. 'Where's it played and how come it's never on T.V.?'

Dixie looked puzzled. 'Sure it is. It's all my brothers ever watch – Firesticks, Dragonball and more Firesticks. They used to want to be like Nitron Dark. He's a world famous player.'

'Is not!' argued Gavin. 'He's had it. My Dad reckons Suberlo Jenks is ten times better than him.'

'Hah!' retorted Dixie. 'Suberlo Jenks isn't even half as good.'

'Is that the name of the team?' asked Sammy, confused by the apparent knowledge of all the first years, apart from Naomi and Helena who seemed to be as much in the dark as he was.

Gavin laughed. 'No, Suberlo Jenks is a Firesticks player, the best in the world!'

'Is sooo not,' said Dixie. 'You know nothing about Firesticks! Next you'll be saying Martinez Vancuez and the Grey Eagles will win this season!'

'Yeah right,' said Gavin sarcastically. 'The Nitromen will probably win.'

'That's Nitron Dark's team,' whispered Dixie. 'They're ten points ahead for the cup. It'll be the twelfth time in a row if they win this one. The final is just before Easter and they're guaranteed to be in it after they knocked out Batwing Joe.'

'Who?' asked Sammy, astonished at the spiel.

'Well that's not his real name,' admitted Dixie. 'He got the nickname when he was at school because of his long arms and baggy jumpers. The name stuck and everyone calls him that. He used to play for Sub-Nation, Suberlo Jenks's team. Without him, the Red Bulls are nothing. They lost to the Nitromen by eight points to seventy-two!'

'Cool,' said Sammy. 'How come you know so much about it?'

'Yeah,' demanded Gavin. 'Most girls aren't interested, but I bet you could write a book.'

'Maybe,' said Dixie, looking like she was giving the idea some serious thought. 'It's because of my brothers, it's practically all they talk about at home. They're hoping to get chosen for the Woodland Ranchers, our local team.'

'Really?' asked Gavin. 'You must live quite close to us. The Woodland Ranchers is our local team too.'

'Yeah,' added Toby. 'We've been to some of their home games with our Dad.'

'Wow,' said Dixie. 'I've never been to a match. It's only a few minutes walk to the entrance from home, or you can squeeze through the garden hedge when security aren't looking.'

'Your house backs on to the Ranchers training ground?' asked Gavin. 'That's so cool!'

Dixie shrugged. 'Not when the balls smash the dining room windows. One nearly landed in my Sunday lunch. Serb, Mik and Jase each got season tickets as an apology, but that was a long time ago.'

'Sounds fun,' said Sammy as the evening bell rang. 'Nothing that exciting happens where I live.'

'Must be nice,' said Dixie, 'peaceful.'

Professor Burlay came up to the boys' tower room just before ten o'clock. 'Is everything ok now Sammy?'

Sammy checked Kyrillan snoozing on the top of his wooden chest of drawers and nodded.

'Yes Sir,' he replied, just hearing the tower door click shut before he fell asleep.

Next morning at breakfast, the school was buzzing with excitement. Someone in the fifth year had overheard Professor Sanchez talking to Professor Burlay about preparations for taking the students to the latest land to arrive above the school.

'Land of the Pharaohs,' said Toby grinning from ear to ear. All the North first years knew about what Sir Ragnarok had said to Sammy in his office.

'More than one Pharaoh,' added Dixie, her eyes sparkling.

'That's awesome,' said Darius. 'My parents are always visiting places with that kind of stuff.'

'What kind of stuff?' asked Sammy, buttering himself a thick slice of toast.

'Pyramids, ancient things, mummies,' said Darius in a spooky voice.

'Creepy,' muttered Milly. 'We don't have to go inside, do we?'

'Dunno,' said Darius. 'They brought me back a really old plate last time, belonged to some king hundreds and hundreds of years ago.'

'Look,' said Dixie pointing to the tapestry at the side of the room. 'Here's Sir Ragnarok. Hopefully he'll announce it today.'

Dressed in his usual dark gown, Sir Ragnarok marched between the tables dropping a pile of leaflets into the hands of the head boy and girl of each house.

'Good morning, good morning,' said Sir Ragnarok in an unusually cheerful voice. 'One leaflet each and pass them on.'

By the time the leaflets reached Sammy's table, they were more than a little crumpled and Sir Ragnarok had started talking.

'You will notice there are several differences between this land and the Floating Circus,' said Sir Ragnarok. 'As the third years and above will know, the Land of the Pharaohs is not necessarily as safe as the Floating Circus. After last time, I must insist that you each receive your parents' permission to be allowed to go.'

The hall erupted with loud groans and boos.

'Yes,' said Sir Ragnarok firmly. 'Even the fifth years must have permission. There will be no excuses and no exceptions.'

'What happened last time?' Sammy asked Dixie who was sitting opposite him.

'Someone got trapped and a pyramid collapsed. It was someone in my brothers' year, a boy from East. I think he was called Paul Preverence.'

'Really?' asked Gavin. 'What happened to him?'

'No one knows,' said Dixie. 'Serberon thinks he got crushed, but there's a rumour he got out but they never found him.'

'Dead or alive,' said Darius. 'My parents definitely have to let me go! Imagine all those pyramids, the ruins will be amazing.'

'Good to see you're all so interested,' said Professor Burlay, coming up to the table with a piece of jammy toast in his hand. 'If you would like to go, I'll need your permission slips after the Easter holiday.'

'No problem,' said Darius keenly. 'Is it true someone died on the last visit?'

'That's right Darius. That's why your parents have been sent letters to send the permission slips back to Sir Ragnarok. He is aware that some of you may be happy to, ahem, forge your parents' signatures. Yes, Sammy?'

'Will Sir Ragnarok have my parents' new address? They're in Switzerland at the moment. I'm not going to see them until the summer.'

'I'm sure he has, Sammy. You received your invitation to the school, didn't you?'

'Yes, but they've moved since then,' said Sammy, frustrated that Professor Burlay had already moved up to the second year table.

'You'll get it,' Dixie reassured him.

'Yeah,' said Darius. 'My parents move around all the time and they'll get theirs.'

'Oh,' said Sammy, feeling a little better. 'By post?'

'Yeah stupid!' said Darius, laughing at him.

'Or Sir Ragnarok will let the fifth years deliver them,' said Dixie. 'By dragon post!'

'Cool,' said Sammy, trying to picture postmen and women riding dragons. 'I wish our dragons would grow so we can do stuff like that.'

CHAPTER 18

AN EASTER SHOCK

The weeks up to Easter soon disappeared with Professor Sanchez setting them a valentine's potion that went horribly wrong. Professor Burlay carried on with the star charts, letting the first years do some night navigation through the school grounds.

He also stopped asking Sammy and Amos to come for extra study after Amos surprised everyone by gaining a rarely awarded triple A for perfect work.

The Land of the Pharaohs was just three weeks away with the Easter holiday in the middle to beg, borrow or steal a parent's golden signature to be allowed to go. Despite having three offers to stay over Easter, Sammy was gloomy, sure his parents wouldn't have received their letter.

To Dixie's disappointment, he had chosen to stay with Gavin and Toby again.

'We won't be far away,' Sammy called to Dixie as she waved to him from the back of her mother's rickety Land Rover, sandwiched between Mary-Beth and Miranda who were staying for the first week of the holiday with Serberon, Jason and Mikhael.

'Promise me you'll visit,' shouted Dixie as she was driven off. 'It's the only house in the village with three chimneys!'

'Ok,' shouted Gavin. 'See if you can get us tickets to the Ranchers!'

A few minutes later, Gavin and Toby's father, Graham Reed, arrived to pick them up in his own modern Land Rover. He helped hoist their suitcases into the boot.

'No dragons?' asked Mr Reed.

'We told you already,' said Gavin, rolling his eyes. 'We don't get to take them home until the summer.'

Sammy was relieved to see Dr Lithoman picked up by a short man he guessed must be her husband. At least she won't be able to get Kyrillan, he thought, as they sped away from the school. On the way to the Reeds' home, they listened first to his, then Gavin's, then Toby's choice of music. After listening to the same track twice in a row when Gavin accidentally-on-purpose dropped the remote control down the side of his seat, Sammy was glad to arrive at their country manor house with "Pine Ridge" written in pebbles on the lawn.

Several of the Reeds' sheep were being herded into the barn beside the house by Euan, the Reeds' farmhand. Euan was twenty and worked full time on the farm. He waved to them, before disappearing into the barn followed by at least sixty sheep and two dogs.

Mrs Reed was standing at the large front door waiting for them. She waved and came over to the Land Rover.

'Hello boys! Come and tell me how you are. Did you have a good term? Take your cases inside and we'll have some afternoon tea.'

They nodded, hustling and bustling as they dragged the heavy cases upstairs. Mrs Reed had prepared the large spare bedroom, across the hall from Gavin and Toby's separate rooms, to share just as they had at Christmas. Sammy remembered Mrs Reed being firm with Gavin when he had wanted to stay in his own room, telling them that one room meant one mess. Sammy took the bed next to the window and slid his suitcase into the space underneath.

Just as they had unpacked and changed into jeans and t-shirts, Mrs Reed called them down for some home-made lemonade and cream cakes that she had laid out in the garden.

Sammy leapt back in shock as Mrs Reed's fully grown dragon flew across the field behind the garden. It was jet black and looked like a small aeroplane as it came into land. It blew a cloud of smoke at Sammy and seemed annoyed to see him again.

'Don't worry Sammy,' said Mrs Reed. 'She'll get used to you soon enough.'

Sammy rubbed the soot out of his eyes. He wasn't so sure.

Gavin and Toby belted down their lemonade and disappeared into the house to fetch Toby's Dragonball set.

'Have you heard from your parents?' asked Mrs Reed. 'Is your mother enjoying her new job?'

'I think so,' said Sammy, nervous at talking to Gavin and Toby's mother alone. 'I had a letter from them at the end of term,' he reached into his pocket for the paper. 'They sent you a cheque to cover things while I'm here.'

'They didn't have to do that Sammy, it's a pleasure, really it is…oh how very generous. I must write and thank them.' She smiled at him, 'we'll make sure your Easter is special Sammy. It's not long until you'll see them in the summer.'

'I know,' said Sammy, feeling a twinge of homesickness. 'Please could you ask them if they got my permission form from Dragamas?'

'Well,' said Mrs Reed, frowning slightly. 'I will ask them. Of course it's up to them, but we're not going to let Gavin and Toby go. It's just too dangerous after what happened to that poor boy.'

'What happened?' asked Sammy, a little keener than he meant to. 'Er, I mean, Sir Ragnarok said it was an accident. Surely is can't have been that bad?'

'Worse Sammy,' said Mrs Reed, 'far, far worse. Of course, in our opinion the school shouldn't allow visits to those lands at all. I went to St. Elderberries School for Girls and although we bred and raised dragons, there were no visits to any lands. We had normal activities, ballet, the theatre or the zoo.'

'Mm,' said Sammy, thinking privately that Mrs Reed didn't have a clue. 'The visits are really well organised,' he lied, remembering Professor Burlay's absence at the circus. 'We went to the Floating Circus before Christmas. That was awesome.'

'I'm sure it was,' said Mrs Reed. 'No doubt there will be lands that Sir Ragnarok feels the need to ask our permission and lands where he doesn't. It says here you'll be there a whole weekend not just for the day. In our opinion, mine and Graham's, we believe you will learn as much on the ground as you will floating in mid-air on some magic carpet land.'

Sammy bit his tongue, about to tell Mrs Reed about Professor Burlay's family and their ice cream caravan.

'Besides,' said Mrs Reed, pouring salt in the wound, 'the Shape are said to have been present when the boy fell into the pyramid, sucked in he was, lured by their evil ways. No, in fact I may write to your parents anyway and advise them not to let you go. It's far too dangerous for a young boy like you to get mixed up with something like the Shape.'

'Wait,' said Sammy as Mrs Reed stood up, 'I've already met them.'

But it was too late. She scooped up the lemonade glasses and disappeared into the house saying something about making a chocolate cake for tea.

Wishing he hadn't raised the subject of the permission form, Sammy followed Mrs Reed and slipped unnoticed upstairs. He found Gavin and Toby seething in their shared bedroom, the double windows overlooking the garden table wide open.

'What did she have to do that for?' demanded Gavin. 'She hasn't even given us a chance to see what it's like.'

'Just says "no" to everything, all the time,' said Toby scowling from his perch on the windowsill.

'Hey,' said Sammy, 'it doesn't look like I'll be going either.'

'Bad luck,' said Toby, not looking entirely like he meant it.

'Maybe I can write to my parents and ask them myself,' said Sammy.

'No point,' said Toby, sharing a knowing look with Gavin. 'Once she's decided something...'

'...it happens,' finished Gavin.

'Oh,' Sammy felt like the fun had been sucked out of the spring term. 'Maybe we can go next year.'

After a filling welcome home tea of sausage rolls, sandwiches, chocolate cake, cheese and biscuits, Sammy went to bed feeling full but empty at the same time, resulting in a fitful sleep worrying about Kyrillan.

He was almost glad to be woken at six o'clock by the Reeds' large rooster, Sentry, crowing at day break. Sammy sat bolt upright, wondering where he was, about to put on his school uniform, then he remembered. 'It's the Easter holiday and I'm at Gavin and Toby's house,' he said to himself.

Gavin and Toby had both slept through Sentry's morning call and woke when Sammy returned from the bathroom, fully dressed and ready for breakfast.

'Come on sleepyheads,' said Sammy, rolling up the sleeves of his blue and grey chequered over shirt. 'Do we get to help with the sheep again?'

'Chase them!' said Gavin throwing back his duvet. 'I'm first in the bathroom!'

'Are not!' yelled Toby, sticking his leg out so Gavin tumbled over him. He pushed Gavin back on his bed, grabbed his towel on the way out and slammed the bathroom door shut.

'Hah!' said Gavin, avenging himself by pouring crumbs from an old packet of crisps over Toby's pillows.

'Boys, keep it down please,' Mrs Reed called up the stairs. 'Breakfast is ready.'

Without waiting for Toby, Sammy followed Gavin who was still in his pyjamas, downstairs and into the kitchen.

'Oh Gavin,' said Mrs Reed shaking her head at his tousled hair and night clothes. 'You'll have to get ready quickly this morning, your father's taking the three of you into the village.'

'Oi!' came a roar from upstairs. Sammy guessed Toby had found the crisps.

'Gavin?' Mrs Reed asked warningly, her cheeks a light shade of purple. 'What have you done to your brother now?'

Sammy guessed this must happen a lot at the Reeds'. It gave him another twinge of homesickness that he cured with a large bite of toast smothered in strawberry jam.

'Nothing mother,' said Gavin opening his eyes really wide, trying hard to look innocent.

'I don't know,' said Mrs Reed, relaxing a little. Sammy was pleased to see her cheeks return to their usual colour. 'Hopeless, the pair of you.'

'Hi Mum,' said Toby leaping from the bottom stair into the kitchen. 'Gavin put…'

'I don't want to know, thank you,' said Mrs Reed, passing Toby the butter. 'I'm sure Sammy doesn't cause his parents any trouble.'

'Well,' said Sammy, thinking back to a number of times his parents had been less than pleased with him. 'It's just me on my own at home, can't really get up to much trou…' he broke off, giggling, as Toby slapped a piece of jammy toast in Gavin's face.

'Ugh!' said Mrs Reed, taking off her apron and throwing it over the back of her chair. 'I don't know what to do with you! Gavin, upstairs, now! I want you washed, dressed and back here by the time your father has the sheep out. It's Euan's day off, so you'll be dropping him in the village and we'll need your help this afternoon to bring the sheep in.'

'Mmm, cool,' said Sammy, finishing the last of the toast.

'Oh yeah,' said Toby rolling his eyes, 'you'll love bringing the sheep in.'

'It's not as easy as it sounds,' said Gavin.

'Gavin, upstairs, now!'

Five minutes later Sammy sat in the back of the Reeds' Land Rover with Gavin and Toby. Euan and Mr Reed were in the front, discussing some lambs that had come early and whether they should sell any sheep at the market.

In the short journey, Sammy watched the fields and hedgerows stream past as they approached the village centre. Mr Reed stopped in a small car park between

Everyday Cuts, the village hair dressing salon, and the Kings Arms pub. He gave Euan a folded white envelope.

'There's a bit extra this week,' said Mr Reed. 'You've helped with the lambs we weren't expecting.'

Euan grinned broadly. 'Thanks very much Mr Reed.'

'Don't mention it,' said Mr Reed, shaking Euan's hand as he got out. 'Right boys, I'll meet you back at the house at seven. Here's a fiver for some lunch and don't get into any trouble.'

Gavin stared at the back of the Land Rover as Mr Reed drove off. 'A fiver? That won't get us much.'

'It will,' said Sammy brightly. He was back in the holiday mood and there were no grown-ups, no responsibilities, just a sunny day ahead of them. 'How about we try and find Dixie's house?'

'Cool,' said Toby enthusiastically. 'If she's near the Woodland Ranchers, it'll be this way.'

'Are you coming, Euan?' asked Gavin. 'Your farm's up that way.'

Euan shook his head. 'Thanks anyway, but I'm getting picked up in a minute. Got some mates coming. We're going to Danny's girlfriend's party. Her parents are away and Danny says she's organised an all-nighter.'

'Cool,' said Toby.

'Yeah, should be,' said Euan. 'Here he is, Danny-boy. I'll see you later.'

Sammy looked enviously at the overcrowded car that turned up. It was jet black with shiny silver alloy wheels and loud music pumping from the stereo.

'Thought you'd got lost,' shouted the driver, 'been round the block twice looking for you!'

'Yeah right!' said Euan. 'I've got sixty-two sheep and twelve lambs now.'

'No excuse,' said another voice, shouting above the music. 'Come on, let's go!'

'Wish we were older,' said Gavin as the car roared away. 'I'd get a car like that.'

'Mum would never let us throw an all-night party,' said Toby, 'not in a million years.'

It was unusually quiet walking through the village. Last time Sammy had been there, the Christmas lights had been up and people were hustling and bustling in and out of the shops buying presents.

At the end of the row of shops, the houses began in lines either side of the road, winding and twisting beside each other, all made from old bricks with silver grey slate roofs. After the houses, the village ended abruptly in a narrow, uneven road with mud and grass growing up the middle and high hawthorn hedges either side. Overhead, birds were twittering and calling in the early morning air.

They walked down the narrow road, leaning back against the hedge to let a large red tractor past. The driver waved at Gavin and Toby.

'That's Euan's Dad,' said Toby. 'He's got a farm up beyond the Ranchers.'

'Yeah,' said Gavin, 'but it's only half as big as ours. Mum and Dad pay Euan for his help on our farm.'

'Until we're grown up,' added Toby. 'Then we'll work on the farm instead.'

'Wow,' said Sammy, 'that sounds like fun.'

'Hard work,' said Gavin. 'Hopefully our dragons will be able to help.'

'Help!' said Sammy, trying to picture fully grown dragons on the farm. 'I can't see Kyrillan helping. Maybe to start a fire or something when he's grown up, but we can do that anyway with our staffs.'

'Mum and Dad use their dragons loads at home,' said Toby. 'That toast we had for breakfast wasn't cooked in a toaster, you know. The dragons help out on the farm as well.'

'Really?' Sammy looked at Toby. He seemed to be telling the truth.

'Yeah,' said Gavin. 'Dad keeps trying to train his dragon to round up the sheep.'

'Except he gets hungry half way through and eats some of them,' said Toby. 'That's why they have Euan to help.'

'Wish my parents had dragons,' said Sammy, plucking a dandelion clock from the hedgerow. 'Everything would have been so much better.'

'At your old school?' asked Toby.

'Yeah,' said Gavin. 'Your parents could've set their dragons on those Rat-Munchers. Then see who's scared.'

'Rat Catchers,' corrected Sammy, keen to steer the subject away from Ratisbury. 'Is it much further? My feet hurt!'

'Should be just around this corner,' said Gavin, standing up from re-tying his shoelace. 'We're just about there.'

They ran the last hundred yards, turning a sharp corner to face a long, white stone building with a pillared archway and stone steps leading to a portcullis that blocked the way through to the grassy pitch. Signs each side of the archway read "Welcome to the home of the Woodland Ranchers" in large green handwriting. Toby ran up the steps and swung on the portcullis bars.

'This is it,' said Gavin, puffing slightly, 'car park on the left and the pitch on the right.'

'Wow!' said Sammy, looking first from the empty gravel car park then to the huge entrance to the firesticks pitch, flanked by two large white marble pillars. At the foot of each pillar there were three terracotta pots, brimming with green and white flowers. Stretching between the pillars were thin iron bars that Sammy recognised as a cattle grid to hide the building from people who couldn't see dragons.

Sammy pointed to the bars. 'What do other people see?' he asked Gavin.

'Dunno,' said Gavin, unhelpfully. 'Anything but what's there I guess.'

'So other people would just see the lane and some trees?'

'Perhaps,' said Gavin, 'I've never thought about it before.'

'Whassat?' asked Toby taking a giant leap down the steps.

'Nothing,' said Sammy. 'Is it open?'

'Nope,' said Toby, 'but I saw a gap in the hedge round the corner.'

'Cool,' said Sammy.

'Wait until you've been inside!'

'Yeah, we've only ever been in for a match,' said Gavin as they walked round. 'I never knew there was a hole in the hedge.'

They stopped beside the gap in the hedge. 'It looks fairly recent,' said Sammy, feeling the edge of one of the snapped branches. 'This twig is freshly cut.'

'Spooky,' said Gavin crawling through the ready-made hole.

'No, wait,' said Sammy, 'I mean like today fresh. There might be someone else in here.'

'Freaky,' said Toby following his brother. 'Wonder who it is?'

'Maybe we shouldn't be here,' said Sammy.

Toby poked his head through from the other side. 'Sure we should. Come on Sammy, or are you chicken?'

With a strong feeling that what they were doing was wrong, Sammy shook his head and said, "yeah right". He crawled through the gap on his stomach and heaved himself out the other side.

Sammy stood up and caught his breath. The emerald pitch was perfectly cut, acres of green stretching out in front of him. Gavin and Toby were ahead, running up the steps into the semi-circle of staggered undercover seating overlooking the pitch. Opposite the stand, a row of houses stood behind a high hedge.

'Come on Sammy,' yelled Toby. 'You can see loads from up here!'

Sammy sprinted over and clattered up the iron steps to the left hand side of the stands. He was about two rows behind Toby when a flash of black distracted him.

'What's that?' said Sammy. 'Over there?'

Gavin shrugged. 'I didn't see anything. You a bit spooked or something?'

Sammy shielded his eyes and looked again. 'I thought I saw something black over there.' He pointed at the far seating, but there was nothing there.

'Let's go have a look,' said Toby, rolling up his sweatshirt sleeves.

'I don't think that's a good idea…' started Sammy, but egged on by the brothers and not wanting to be the one who said "no", Sammy followed a short distance behind them.

A flash of black on his left made Sammy look round. 'There!' he shouted. 'Did you see it?'

'See what?' asked Gavin. 'Are you feeling ok Sammy?'

'No Gav – Look!' yelled Toby.

Sammy swung round. There were five figures dressed all in black standing with their backs to the hole in the hedge that Sammy, Gavin and Toby had crawled through.

'We can't get out!' shrieked Toby. 'The gates are locked and they cut that hole!'

'They might just let us go,' said Gavin, his voice trembling.

'The Shape. No one has met the Shape and survived,' said Toby.

'I have,' said Sammy. 'The first day, I met them in the woods. Dixie ran through them and they dissolved.'

'That's it then,' said Toby. 'We'll run at them.'

'No,' Sammy caught Toby's sleeve. 'It won't work. Commander Altair said, uh, Dixie, um, Dixie ca...'

'Dixie what? Sammy tell us!'

Sammy took a deep breath. 'Dixie-cared-more-for-me-than-herself,' he ran the words together.

'Woohoo!' said Gavin grinning. 'Sammy's got a girlfriend!'

'Shut it Gavin,' snapped Toby. 'Shall we try it? They seem to be coming towards us.'

'No,' said Sammy. 'There has to be another way out.'

'Dixie's house!' said Gavin. 'She said it backs on to the pitch.'

'But which one?' asked Toby pointing to the row of identical looking terraced houses. 'There are loads to choose from.'

'She said it had three chimneys,' said Sammy, remembering suddenly. 'It has to be that one!'

Across the pitch, the house with three chimneys protruding from its grey slate roof was the closest to the black figures and where the hedge grew highest.

Gavin spat on his hands and rubbed them together. He took a deep breath. 'Come on, let's RUN!' he shouted, leaping down the steps.

Sammy ran. He leapt down the last five steps and scrambled across the pitch. Behind him, he knew the figures were chasing them. He splashed through a shallow stream running along the edge of the pitch and threw himself at the hedge behind Gavin. He could feel the Shape reaching for him. They were just a few paces away. He thrashed a path through the hedge, spinning his arms like a windmill, tearing the branches. He dived through into the garden behind and careered into someone.

Sammy yelled as he was caught and shook.

'Hello Sammy.'

Sammy wrenched open his scratched eyes. It was Dixie's brother, Serberon.

'Serberon!' breathed Sammy, relief pouring over him like a bucket of cool water. 'You have to help, quick. Toby's coming through. The Shape are after us.'

'What...' started Serberon. 'No - you - don't,' he yelled, grabbing hold of Toby's arm. The Shape glared at Serberon and dissolved into the brambles.

'Wow! Thank you,' said Toby, shaking Serberon's hand over and over. 'They had my foot, pulling me back. They said, "give us the boy and you'll go free".'

Serberon stared at Toby, then at Sammy. He frowned and shook his head. 'They're after you, Sammy?'

Sammy stared back blankly. 'The Shape are after me?'

'Have they gone?' asked Toby, rubbing his ankle.

Serberon pulled apart the branches and looked through. 'Yes,' he said matter of factly. 'They've gone.'

Sammy nodded, his legs felt like jelly. He caught sight of Dixie for the first time since they'd burst into her garden. 'Hi,' said Sammy, glad to find his voice sounded almost normal. 'How're you doing?'

'Hi,' said Dixie, hastily stuffing some plastic figures under the blanket she was sitting on. 'Thought you'd be coming in the front way,' she laughed nervously. 'Were they really after you?'

Sammy nodded, trying to laugh. 'They were after me,' he shivered, grateful as Dixie linked arms with him.

'Come inside,' said Dixie. 'I've told my Mum all about you.'

Sammy, Gavin and Toby followed Dixie through her untidy garden littered with weeds, plants and toys amongst the grass and pathways.

Sammy spotted something in one of the tall trees overshadowing the house. 'Hey you've got a treehouse!' he said, pointing to a neatly constructed mushroom shaped building, painted in white with a red roof complete with white spots, nesting halfway up one of the tallest trees in the garden.

'Uh, yeah,' said Dixie, 'Dad built it. I haven't been in it since he's gone.'

'Oh, sorry,' said Sammy.

'Can we go in it later?' asked Toby.

'If you want,' said Dixie, staring hard at something in the distance. 'The ladder should still be there.'

'We could look out and see if the Shape are still there,' said Gavin excitedly.

'They're not,' said Serberon, catching them up and play wrestling Dixie. 'They dissolved when they saw they couldn't get in.' Serberon looked seriously at Sammy. 'I don't know what you've done to upset them, but you're going to have to be careful. I'll ask Mum to drop you home. It's just the other side of the village, isn't it?'

Gavin nodded. 'This is a really nice house.'

Serberon smiled at Gavin. 'It's home,' he said, opening the back door that led into the kitchen.

Inside, the Deane's house was a reflection of the garden. More toys, books, games and magazines cluttered the table tops and work surfaces. It was a complete contrast to the luxury and order Mrs Reed maintained at Gavin and Toby's house. It felt warm and welcoming and reminded Sammy of Mrs Grock's house in the grounds at Dragamas.

Doors from the kitchen led into the hallway and the lounge, where Mrs Deane was sitting with Mary-Beth and Miranda. They were watching a small television whilst she was teaching the two girls to knit. By the look of Mary-Beth's effort Sammy thought privately she would have been better off playing Dragonball in the garden.

Dixie coughed to get her mother's attention. 'Hi Mum, these are some of the boys from school I was telling you about.'

Mrs Deane looked up from her knitting. 'Blond hair and blue eyes, you must be Sammy,' she said, smiling at them. 'And you must be Gavin and Toby, alike as two peas. You'll have to tell me which is which!' Mrs Deane laughed merrily. 'Can I get you a morning snack, perhaps some tea and biscuits in the garden. It looks like a nice day.'

She stood up and let her knitting fall to the ground in a thin spiral. 'It's a scarf for next winter,' she explained. 'Dixie, please fetch your brothers. They were supposed to be weeding the garden, but by the noise from upstairs, I think they're playing on that computer again.'

'Serberon was outside,' said Sammy. 'He just saved our lives.'

On the sofa, Mary-Beth and Miranda giggled politely.

'No,' said Sammy. 'It's not a joke. The Shape were outside. That's why we came through the hedge.'

Mrs Deane looked hard at Sammy, as if she were deciding for herself whether he was telling the truth. Finally, she nodded. 'Well, you are lucky to be here,' she concluded, whisking herself into the kitchen.

'You're the boy who got me Goldie,' said Mary-Beth. 'I never got the chance to thank you.' And without any

319

warning, she got up from the sofa and planted a kiss on Sammy's burning cheek.

'Oi!' said Serberon, coming back inside carrying a basket of weeds. 'She's my girlfriend!'

Mary-Beth laughed and kissed Serberon on the cheek as well.

'That's better,' said Serberon. 'Where's Dixie?'

'Here,' called Dixie, jumping down the stairs two at a time. 'Jason and Mikhael are coming in a minute. They're on level eight hundred and eleven, just got to find the key for the Monk's chamber, or something.'

'Aha,' said Serberon. 'I got there yesterday. You get the key be giving the peasant outside the chamber some food.'

'Dragon Questers,' explained Dixie, rolling her eyes. 'They got it from Mum for Christmas and haven't stopped playing it since they got home.'

'Sounds like fun,' said Sammy.

'It is,' said Gavin. 'I got it last year as a birthday present.'

'Really?' asked Serberon looking interested. 'Did you finish it?'

'No, got to level three hundred and fifty-two from memory,' said Gavin. 'Couldn't get past the hornless unicorn.'

'You need to collect the missing horn from the temple in the jungle,' said Serberon. 'It's quite tricky but once you get it you can...'

'Yeah all right Serb,' snapped Dixie. 'I'm sure he can make it.'

Serberon grinned. 'Come on, Mum's got the drinks ready in the garden.'

Soon the ten of them were sitting on garden chairs and picnic rugs in the garden enjoying Mrs Deane's tea and eating sun and moon shaped cracker biscuits.

Mrs Deane had brought out her knitting and started click-clacking her needles, changing thread every few minutes to another garish colour that added to the odd appearance of the scarf.

When all of the biscuits had been eaten, Serberon, Jason and Mikhael disappeared back inside to play Dragon Questers. Miranda and Mary-Beth went with them, Miranda asking whether she could play too.

Mrs Deane folded up her knitting. 'Just going to check on Penelope next door,' she said getting up.

Dixie nodded. 'See you later.'

'I'll be back soon,' said Mrs Deane.

When she had gone out of the garden gate, Dixie turned to Sammy, Gavin and Toby. 'Do you want to see the treehouse now?'

'Yes please,' said Gavin. 'I've always wanted one, but Dad doesn't think they're safe. Uh, sorry Dixie, I forgot, your Dad isn't here.'

'It's ok,' said Dixie, giving them the impression that things were far from "ok". 'The ladder's still here,' she added, unhitching a rope ladder from a notch in the tree trunk.

'Cool!' shouted Gavin. 'Can I go first?'

'Sure,' said Dixie. 'Watch out for the top rung, it always used to be a bit loose.'

Gavin swung up the ladder. 'Is this the loose one?'

Dixie stared at the rung he was clutching. 'Yeah, just don't pull it too hard.'

'Ok!' shouted Gavin, disappearing from sight. 'I'm up!'

'Go on Sammy,' said Dixie, grinning at him. She looked much more excited about going back into her treehouse than before. 'You go next.'

'Ok,' said Sammy, climbing the ladder more easily than he expected. He paused to check the wobbly rung at the top. It held his weight and he grabbed Gavin's hand to hoist himself into the treehouse.

'Cup of tea?' asked Gavin, laughing and pointing to a collection of dolls arranged around some red and yellow plastic cups and saucers.

'Oh no!' shrieked Dixie, hoisting herself into the treehouse. 'I thought I'd put all of that away!' She hastily scooped up the dolls and their tea party and shoved them into a cupboard.

'Lemonade anyone?' she asked, pulling out a dirty bottle half full of a murky brown liquid.

Sammy shook his head, laughing at the old bottle. He rubbed a hole in the dirt caked on the window and peered out. 'You can see for miles.'

'Yep,' said Dixie, helping Toby up. 'There's a trapdoor up there into the roof. Dad used to let me sleep up there once in a while. You can see the whole of the pitch,' she added, pointing to a small hinged square in the wooden ceiling.

'Wow!' said Gavin at the same time Toby said, 'that's cool!'

'Yeah, I've never been in the grounds, but I used to watch some of Nitron Dark's games from up there.'

'We might have been at a game you were watching!' said Gavin. 'Can we go up?'

'I suppose,' said Dixie thoughtfully. 'I'll just check it's clear, then you can come up if you want.'

'Cool,' said Gavin, standing on tiptoe to unhook the trapdoor. It swung open, revealing a dark square in the ceiling.

Dixie climbed on to the cupboard and pulled herself into the roof. From the room below, Sammy heard a click and a light came on.

Dixie stuck her head back down, her green ponytail falling over her eyes. 'It's safe,' she giggled, 'no dolls up here, just some cushions and an old book – Dragon Tales For Seven Year Olds, wow, that's old. A birthday present if I remember.'

'Can we come up?' Toby asked eagerly. 'Can you really see the whole of the pitch?'

'Yep,' said Dixie, her voice muffled as she withdrew back into the roof. 'Hey look! There's someone on the pitch.'

'Where?' demanded Gavin, pushing past Toby. 'Help me up.'

Sammy stayed at the window, rubbing a bigger hole to get a better look. 'Yeah, there's someone wearing black.'

Torn between wanting to go into the roof and seeing the figures, Gavin jumped down from the cupboard and stood next to Sammy to look through the window. 'It's the Shape,' he whispered. 'They've come back.'

Bunched together at the window, the three boys watched the figures in silence for nearly five minutes. Just as Sammy felt certain the Shape would know they were being watched, the cloaked figures disappeared from view.

'Woah,' said Dixie, leaning down to the main room. 'Are they really after you Sammy?'

A shiver ran down Sammy's spine. 'I think so,' he whispered.

'But why?' asked Toby. 'What could you possibly have done to get on the wrong side of the Shape?'

'Yeah,' added Gavin. 'You aren't even from a dragon family.'

'I don't know,' said Sammy quietly. 'But I hope I find out before they find me.'

'It's all right Sammy, we're here for you,' said Dixie climbing down from the roof, the copy of Dragon Tales

For Seven Year Olds tucked into the back pocket of her jeans.

They sat in the treehouse talking about the Shape until Mrs Deane called them down to ask if Sammy, Gavin and Toby wanted to stay for lunch.

'I'll drop you home later on if you like,' she added. 'If the Shape are looking for you Sammy, it might be safest.'

'Ok, thank you Mrs Deane,' said Sammy. 'As long as it's no trouble.'

'None at all,' said Mrs Deane, beaming at him. 'I've cooked plenty, just come into the dining room when you're ready.'

'She means in about half an hour,' said Dixie. 'That's how long it'll take to make my brothers leave that stupid computer.'

After a long lunch and an afternoon playing in the garden, Mrs Deane called them inside. 'I think it's time to take you boys home now. Your parents will be worried about you.'

They piled into Mrs Deane's shaky old blue Land Rover. Dixie sat in the front and Sammy crouched with Gavin and Toby on the benches in the back. It only took about ten minutes to get to Gavin and Toby's house, lurching down shortcuts that Mrs Deane knew like the back of her hand.

All the way back she talked at the top of her voice, above the rumble of the engine and mostly for Sammy's benefit, about all of the people she knew in the village.

'That's Mrs Eccles's bakery,' she said pointing to a large white building sliced between two shops on the high street. 'All home-made and she bakes the most wonderful fresh bread. Oh and there's Penelope from next door, doing her shopping by the look of it – woohoo Penelope!'

A portly lady in a large green overcoat turned and waved at them. She leapt back as the Land Rover came a little too close to the pavement.

'You'll like the next shop Sammy, it's the jewellers, just there on the right,' Mrs Deane carried on. 'It's the shop everyone here knows Sir Ragnarok is using to move the diamonds.'

Sammy looked keenly as they trundled past a shop with Pickering & Co. written above the door. He tried to see inside the darkened windows, but the shop appeared to be closed. A sign on the door confirmed this with "Closed by order of the Management" written in large black letters.

'That's odd,' said Mrs Deane. 'I came here before Christmas and they were open, how strange.'

'Perhaps it's not needed anymore,' suggested Sammy, remembering his meeting with Sir Ragnarok.

'Oh no Sammy, the word is Sir Ragnarok has only raised three quarters of the money. If the rest isn't found by the end of the summer term, you'll all be looking for new schools.'

'We won't Mum,' said Dixie. 'Sir Ragnarok will fix it.'

'I'm sure he will honey,' said Mrs Deane, amidst giggles from Gavin and Toby.

'Honey,' snickered Gavin.

'He's asked for donations with the permission slip for this land you're supposed to be visiting,' said Mrs Deane, looking reprovingly in her rear view mirror.

'Our Mum won't let us go,' said Gavin, his laughter vanishing. 'She doesn't think it's safe. It's not fair, everyone else will be going.'

'Perhaps it's for the best,' said Mrs Deane, turning down Gavin and Toby's road. 'It was a tragic accident with that poor boy.'

'I can go Mum, can't I,' asked Dixie.

'I'll have to see,' said Mrs Deane, squinting as she looked up the road for the right house. 'Perhaps I could talk with your mother in a moment, if she's home.'

'She should be,' said Gavin, pointing at the entrance of his home. 'It's just here.'

They rumbled over the cattlegrid into Pine Ridge. Mrs Deane parked next to Mrs Reed's newer Land Rover.

'My, they've made some improvements,' said Mrs Deane, looking enviously through the windows.

Gavin and Toby raced each other to ring the doorbell. Toby won by elbowing Gavin out of the way.

'Hi Mum!' they yelled, bursting through as Mrs Reed opened the door, leaving Sammy, Dixie and Mrs Deane waiting outside.

'Hello,' Mrs Reed greeted Mrs Deane with a stiff handshake. 'Thank you for bringing the boys back. I hope they haven't been any trouble.'

'None at all,' said Mrs Deane. 'This is my daughter Dixie. She's at Dragamas with the boys.'

'Oh,' said Mrs Reed, staring disdainfully at Dixie's green hair. 'Well I suppose they take all sorts.'

Sammy felt uncomfortable. But if Mrs Deane had noticed Mrs Reed's snobbery she chose to ignore it.

'You have a lovely house Mrs Reed. I don't suppose I could stop for a moment? I was hoping to talk with you about the land the children will be visiting.'

'Oh, I see,' said Mrs Reed, looking looked torn between wanting to be rid of the woman at her door and not wishing to seem ungrateful. 'Well I was just preparing tea for the family while my husband brings in the sheep.'

'Another time perhaps,' said Mrs Deane.

'No, it's fine.' Mrs Reed gave a forced smile. 'Please come in. I'll just turn the potatoes and put the kettle on.

Sammy, you and Trixie may help the boys bring in the sheep.'

'Yes Mrs Reed,' said Sammy as politely as he could, grinning at Dixie's glare. 'We'd love to help with the sheep, wouldn't we,' he nudged Dixie.

'Of course,' beamed Dixie. 'Why, that would be lovely.'

Mrs Reed looked at Dixie. 'A sweet child you have there,' she said, showing Mrs Deane into the lounge.

In the yard outside, Gavin and Toby were fighting with a large sheep, trying to coax it into the barn. The sheep, an old ewe, was stubborn and refused to budge. She kept baaing and looking back towards the field.

'Have you left one behind?' asked Sammy, stroking the rough wool on the ewe's back.

'Dunno,' said Gavin. 'Including the lambs, there should be seventy-four. I'll count them.'

Gavin disappeared into the barn reciting the numbers out loud. He came out a minute later. 'Well done Sammy, we're two short, could be her lambs. Let's check the field again.'

Sammy and Dixie followed a few steps behind Gavin and Toby who vaulted the style in one easy jump. They were halfway into the middle of the field by the time Sammy had helped himself and Dixie on to the step to climb over the wooden fence.

Spotting something in the far corner, Sammy shouted, 'over there!'

Gavin and Toby turned to where Sammy was pointing. There was a huge black shape in the corner of the field. As they ran closer, it looked suspiciously like Mrs Reed's dragon. She didn't move, even when they got right up beside her.

Sammy hung back a little. He was as close as he had been in the garden when she had belched smoke at him. 'What's wrong with her?' he asked.

'There's the missing lambs,' said Toby, white with shock as he pointed to underneath the dragon's front paws. The white blobs were as motionless as the dragon herself.

'What happened?' asked Sammy. 'Why aren't they moving?' He followed Gavin round the dragon's sixteen-foot body, clapping his hand to his mouth as he saw why neither the lambs nor the dragon were moving.

'They're dead!' screamed Gavin. 'Look they're all dead!'

Toby ran round and pulled his brother away from the dragon and the wooden spear that had pierced the side of her head.

Sammy knelt down to take a closer look. With a rough idea of the colour and shape of draconite, he wanted to check for himself whether it was the Shape who had killed the dragon. He turned to go but paused at a shout from Dixie.

'The lambs are still alive Sammy! Help me lift her feet. I think we can save them.'

Sammy looked hard at the gaping hole in the dragon's head. 'She was trying to protect them,' he said quietly.

With Dixie's help, he lifted the dragon's heavy paws away from the quivering cotton wool lambs. Even with the restricting paw removed, the lambs stayed still.

'Hold it higher Sammy, I'm going to have to pick them up,' said Dixie. 'Where have Gavin and Toby gone?'

'Back to get help hopefully,' puffed Sammy. 'Mrs Reed won't be happy about this.'

Dixie pulled both lambs to safety and they carried one each, running into a party of people at the style.

Mr Reed vaulted over the fence, followed by his sons. Mrs Reed and Dixie's mother climbed over more carefully.

'Thank you Sammy, thank you so much.' Mr Reed took the two lambs from Sammy and Dixie.

'Dixie helped,' said Sammy.

'Well, thank you too Dixie, very kind,' said Mr Reed, staring at her green hair. He carried the lambs, one under each arm, back over the style towards the farm.

'Mum,' said Gavin hesitantly. 'Your dragon's over here. She's…'

'Hurt,' said Sammy quickly. 'It looks like she might have been attacked.'

'Attacked!' shouted Mrs Reed, looking very angry. 'This is a safe village. No one, nothing gets "attacked" here.' She stormed ahead, Gavin and Toby running to catch up with her.

Mrs Deane put her arm round Sammy's shoulders. 'The dragon is dead, isn't she?'

Sammy stared at her. 'How did you know?'

'That was kind of you to break it to her like that, although she may not appreciate it now. The Shape haven't been seen in these parts for many-a-year.'

'But,' started Sammy, interrupted by an inhuman shrieking from Mrs Reed.

'Dead!' she wailed, shaking Gavin. 'How could you let this happen?'

'Mrs Reed, take hold of yourself,' said Dixie's mother. 'Let your son go. This isn't his fault.'

Mrs Reed turned to Mrs Deane, her eyes bloodshot and glaring. 'And just what would a peasant woman like yourself know better than me what has happened on my own farm?'

With an equally intense stare, Mrs Deane spoke quietly and firmly to Mrs Reed. 'This happened this afternoon, when your sons were at my house. They were chased by the Shape and would not be here if it hadn't been for my son pulling them through our hedge. This is the work of the Shape, as I suspect you already know.' Mrs Deane turned and walked back to the style with Dixie. Sammy desperately wanted to go with them.

Mrs Reed scooped up her long skirt and marched after Mrs Deane. 'What do you mean?' she shouted. 'The Shape aren't here.'

Mrs Deane turned to face her. 'Then who else could it have been? They're after Sammy. There is something even he doesn't know about himself that they cannot stand. He has been attacked at school and now here. This is the work of the Shape, Mrs Reed. They may be trying to scare you, to get to Sammy.'

'They can have him,' snapped Mrs Reed. 'My dragon is dead. They have stolen her stone. The boy cannot stay here. He is no longer welcome.'

Sammy felt his knees shaking again, terrified of Mrs Reed. He knew he had to get away, perhaps back to school, anywhere, he had to get his things and go. Without realising it, he was running back to the farmhouse, upstairs in the bedroom, packing his possessions into his school suitcase, his books, clothes, even his toothbrush and flannel. He sat on the bed and, everything catching up with him, he cried, not caring if anyone heard or saw him.

A few minutes later he stopped, looking up at a pink and white handkerchief waving in front of his nose. He looked up to see Dixie standing in front of him.'

'Come on,' whispered Dixie, her eyes sparkling. 'You're staying with us for the rest of the holiday. Mum's arranged it all with that woman.'

'She hates me,' mumbled Sammy. 'I don't even know what the Shape want with me.'

'Doesn't matter,' said Dixie, heaving Sammy's suitcase out of the door. 'Blimey, this is really heavy.'

'I'll take it,' said Sammy. 'Did your Mum really say I can stay?'

'Yep,' said Dixie, carrying on down the stairs with the trunk. 'She said one more won't hurt. Gavin and Toby's Mum gave her some money from your parents. I think she's glad to get rid of you.' Dixie giggled. 'Mum's not happy with her after being called a "peasant woman". She won't forget that in a hurry.

Mrs Reed didn't say a word as Sammy and Dixie walked past her. She said nothing when Sammy thanked her for the time he had spent there and she pulled Gavin and Toby back inside, slamming the door the second Sammy, Dixie and Mrs Deane had left the house.

'What a horrible woman,' exploded Mrs Deane. 'Peasant woman indeed,' she spluttered. 'Those poor boys, growing up with a mother like that.'

Dixie grinned. 'Never mind, we get Sammy for the rest of the holiday!'

Sammy smiled too, tired from the eventful day. 'Thank you so much,' he said to both Mrs Deane and Dixie, and he really meant it.

'No trouble at all,' said Mrs Deane firmly. 'I think the first thing to do is to write to your parents to tell them where you'll be staying for the remainder of the holiday. We'll see if we can get you that permission slip for the Land of the Pharaohs as well.'

'For me as well?' asked Dixie, grinning at Sammy.

'Of course,' Mrs Deane smiled as she started the engine. 'Can't have one rule for one, can we? I'd never hear the end of it!'

They laughed and Sammy relaxed for the first time since leaving the Reeds', confident he was going to enjoy the holiday and looking forward to staying with Dixie's brothers and Mary-Beth and Miranda.

It was getting dark when they arrived at Dixie's house with the three chimneys. Sammy was nervous in case the Shape knew he was no longer staying at the Reed's. Mrs Deane didn't seem bothered in the slightest. She heaved Sammy's suitcase out of the Land Rover single handedly, simultaneously throwing the door key to Dixie and volleying instructions to Sammy.

'You'll sleep in the boys' room. We've got a spare sleeping bag, so you can either use that or toss a coin with the boys for the beds.'

'Thank you Mrs Deane, the sleeping bag sounds fine,' said Sammy.

'It's Sylvia, Sammy, not Mrs Deane. That's far too formal for a "peasant woman",' she burst into a fit of the giggles. 'If only Jacob was here, he'd love to have heard that.'

'That's my Dad,' whispered Dixie. 'He's the one who built my treehouse.'

Sammy nodded. Nothing needed to be said.

Mrs Deane carried Sammy's suitcase almost effortlessly into the house and put it upright at the bottom of the stairs.

'Serberon,' she called up the stairs. 'Help Sammy with his suitcase. He's staying with us for the rest of the holiday.'

Serberon's greenhaired head emerged over the banister. 'Cool, I'll get Jason to make some room.'

'Thank you honey,' called Mrs Deane, then turning to Sammy, 'what would you like for tea?'

'Anything sounds good,' said Sammy, deciding he was going to enjoy every minute at the Deane's house until it was time to return to Dragamas.

A few days later Sammy woke up to the now-familiar sound of Dragon Questers. Serberon, Jason and Mikhael were up to level nine hundred and thirty and, much to

Dixie's annoyance, they had let Sammy play on several occasions.

Since his eviction from the Reeds, they had played in the garden almost constantly, swapping between Dragonball and football, both of which Sammy was pleased to see he was as good as Dixie's brothers. He had even stayed in the room at the top of the treehouse one night with Dixie and Mikhael, taking turns to keep watch for signs of the Shape.

Fortunately, it seemed that the Shape had vanished as quickly as they had appeared. Sammy knew he wasn't the only one relieved about this. He wondered briefly how Gavin and Toby were getting on, wishing they would visit to let him know if things were ok at their house.

In the quiet moments, Sammy thought about the Shape; why had they reached for Toby and why they had killed Mrs Reed's dragon, stealing her stone. He worried about how much money Sir Ragnarok needed to pay the Shape's ransom, if indeed he planned to pay it at all.

'Morning Sammy!' said Serberon from the corner of the room. He held out the Dragon Questers handset to Sammy. 'Do you want a go?'

Sammy nodded, still half asleep. He took the grey handset and punched the keys to make his on-screen figure fly on a firebreathing dragon, over a lake to the gates of a castle which were guarded by two mean looking trolls with bright green hair.

'There's Uncle Joe,' laughed Mikhael.

'Really?' asked Sammy, rubbing his eyes, not quite awake.

'Well, no, not really Uncle Joe,' said Mikhael, 'just our on-screen relatives.'

Seeing Sammy's blank look, Serberon explained, 'we have troll blood. That's why we have green hair and hook noses.'

'You don't have hook noses,' said Sammy, laughing.

'No joke, Sammy,' said Serberon, 'we are related to trolls. It's why dwarves like Dr Lithoman hate us so much.'

'Yeah,' added Jason. 'She never gives us good marks.'

Sammy scratched his head, guiding his dragon over the castle wall. 'But why doesn't she like you?'

'Cos our ancestors squashed hers,' said Mikhael viciously. 'Trolls and giants used to crush dwarves like her for breakfast.'

'Oh.' Sammy felt suddenly nervous.

'It's ok Sammy. It's only at full moon when we eat people!'

'I'll be right back,' said Sammy, hurriedly leaving the room to a volley of laughter. Not watching where he was going, he bumped straight into Dixie.

'Oi!' she shouted, pulling her pale green dressing gown tight. 'Watch where you're going.'

'Sorry,' Sammy grinned at her. 'Is the bathroom free?'

'No,' grumbled Dixie. 'Miranda's been in there for forty minutes.'

'Forty!' said Sammy. 'Even my Mum doesn't take that long.'

'Stuffit,' said Dixie. 'Let's go downstairs, get something to eat and take it up to the treehouse.'

'Not in our pyjamas?'

'I suppose not,' said Dixie. 'Meet me downstairs in a minute.'

Sammy slipped into the boys' bedroom and grabbed his jeans, t-shirt, socks and shoes without any of Dixie's brothers noticing. He dressed in the hallway and ran downstairs to find Dixie had beaten him.

'Slowcoach. How long does it take to put on jeans and a t-shirt?'

They ran through the house and past Mrs Deane, who was baking bread rolls in the kitchen.

'Morning Sammy, morning honey!' she called, not noticing Dixie pluck some of the fresh rolls from the wicker basket on the kitchen table.

When she realised and reproved them, Sammy and Dixie were out of sight, sitting in the treehouse munching the warm crusty rolls.

About half an hour later, Mrs Deane came to find them.

'Dixie!' she called from the bottom of the ladder.

Looking guilty, Dixie leant down. 'What do you want?'

'Shopping,' came the muffled reply.

Dixie looked furious.

'What's up?' asked Sammy.

'Mum wants me to go into the village with her. She always lets my brothers stay here on their own. Just because I'm a girl,' she grumbled.

'It's probably because of me,' said Sammy. 'If the Shape come back it's probably safest to go out. Anyway, some of the shops look really interesting.'

Dixie stared at him. 'Really, you'll come? Mum should only be a few hours. We can get loads of food and look round all the shops you want.'

'I'd like to visit the jewellers,' said Sammy when Mrs Deane had parked in the village, having bought half the local supermarket.

'Just got to get my hair done,' said Mrs Deane smoothing her green curls. 'Go wherever you like, but please meet me at the car in an hour.'

'Cool,' said Dixie. 'She never normally lets me go round the village by myself. So anyway, why do you want to go to the jewellers? Are you hoping he'll tell you how much money Dragamas needs?'

'No,' said Sammy thoughtfully, 'well, maybe. My uncle runs a jewellers. I used to love going in there with him a few years ago.'

'It's my Mum's birthday soon. We could say we're getting her a present.'

'Yeah,' said Sammy. 'Just hope he doesn't take us seriously. I haven't got much money on me, a few coins at most.'

'Don't worry silly – it's just to get him talking, then we can ask him about Dragamas.'

'Ok,' said Sammy as they reached the quaint doorway with the sign "Pickering & Co. – International Jewellery Services" hanging above the door. On the security meshed door, the sign reading "Closed by order of the Management" in large black letters was still there.

Sammy peered through the top window jostling with Dixie.

'There's someone inside!' shouted Dixie. 'Look, something moved!'

Without waiting for Sammy to reply, she banged on the door with both fists.

Almost as if he'd been waiting for them, a man appeared at the window, his face thin and cheekbones prominent. He was frowning at them, pointing at the sign. 'Can't you read? We're closed.'

'But we want to buy my Mum a birthday present,' shouted Dixie, clearly unaware that several people in the street were watching them.

'Come on,' whispered Sammy. 'He's not going to let us in.'

Dixie ignored him and hammered harder on the door.

The man looked out past them and jolted backwards. Sammy heard a click as bolts were drawn back. Then the man opened the door, tutting and tapping his watch. 'Haven't got all day you know.'

'Neither have we,' said Dixie, grinning at him. 'My Mum asked us to be back at the car in an hour.'

'I see, and who might your mother be?'

'Sylvia Deane,' said Dixie, without a moment of hesitation. 'We live behind the…'

Sammy coughed loudly.

'What?' snapped Dixie. 'He just asked a question.'

'Not at all,' said the jeweller. 'In fact quite understandable with the Shape lurking in every corner.'

'What do you know about the Shape?' asked Sammy. 'How do you know they're here?'

'They were watching you from across the street.'

Sammy stared at the jeweller, half hidden in the shadows behind the cabinets of treasures in his dark shop. He felt his knees weaken, resting his hand on a counter of rings, his eyes hurt feeling suddenly dizzy.

'Sammy? Are you ok?'

Dixie was kneeling beside him, the room felt suddenly tall and Sammy realised he was lying sprawled out on the carpet floor. The jeweller passed him a glass of cool water he had fetched from a room at the back.

'Are you all right, young man?' asked the jeweller, staring uncomfortably at Sammy. 'Why if I'm not mistaken, you're my nephew, Samuel Rambles, Charles and Julia's son, am I right?'

Dixie stared first at the jeweller, then at Sammy. 'Yes,' she said. 'He's Sammy Rambles.'

'Uncle Peter?' whispered Sammy, still feeling a little bit sick.

'Why yes,' said the jeweller. 'What brings you to my part of the world?'

'I go to school near here, to Dragamas.' Sammy pulled himself upright and handed back the empty glass.

'But of course you do,' said the jeweller. 'This has been a lovely surprise, and look, you're still wearing the watch I gave you.' He turned to Dixie. 'Now, to find something for your mother young lady. What month was she born in? I have sapphires for April, or emeralds for May.'

'Um.' Dixie stared desperately at Sammy.

Sammy understood. They didn't have enough money to buy anything in the shop. 'Uncle Peter, could we come back another time? We said we'd meet Dixie's Mum in a few minutes.'

'Of course. You must come back.'

'Thank you Mr Rambles, we will,' said Dixie, reaching for the door handle.

'Oh no dearie, it's Pickering,' said the jeweller. 'I'm Sammy's mother's brother, Peter Pickering.'

'Nice to meet you, Mr Pickering,' Dixie smiled at him. 'Come on Sammy, it looks like the Shape have gone. We should be safe.'

Sammy shook hands with his uncle and followed Dixie, his head still spinning. He was glad when they got back to Mrs Deane's Land Rover.

When Mrs Deane arrived, they saw that her hair appointment at Everyday Cuts had been an improvement. Her short green curls were now pulled into long waves that reached her coat collar. 'Thank goodness you're here,' she said, sweeping Dixie into a hug. 'They said the Shape have been in the village.'

'We know,' said Dixie, grinning at her mother. 'Sammy's uncle saved us.'

Back at Dixie's house, they sat in the lounge eating the fresh rolls Mrs Deane had cooked earlier.

'So, Peter Pickering is your uncle, eh Sammy? Serberon asked, helping himself to the butter.

'Yeah, I knew he had a jewellery shop somewhere,' said Sammy. 'I never thought he was anything to do with Dragamas. He's the most un-dragonish person you'll ever meet.'

Mrs Deane burst out laughing. 'It'll interest you Sammy that he has three fully grown dragons in his back garden. Only ever used to have the one orange one, but he took in a black one and a small green one, ooh, several years ago.'

'That means they could be my parents' dragons,' Sammy thumped the settee arm. 'I have dragons in my family!'

'It would explain a lot,' said Dixie. 'It was weird when Kyrillan hatched so quickly and how you taught him to fly so easily, especially with people like Gavin and Toby taking ages to bond with theirs.'

'It's just a thought,' said Mrs Deane. 'Your parents will be home soon and I'm sure they'll tell you all about it.'

'About what?' asked Sammy. 'Why haven't they told me anything?'

'For your safety I presume,' said Mrs Deane. 'The Shape are after you, you know.'

'Maybe I found out something in class, Dr Lithoman's draconite stone. She's part of the Shape, that's why they're after me!'

'Sammy!' exclaimed Mrs Deane. 'You shouldn't say things like that…'

'…without proof, yeah I know,' snapped Sammy. 'That's what Sir Ragnarok said.'

After receiving a large dragon shaped Easter egg, Sammy was glad nothing more was said about his parents and dragons for the rest of the holiday. Serberon, Jason and

Mikhael reached level four thousand and two and Miranda and Mary-Beth went back to their homes.

Mrs Deane ferried them to and from the village stores to buy supplies of pens, paper and pencils. It wasn't that he hadn't wanted to go back to his uncle's jewellers that had kept Sammy away, he desperately wanted to go back, but on hearing about the Shape and how they seemed to be stalking him, Mrs Deane kept her eye firmly on him for the whole holiday and wouldn't even let him get close to places where they had been seen.

In fact, other than defeating a three-eyed monster on Dragon Questers, the only piece of good news Sammy received was a postcard from his parents saying he could go to the Land of the Pharaohs.

In almost no time at all, Sammy was packing his suitcase and piling into Mrs Deane's Land Rover with Dixie in the front and himself with Dixie's three brothers sitting hunched up on the benches resting their feet on their suitcases, their three dragons flying overhead.

'Dragamas!' squealed Dixie as they pulled into the lay-by opposite the school gates.

Sammy craned his neck to spot the North tower amongst the black and gold Dragamas flags flying from the turrets. In the Easter sunshine, the castle looked more friendly and inviting than September when he had first arrived with his parents.

Ten dwarves, led by Captain Stronghammer, touched their caps to Mrs Deane and Dixie and carried their suitcases, two dwarves per suitcase, into the school.

Sammy felt a little homesick as he waved goodbye to Mrs Deane.

Serberon elbowed him as Mrs Deane sped away. 'Come on, race you to the door!'

Sir Ragnarok greeted everyone in the Main Hall with a lively welcome-back speech followed by more food than Sammy had seen in his entire life.

Sammy ate and drank as much as the others, even though he felt weighed down by the possibility of the Shape coming after him at school and the fact that neither Gavin nor Toby had spoken to him since he had got back to Dragamas.

He was glad when Sir Ragnarok read through the school announcements and sent them to their tower dormitories to unpack. Even the threat of the summer exams and the penalty of repeating the year didn't worry Sammy. He was glad to be back.

Up in the North tower Sammy unpacked his suitcase and kicked it under his bed. Kyrillan was asleep on his chest of drawers and Sammy tickled under his scaly chin, trying to wake him up, hoping Kyrillan would be pleased to see him even if Gavin and Toby weren't.

Kyrillan snapped his black bead eyes open and blew a jet of fire up towards the ceiling. Sammy leapt back, his mouth wide open. He checked around, desperate to share it with Darius, even Amos, but everyone's curtains were pulled shut.

'Wow Kyrillan! What did they teach you over Easter?' Sammy asked, tucking himself into bed.

CHAPTER 19

SAMMY'S DISAPPOINTMENT

With Gavin and Toby still cool towards him after the events during the Easter holiday, Sammy was almost pleased that he, Darius and Amos were allowed to go to the Land of the Pharaohs and, despite many letters home, Gavin and Toby were not.

'It's tomorrow!' squealed Dixie on Friday morning at breakfast. 'Just Alchemistry, Astronomics and Armoury to go, then we'll be at the Land of the Pharaohs for the whole weekend!'

"Just Alchemistry, Astronomics and Armoury" couldn't have been further from the truth when Professor Sanchez chose that Friday morning to spring a surprise test on all the plants and potions they were supposed to have revised over Easter. The test was followed by a demonstration of their mind controlling abilities using a set of coloured cards, each with a different symbol.

Sammy, Dixie and Darius formed their usual group of three and took it in turns to read each other's mind and pick out the card that the other person was thinking of.

Having had limited success, Sammy was glad when the bell finally rang, giving them a few minutes break before going to room 37 for their Astronomics lesson with Professor Burlay.

As usual, Professor Burlay turned up seven minutes late. When questioned, he explained that he set his watch by the land above the school so he knew what time it was for his family at the Floating Circus.

For Sammy and some of the others, this explained as much as it didn't and Sammy found the entire lesson had passed whilst he had been doodling pictures of lions on the inside cover of his Astronomics book. To his dismay, Professor Burlay had been scribbling dictation in his illegible scrawl on the blackboard and Sammy hadn't written a single word down.

'Can I borrow yours at lunch?' Sammy whispered to Darius who was sitting on his left.

'Ok,' said Darius, 'but you'll miss the slide show Dr Shivers is putting on about the history of the pyramids.'

'Well…' Sammy thought hard, torn between catching up with the work for their exams and seeing the presentation, 'I really have to catch up with the work. I'll see the pyramids tomorrow anyway.'

Darius gave him a dirty look. 'Swot,' he said handing over his papers.

Feeling envious as everyone left Astronomics to go to Dr Shivers's presentation, Sammy took Darius's notes to the school library on the top floor, just along from the Alchemistry classroom.

As he was about to go into the library, he almost bumped into another teacher who was on his way out. Sammy vaguely recognised him as one of the other Alchemistry professors who taught some of the older students.

'Hello Sammy,' said the professor who, despite looking as if he was ninety, old and frail under a pair of spectacles and wearing the same dark robes as Professor Sanchez, he seemed to have his wits about him.

'Hello Professor,' said Sammy, without thinking how the professor knew his name.

'Mind control,' said the Professor. 'I ask the questions and your subconscious answers without you realising.'

Sammy stared at the old man.

'You are on your way to the library, are you not?'

Sammy nodded, fascinated. 'But I didn't say anything.'

The Professor wheezed with laughter. 'You are easily led. Your name is on your book along with papers in writing not of your hand. Carry your books better, it will extend their life for future students.'

Sammy looked down, he hadn't touched his book, but it was there, inside out, his name and lion drawings and the papers with Darius's notes. 'How did you do that?' he asked. 'I didn't put them that way round.'

The Professor laughed again. 'You will be a fine example to tell my fifth years this afternoon. I'm sure they will enjoy the tale.'

'Could you teach me?' asked Sammy, excitement getting the better of his nerves.

'I can try,' said the Professor, wheezing slightly. 'Come, there is a spare classroom here and it's not tricky to master. Nice to have a keen student at last, the fifth years are too busy dating each other to care about my lessons, or their exams.' The old man laughed again and extended his hand. 'I am Patrick Preverence, Professor Preverence to you my boy. Now, let me see what you are made of.'

Sammy followed Professor Preverence into room ninety-five, three rooms up from Professor Sanchez's classroom. It was laid out in exactly the same way, with the same rows of bookshelves and chairs tucked neatly under their desks, but it smelt older, the air full of magic and heavy with dust. It reminded Sammy of his uncle's jewellery shop where the coloured glass and gemstones were surrounded by old wooden furniture and the same musty smell.

'Let us begin,' said Professor Preverence. 'Pass me your friend's notes and I shall show you some magic.'

Sammy passed across Darius's notes and several sheets of lined paper.

'I shall do the first,' said Professor Preverence, screwing up his eyes in utmost concentration. 'There,' he handed Sammy a copy of the first page of Darius's notes.

'Wow!' Sammy looked at the paper. 'It's like you've photocopied them.'

Professor Preverence frowned. 'Fo-to-cop-eed?'

'Never mind,' said Sammy. 'This is much better.'

'Your turn,' said Professor Preverence. 'I take it you have a staff?'

Sammy nodded and quickly extended his staff from his pocket, glad he had practised over the holiday. He added the black onyx crystal once the three pieces were assembled.

'Good,' said Professor Preverence, looking closely at the gnarled staff. 'There is a strong energy in that staff. I feel you could put many of my fifth years to shame.'

Sammy ignored him, concentrating hard on the words in Darius's notes, reading them through in his mind. He closed his eyes, frowning and concentrating on the blank piece of paper under his staff.

In his grasp, Sammy felt the staff quiver and shake. He opened his eyes. A large drop of ink had fallen on to the paper in the shape of an "A" which was the first letter of Darius's notes.

'Good!' roared Professor Reverence. 'Some fifth years don't even get a single drop, let alone a letter. Keep going boy!'

Sammy closed his eyes again, listening for the "plip" of a drop of ink falling on the page. After thirty seconds, he opened his eyes and stared as he saw an identical page of the Astronomics notes.

'Wow!' was all he managed to say.

'Quite,' said Professor Preverence, taking off his spectacles. 'I am most impressed. Would you mind trying an experiment for me on the last page of notes?'

Sammy nodded. 'Ok.'

'Give me your staff,' said Professor Preverence, taking it from Sammy. 'Now try.'

'Without my staff?' asked Sammy. 'But how?'

'Exactly as before,' said Professor Preverence. 'The staff, though useful in many ways, is often best used for stirring potions. The greatest of Dragon Knights need only their minds alone.'

'I want to be a Dragon Knight,' said Sammy, closing his eyes for the third time. 'Mrs Grock said I may be able to become one in time.'

'Perhaps you already are,' said Professor Preverence.

There was a faint hiss and Sammy opened his eyes. Professor Preverence was nowhere to be seen. Sammy's staff lay motionless on the desk and the classroom door was closed. He was alone in the room.

'Professor Preverence? Are you there?' Sammy looked down and grinned. He had created an exact replica of Darius's notes.

Sammy picked up the notes and his staff. He looked for Professor Preverence all along the top floor, but he was nowhere to be found. Giving up, Sammy walked down to the canteen to get himself some sandwiches from the lunch machines. He was glad when the afternoon bell rang and he could join the rest of the first years for their Armoury lesson with Commander Altair.

'Hey Sammy!'

Sammy looked up, Darius and Dixie had saved him a seat in the back row. He sat down on the wooden chair, unpacked his Armoury book and assembled his staff.

'Put your books away please.' Commander Altair's voice came out of nowhere, his body appearing through a thin red mist. Sammy hated the way Commander Altair made his entrances, he was never sure if his teacher was there or not and, more often than not, Commander Altair was on the lookout for any students even daring to think about causing any mischief.

'What are we doing this lesson, Sir?' asked Gavin from the row in front of Sammy.

'All will be revealed,' said Commander Altair with a wink. 'Take out your staffs and hold them horizontally, black crystals in your writing hand, like this,' Commander Altair demonstrated with his own staff, a glittering diamond where the first years had the black onyx stones. He rolled the staff over in his hands sending rainbows ricocheting on the blackboard. 'Milly, stand up please.'

'But I was listening,' protested Milly.

'I know,' said Commander Altair, tapping the side of his head. 'All I can hear in your head is "red hair slides for tomorrow or blue".'

The class laughed and Milly went bright pink.

'Well?' asked Commander Altair. 'Red or blue?'

'Red,' said Milly, looking extremely puzzled. As she frowned, Commander Altair fired a volley of red sparks at her.

Sammy wasn't convinced she did it on purpose, but Milly raised her staff and deflected the sparks around the room, squealing as they bounced around her.

'Don't worry, they're harmless,' said Commander Altair. 'Let's try it again, Gavin, your turn.'

Gavin stood up, his staff clenched in his hands. Knowing what to expect, he easily punched the sparks away from himself.

'Good,' said Commander Altair. 'This lesson we're learning the basics of self-defence. Sir Ragnarok thinks it's wise for all students to be prepared for anything this weekend and I happen to agree with him.'

'He's worried about something,' muttered Sammy as he stood up to take his turn. He stood feet apart, staff clenched, staring solidly at Commander Altair.

'Ready?' Commander Altair smiled at him. 'Let's try something different…'

Sammy nodded, bracing himself as Commander Altair fired a huge volley of red and blue sparks at him. He held out his staff, onyx pushed forward, deflecting the red sparks as they came towards him. Several students ducked out of the way as they came close then fizzled out.

The blue sparks hit Sammy's staff with a force that threw him back in his seat with a bump. His staff felt white hot and clattered to the floor. He screamed. His hands were hot, burning hot. Sammy stared as they blistered in front of him.

Commander Altair's smile vanished. 'Mrs Grock's. Now,' he commanded. 'Dixie, Darius go with him. Toby, try these…' Commander Altair fired a volley of red sparks at Toby. Sammy, Dixie and Darius ducked under the sparks and fled out of the classroom, red sparks bouncing round them as they left.

Outside, Sammy checked his hands. They were a nasty shade of purple and were starting to flake, pieces of burnt skin dropping to the floor.

'Quick,' muttered Sammy. 'It hurts.'

They ran to Mrs Grock's house, tucked into the edge of the woodland surrounding the school. Darius knocked on the green front door and pushed it open.

'Ooch, hello,' beamed Mrs Grock, a tray with three mugs of hot chocolate in her hands. 'I've been expecting you. Sit on the couch, I'll get my things and I'll soon get these hands fixed up for you.'

Sammy stared. 'How does she know,' he whispered.

'Mind control?' asked Dixie.

'No,' stormed Darius. 'This is a set up, to stop Sammy going tomorrow.'

'What?' said Dixie, screwing up her nose. 'Sammy got injured in Armoury. It was an accident, how can that be a set up?'

'I was the only one to get blue sparks,' said Sammy thoughtfully. He perched himself on the arm of the sofa. 'Look at my hands.'

'Eugh!' squealed Dixie. 'They're all flaky.'

'Exactly,' said Darius, gulping down his hot chocolate in one go. 'Sammy's not going anywhere tomorrow.'

'But that's not fair.' Sammy glared at his hands. 'If only I'd been able to fight those sparks, I bet I could've controlled them. I was even told earlier today that staffs are best used for stirring potions. I just let the staff take it. How could I have been so stupid. I should have tried harder.'

'Ooch Sammy, you canna cry over spilt milk,' said Mrs Grock, returning with a roll of tape and some cotton bandages. 'What's done is done.'

'Hey!' exclaimed Sammy. 'You can't put bandages on them, what about your magic potion, the eggs, turnip and amberoid juice?'

Mrs Grock looked sympathetically at him. 'Ooch see, the hens haven't been too well lately. They just don't seem to want to lay any eggs. It's a pity, I could've had you back together in no time. Hold out your hands and I'll get these on you. You two had better get back to class, hadn't you?'

Before Sammy had time to object, Mrs Grock ushered Dixie and Darius out of the house and closed the door behind them.

'Conspiracy,' Sammy muttered as he held out his hands for Mrs Grock to wrap. 'Ow! That hurt,' he said as she pulled the bandages tight.

'Ooch don't you look in the wars,' said Mrs Grock. 'You should still be able to drink your hot chocolate now the bandages are on.'

Sammy reached for the cup, but found the bandages were too thick and he couldn't wrap his fingers round the handle.

'Ooch dear my little Dragon Knight. Perhaps I canna find you a straw.'

'Are they keeping me here?' asked Sammy when Mrs Grock returned from the kitchen with a packet of coloured straws.

'Keeping you here?' repeated Mrs Grock. 'I don't know anything about that. My job's to make sure you're all right.'

'Oh,' said Sammy. 'Thank you.'

'Why don't you lie down? I'll make you up a bed, you canna stay with me over the weekend and you'll be back with your friends on Sunday evening.'

'No!' shouted Sammy, knocking his hot chocolate flying. 'I want to go to the Land of the Pharaohs. My parents signed the form. I got a postcard from them. They said I can go.'

'Well I don't know anything about that,' said Mrs Grock, frowning at the mess. 'Sir Ragnarok said...'

'So it is a conspiracy!' shouted Sammy. 'Just because the Shape are after me. Why can't I go?'

'As I was saying,' said Mrs Grock, ignoring him, 'you canna stay with me over the weekend. The circus is coming later this term. You canna go to that land I'm sure.'

'I've been there,' yelled Sammy. 'I want to see the pyramids, the Pharaohs, the sand and temples. Darius said his parents go there. I want to go.'

'Yelling and a screaming like that won't make you a Dragon Knight,' Mrs Grock shook her head, 'I'm disappointed in you, I would have thought you'd understand.'

'Understand what?' yelled Sammy.

'That I have your best interests at heart,' said a quiet voice.

Sammy jumped. Sir Ragnarok was sitting beside him on the sofa, drinking his own mug of hot chocolate. 'Yes,' said Sir Ragnarok. 'I have been sitting here the whole time.'

'Oh,' said Sammy calming down. 'Then why can't I go? Is it true I've been injured on purpose?'

'Tell me why you want to go, and I will tell you why it is imperative that you do not.' Sir Ragnarok flashed his eyes over to Sammy, challenging him.

'I would like to go to the Land of the Pharaohs because,' started Sammy, the words drying up in his mouth, 'because, um, the pyramids, the Pharaohs...I'm not afraid of the Shape.'

Sir Ragnarok nodded. 'That is good to hear Sammy, but sadly you will change neither my mind, nor the fact that you have blistered hands.'

Sammy looked down at his hands. They were still sore and blood and puss had soaked through the white hospital bandages. 'So, really, why can't I go?' asked Sammy.

'I imagine you already know the answer.' Sir Ragnarok smiled sadly at him. 'The Shape are troubling us greatly. Your safety has been entrusted to me as your guardian whilst you are at Dragamas. They have been more devious than even I had foreseen.'

'But I got a postcard with their permission. Please let me go,' begged Sammy.

'Do you have it with you?'

'Yes,' said Sammy, pulling the creased card out of his shirt pocket with his teeth and dropping it into his lap. 'It says "P.S. We give our permission for you to go on the school visit to the Land of the Pharaohs".'

'Yes,' said Sir Ragnarok, 'but look at the stamps, British stamps, with a postmark from the village if I'm not mistaken.'

Sammy stared at the head on the first class stamp.

'Didn't you wonder how it arrived so quickly? The Shape must have been standing at the postbox, waiting for Mrs Deane to post her letters.'

'And read her letter asking my parents for permission? Impossible.'

'On the contrary, quite possible,' said Sir Ragnarok. 'You only confirm my opinion that you do not respect your enemy. You cannot fight what you do not believe to be a danger. You are to stay here for the weekend and I will send your friends with a change of clothes and your dragon. Perhaps you could teach him to fly, that's quite an achievement for one so young.'

Sir Ragnarok stood up and fastened his cloak. 'I'll see you on Sunday Sammy,' he added and walked out of Mrs Grock's, closing the door behind him.

'Stuffit,' scowled Sammy. 'Kyrillan can fly and I want to go!'

At half past six that evening, Dixie and Darius brought Kyrillan, some sweets and a change of clothes as promised. Dixie also brought a photo album lent by Serberon, with pictures of his visit to the Land of the Pharaohs a year ago. Halfway through looking at the pictures of a land he wouldn't see, Dixie and Darius left to go to dinner, promising to bring Sammy a souvenir from the pyramids.

After they'd gone, Mrs Grock changed Sammy's bandages and the weekend dragged at a snail's pace.

By the time Mrs Grock had checked on him for the last time on Sunday afternoon Sammy was bored out of his skull. Even teaching Kyrillan near-perfect loop the loops and walking round the entire school hadn't made up for being stuck on the ground on his own, apart from bed-ridden Ern, a boy from the fourth year who was recovering from measles he'd picked up from his cousin over the Easter holiday.

Sammy was glad at eight o'clock when Sir Ragnarok finally visited to check on his hands and dropped off some eggs from the village.

'Can't have you missing lessons, Sammy,' said Sir Ragnarok with a smile.

'Thanks,' said Sammy, keeping his mouth firmly closed in case he added something rude.

'There's no need for that,' said Sir Ragnarok. 'You'll be able to go to the Floating Circus before the end of term and of course, there'll always be next year.'

'You hope,' Sammy muttered when Sir Ragnarok was out of earshot.

'That'll be a star my Dragon Knight,' said Mrs Grock, using her staff to draw a black star. 'Sir Ragnarok said specifically for you not to discuss the school closing.' She tapped the star out of the open window and watched it fly up to the castle.

'But he hasn't raised all of the money,' said Sammy. 'It can't be long before the end of term.'

'Long enough you'll find. In all my years of knowing Sir Ragnarok, he's not let me down yet.'

'He said he might not pay it,' said Sammy defiantly as Mrs Grock mixed up the foul smelling lotion for his hands.

'Well,' said Mrs Grock as she stroked the slice of turnip over Sammy's blistered hands. 'It's not really my place to say it, but I think it'll turn out for the best. If there's anyone who can defeat the Shape and save you and your dragons, it's Sir Lok Ragnarok.'

'Do you have a dragon Mrs Grock?'

'Ooch yes Sammy, but I canna tell you where she is.'

'She's under the house, isn't she?' Sammy grinned. 'We saw her on Halloween.'

'That'll be for me to know and you to wonder,' said Mrs Grock firmly. 'There, you're done.'

Sammy looked at his hands, flipping them over to check the front and back.

'Thank you,' he said, grateful to be back to normal. 'I just wish Sir Ragnarok could've got the eggs on Friday.'

Mrs Grock laughed. 'Aye Sammy, perhaps he could have. Anyhow, gather your things and I'll give you a full report for good health. Enjoy your lessons my Dragon Knight.'

"Pah" was all Sammy could say as he packed his clothes, sweet wrappers and the photo album into a carrier bag and picked up Kyrillan from his bed beside the fireplace. He waved goodbye to Ern and Mrs Grock and stomped back to the North tower.

The castle was quiet and empty as Sammy got back. He met Tom Sweep the caretaker in the main corridor and learnt the school wouldn't be back for another hour. He packed his clothes away and went to wait for them on a beanbag in a corner of the common room with Kyrillan curled in a ball at his feet.

He heard the North house almost two minutes before they burst into the common room, talking and shouting as they recounted the weekend away.

Sammy stood up as they came in. Dixie and Darius spotted him and came straight over.

'It was amazing,' shouted Dixie above the racket. 'You'd have loved the pyramids, even Milly climbed one!'

'Here,' said Darius, holding a small parcel. 'We clubbed together, all the first years, to get you something.'

'Yeah, to make up for you not being able to go,' added Gavin standing closer to Sammy than he had since the Easter holiday. 'We're both really sorry you couldn't go.'

'Yeah,' said Toby. 'It wasn't your fault.'

'How come you went?' asked Sammy.

Gavin blushed. 'Mum said it was ok when she heard you weren't going.'

'Oh,' said Sammy.

'Open it then,' said Dixie. 'We all chose it.'

Sammy pulled open the purple and green tissue paper, revealing a small triangular pyramid inside a snow shaker. He shook it and gold and silver glitter shimmered through the pyramid.

'Hold it upright to see inside,' said Dixie impatiently. 'Look!'

Sammy tilted the pyramid and held it up to the light. He could just make out what looked like a statue, some coloured jars and a chest with coloured gems to represent the treasure.

'This is great,' said Sammy, turning the pyramid to show Darius. 'Thanks for bringing it back, I wasn't expecting anything.'

'What are friends for?' said Darius, handing him back the coloured pyramid.

'Like it?' asked Serberon, coming up to Sammy with a number of other students. 'You're not infectious, are you?'

Sammy laughed. 'No, Ern was the one with measles, I had an "accident" in Armoury.'

Serberon frowned. 'Yeah, we heard.'

'Do you think it was on purpose?' asked a girl from the fifth year that Sammy had never spoken to. He nodded and she looked closely at him as if trying to read his mind. 'That's terrible,' she said and went back to her friends in the far corner of the common room.

'Like she'd know anything,' said Serberon. 'Pricilla by name and silly by nature. Don't know how she got into Dragamas, let alone made a dragon minder.'

'We don't have dragon minders,' said Dixie. 'Or if we do, I've never seen them.'

'You only get them from the second year up,' explained Serberon. 'Until then, Professor Burlay and the other house heads do it for you.'

'Oh,' said Dixie. 'I didn't know that.'

Serberon laughed. 'Come on, there's time to get something to eat from the canteen before bed.'

'I'm too tired,' said Sammy, yawning suddenly. 'Thanks anyway, being "ill" takes it out of you. Oh, here, thanks for letting me borrow the photos, it was as good as going.'

Serberon laughed and took the album. 'Bet Sir Ragnarok said you can go next year.'

Sammy nodded. 'Yeah, but he's safe saying that.'

'One star, Sammy,' Professor Burlay called across from the common room door, 'and you can all go to bed. I want all first years awake for some serious Astronomics, starting at six thirty in the morning. I want to show you the seven sequences of daybreak.' Professor Burlay raised his voice over groans from the first years. 'Bring your notebooks and pens. This may just come up in your end of year exams.'

CHAPTER 20

THE MOCK EXAMS

Having spent half the night listening to Gavin, Toby, Darius and Amos recount minute by minute their adventures at the Land of the Pharaohs, and the other half in a fitful sleep worrying about the end of year exams, Sammy wasn't impressed when Professor Burlay knocked on their tower door at quarter past six in the morning.

'Morning boys!' said Professor Burlay, blissfully unaware of the bags under their eyes. 'We'll have to be quick. My calculation says that daybreak is less than ten minutes away.'

True to his word, they stood in the semi-darkness outside Mrs Grock's house at twenty-five past six in the morning, watching as the sun emerged over the distant horizon.

'Stage one,' said Professor Burlay. 'Observe the shape, diameter and colour of the rising sun. A dragon knight pays close attention to this as it guides him, or her, throughout the day,' said Professor Burlay, clearly enjoying himself.

'Stage two is where the colours widen, which tells us what, Darius?'

'If it's going to rain,' said Darius, covering a giggle unsuccessfully with his hand.

'Correct!' said Professor Burlay smiling broadly.

Darius stared. 'It was a joke,' he whispered to Sammy and Dixie. 'Hope the rest of the lesson is this easy!'

'Stage three,' said Professor Burlay, holding up his staff. 'Observe the colours. It won't rain today. The colours and the shape are the most important.' He lowered his staff and surveyed the class. 'Take as many notes as you wish, they're your exams not mine.'

'Take notes,' grumbled Dixie. 'Size and colour, that's all he's said so far.'

'Stages four and five,' said Professor Burlay. 'Watch closely at the back, or you'll miss the end. Six, the crest rising and seven, the sun is on its upward ascendant, ready to form the day.'

Professor Burlay looked from the sun to the class and back again. 'Write this up in my lesson please. I won't be there as I have a meeting with Sir Ragnarok, however Dr Lithoman has kindly offered to supervise your work.'

'I bet she has,' muttered Sammy, 'and plot which dragon to kill next.'

'Come on,' said Dixie, stuffing her notes into her shirt pocket. 'Hope there's something hot for breakfast.'

The rest of the day passed uneventfully, with an unofficial game of Dragonball played inside the North tower against students from the East house. Despite only twelve people coming from East, it had been a close game. Still concerned about his hands not being completely back to normal, Sammy kept score for both sides.

'Eleven – Eight,' shouted Sammy as a ball whizzed over his head. 'Good goal Mary-Beth, get us another three!'

The game finished at a quarter past ten, when Professor Burlay shooed them to their tower rooms. The score by Sammy's reckoning was fifteen all.

'That'll be all boys, and girls,' said Professor Burlay, catching Dixie's eye. 'I would have hoped to see you revising for your exams, not playing games. Sleep well. Your lessons have been easy today to get you back into the routine after the holiday and tomorrow you start in earnest.'

'In earnest?' groaned Darius when Professor Burlay had gone. 'Getting up at sunrise this morning was hard enough!'

The following morning, Professor Sanchez had prepared her own mock exam. It was also Simon's birthday and she made them stand up to sing him "Happy Birthday" at the beginning of the lesson.

'Very good,' beamed Professor Sanchez, handing her son a small present wrapped in yellow foil tied with a gold ribbon. 'Just a little something for my eleven year old. Open it later Simon, we must get on with the lesson.'

Barely pausing for breath, Professor Sanchez whisked around the class, dropping test papers on their desks.

'Separate the desks, please,' she barked and with some creaking and groaning, the class pulled their desks away from each other.

Back at her own desk, Professor Sanchez picked up a large brass egg timer. 'You have one hour.' She tipped the timer upside down and placed it at the front of her desk. 'You may start...now.'

Sammy flipped over his test paper, wishing he'd spent the evening revising, sure Professor Sanchez hadn't mentioned the test before the Easter holiday.

The paper was filled with Professor Sanchez's handwritten questions. Sammy found himself thinking it would have taken her hours to write a copy for each of them. He guessed she hadn't and that she'd used the mind control technique Professor Preverence had shown him.

'Question one,' Sammy whispered to himself. 'Using information you have learnt, draw a close representation of three of the plants we have discussed.'

Sammy squiggled a collection of lines into the shape of one of the plants he remembered from an earlier lesson.

Question two was a "fill in the blanks" question, covering Mrs Grock's self-healing potion. Having used the foul smelling mixture on more than one occasion, it was easy and Sammy filled in the words "eggs", "turnip" and "amberoid".

Questions three and four were based on some of the studies they had carried out. They were fact based questions that you either knew, or you didn't. For "What is the boiling point of silver", Sammy left the answer blank and for "Name two places you would find gold ore", he wrote "mine" and "jeweller" which were the first two places that came into his head.

Question five, the last question, intrigued him. It simply read "What do you see?"

'Mind control,' muttered Sammy. He checked the timer on Professor Sanchez's desk. Most of the sand had fallen.

'Think,' muttered Sammy. 'What do I see?' He focussed hard, trying to read Professor Sanchez's mind. All he could see beyond the classroom, in his mind's eye were swirls of white smoke.

'That can't be right,' he whispered. 'Look harder.' He sharpened his pencil, staring desperately at the paper.

At the front of the classroom, Professor Sanchez stood up and surveyed the class. Out of the corner of his eye, Sammy saw her check the timer. The last grain of sand had fallen.

'Time,' said Professor Sanchez. 'Put your pens down.'

'Dragon!'

Sammy spun round. No one had spoken. Everyone else had put their pens down and were facing the front of the class. Without thinking, Sammy scribbled the word on to his test paper and put his pencil flat on the desk.

'Good.' Professor Sanchez smiled briefly. 'Let me see what we have. Pass the papers to the front.'

Sammy reached behind him to take Gavin and Toby's papers. They had both written "nothing" for question five. Sammy wanted to change his answer, but he had already passed his paper forward. Had he been looking too hard for something that wasn't really there?

Almost before Professor Sanchez had received all of the papers, the end of lesson bell rang.

'Wait for the results,' barked Professor Sanchez. 'Nobody leaves.'

Sammy tucked his pencil into his bag and sat down.

'The top marks,' said Professor Sanchez, shuffling through the papers at lightning speed, 'go to Simon and Sammy. Well done. I will give each house a gold star.'

With expert precision, she flicked her staff and drew two large gold stars, tapping them to send them out of the classroom window where Sammy knew they would land on the noticeboards in the Main Hall.

'But I left one question out,' Sammy said to the North table at lunchtime.

Dixie giggled at him. 'You left one question out, rumour is most of the class left all five out!'

'What?' Sammy was shocked. 'All of them?'

'Yeah,' added Darius. 'I put answers down for all of them, but I know they were wrong. Hey, what did you put for that last question? I put "white smoke".'

'I put "dragon",' said Sammy. 'It came to me at the last minute.'

'Oh no,' groaned Dixie. 'I was going to put dragon, but I crossed it out and wrote "smoke". It was really hard to make anything out, even with my eyes shut.'

'Shut!' Gavin laughed at her. 'How did you expect to see anything with your eyes shut?'

'With your mind's eye, stupid,' said Dixie. 'Of course there was nothing on the paper!'

'Oh,' said Gavin, hastily finishing his lunch. 'Got to go…er…somewhere,' he said leaving the table in a hurry.

Dixie looked at Toby who simply shrugged. 'Dunno where he's going.'

'Look at our stars,' said Dixie, ignoring Gavin's sudden departure. 'They look really impressive.'

Sammy followed her pointed finger and saw the coloured house noticeboards. High above any student's reach were a large number of glittering gold and silver stars. On the green, North noticeboard Sammy counted five gold stars and over fifty silver stars, awarded to students from the first to the fifth year. One of the gold stars was his, Sammy thought as he tucked into the roast chicken they were having for lunch.

As they started dessert, Sammy's personal favourite; strawberry Swiss roll and custard, two more silver stars burst into the Main Hall, squabbling with each other to be first to stick to the West noticeboard.

'Look, there's some more,' said Dixie, pouring a large dollop of custard into her bowl. 'Wonder what they did to get those.'

'Knowing Dr Lithoman,' said Darius darkly, 'she probably put them there herself.'

As they finished, Sammy scraping every last drop from his bowl, knowing they wouldn't have Swiss roll again for a while, Sir Ragnarok came into the Main Hall. He stood at the front, his great staff in his hand, waiting for the school to stop talking. A group of boys in the East house were the last to stop talking, their argument over the last of the custard dwindled as they realised the whole school was listening. Sammy saw them go bright red and they stopped talking at once.

'I have good news,' said Sir Ragnarok. 'The end of term is only six weeks away.'

The whole school cheered and Sir Ragnarok waved his staff for quiet.

'Six weeks,' he added, eyeing the students keenly, 'to learn everything you can from Dragamas, the school, the staff, our way of life.'

Everyone cheered again. Some students stamped their feet under the table and others clapped. The noise was deafening.

'As usual,' Sir Ragnarok went on, 'the school exams will take place in the penultimate week.'

'Last but one,' Darius whispered to Sammy as the school groaned.

'And then,' Sir Ragnarok dropped his voice to almost a whisper, 'then, we take on the Shape.'

The school had been ready to give Sir Ragnarok a standing ovation at the end of his speech, but everyone stopped, silent and in shock. "We'll take on the Shape" rang in the ears of every boy, girl and teacher.

Sir Ragnarok stared solidly into the crowd of frozen students, waiting, daring them to challenge him, to question his words. He stared straight at Sammy, his eyes deep and penetrating.

Feeling it was somehow up to him, Sammy stood up and started clapping. He had only put his hands together twice when the rest of the North house stood up and clapped with Sammy at Sir Ragnarok's speech. Sammy heard a chant start further up the table as the rest of the school stood up and joined in and sang: "We will fight the Shape! We will fight the Shape! We will fight the Shape!"

If Sir Ragnarok was taken aback by the unanimous support, he didn't show it and waved his staff for the school to stop and sit down.

But the chant didn't stop and singing "We will fight the Shape!" the fifth years led the students of each house around the tables, snaking between the four rows and out of the Main Hall and on to their next lessons.

As they reached the Armoury classroom, Sammy could tell something was different about today's lesson. Commander Altair was waiting outside for them, the window in the classroom door blacked out and he wouldn't let them in.

'For your mock exam, I have prepared an obstacle course,' explained Commander Altair. 'One by one you shall go into the left hand side of the classroom, along a passage I have created with desks and chairs, until you come out the other side. It should take less than five minutes each and while you wait I encourage you to revise both theory and practical tests from your Armoury textbooks. Yes Gavin, you may go first.'

Commander Altair opened the classroom door, let Gavin inside, then closed the door again. As the door swung shut, Sammy saw why they couldn't see inside the classroom. Commander Altair had sticky taped some black card to stop them peeking while they were waiting for their turn.

About three minutes later, there was a knock on the classroom door. Commander Altair let Gavin out, pressed a finger to his lips and motioned for Gavin to go down the corridor. 'Finish the lesson in the library please. Make notes on what you saw, how you dealt with it and what you would do differently next time.'

Standing at the back with Toby, Dixie and Darius, Sammy didn't like the way that Gavin's usually tidy hair seemed to be standing up on end, nor that he left sooty footprints on the stone corridor floor as he made his way up the stairs to the library.

'I don't like the look of this,' Sammy overheard Tristan Markham say to another boy from the South house. 'Me neither,' came the reply.

Sammy felt a little better when Milly came out, smiling crookedly with a smudge of dirt on her cheek. "It can't be that bad", he thought to himself.

At the halfway mark, with twenty students left to walk through the classroom, a bell ring twice.

'Is that the end of the lesson?' asked Dixie. 'I actually wanted a go at that.'

'Fire alarm?' suggested Darius.

'Both wrong,' said Commander Altair. 'When you get further up the school, you'll have two morning lessons and two afternoon lessons. You only hear the bell if it ties in with your lessons.'

'Oh,' said Dixie. 'So we don't need to do anything?'

'Just concentrate on the lesson,' said Commander Altair. 'You don't get out of it that easily.'

Dixie grinned at him. 'Can I go next?'

Commander Altair nodded and opened the classroom door almost before Simon Sanchez knocked to be let out.

'Good,' said Commander Altair. 'A good use of your staff and you have finished inside the five minute mark.'

Simon looked a little flushed, but he'd come out clean compared with Gavin and Milly. He nodded at Commander Altair, picked up his bag and disappeared up the stairs at the end of the corridor.

'Ok Dixie, your turn.' Commander Altair stepped aside as Dixie assembled her staff. She marched confidently into the classroom. Commander Altair checked his watch and closed the door.

Sammy caught a glimpse of the watch out of the corner of his eye. It was a larger version of his own, with the big "C" for the brand "Casino" stamped around the Roman numeral dial.

Almost like a hologram, Commander Altair twisted his wrist so that the clock face merged with a silver image with tiny lines across it. Sammy guessed it was the contents of the classroom, a red and yellow thermal dot where Dixie was walking.

'No cheating,' said Commander Altair firmly. 'I see you have the same watch, Sammy, slightly smaller, but as efficient. Perhaps I could borrow it for the lesson.'

Almost in a trance, Sammy found he was unstrapping the watch his uncle, Peter Pickering the jeweller, had given him on his seventh birthday.

Commander Altair pocketed the watch and simultaneously opened the classroom door. 'Very good Dixie. Dixie? Are you all right?'

Dixie shook her head, scooped up her bag and ran down the opposite stairs towards the North tower.

Commander Altair shrugged. 'She'll be back. She's got the makings of a Dragon Knight. No one's ever done it that fast. Two minutes and fifteen seconds to beat boys and girls. Who's next?'

Toby pushed to the front. 'I'll go.'

Commander Altair held open the door and stared down the corridor in the direction that Dixie had left. 'Perhaps someone should go after her,' he murmured.

Four minutes later, Toby finished the course as dirty as Gavin. 'It's easy,' he mouthed, dusting himself off before heading towards the library.

Several minutes later, Sammy and Darius were the only ones left and no one had come close to Dixie's time. While they waited, they tested each other on some of the self-defence moves they had learnt and practised against the wall.

Stepping around a high kick from Darius, Commander Altair opened the door and let a worried looking West girl out of the room.

'The fear of fear is as fearful as fear itself,' said Commander Altair, checking his watch. 'Seven minutes Megan, a little too long for the obstacles inside. Keep practising and you'll be fine in the exams.'

Almost in tears, Megan shuffled past Sammy. She picked up her bag and walked off, her staff tucked under her arm.

'Darius, are you ready?' asked Commander Altair.

'Yes Sir!'

Darius ducked under Commander Altair's arm and disappeared into the classroom, leaving Sammy alone with Commander Altair in the corridor.

'So Sammy,' began Commander Altair, 'what do you think of Dragamas?'

Sammy put down his Armoury book, wondering what the right answer was. 'It's good so far, Sir. A lot better than my old school.'

Commander Altair nodded. 'That's good. What did you want to be Sammy, when you're older, a job, a profession?'

'I, um,' started Sammy, looking nervously at the door, 'I wanted to be a taxi driver or a racing driver, something to do with cars, maybe, but since I've been at Dragamas, I want to be a Dragon Knight,' he finished in one breath and looked up at the Armoury teacher.

'A worthy choice.' Commander Altair smiled at him. 'You have the mind for it, a few more years at Dragamas and I believe you would make a fine Dragon Knight.'

'But...'

Commander Altair put his finger to his lips. 'Trust Sir Ragnarok. He knows a lot more than he lets on. I can see Dragamas outliving either you or I.'

'Sir,' started Sammy.

'In good time,' said Commander Altair. 'You will find out your duties as a Dragon Knight in good time.'

Sammy nodded as Commander Altair pulled open the door at the split second that Darius knocked.

Darius burst out of the Armoury classroom covered from head to foot in a thick layer of jet black soot. He sent it flying in all directions as he shook himself and ruffled his hands through his hair.

'Hey, watch it,' said Sammy as a cloud flew towards him.

'That was awesome,' said Darius, his eyes glazed over. 'Awesome,' he added, picking up his bag, staff and the self-defence chart they had been working on. 'Good luck Sammy.'

'Thanks,' said Sammy as he walked through the door Commander Altair held open for him. He caught a glance from Commander Altair that unsettled him. There was something in his eyes Sammy couldn't figure out. He couldn't be sure, but as Commander Altair closed the door, Sammy couldn't help feeling that he wasn't alone in the classroom.

The door clicked shut and Sammy blinked to make sure his eyes were open as the room seemed as dark either way. He couldn't see how Dixie had made it out so fast. She was afraid of the dark and must have run through the course at top speed.

Sammy felt a strange feeling creep into his stomach and felt goosebumps break out across his shoulders and down his arms. He jumped as he stumbled into a wooden table. He reached for his staff, the command "fire" burning on his lips, sure he had heard a footstep behind him. He crouched under the desk as someone, or something, walked past him. He felt the hairs stand up on the back of his neck.

As quietly as he could, Sammy tiptoed back to the door. He twisted the handle, but it was locked.

'I must go right round,' Sammy whispered to himself as he retraced his steps in the darkness. Commander Altair had blocked all of the classroom windows and Sammy could hardly see his hands in front of him. He could still hear footsteps across the other side of the classroom.

Crouching on all fours, Sammy crawled his way to the front, wishing he hadn't given his watch to Commander Altair. With a bit of practice, he was sure he could have conjured the lines and dots to show him which way to go. He checked his empty wrist and guessed he would be way past Dixie's time of two minutes and fifteen seconds.

Sammy stopped at a thick object and using his hands, felt the ornate legs of Commander Altair's wooden desk. He stood up, desperately trying to make out the shapes of the obstacle course in the darkness. Panic got the better of him and he reached for his staff and whispered "fire".

As if his staff understood the situation, instead of the normal sized fire, it gave him a flame no larger than a candle flame. It gave an eerie orange glow to the classroom.

Sammy looked up from the flame and clapped his hand to his mouth in horror. Standing with their backs to him were five black hooded shapes. They towered above him, their shadows wavering almost to the ceiling in the firelight.

Shaking and with his heart pounding, Sammy used the flame to guide him to the door. He focussed on the flame, willing it to go out. With a faint hiss, the flame disappeared and the room plunged into darkness.

Sammy tapped quietly on the door. He tried the handle again, but it was still locked. He pulled it harder and it seemed to come with him.

'Bolts,' whispered Sammy, clutching the broken doorknob. 'It's locked from inside!'

He crouched down, feeling for the lever, any metalwork sealing him in with the hooded figures. His hand closed around a cold metal handle and he pulled it, flinching as it grated and grumbled from locked to unlocked.

Sammy tried the handle again but it didn't budge. There seemed to be a second bolt out of his reach at the top of the door. He froze as he felt something close in behind him, something warm and silky, the cloaks of the hooded figures. Sammy yelled as he looked straight into the red eyes of the masked figure, feeling hands close in around his neck.

The last thing he remembered was falling to the floor, hearing his staff clatter beside him.

'And that's how it happened?'

Sammy opened his eyes again and nodded, his head still spinning. He'd woken up a few minutes ago to find himself back in bed at Mrs Grock's. Ern was lying opposite him, his face still swollen with the measles, the rest of him tightly tucked into the hospital sheets.

Sammy looked around. The bedside table was overloaded with home-made cards, a bunch of flowers and several boxes of chocolates. Someone had even brought Kyrillan to him. He wriggled his feet as Kyrillan blew a jet of warm smoke between his toes.

'Sammy.'

His head feeling like a lump of lead, Sammy turned to see who had called him. Ern was asleep and he couldn't see anyone.

'Sammy!'

The voice sounded more urgent this time and Sammy sat up, coming face to face with Dixie, who was leaning against the window, perched on a branch of one of the apple trees in Mrs Grock's garden.

'Hurry!' hissed Dixie. 'It's me and Darius. She won't let us in and I can't hold on forever.'

'Hang on,' whispered Sammy, throwing back the covers and finding himself dressed in his pyjamas, which he was sure he hadn't been wearing in the Armoury mock exam.

'Thanks,' whispered Dixie. 'Another ten seconds and the branch would've broken!'

'Come in,' whispered Sammy. He held the second floor window open and Dixie jumped from the branch to the windowsill.

Ern looked up as she jumped down into the bedroom.

'This is nice,' said Dixie. 'Hey, you've had loads of cards. Hi Kyrillan, are you looking after Sammy?'

Sammy helped Darius down into the bedroom as well and Ern stared at the three of them.

'I'll tell Mrs Grock,' hissed Ern. 'No visitors, that's what she said.'

'No you won't,' said Dixie, brandishing a bright red lipstick. 'One word and I'll paint a thousand measles on you with this. You won't be back at school before the summer holidays.' She took off the lid and waved it at Ern. 'Milly lent it to me,' she explained, giggling as Ern shrank out of sight under his sheets.

Feeling a little shaky, Sammy sat on the bed, pulling the covers around him. Kyrillan edged closer. In his dragonish way he seemed to know what Sammy was thinking and puffed a warm jet of steam into Sammy's hands.

'Kyrillan is so well trained,' said Darius, looking very envious. 'Even with two eyes, my dragon keeps bumping into things.'

Noticing a pile of books under the bed, Dixie picked one up and flicked through it. 'You haven't done any of the crosswords I sent you,' she looked put out.

'He's only just woken up this morning,' said Ern, looking warily for Dixie's lipstick. 'Three weeks he's been in here and he's only just woken up,' he cackled with hoarse laughter that ended in a coughing fit. Dixie had to slap him hard on the back before his face changed from purple to normal.

'Thanks,' wheezed Ern. 'Three weeks!'

'No,' whispered Sammy, feeling cold suddenly all over. 'It's not true.'

Darius nodded solemnly. 'Three weeks out cold. Didn't think you'd make it personally.'

'All I remember is falling,' said Sammy. 'Falling in Armoury, Commander Altair's test.'

'Sir Ragnarok sorted him out for that,' said Dixie. 'Didn't think putting Mrs Grock's firebreathing dragon in the room was the way to teach first years.'

'Mrs Grock's dragon?' Sammy stared.

'Yup,' said Darius. 'She blew clouds of smoke everywhere. Everyone came out dirty, remember?'

'Except Simon Sanchez,' said Dixie. 'He said he controlled her. That's what he told everyone but we reckon the dragon left the room when he went in.'

Sammy smiled faintly. 'Did they say what I had to get past in the room?'

'No Sammy,' said Dixie. 'It wasn't like that, you should have seen Mrs Grock's dragon like the rest of us.'

'No one knows how the Shape got in,' added Darius.

'They locked me in,' whispered Sammy. 'Put their hands around my neck.'

'Commander Altair saved you,' said Darius. 'That's why Sir Ragnarok didn't sack him. He saved your life.'

'He must have come in after you,' said Dixie. 'Perhaps he knew it would happen.'

Darius nodded. 'The Shape are after you, remember?'

'The door was bolted from the inside,' said Sammy, thinking back to the darkened classroom. 'No one came in after me.'

'So,' whispered Dixie, 'that means…'

'…they were already there,' finished Darius, his eyes white. 'Any of us could have met them.'

'Perhaps they were after the dragon,' said Ern from the other side of the room. 'Didn't mean to listen in but you're not exactly quiet. If they're after draconite, a big dragon like that would have plenty of powers.'

'Yeah Sammy, maybe Ern's right,' said Darius. 'Maybe that's what it was.'

Sammy shook his head. 'No, they were after me. Commander Altair made me go last on purpose.'

'Wait until I see him,' said Dixie, standing up her fists raised. 'I'll show him.'

'I'm sure you will lassie,' said a voice from the bedroom doorway.

Dixie dropped her fists, her cheeks the colour of beetroot. 'Hello Mrs Grock.'

'Hello yourself, lassie. What do you think you're doing in my patients' room? Are you ill?'

Dixie shook her head. 'No Mrs Grock.'

'Are you staying?'

As Darius started to say "yes" Dixie grabbed his hand and pulled him through the bedroom doorway and past Mrs Grock.

'See you Sammy,' she shouted up from the bottom of the stairs.

Two seconds later, the front door banged and Sammy could hear them running back to the castle.

'Ooch, I don't know, that girl, all the greenhairs, all they do is cause trouble. Are you all right my Dragon Knight?'

Sammy smiled at her. 'I feel loads better. Can I go yet?'

'Well,' said Mrs Grock, examining him closely. 'Let me take your temperature and if it looks all right you canna go. Gave us all a mighty scare you did. Sir Ragnarok called your parents out twice, thought you were a gonner.'

'My parents have been here?' Sammy was surprised. 'They're not supposed to be back until the start of the summer holidays.'

'Ooch yes, I remember your parents all right. Lovely folk, a bit too city folk for my liking, if you know what I mean.'

'Did they say anything? Any messages?'

'Not that I canna remember,' said Mrs Grock thoughtfully. 'Your ma said she might have to work on a few days of the summer holiday. Sir Ragnarok said you canna stay with me, or you canna go to one of your friends if you'd prefer.'

'Thanks,' said Sammy. 'Can you ask Dixie's Mum if I can stay and get picked up from her house?'

Mrs Grock smiled. 'I'm sure that canna be arranged my Dragon Knight.' She pulled at Sammy's cheek affectionately. 'A fine young knight you'll be one day.'

Sammy nodded, his mouth full of the thermometer resting under his tongue. 'Can I take Kyrillan home for the summer,' he mumbled.

'Of course,' said Mrs Grock. 'I shouldn't really be telling you this, but Sir Ragnarok wants all dragons out of the school this summer. In case we don't come back,' she added ominously, rearranging her hairpins with trembling hands. 'There is some good news however. You have a visit to the Floating Circus at the end of term. John's invited me, so I'll need you both out of here before then.'

Sammy took out the thermometer for Mrs Grock to read. 'I'm not missing this visit!'

'Me neither,' said Ern, surveying the last of his measles in a long handled mirror.

As Mrs Grock turned to go, Sammy had a sudden thought. 'What lessons have I got this afternoon?'

Mrs Grock laughed. 'Ooch no lessons laddie, it's a Sunday. Probably wouldn't hurt to go over your notes this afternoon and this evening. Word is, your exams start tomorrow.'

Sammy sat bolt upright. 'Mrs Grock, I think I have a temperature now!'

Mrs Grock threw back her head and laughed. 'It'll take more than a temperature or the measles to keep you away from those exams. If you don't pass, you'll both be kept down a year.

The prospect clearly terrified Ern. 'Sir Ragnarok can't do that! My parents will kill me even if the measles doesn't!'

CHAPTER 21

CHEATERS

Having spent the whole afternoon studying with Dixie, Darius, their dragons and Kyrillan, Sammy woke the following morning feeling confident. He was sure he knew everything it was possible to know about all of his subjects.

His brain hurt as he ran through the star charts from Astronomics, the gemstones from Gemology and potions and mind control tips from Professor Sanchez.

Commander Altair had called into the North common room to apologise and wish Sammy "good luck". Still reeling from the possibility that Commander Altair had set him up, or worse, was part of the Shape, he had been almost silent whilst the Armoury teacher had been in the North common room.

Sammy dressed quicker than usual, tickled Kyrillan's ears and threw his duvet neatly up to the pillows.

When he pulled back his curtain, Amos was pacing around his bed with his dragon, Morg, perched on the chest of drawers. Gavin and Toby were testing each other from a Gemology book and Darius was fast asleep.

'Are you ready for the exams?' asked Sammy.

'Ready?' groaned Amos. 'Even with all the revising I've done, I'll never be ready.'

'Me neither,' said Toby, giving Sammy a puzzled look.

'What?' asked Sammy, straightening his staff and checking the onyx was secure.

'Well, you've just had three weeks knocked out in Mrs Grock's and you want to do the exams?'

'Weird,' added Gavin, tapping his head. 'You sure the Shape didn't knock you out a bit too hard?'

Darius gave a loud snore and sat upright. 'Someone say something about the Shape? Not here are they?'

Gavin laughed nervously. 'No, but it's Monday morning and we've got the first of our exams.'

'Oh no!' shrieked Darius, leaping out of bed. 'I told you to wake me up early. I've got fifty-seven pages I wanted to revise before the Gemology exam!'

'Doesn't make any difference now,' said Amos, staring out of his tower window. 'Besides, if Dr Lithoman's marking them, she'll have us marked down from the start.'

'Yeah,' said Toby, 'top marks for her fishies.'

'Ooh my little fishies,' sniggered Gavin. 'Wish Professor Burlay gave us top marks.'

'I'm glad he doesn't,' said Darius. 'At least I know I've worked hard for my marks.'

'Not that he's been here much,' Amos scowled at Sammy. 'Three weeks off just to revise, can't be bad.'

'Hey wait a minute,' Sammy snapped. 'I don't remember anything since that Armoury lesson. I was in a coma.'

'Yeah Amos,' said Darius, 'his parents came down and everything.'

Amos shrugged. 'I suppose we'd better get going.'

Sammy tapped Darius's shoulder at the top of the stairs. Gavin and Toby had followed Amos and were already two spirals down.

'Does everyone think that?' asked Sammy. 'That I've had three weeks off to revise, swot up, practise maybe?'

Darius shrugged. 'Amos is just jealous. He's worried he'll be kept down a year.'

Sammy pointed at Amos's bed plaque. 'It still says one year.'

Darius looked across. The plaques with each of their names, North house and the mysterious dates were still there, as shiny as they had been on the very first day. Morg was asleep at the end of Amos's neatly folded bed, his tail hanging down over the edge.

'I suppose you're right. He might get kept down a year.'

Sammy checked his watch, remembering he'd felt glad to see it on the dresser at Mrs Grock's. Commander Altair must have returned it to him while he was in the coma. It read ten minutes to nine.

'We'll be kept down a year if we don't get a move on.' Sammy raced Darius down the spiral stairs and arrived in the Main Hall just in time for the start of the Gemology exam. Dr Lithoman gave them a frosty stare as they flung themselves into two empty seats.

In the Main Hall, the four dinner tables had been replaced with about a hundred classroom desks and chairs. Sammy was sitting two rows from the front. Commander Altair was the supervising teacher closest to him. Sammy's desk was directly behind Amos, with Dixie on his left and Darius on his right. Dixie mouthed "good luck" to him and Sammy nodded, hoping his answers would be good enough so he could go up to the second year and not be kept back to repeat the first year.

At precisely nine o'clock, Dr Lithoman rang a small silver bell on her desk at the front of the Main Hall and upended a wooden sand timer. Sammy flipped over his exam paper and picked up his pen.

The first question had two parts: "In three pages or more, describe in detail the process involved with the formation of the crystals found in the caves of Mount Vinegar".

Sammy didn't even remember studying Mount Vinegar and he crossed out the question and went on to the second part: "Choose three gemstones and write one page of detailed information about each stone".

'Sounds good,' Sammy whispered to himself, choosing onyx, diamond and emerald.

He was midway through the second page on diamonds, having covered onyx easily inside the first twenty minutes. He stretched and caught a glimpse out of the corner of his eyes at Dixie's paper. Like him, she seemed to have chosen the second question and was writing furiously in amongst sketches that Sammy guessed were the gemstones she had chosen. He looked away as Dixie flung her left hand in the air whilst still scribbling with her right.

Commander Altair stood up to answer her question. He briefly glanced at Sammy's paper as he wove between the desks.

'Yes Dixie?'

'Please can I have some more paper?'

Commander Altair nodded and dropped some lined sheets on her desk.

'Twenty-five minutes remaining,' said Dr Lithoman from her desk on the stage at the front of the hall. 'Just twenty-five minutes left.'

Sammy stared around the room. He could see that Gavin and Toby had finished, each laying their pens on top of their answer papers. They seemed to be using the time to pull faces at each other. Sammy turned back to his page on emeralds. He had written three quarters of a page, starting with the locations where emeralds were found, the formation and polishing techniques they had been taught.

When Sammy next looked up, Dr Lithoman was checking her wooden sand timer. Most of the sand had fallen through. He saw her shake it a little and check her watch. Discretely, he looked forward at Amos's paper and stared. It was completely empty. Amos hadn't even started. Sammy could see him visibly shaking as Amos twisted his pen as if he was desperately trying to shake out some words. All Sammy could see fall out was a dribble of blue ink. He racked his brains, wishing Amos would start.

And then it came to him. He would write Amos's paper for him, using the technique Professor Preverence had taught him. Sammy focussed on the paper, concentrating, visualising the ink appearing on Amos's sheets.

By the way Amos's back suddenly straightened, Sammy could tell it was working.

'Don't give the game away,' Sammy said to himself, grateful when Amos hunched over the paper and picked up his pen.

Just a few seconds later, Dr Lithoman stood up and rang her silver bell.

'This is the end of your exam,' she said with a smile. 'Put down your pens, keep your papers on the desks and leave by the nearest door.'

Sammy didn't need telling twice. He dropped his pen on top of his answers and walked to the back of the Main Hall followed closely by Dixie and Darius.

'That was really easy,' said Darius, grinning at them. 'The way she's been going on about it, I thought we were going to have to grow our own crystals or something.'

'I don't know,' said Dixie. 'I hope I wrote enough. I chose onyx, diamond and emerald.'

'Me too!' said Sammy, turning round at a tap on his shoulder.

'Not cheating are we?' asked Simon Sanchez.

'What did you choose?' demanded Dixie.

Simon grinned. 'Mum told me Dr Lithoman would give top marks for onyx, diamond and sapphire, so that's what I chose.'

'Sapphire,' groaned Dixie when Simon had gone. 'We should have known.'

'What?' asked Darius, turning round from a conversation with Gavin and Toby.

'Blue sapphires for top marks,' said Sammy.

'That was obvious,' said Darius, grinning smugly. 'What did you choose?'

The rest of the exam week passed smoothly. Sammy felt confident that he had done reasonably well in most of the exams. He had got used to swapping exam papers in the morning for rigorous games of Dragonball and Firesticks in the afternoon. Sports master Mr Cross told them he wanted all the first years physically as well as mentally fit and wouldn't excuse anyone from his warm ups, or from their full length games.

On the last night of the exam week, Sammy headed back to the North common room with the other North first years.

'Hey look!' squealed Dixie as she pushed open the oak panelled door. 'A feast!'

'Where?' demanded Darius pushing past. 'Wow, look!'

Sammy looked. The common room at the foot of the North tower had been rearranged into a restaurant like setting, with enough tables and chairs to comfortably seat everyone in the North house.

Sammy stared at the transformation. The comfy chairs had been pushed to the side of the room and the study tables had been pushed together and piled high with food. There were plates of crisps, sweets, sausages on cocktail sticks and sandwiches with every filling imaginable. The North students milled around the tables, helping themselves to a little of everything.

Professor Burlay was already in the room along with several other teachers, including Dr Shivers who waved when he saw Sammy, Dixie and Darius come in to the common room.

Sammy joined the line of students, shuffling around the tables, filling his plates with a bit of everything in the feast. As he reached the internal noticeboard, two large notices caught his eye.

The first was a handwritten note that said "Sir Ragnarok requests Dixie Deane, Amos Leech and Samuel Rambles visit his office at nine o'clock on Monday morning" and the second said "Visit to the Floating Circus next weekend!" in bright pink letters.

'Sammy look!' squealed Dixie, clutching Sammy's arm and making him jump. 'We've got to go to Sir Ragnarok's office.'

'Probably failed my exams,' said Amos, staring gloomily at the board. 'This really weird thing happened in the Gemology exam,' he said, explaining what had happened.

'Wow,' said Dixie a minute later. 'Wish that had happened to my paper. I just wrote any old thing.'

'Yeah, but at least it was your own work,' said Darius. 'Whatever mark you get, it's yours.'

Dixie nodded, scratching her head. 'Wonder why we have to see Sir Ragnarok.'

'He probably thinks we cheated,' said Amos stiffly. 'We all wrote about the same stones, didn't we?'

The thought hit Sammy like a punch in the stomach. 'Cheating,' he gasped. 'Surely other people chose the same stones?'

Gavin shook his head. 'I spoke to Tristan in the corridor after the exam. He knew what everyone chose. Loads of people chose onyx, but I don't think anyone else chose diamond and emerald.'

'They must have,' said Toby, grinning. 'You're making that up!'

Gavin coughed. 'Yeah well, Sammy fell for it!'

Sammy grinned as well. 'It can't be that.'

'We'll find out on Monday,' said Dixie, shoving her hands in her pockets defiantly. 'Come on, this feast looks great!'

Halfway through the meal, Sammy decided he'd never eaten so much in his entire life. He'd tried everything from the ice cream with pink marshmallows to the toasted sandwiches, munching cakes, biscuits, crisps and taking several mouthfuls of a combination of everything he could reach.

Throughout the evening, Professor Burlay kept coming over to their table, carrying a silver tray stacked with coloured drinks. He handed out glasses of strawberry and raspberryade, limeade, cherryade, orangeade, blueberry juice and cola before retiring back to his own table to share a bottle of something stronger with Dr Shivers that brought colour to Dr Shivers's grey ashen face. They giggled louder and longer than any of the North students, stopping only when Mrs Grock called in, bringing a tub of capsules, "to prevent stomach ache", Sammy heard her say as she whisked past him.

As the grandfather clock beside the fireplace struck midnight, Professor Burlay walked over to their table with the capsules. 'Anyone ill over here?' he asked.

Darius raised his hand. 'Are those for stomach ache?'

Professor Burlay nodded. 'Anyone else eaten too much?' he asked, handing capsules to Darius and Gavin. 'These will clear anything up in two minutes flat.'

'My parents make these at home,' said Darius. 'Once I ate three plastic bags and a mouthful of engine oil. I took one of these and I was fine.'

Sammy stared. 'Really?'

Darius nodded. 'I chucked up twice before they let me have one. They said it would teach me not to do it again!'

'Did it?' asked Gavin. 'If me or Toby did anything like that, Mum would have put us both in hospital. She doesn't believe in those kind of medicines.'

Darius shrugged. 'Works fine for me,' he said, washing the capsule down with a large swig from his glass of blueberry juice.

'What's in them?' asked Sammy. 'Back home we have pills. You can get them from the supermarket.'

'Really?' asked Darius. 'So you don't have to make your own?'

Sammy laughed. 'I don't think my parents would know where to start!'

'I wouldn't be too sure of that Sammy,' came Dr Shivers' voice from behind Sammy's chair. 'I knew them well at one point, I did,' Dr Shivers swayed from side to side.

'He's drunk,' said Dixie disgustedly. 'I think we're supposed to go to bed. Professor Burlay's just been over to Milly's table.'

'Come on,' said Darius, picking up a handful of biscuits and another toasted chocolate sandwich. 'I can't believe we're going to the Floating Circus next weekend.'

'Should be awesome,' said Gavin, stuffing two bottles of limeade up his jumper. 'Get those crisps Toby, they were really good.'

The four boys waved to Dixie as she went across to the girls' staircase, pursued by Serberon. In their tower room Amos had already changed into his pyjamas and was sitting up in bed, stroking Morg and reading a book by candlelight.

'More food?' Amos looked surprised.

'Yep!' Sammy grinned and threw crisps, biscuits, a squashed piece of cake and a handful of toasted sandwiches on to their shared table.

Gavin pulled the bottles of drink out of his jumper and Toby emptied a heap of crisps on to the pile.

'What did you get, Darius?' asked Toby. 'We all brought stuff.'

Darius reached inside his own jumper and pulled out five plates and five cups.

'Good thinking,' said Sammy, pouring the drinks. 'Come on Amos, there's plenty.'

Amos looked up from his book. 'It's ok, I'm fine, really.' He stood up and drew his curtain.

'Weirdo,' muttered Gavin. 'Still, more for us.'

'Do you reckon he's ok?' asked Darius. 'Seeing his name on the board must've freaked him out.'

'It freaked me out,' said Sammy.

'Wonder what Sir Ragnarok wants,' said Gavin, piling crisps into his mouth. 'Fwenty,' he mumbled.

'Twenty?' said Toby. 'Can't hear you!'

'Fwenty,' Gavin repeated, pointing at the crisps and then his mouth. 'Fwenty,' he said again, a shower of crisps flying out of his mouth.

Darius giggled hysterically. 'Let's have a go.'

Sammy grinned, his thoughts of Amos forgotten. He joined in the game, piling crisps on his tongue. He reached ten easily and was about to lay his eleventh when there was a quiet knocking at the door.

'You're in trouble now,' came a mutter from behind Amos's curtain.

'Quick!' said Toby. 'Hide the food!' At lightning speed, he pulled his duvet over the table, his dragon squawked and flew out of the way.

Sammy and Darius ducked down and hid behind Toby's curtain.

Gavin opened the door, an innocent smile on his face. 'Professor what's…uh Dixie?'

Sammy peaked round the curtain. Dixie was alone at the top of the tower staircase, dressed in her nightdress and some pink rabbit slippers. She had her duvet in one hand and a rope lead in the other.

'Hi Dixie,' said Sammy. 'What are you doing here?'

'Yeah, this is the boys' tower,' added Toby. 'Hey, what's up?'

Dixie wiped her eyes. 'They don't understand me,' she said, walking past the hidden feast to sit on the end of Sammy's bed.

'Hey,' started Gavin.

Sammy elbowed him in the ribs. 'It's ok,' he reassured Dixie, stumbling as her three foot long dragon, Kiridor, followed her into the room.

Amos stuck his head round the curtain. 'We'll see what Sir Ragnarok has to say about this,' he sneered. 'Keep it down, I'm trying to sleep.'

'Hey!' said Toby. 'Mind your own business.' He picked up his duvet and threw it around Dixie's shoulders. 'Do you want anything to eat?'

Dixie sniffed and nodded. She tucked into one of the now-cold toasted sandwiches. 'You've got loads,' she said. 'I took some up to our tower room, but everyone had gone to sleep.'

'What's wrong with that?' asked Gavin. 'I bring up loads of food at home. It's better when Toby's asleep.'

'Liar,' said Toby. 'I always get the best food, and the most.'

'Hey,' said Sammy, nodding towards Dixie. 'So what happened?'

'Serberon,' said Dixie, shaking slightly. 'He said I was a cheat and a disgrace to the family. He said I hang around with boys too much. He said I have the wrong friends, leading me into trouble. When I asked if he meant you as well,' she pointed at Sammy, 'he said he'd rather have you as a brother than me as a sister.'

Sammy felt his jaw drop. 'He what?'

Dixie burst into tears, coughing as some of the toasted sandwich caught in her throat. 'He told me not to come home. He said Mary-Beth could have my room. He said our Mum would throw me out and that Daddy...' she coughed even more violently and rubbed her eyes with the corner of Toby's duvet, '...that Daddy would hate me.'

'Ouch,' said Gavin.

Dixie shook her head. 'He meant it, started packing my stuff up, said I'd be expelled.'

Sammy stood up. 'If you're going to be expelled, so are me and Amos. Let's go and tell him that.'

'He thinks you're getting awards for top marks, or a prize for telling on me. I hate him.'

Sammy had already thrown on his jumper, over the top of his pyjamas. 'Come on, let's go.'

Dixie stared at him. 'Really?' she whispered. 'You'd do that for me?'

'Course we would,' said Sammy. 'What are friends for?'

Dixie dried her eyes, fresh tears forming.

'Hey, don't cry,' said Sammy nervously.

'I'm not,' said Dixie, wiping her eyes again on the duvet.

'Liar,' said Gavin and Toby at the same time.

'I'm...I'm just, well, really happy, uh, so how many crisps did you get up to?' she coughed again. 'I had to stand outside the door for a few minutes to let Kiridor catch up. Fwenty, wasn't it Gavin?'

Gavin laughed. 'Bet you can't beat it. How many can you do?'

'Fifty,' said Dixie. 'Watch.' She stuck out her tongue and loaded the first crisp. 'Uhn.'

'One,' said Darius, passing her the bowl. 'Two, three...six...ten...fifteen...eighteen, nineteen.'

'Twenty,' said Gavin, looking surprised. 'Even Toby can't do more than fifteen.'

'Fenty-uhn,' mumbled Dixie, 'afwenty-tuh.'

'Yeah well done,' said Gavin, still in shock. 'I'll have to practice a bit more.'

At a thud from the direction of the door, Sammy spun round, watching as it creaked open.

'Uh-oh,' said Toby, seven crisps stacked on his tongue.

'Professor Burlay,' said Gavin, putting on his well-practised wide-eyed innocent stare. 'What do you want?'

'Crisps?' asked Darius, holding out the bowl.

'Noise,' giggled Professor Burlay, holding tightly to the banister. 'Complaints,' he pointed to the floor below, pausing as he caught sight of Dixie. 'Green-hair.'

'Yes Professor,' said Dixie, standing up.

'Bed,' said Professor Burlay, holding open the door.

Dixie stared at Sammy.

'It's ok, I'll speak to Serberon tomorrow, I promise,' he said, holding out the remainder of the biscuits.

'Now,' giggled Professor Burlay, 'the dragon ashwell.'

'Come on Kiri,' said Dixie, coaxing her dragon out from under Sammy's bed. She walked slowly out of the tower room, followed by Kiridor. As they reached the door, Kiridor flicked his tail up to the table and seized a packet of crisps into a hidden coil in his tail. They sloped out of the tower each looking as miserable as the other.

'Blimey,' said Gavin when Professor Burlay, Dixie and Kiridor were out of sight. 'How about that.'

'Wait until I see Serberon,' said Sammy, his teeth clenched. 'He'll wish he'd never said that.'

'Then you will get expelled,' muttered Amos from behind his curtain.

'Shut up!' said Toby. 'Sammy's not getting expelled.'

'Go to sleep,' added Gavin. 'It'll be ok in the morning.'

'Yeah,' said Sammy, cheering up. 'We've got a game of Firesticks first thing, then Dragonball all afternoon.' He took off his jumper and got into bed. 'Night everyone,' he said out loud, then, 'night Kyrillan,' he whispered to Kyrillan who was curled in a ball under his bed.

After the feast, the weekend seemed to disappear as if being sucked up by some giant vacuum cleaner. Monday morning seemed perilously close as Sammy threw his muddy clothes into the laundry bin.

'Good game of Dragonball,' he said climbing into bed.

'Yeah,' agreed Toby. 'Can't wait until we get to ride our dragons.'

'Me neither,' said Sammy. 'I can't believe it's Monday already.'

'Did you speak to Serberon?' asked Amos.

The room fell silent as Sammy cursed himself. 'Tomorrow,' he said firmly. 'I'll see what Sir Ragnarok wants, then I'll talk to him...even if it means I can't stay with them in the summer,' he added.

'You can always stay with me,' said Darius. 'My parents sent me a letter after they heard about you and the Shape. They really want to meet you.'

'Thanks,' said Sammy, accepting some of Darius's chocolate. 'You still get a bar every day?'

Darius grinned. 'Every day.'

'Wonder if you'll get them next year?'

Darius shook his head. 'I didn't get any at home. I guess it only works for this bed.'

'Someone's in for a surprise,' said Sammy, taking a bite of the bar.

'Oh, yeah.' Darius slapped his forehead. 'We're not in this room anymore, are we. It'll be a bit sad to leave.'

'Yeah but it's one step closer to finishing school. Start at the top of the tower, move down each year and after the fifth year, you're out.'

'We should leave something behind,' said Darius.

'Like what?'

'Darius woz ere,' said Darius, giggling. 'We could write it on a wall somewhere.'

'Shh,' came a voice from behind Toby's curtain.

'So what,' said Sammy. 'I'm probably getting expelled in ten hours time!'

"Expelled in ten hours time" Sammy muttered inside his head, thousands of questions racing in his brain: "What would his parents say?" "Who would look after Kyrillan?" As the questions buzzed louder inside his head, he realised it was Monday morning. He'd fallen asleep without realising, his questions unanswered.

Sammy sat bolt upright in bed, accidentally knocking Kyrillan on to the floor.

'Sorry Ky,' whispered Sammy. 'I've got to see Sir Ragnarok this morning.'

He got up and dressed, paying particular attention to ensure his tie was neat and his shirt was tucked in. Sammy tightened his belt and threw on his school blazer. He added a slick of gel to his hair and pulled open his curtain.

Amos was standing in front of him, identically dressed, his face paler than his white shirt.

'Look at you,' said Gavin, peering round his curtain, Toby at his side. 'You're smarter today than when we first met you.'

'Thanks,' Amos replied stiffly. 'If things don't go well, it might be the last...'

'Cheer up,' said Sammy. 'It'll be ok.'

'Yeah, you're right.' Amos glared at Gavin and Toby. 'Whatever happens, it's been better here than learning at home with my parents.'

'It's better than my old school too,' said Sammy, marching quickly out of the tower room, afraid he'd say something stupid or worse, burst into tears. He climbed down a little quicker than normal and had to stop quickly as he bumped into Dixie who was climbing up.

'Getting a bit regular this,' sneered Amos. 'People will start talking.'

'Yeah whatever,' snapped Dixie. 'Guess what Sammy, Serberon tried to apologise this morning but I ignored him, pretended I couldn't hear him. Turns out Mikhael and Jason had a go at him for having a go at me, let him stew I reckon.'

'Oh,' said Sammy. 'I'll still say something to him, you know, like I promised I would.'

'Here's your chance,' snapped Amos. 'You wouldn't think we had an expulsion to get to.'

'Hey Sammy!'

Sammy turned around. Serberon was behind him.

'Has Dixie said anything,' asked Serberon, looking uncertainly at them.

Sammy just had time to nod as Dixie gripped his wrist and dragged him into the corridor.

'No one speaks to him, ok?'

'Uh Dixie,' Sammy started, freezing under her icy stare. 'Ok, let's get this over with first.'

'How do we get to Sir Ragnarok's office again?'

'Through the passage in the Main Hall behind the knight picture,' said Sammy.

'Go there a lot, do you?'

'Just here,' said Sammy, pulling the tapestry aside to reveal the steps. He found he had butterflies in his stomach by the time they climbed to the first of Sir Ragnarok's office doors.

Sammy hung back as Amos knocked twice on the solid oak door.

The door creaked open. Sir Ragnarok's smoke grey cat, Lariston, stared at them, his large amber eyes glowing as he surveyed them.

'Come in please,' said Sir Ragnarok, in an unusually firm voice.

They walked up the seven steps into Sir Ragnarok's office under Lariston's watchful eyes. There was no "please sit down" like on Sammy's last visit to the office. In fact, he was frowning so hard both his eyebrows seemed to be knotted together. He sat at his desk, tapping his fingers on some papers.

'I will not tolerate cheating,' he said quietly. 'The three of you have near identical Gemology papers and I understand you were sitting next to each other in the exam,' he shook his head. 'Each one of you should be ashamed. At Dragamas, cheating is an expellable offence.'

Sammy felt the butterflies leap into his throat as he nodded with Dixie. Amos was still as white as his shirt.

'Are we…are we…' started Amos.

'Expelled? No, I am offering you the chance to leave.'

'Ttt…tto leave?' stuttered Amos.

'Do any of you have anything to say for yourselves?'

Sammy gulped down the butterflies and, with a lump of lead forming in his stomach, he raised his hand.

'Yes Sammy. If you have excuses, save your breath.'

Sammy gulped again. 'No Sir, it was me, my memory, mind, paper…'

'Slow down boy, are you saying you projected your answers on to Amos's and Dixie's papers?'

Sammy shook his head. 'Just Amos. He hadn't written anything so I…'

'You thought you'd help out. It didn't cross your mind we create an illusion so the row in behind can't read the answers of the row in front. Usually it's the other way round. We don't get many students trying to project their answers elsewhere.'

Sammy felt his cheeks burn. He stared firmly at his freshly polished shoes. 'I'm very sorry.'

'Quite,' said Sir Ragnarok. 'None the less, I admire you for owning up. That must have taken some courage…yes Dixie, is something funny?'

'No sir,' Dixie grinned. 'Just Sammy not realising.'

'Hmm, I would have thought Professor Burlay would have said. Anyhow, I have a meeting to attend to. As punishment, I would like you to retake the exam Sammy. You and Dixie may leave now.'

'Great,' groaned Sammy as they left. 'Let me guess, I'll have to do it when everyone goes to the Floating Circus.'

'How come Sir Ragnarok wanted to see Amos?' asked Dixie.

'Dunno,' said Sammy. 'Seriously, do you think he'd do that, make me miss the visit?'

'Maybe,' Dixie looked thoughtfully at him. 'Perhaps he'll speak to Professor Burlay and let you do it one night this week.'

As they reached the bottom of the stairs, Amos came flying down behind them.

'Hey! He did it!' yelled Amos, dancing his way through the knight tapestry.

'What?' asked Dixie. 'What did he do?'

'Everything!' shouted Amos. 'Everything is fine!'

'Why?' snapped Dixie. 'It was really brave of Sammy to own up.'

Sammy coughed. 'Yeah but it was my fault. I shouldn't have tried to help. It's so stupid and didn't even work anyway.'

Amos stopped dancing. 'It did work,' he said in a serious whisper. 'I hadn't written anything. Sir Ragnarok just didn't want to make me look bad in front of you.'

'But he said it didn't work,' said Dixie.

Amos sighed. 'You'd think getting the top mark for Gemology would mean you're not stupid, but you don't get it.'

For the second time that morning, Sammy looked at his shoes, thinking hard. 'So, if I cheated and it worked, but Sir Ragnarok said it didn't, do I still have to retake the exam?'

Dixie shrugged. Amos started dancing again, still wearing his massive grin.

'What?' snapped Dixie. 'You not answering your questions got Sammy into trouble.'

'Who cares,' Amos carried on grinning. 'I've changed houses!'

'What!' Dixie exploded with rage. 'You can't have.'

'I can and I have,' said Amos. 'Starting next term, I'm in East with Simon Sanchez.'

Leaving Sammy and Dixie open mouthed, Amos danced his way out of the Main Hall.

'He can't do that,' said Dixie. 'It's not fair.'

'Fair or not, it's happened.'

Sammy and Dixie jumped. Professor Burlay had come down the staircase after them.

'Secret passages,' he explained.

'It's not fair Professor Burlay,' said Dixie. 'How come Sammy has to retake the test...'

'...when Amos didn't even try? Yes, I see what you're saying but I'm sure Sir Ragnarok has his reasons.'

'When do I have to retake the test?' asked Sammy, keeping his fingers crossed.

'Soon,' Professor Burlay checked his watch. 'Actually, now. Dixie, you have a free lesson. Take the girls from your tower to practice flying with your dragons. No, not on them, with them. You stay firmly on the ground please. Anyhow, Sammy, my office if you please and a word of warning, don't write about any of the stones you chose before.'

'Ok.' Sammy exchanged an "it'll be all right" glance with Dixie and followed Professor Burlay up to the Astronomics classroom.

Once inside, Professor Burlay closed the door and pointed his staff at the blackboard. He muttered something under his breath and Sammy stared open mouthed as a pile of books shuffled out of the way, revealing a small square door at knee height.

'I've been meaning to ask Sir Ragnarok to make it bigger,' said Professor Burlay, bending down to crawl through the opening.

On his hands and knees, Sammy followed Professor Burlay through the door, into a low-ceilinged L-shaped passageway and out into a small rectangular room.

'We're under the stargazing balcony,' said Professor Burlay, straightening himself. 'Welcome to my office.'

Sammy stood up and took in the tiny room with its leaning stacks of paper, overcrowded bookshelves and two desks with high-backed emerald green office chairs. The room was lit by a large green candle and four diamond shaped lattice windows which overlooked the Dragonball pitch.

Sammy peered out of the nearest window. He thought he could just make out the Dragamas constellation and compared it with a chart on the opposite wall.

'Take a seat Sammy,' Professor Burlay pointed to the smaller of the two desks. 'I have some marking to do and you'll need to concentrate if you want to go to the Floating Circus.'

Some two hours later, Sammy put down his pen as Professor Burlay called the end of the exam.

'Put down your pen Sammy. Oh, good, you're finished. Was that any easier?'

"Not really" was what Sammy wanted to say. It wasn't fair that he'd had to do two Gemology exams. Instead he nodded. 'Hope that's ok.'

Professor Burlay laughed. 'I'm sure it is. Thought you might have tried projection to get it over with.' He stared straight into Sammy's eyes. 'Sir Ragnarok was right. There is good in you. Although we have dark times ahead, I'm proud to have you in my house.'

Leaving Sammy puzzled, Professor Burlay stacked up his papers and blew out the candle. He stood up and went to the door.

'After you Sammy,' Professor Burlay smiled. 'I'll give these to Dr Lithoman. You'll have your results at lunchtime.'

Still feeling puzzled, Sammy joined the first years in the underground mine for the last ten minutes of Gemology. Dr Lithoman gave him a frosty stare and pointed a stubby finger at him.

'Here comes the cheater,' she whispered, loud enough for the class to hear.

Sammy found himself staring at her hand. On the third finger of her right hand she wore a large ring with a blue-green stone flashing in the centre. When he was sure no one else was looking at him, Sammy mouthed "draconite" at her. Dr Lithoman seemed to flinch as she waved him to an empty seat.

She returned to the front of the class and began sketching a small red formation on the blackboard. Although he'd missed most of the lesson, Sammy leaned over Darius's notes and learned that it was a stone they would be using next year on the end of their staffs.

'More power,' said Dr Lithoman, scraping the chalk across the board with a flourish. 'More knowledge! More work! More power!'

Sammy was distracted from her speech as Captain Stronghammer rumbled through the classroom with an empty wheelbarrow. He disappeared into the mine as the bell chimed. Dr Lithoman gave him a frosty glare and erased the chalk drawing from the blackboard.

'How did it go?' Dixie asked Sammy as they poured out of the classroom. Behind them Gavin and Toby were high-fiving each other. They ran past shouting "last Gemology lesson" to anyone who'd listen.

'Uh yeah,' said Sammy, staring after Gavin and Toby. 'I think I did ok. Professor Burlay said I'll get the results after lunch.'

'Great,' said Dixie. 'Guess what, it's chicken pie for lunch, again.'

'Again?' said Sammy. 'That's all we've had since last Thursday.'

'Sir Ragnarok's clearing everything out for the holiday,' grumbled Darius, heaving his bag over his shoulder. 'Chicken pie must be all that's left.'

The lunch hour passed painfully slowly for Sammy. He kept looking out for Professor Burlay, ignoring Dixie and Darius's efforts to distract him. He was so busy checking the door that he didn't notice Dixie pouring salt over his slice of chicken pie, or when Darius swapped his water for a cup of vinegar. He took a swig from the cup as Professor Burlay finally arrived and spat it back in disgust at the bitter taste.

Professor Burlay looked worried as he approached the North table. He stopped opposite Sammy, a frown etched between his eyebrows.

'I failed, didn't I,' said Sammy, miserably picking grains of salt out of his pie with his fork.

Professor Burlay smiled. 'On the contrary Sammy, Dr Lithoman has given you a fair mark.'

'Nothing is fair about Sammy retaking the exam,' stormed Dixie. 'Nothing!'

Professor Burlay leaned close. 'I couldn't agree more,' he whispered. 'She hasn't given anyone in North or South an "A" for twenty years.'

Sammy stared 'Twenty years?' he exclaimed. 'Why not?'

Professor Burlay shrugged. 'Who knows. Anyway, Simon Sanchez got the first Gemology "A" for the East house. They've never had an "A" for as long as I've been teaching here.'

'But Simon said he cheated,' said Dixie, her face flushed pink against her green hair. 'He said Professor Sanchez told him the stones Dr Lithoman would give top marks for.'

'I'm sure,' said Professor Burlay. 'But at least you know your marks were earned.'

'I'd rather have an "A",' said Dixie, crossing her arms defiantly.

Professor Burlay raised his right eyebrow. 'Would you?' he asked quietly as he walked away from the table.

CHAPTER 22

THE END OF YEAR AWARDS

The rest of the week flew past. Most of the teachers spent the lessons marking exam papers. As well as the first years', they had papers from all five years in the school and let the lessons drift in organised games that required little or no intervention.

Whilst marking papers on the Friday afternoon, Commander Altair organised a fencing competition where two students at a time stood on chairs three feet apart and practised knocking the staff out of the other person's hands. The winner stayed on their chair until their own staff was knocked out of their hands.

Sammy was particularly pleased to beat both Simon and Amos using nothing more than his thoughts and a light tap from his staff. It earned him a "good Sammy" and a silver star from Commander Altair as well as a very black look from Amos.

Tristan Markham finally knocked Sammy's staff out of his hands as his concentration broken by the loud chime of the school bell, ringing for the end of the last lesson on the last day of term.

Sir Ragnarok had given each student a strict timetable for the evening and an orange wristband for their visit to the Floating Circus taking place the following morning.

Sammy checked his timetable. It started with an awards ceremony in the Main Hall. Dressed in his last clean white shirt and school trousers, he walked with Dixie, Darius and the rest of the first years into the Main Hall and sat at the North table.

Sir Ragnarok raised his cup. 'A toast to all of our students and teachers.'

Sammy joined the rest of his table, standing up and clapping. They drank from their glasses of orange juice, toasting the end of the year.'

'Now,' said Sir Ragnarok with a broad smile. He pushed a stray hair away from his eyes and stroked his freshly trimmed silver beard. 'To the awards,' he added, waving in the direction of the noticeboards which were covered from top to bottom with gold and silver stars of all shapes and sizes.

'In fourth place this year,' roared Sir Ragnarok, in a voice so loud, Sammy thought he'd have heard if he'd stayed up in the tower dormitory, 'is the West house.'

A volley of "boos" came from Dr Lithoman and the students in the West house, matched equally by cheers from everyone in North, South and East. Sammy clapped especially loudly, glad Dr Lithoman had lost.

'In joint second place,' continued Sir Ragnarok, 'with a total of two thousand and three silver stars and fourteen gold stars are the East and South houses.'

'We won!' shrieked Dixie. 'North's first! We won!'

Sammy clapped louder than ever. Professor Sanchez and Commander Altair glared at each other.

'This cannot be,' Professor Sanchez said loudly. 'North do not win.'

Commander Altair clapped sportingly as Professor Burlay collected a large silver Dragamas shield with the year and the word "winner" embossed in gold.

Professor Burlay held up the shield and mouthed "well done" in the direction of the North table.

'Now,' said Sir Ragnarok when the clapping and foot stamping had died down. 'We have three school honours to hand out, a medal for bravery plus the exam results I know you've all been waiting for. The results will determine your careers based on your knowledge and application of that knowledge. Dragamas is merely a stage for you to perform on, a book for you to learn from and a place for you to show everyone, including yourself, that you are strong, wise, brave, noble, courageous and honourable with integrity and valour.'

'Blimey,' Dixie whispered in Sammy's ear. 'What's he been drinking?'

Sammy giggled. 'Dunno, but I hope he hurries up, I'm hungry.'

Sir Ragnarok paused at a nudge from Professor Sanchez. 'Ah yes, well,' he coughed, ending the list. 'School honours go to Ernest Westbridge of the West house. Despite having measles for a large portion of the summer term, he has passed all of his exams with grades A and A*. Congratulations Ern!'

Sir Ragnarok held out a long paper scroll tied with a blue ribbon. Ern marched proudly up the steps and on to Sir Ragnarok's stage to accept his prize. When the clapping died away, Sir Ragnarok picked up a second rolled parchment.

'School honours are also awarded to Genevieve Rivers for her outstanding results. Genevieve has been accepted into the University of Rock where she will study a degree in Gemology with the aim of becoming a qualified Healer.'

'Like my parents,' whispered Darius. 'They went to Rock and now they're some of the best Healers in the world.'

'Anyone getting a scroll that's not in West?' grumbled Dixie, looking up as Genevieve left the stage and Sir Ragnarok picked up the third scroll.

'Matthew Silver,' said Sir Ragnarok. 'Matthew has more than earned his School honours for the tireless work he has put in, helping Captain Stronghammer and the dwarves, to take care of our dragon population. Matthew of the West house has helped feed nearly seven hundred dragons all year and hasn't missed a single day of study.'

'Ugh,' whispered Dixie, 'another one from West.'

'Didn't save Mary-Beth's dragon, did he?' Sammy muttered under his breath.

Matthew Silver walked up the steps and whispered something to Sir Ragnarok.

'My mistake,' said Sir Ragnarok. 'Matthew is in East.'

The school clapped twice as loudly as Matthew returned to his seat. Sir Ragnarok let the clapping continue for several minutes while he fumbled with a small black box on his table. He took it to the side and asked Mrs Grock to prise it open.

The clapping subsided as a white light shone from a metal object inside the box, reflecting in the faces of each and every student in the Main Hall.

'Ah yes,' said Sir Ragnarok. 'The award for bravery, rarely given to someone so young and inexperienced. Someone who has bravely faced mortal danger.

Sammy felt his heart skip a beat. Sir Ragnarok couldn't mean him. Just looking at the brightness flowing from the metal object, a cross, he decided, was so pretty, so bright, his eyes were drawn instantly to it.

'None the less,' Sir Ragnarok went on, 'the boy, or girl, who receives this medal should remember this is an award for events accomplished. It is not a talisman or an invitation to danger. The wearer, however the award is won, must remember...'

Sammy was sure Sir Ragnarok looked directly at him.

'...must remember that they too are human.' Sir Ragnarok paused, letting the school whisper excitedly, wondering who would get the shining cross.

'It's you,' Dixie whispered to Sammy. 'It has to be, mortal danger, you faced the Shape three times this year.'

'Four,' replied Sammy, 'if you count the first day. But it's not me. Other people have done better, braver things.'

'Samuel Richard Rambles!' Sir Ragnarok shouted above the din. 'Come! Receive your medal for bravery. The cross of the Dragon Knight – Validus Aureus Draco – Mighty is the Golden Dragon. Here,' Sir Ragnarok swung the cross over Sammy's head.

Sammy was in a spin, he felt dizzy, the award, for him, against the Shape.

'I will remember,' he whispered. 'Mighty is the Golden Dragon.'

'Mighty indeed,' whispered Sir Ragnarok. 'We are all proud of you.' Then he gripped Sammy by the shoulders and so the whole school could hear, he recounted Sammy's encounters with the Shape.

'Dark times we have ahead indeed,' finished Sir Ragnarok. 'The ransom if you remember, may be paid by the end of the summer term, or it may not. Time will tell.'

Sir Ragnarok squeezed Sammy's shoulders one last time and let him go back to the North table.

As Sammy sat down, he was handed the Dragamas shield, passed down from Professor Burlay. It was as shiny as his cross, but it didn't glow. He touched the embossed "winner" and passed the shield to Dixie so it could travel back up the other side of the table to Professor Burlay.

'That cross is so cool,' said Dixie, reaching over and holding it. 'Oooh, it's cold too.'

'Really?' asked Darius. 'You'd think it would be hot with all that light coming out of it.'

'Yeah but if it was too hot, you couldn't wear it,' said Gavin. 'Wish I had one.'

Darius let go of the cross and stared at Gavin. 'No you don't. To get this, Sammy had to face the Shape. If the stuff he says happened to him happened to me, my parents would have taken me out of the school.'

'I suppose,' said Gavin, unable to take his eyes off the medal.

'My parents don't even talk about the Shape at home,' added Darius. 'The sooner they're defeated the better.'

'Dr Lithoman's a Shape,' said Sammy. 'She's not defeated.' He pointed to the staff table where Dr Lithoman and Commander Altair were drinking from the same goblet of wine.

'Part of the Shape,' Darius corrected him, 'and you don't have any proof.'

'Then we'll get some,' said Sammy, gripping his cross for bravery. 'If it's the last thing we do.'

Dixie nodded. 'I'm in.'

Sir Ragnarok stood up again. 'Exam results,' he said, reaching for another box of scrolls. 'Astronomics first. Professor Burlay will read out the name, the house and the result as usual. You'll find the full table of results on the noticeboards in each common room later this evening. Now, while the results are read out, please eat.'

Sir Ragnarok spread his arms wide and thousands of dishes appeared on the house tables, each piled high with hot and cold snacks.

'When you're ready, Professor.'

Professor Burlay took the top scroll and cleared his throat. 'Starting with the North first years, Amos Leech, C, Darius Murphy, B+, Dixie Deane, A*...'

'A*,' shrieked Dixie, her eyes shining like emeralds, 'A*!'

Professor Burlay was drowned out as Serberon, Jason and Mikhael leapt across to the first year table and lifted Dixie on to their shoulders. In that split second, Dixie seemed to forget her quarrel with Serberon and accepted his bear hug with a huge smile, her green hair ruffled in the scrum.

'Sammy Rambles, A. Well done Sammy,' Professor Burlay beamed. 'From South, Simon Sanchez, A.'

The list went on, but Sammy had stopped listening, his mouth wide open.

'Grade A,' he whispered. 'I've never got grade A.'

'A*,' grinned Dixie. 'Beat-cha!'

'I bet Professor Burlay marked you up,' teased Darius.

Dixie's smile vanished. 'He didn't, did he?'

'No Dixie.' Professor Burlay had finished reading the Astronomics marks and was standing behind her chair, pouring drinks for Gavin and Toby from a double-necked bottle. 'Those big eyes and green hair don't work on me,' he paused and smiled. 'You got your own mark. In fact, I double checked it!'

'So it's all mine?'

'Yes Dixie, all yours,' Professor Burlay looked across at Sammy and pointed at the medal around his neck. 'I think we'd all prefer it if you don't get another one of those next year.'

Sammy laughed, not sure if Professor Burlay was joking or not. "Joking" he decided as he tucked into a chocolate Swiss roll. Professor Sanchez stood up on the stage and began reading from the Alchemistry scroll of marks.

By the time the feast and the exam results had finally been read out, Sammy had received four A's for Astronomics, Alchemistry, Armoury and Dragon Studies and an E for Gemology which he couldn't care less about since he knew that Dr Lithoman had marked him down.

On one hand he wished he'd got five grade A's, he knew his parents would be pleased, but on the other hand, as Sir Ragnarok had said, he was only human after all.

'Last day tomorrow,' Darius whispered as they turned out their dormitory lights.

In the darkness, Sammy nodded, torn between wanting to see his parents and wanting to stay at Dragamas with his new friends. It took him a long, long time to fall asleep, Kyrillan tucked into a fold of the duvet down by his feet.

CHAPTER 23

DRAGON CLIPPERS

Next morning, Sammy woke to the familiar warm sunlight streaming through the windows. He sat up, rubbing the sleep out of his eyes.

'Last day today, last night tonight,' he whispered to Kyrillan.

As he was about to get up, a pair of trousers flew over his curtain rail, followed by a volley of rolled up socks and hysterical laughter. Sammy brushed the trousers aside and opened the curtain. Gavin and Toby were bombarding their room-mates with anything they could lay their hands on. Darius joined in, throwing his bath towel over Gavin's dragon, who promptly ripped a hole trying to get out.

'Ooops!' giggled Darius, scooping up an armful of t-shirts. Even Amos joined in, if only to throw back what wasn't his.

They stopped at a knock from Professor Burlay on their tower door.

'Come in!' yelled Gavin, throwing the last of his clothes at Darius.

Professor Burlay pushed open the door and surveyed the mess with a gasp. 'You'll have to leave this boys, we're late already,' he said, shaking his head in despair. 'Sir Ragnarok wants North to go first and since you're first in the North house, you'd better get a move on. The girls are already on their way with Professor Hilton.'

Sammy looked out of his window. He could easily make out Dixie by her green hair, amongst the snaking line of students.

Professor Burlay stepped backwards out of the tower room, still shaking his head at the mess. 'Downstairs in five minutes please, and don't forget your orange wristbands.' He held up his left wrist and pointed at the orange band. 'Hurry!'

Sammy, Darius, Amos, Gavin and Toby dressed at lightning speed, throwing on whatever was closest. Sammy put on a pair of odd socks, one slightly blacker than the other. He threw on black jeans and a faded green t-shirt, tying his favourite chequered shirt around his waist. He hopped on one foot trying to tie his shoelaces faster and ended up falling over, nearly squashing Kyrillan.

'Come on,' said Gavin, swinging open the door.

'Ready!' shouted Toby, threading his hand through his orange wristband. 'Let's go!'

Sammy ran with them, down the five flights of stairs, through the common room and out into the corridor.

Professor Burlay was waiting for them, staring at his watch.

'Good timing boys. You should be able to get to the cave in time for the next lift.' Professor Burlay pointed at the window.

Through the murky glass, Sammy could just make out a marshmallow coloured blob streaming up the pearlescent

410

tube. More students were on their way to the Floating Circus.

Professor Burlay held the castle door open and they ran out into the sunshine, racing each other to be first to get to the clearing. There was a slight breeze in the air that rustled the grasses and tickled their legs as they ran past.

They reached the clearing as Professor Sanchez disappeared into the Dragon's Lair, followed by several students from the East house. Sammy leaned over to get a stitch out of his stomach. He looked up at the sky, through the dense branches and rays of sunshine filtering down into the quiet forest.

Sammy heard some birds calling high in the trees and stood up straight, facing the large black mouth of the Dragon's Lair. The milk white Dragon's Teeth stones seemed to glow as the sunlight shimmered on and off in time with the trees swaying in the breeze.

Sammy leapt up the steps, in front of Amos, behind Gavin and Toby. Darius followed, pausing to watch as Professor Sanchez and the East students flew up the pearlescent tube.

'Come on Darius,' shouted Sammy. 'There's no one else here. We're next!'

Darius ran in as the lift came rumbling back down into the cave. They showed their wristbands to Captain Firebreath, who grunted and waved them into the lift cubicle, slamming the door shut once they were inside. He pulled the lever towards him and they had the familiar "whooshing" feeling in their stomachs as they were flung to the top of the tube and out into the busy reception office at the top.

Sammy flashed his orange wristband at Sargent Rockhammer, who let him through the turnstile. As soon as he was out into the land, he spotted Dixie and her green haired brothers eating ice creams from Merry Megan's ice cream caravan.

'Hello Sammy,' shouted Serberon.

'You took your time.' Dixie took Sammy and Darius's hands and dragged them to the caravan counter to get ice creams.

'Oh, hello lovvie,' Molly Burlay beamed at them. 'Strawberry and lime again? One each?'

'Ok,' said Sammy. 'Just a small one.'

'Small strawberry and lime Mum,' Molly called into the back of the caravan. 'Yes, put it on Dragamas bill, they've all got orange bands today.'

'The Dragamas bill?' exclaimed Sammy.

'Aye lovvie, you don't have to pay a penny.' Molly turned back inside the caravan. 'Yes Mum, Dra-ga-mas.' She turned round and sighed. 'If I've told her once today, I've told her a thousand times.'

'Er Molly,' started Sammy. 'Could you cancel my ice cream please. Sir Ragnarok needs the money to fight the Shape more than we need ice creams.'

Molly stared at him. 'Why bless you lovvie, how sweet,' she turned back into the caravan. 'Cancel that Mum, yes, no charge to Dragamas.' She turned back to Sammy, Dixie and Darius. 'Right, now they're free, do you want one?'

'Three large with everything,' Dixie grinned. 'It's ok, it's a joke. Could I get a small lime ice cream, please?'

Molly laughed. 'A small lime it is lovvie. What would you like boys?'

'May I have the same please,' said Sammy.

'Strawberry and lime for me please,' said Darius, 'with a flake.'

'Right you are,' Molly beamed at them. 'Have a seat, I'll bring these over in two shakes of a dragon's tail.'

True to her word, they only had time to sit at the table with Gavin, Toby and Dixie's brothers before Molly returned with three mouth-watering ice creams, each with a giant flake. Sammy remembered from their last visit that the flake went from the top of the ice cream to the bottom of the cone.

'Here you are lovvie,' said Molly, handing Darius his ice cream.

'Mmm,' said Darius, taking a huge bite out of the flake.

'Lime for you Sammy,' said Molly, handing him a tall green ice cream with a giant flake towering out of the top. 'And a green ice cream for a green haired girl,' chuckled Molly.

Dixie frowned as Serberon, Jason and Mikhael laughed as well.

'Thanks Molly,' she said stiffly. 'Have you heard from your father yet?'

Molly took a step closer to the table and put her finger to her lips. 'Shh,' she whispered. 'We don't talk much about it at the best of times, but it's said that they will return soon.' She tightened her apron and walked back to the caravan where Simon Sanchez and Amos were queueing up with other students from the East house.

'Come on,' Sammy heard Simon call. 'Let's get some service around here.'

'What was that about?' demanded Serberon. 'What did you mean Dixie, about her father?'

Darius answered, his mouth full of flake. 'Her Dad and Dixie's Dad are together somewhere.'

'Oh,' said Serberon, putting on a serious face. 'Then I guess my Dad's there too.'

'Yeah,' added Mikhael, 'mine too.'

'Perhaps,' said Darius, the joke sailing over his head.

Sammy let out a laugh he'd been holding in.

'You're stupid sometimes,' giggled Dixie. 'My Dad, our Dad, it's the same person!'

Darius went red and slapped his forehead. 'Of course it is!'

'Shall we go and explore?' asked Gavin as soon as Darius had finished his ice cream.

'Mmm, good idea.' Darius nodded and stood up.

'Yeah, we're off as well,' said Mikhael. 'We promised Mum we'd bring back some clippers to do her dragon's toenails. Her old pair snapped last month.'

'Apparently they have,' said Jason, who up until then had been silent. 'We think it's her idea of getting a second pair so we can help.'

Serberon nodded. 'Yeah, we'll meet you at the Big Top later.'

'Ok,' said Dixie. 'See you later.'

'We're going as well,' said Gavin. 'I owe Toby a ride on the ghost train.'

Toby grinned. 'I won the boat race.'

'Boat race?' asked Sammy. 'We didn't see anything like that.'

'You should keep your eyes open,' said Toby. 'There's loads of stuff beyond the Big Top.'

'Come on then,' said Darius excitedly. 'Let's go!'

They split up at the entrance to the Big Top. Gavin and Toby ran off towards a large grey train suspended between two trees.

'The ghost train,' said Dixie with a shiver. 'Glad we're not going that way.'

'We could,' suggested Darius, laughing at Dixie's face.

'No way,' said Dixie. 'There is no way I'm going on the ghost train.'

'Not even for this?' asked Darius, snatching Dixie's hairband.

'Give it back!' shouted Dixie, chasing Darius around the popcorn stall, her green hair streaming out behind her.

Sammy laughed as Darius dodged Dixie, waving the hairband just out of her reach. He looked around as something caught his eye. It was Dr Lithoman, scurrying to the back of the Big Top, carrying a brown parcel tied with string.

'Odd,' muttered Sammy, waving as Professor Burlay and Mrs Grock came towards him.

'How's my little Dragon Knight?' beamed Mrs Grock. 'Are you well?'

'Not here alone are you Sammy?' asked Professor Burlay, looking concerned.

'I'm fine, thanks,' said Sammy. 'I'm not alone. Dixie and Darius are here somewhere.'

Professor Burlay looked around anxiously. 'Dixie, Darius, over here please,' he said, relaxing a little as they came over. Darius looked slightly guilty and more than a little ruffled.

'You're supposed to stick together.' Professor Burlay frowned and held out his hand.

Meekly, Darius put the green and gold hairband into Professor Burlay's outstretched palm.

'Yours I presume?' said Professor Burlay looking at Dixie and her dragged-through-a-hedge hair.

'Yes Professor,' said Dixie. 'Thank you.'

Behind Professor Burlay's back, she stuck her tongue out at Darius.

Satisfied they were back in a group, Professor Burlay and Mrs Grock moved over to the popcorn stall. Professor Burlay bought a bucket sized container filled to the brim with multi-coloured popcorn.

Sammy turned to Dixie and Darius. 'What do you want to do? There's the boats on the lake over there, or we can go to the stalls to win prizes.'

'Boats,' said Dixie.

'Prizes,' said Darius.

Sammy groaned. 'Boats then prizes?' he suggested.

'Ok,' said Darius. 'Bumper boats, one each and whoever stays the driest wins.'

Sammy looked at the large lake across from them. There were hundreds of tiny boats following a man-made course, complete with a beach and a lighthouse at each end.

'I don't think it's those kind of boats,' said Sammy.

'Remote control!' yelled Darius as they got closer. 'I always wanted one of those.'

'They're fixed,' said Dixie, pulling the controls as far as they would come out of the wall. 'I'm number ten,' she said, standing on tiptoe to look over the rail. 'Can you see it?'

'Over there,' Darius pointed across the lake. 'You've got a ferry boat.'

'Great!' said Dixie. 'What are you?'

Sammy searched the lake for his number four boat, but it was nowhere to be seen.

The man running the stall came up behind them.

'Aye, she's in for repairs, number four. Try this one,' he said, handing Sammy the controls for number thirty-three.

Number thirty-three turned out to be an orange rescue boat. By the time Sammy had finally got the hang of the heavy steering wheel and the "stop" and "go" buttons, nearly two hours had gone by playing games and running pretend rescue missions on the lake.

'Come on,' said Darius, steering his boat, another ferry as big as Dixie's, into the harbour. 'Let's try something else.'

They spent the next few hours exploring the exotic market stalls set out by people from the land. Almost anything you could think of seemed to be for sale. There were dwarves selling coloured jewels in every shape and size, young women selling hand woven oriental rugs, talking nineteen to the dozen and bartering with passers-by to buy their rugs with matching cushions.

Other stalls sold fruit, pastries, cakes and every kind of sweet Sammy had ever seen. He recognised the foil wrapped sweets Sir Ragnarok liked amongst the rows of truffles, candies, chocolate buttons and brightly coloured jelly beans. He bought a bag of curly candy from an old woman who put in some extra chocolates when he handed her the money and wrote the amount in her sales book.

'Saves me asking me grandson to write it down for me,' she cackled. 'He's good with them letters and numbers, but I can't get him away from the ghost train. He runs it, you know,' she added proudly.

Munching on red and yellow curly candies, Sammy made his way with Dixie and Darius to the very edge of the land, where the edges curled back over their heads, slippery and impossible to reach.

'You'd never get out,' said Dixie, after trying to jump up and reach the curve.

Darius bent down into a crab on his hands and knees and helped hoist her up so she could see over.

'Sky! Just clouds and sky,' she called, reaching up over the curb. 'Ow!' Dixie shrieked as she was thrown backwards and landed on the grass.

'You canna get out that way lovvie,' the old woman from the sweet stall cackled. 'The only way in and out is through the glass building at the other end. Never been there meself, but I've heard of it many a time from me grandson.'

'Wow,' said Dixie. 'So you've been here your whole life.'

'Aye,' said the old woman, 'and me parents before me. Been here for twelve generations as I know and I'm a hundred and seven.'

'A hundred and seven,' echoed Darius. 'You're really old.'

The old woman laughed. 'You remind me of meself at your age. Thought I'd be young forever!'

'There's no way I'll get that old,' whispered Darius. 'Come on, let's see if the Big Top's ready.'

They left the old woman chuckling to herself and walked back towards the large red and yellow tent in the centre of the land.

Dixie stopped at one of the hardware stalls and bought a pair of long handled dragon toenail clippers from a young man. He winked at Dixie as she handed over her coins and slipped a trial-size sachet of nail moisturiser into her bag.

'My brothers will have forgotten about them,' said Dixie as they walked on. 'How old do you reckon he was?'

Darius laughed. 'Too old for you. Besides, you've got me and Sammy, what more do you want?'

Dixie rolled her eyes. 'Come on, there's a show at three. I want to see that lion again.'

'Rolaan the lion,' said Darius, holding up a crumpled circus leaflet. 'I want to see the acrobats.'

Sammy checked his watch. It was five to three. 'We've got five minutes,' he said. 'We should be able to get a good seat before it starts.'

They went straight through the Big Top ticket entrance. The clown who had previously squirted them with water was shaking his head at one of the acrobats. He had taken off his orange curly wig and was mopping his forehead with a red and white handkerchief. Curious, Sammy held

Dixie and Darius back and crouched behind the ticket booth.

'Don't know what the boss will say if he doesn't make it,' muttered the clown. 'He's not been in the best of moods lately.'

'That he's not,' replied the acrobat, shaking his head. 'Not since the Shape threatened Dragamas.'

'His best mate and everything,' added the clown. 'Him and Sir Ragnarok go back to the beginning of time.'

'It's a sad, sad day,' said the acrobat. 'Still, we must go on with the show.'

The clown laughed half-heartedly. 'Two of my clowns short and no lion,' he grumbled. 'Chin up eh?'

The acrobat nodded and helped the clown straighten his wig. In return, the clown held up a mirror and the acrobat dusted his Lycra suit with a cloud of glitter.

'On with the show,' said the acrobat.

They marched through the "Circus Staff Only" door and disappeared into a canvas corridor in the folds of the Big Top.

'What was that about,' whispered Darius as they ducked under the empty ticket barrier. 'They've lost two clowns and the lion.'

'I wanted to see that lion,' said Dixie, jumping as a figure appeared beside them.

The man was tall and dressed in a black suit with a white shirt with ruffles down to his bulging waist and a black bow-tie tucked under his chin. His face was large and red with coal black eyes, eyebrows and a bushy black twirling moustache. His hair was slicked back with gel and coiled out under his tall black circus top hat. He didn't look happy to see them.

'What,' he roared, 'are you three doing here?'

419

Sammy held up his wrist with the orange wristband. 'We're here for the circus – Ow!' The man had seized his wrist to take a better look.

'Humph,' replied the top hatted man. 'Well it won't be much of a show today.'

'We heard,' said Dixie, a little too enthusiastically. 'Um, I mean, there was a clown.'

'Don't talk to me about those miserable, good for nothing, waste of space, clowns. More useless than the acrobats and that's saying something.'

'Hey!' interrupted Darius. 'We love the circus.'

'Are you the ringmaster?' asked Sammy timidly.

'I am,' the man frowned. 'For my sins I am the Andradore of Andradore's Floating Circus. Bunch of kids my lot. I'd swap with Ragnarok any day.'

'We'd better go in,' said Dixie, looking a little in awe of the ringmaster.

'Don't bother,' said Andradore. 'The show won't start until I say so and with Rolaan ill, I'm not sure I can be bothered.'

'Your lion's ill?' said Dixie. 'But I loved the lion. My brothers brought me back a…'

'Stuffed toy lion?' finished Andradore. 'Not quite like the real thing I'm afraid.' He rolled up his sleeves showing off a series of scratches and tooth marks. 'Still I'm sure it kept you amused until the batteries ran out – Grrr!'

Andradore laughed. 'Look at me, the worst day of my life and I'm laughing with a bunch of kids!'

'Laughing's good for you,' retorted Darius. 'Everyone knows that!'

'Ah yes, the wise one,' said Andradore, smiling. 'But if you'd had the day I've had, you wouldn't know whether to laugh or cry.'

'So tell us,' said Dixie impatiently. 'What can be so bad?'

'Well,' said Andradore, sitting down on an upturned barrel. 'My two best clowns have fed themselves and Rolaan some poison,' he said flatly. 'The clowns will be fine in a week or two, thanks to your Mrs Grock. My lion, I'm afraid, he's…he's…' Andradore's face cracked, 'he's going to die.'

He pulled an enormous handkerchief out of his coat pocket and blew his nose loudly. He rested his arm on an empty barrel. 'Mrs Grock has done everything she can, bless her. Most upset she was. Your Professor Sanchez is there now but unless Sir Ragnarok comes, I fear Rolaan will die.'

'Why?' asked Sammy. 'What can Sir Ragnarok do?'

'He drinks the juice of the red berries,' said Andradore. 'His own red berry potion. It changes his blood. One drop has the healing power of a thousand draconite crystals. It is so important that he can come.'

'Why wouldn't he?' asked Dixie. 'That clown said you've been friends for a long time.'

'Since the beginning of time,' added Darius.

Andradore sighed. 'We fell out just a few weeks ago. Over something so stupid,' he groaned. 'Well, he's probably told you…' Andradore looked at them expectantly.

Sammy shook his head. 'Sir Ragnarok told us everything would be fine. He gave out notices for next year.'

'At Dragamas?'

Sammy thought back. 'Well not exactly. We had our awards.'

'Sammy got a cross for bravery,' beamed Dixie.

Andradore shuddered. 'The cross for surviving untold danger.'

Dixie nodded. 'Sammy beat the Shape four times!'

421

'My, my,' Andradore whistled. 'What a surprising day. Anyhow, I plan to check on Rolaan once more, then,' he sighed, 'on with the show.'

'May we come too?' asked Dixie. 'I do love that lion as much as you. Ever since my brothers brought back the toy, the photos and the stories. Please may we meet him?'

Andradore looked keenly at them. 'Very well,' he said at last. 'But one at a time. I don't want to cause any more suffering than poor Rolaan needs. Those stupid clowns.'

Sammy, Dixie and Darius had to run to catch up with Andradore's long strides. They went through the "Circus Staff Only" door and out into a lounge area where two clowns, still fully dressed in their baggy costumes, were lying on two sofas. A young girl, no older than they were, was sprinkling drops of water on to the clowns from a sponge which she dipped into a jug of water. She looked up as they came in.

'All right Sarah?' Andradore called to the girl.

She nodded. 'Yes father. Phillipe and Borgios will be fine in a few days.'

'Ah oui,' said one of the clowns. 'L'eau de navet est magnifique.'

'Turnip water?' laughed Darius.

'You speak French?' asked Sammy.

'A bit,' said Darius. 'I had a French au pair for two years called Morgana. She taught me a few words.'

'Very interesting,' said Andradore. 'Now, may we get on, unless you think speaking French will help my lion?'

'No sir,' said Darius solemnly.

They left Sarah and the clowns behind and walked through the lounge and out of a door on the other side of the Big Top. They could hear the sound of clapping from behind the tent canvas. Sammy guessed that the performance had started. The clapping was followed by a series of boos then cheers as the show, indeed, did go on.

Sammy, Dixie and Darius followed Andradore past some of the homes of the people who worked at the circus. They lived in tiny caravans painted in bright colours, some with windows with clashing coloured curtains, greens with blues, oranges with pinks. Each horse-drawn caravan was made of wood and had a single set of tall wheels balanced with a wooden stake at either end.

'Rolaan used to pull my caravan,' said Andradore when they stopped beside a larger caravan, easily three times as big as the others.

Andradore's caravan was painted from top to bottom in a sky blue with bright yellow door and window frames. It had a large yellow "A" in the shape of a pyramid on the side. A set of wooden steps led up to the front door.

At the bottom of the steps was a large ball of golden yellow fur that raised its head at Andradore when he bent down to stroke its giant nose.

'That's my boy,' whispered Andradore. 'You'll be fine soon.' He took out his handkerchief.

Sammy looked away. He felt they shouldn't be there.

'Come on, let's go,' said Darius awkwardly.

'A good idea,' said a steely voice behind them. 'The lion does not need the attention of children.'

Andradore looked up. 'Let them stay Professor Sanchez. Do you have an answer for me from Sir Ragnarok?'

Professor Sanchez shook her head. 'No Andradore, I am sorry. It is not possible to reach him this afternoon.'

'If only I'd said I'd help him fight the Shape,' moaned Andradore, his head in his hands. 'All he asked for was a few pounds, spare change to me, but I said no. I said he could do it himself. That's why he hasn't come, to teach me a lesson.'

'Andradore, take hold of yourself,' scolded Professor Sanchez. 'Sir Ragnarok is not like that. He could not be reached.'

'I'm sure he'd be here if he could,' added Sammy.

'Just the juice of the red berries and he would be saved,' said Professor Sanchez, touching her eyes with her own ivory lace handkerchief.

'Sir,' said Sammy, an idea forming in his head. 'What does the red berry potion look like?'

Andradore sniffed. 'It's red, of course. A thick potion that tastes bitter-sweet. Why do you ask?'

'Sir,' said Sammy with a lot more confidence than he felt, 'I think I can help.'

Darius let out an explosive giggle. Professor Sanchez looked furious.

Andradore stood up straight. 'This is not a time for jokes, boy.'

'Perhaps he has a touch of the sun,' Professor Sanchez growled, her eyes trained menacingly on Sammy.

'This is no place for the likes of you,' bellowed Andradore, stamping his foot.

'This is a matter for Sir Ragnarok alone,' said Professor Sanchez.

'But I can help,' repeated Sammy. 'Please, let me try.'

'Darn it Simone,' said Andradore. 'Let the boy try. I could do with a laugh at a time like this.'

'Laughing's good for you,' started Darius, silenced by a glare from Professor Sanchez.

'Dixie,' whispered Sammy. 'Can I borrow your clippers.'

As if she was in a trance and with very wide-eyes, Dixie opened her carrier bag and pulled out the golden clippers. They were the shape of a large spanner, at least the size of a cricket bat and twice as heavy.

'Cut my arm,' instructed Sammy, his heart pounding. 'Just below my shoulder.'

Dixie closed her eyes and wielded the clippers like a pair of long handled garden shears. Standing two feet away from Sammy, she opened her eyes and extended the mouth of the clippers. Sammy rolled up his t-shirt sleeve.

Professor Sanchez looked torn between wanting to laugh and wanting to stop Dixie from using the clippers. She did neither and watched open mouthed as Dixie frowned, bit her lip and closed the clippers around Sammy's arm.

The pain hit Sammy first. The cold metal seemed to close around his arm in slow motion. The crunch as it bit through his skin, the wet feeling prickling the short hairs on his arm as blood dribbled from the wound.

'What has this achieved?' demanded Professor Sanchez. 'Now you and the lion are injured.'

Sammy stood up, his head dizzy and his legs like jelly. Braver than he felt, he knelt down by the lion's front paws.

Rolaan opened his deep black eyes. Sammy felt his heart skip another beat as he wiped the blood off his left arm with the fingers on his right hand.

Rolaan opened his mouth to yawn and let out a soft growl in the process.

As fast as lightning, Sammy pressed the blood on to Rolaan's tongue. He pulled his hand out as Rolaan's jaw closed tight.

Sammy stood up and rubbed his cut arm. He stared at Rolaan and wished the lion would do something, anything.

Rolaan yawned again.

Professor Sanchez took her hand away from her mouth. 'See, the boy can do nothing for your lion.'

Andradore frowned at Sammy. 'Thank you for trying,' he sniffed, wringing out his soggy handkerchief.

Dixie linked her arm in Sammy's. 'Let's go to Mrs Grock.'

Sammy looked down at Rolaan. 'Get up,' he said inside his head. 'I know it worked. Sir Ragnarok gave me that potion. I know it worked. You're better. Stand up. Help me show them.'

Rolaan opened his eyes. Sammy knew he had understood.

The lion lifted his head towards Andradore, a sparkle in the jet black eyes that hadn't been there a moment ago. He arched his back, kneeling, then standing. Rolaan opened his mouth and let out a breath-taking roar that sent a breeze past Sammy that made him take a step backwards to steady himself.

Screams came from behind them in the circus tent. Circus staff, including Phillipe, Borgios and Sarah came running out to see them.

Rolaan carried on roaring as if nothing could stop him. Professor Sanchez put a protective arm around Dixie and Darius.

Sammy took a step forward, holding out his hands, palms raised to the sky. Rolaan ignored him, roaring as loud as before. Sammy edged closer and it wasn't until he lay his hands on Rolaan's nose that the lion closed his mouth, ending the roar with a low "grrr".

Andradore clapped his hands. 'My assistant,' he said gleefully. 'You can be the ringmaster when I retire.'

'Uh,' started Sammy, holding on to Rolaan for support. 'Thank you sir, but I want to be a Dragon Knight, to fight the Shape.'

Andradore stared at Sammy in horror. 'To fight...the Shape?' he said in disbelief. 'But why?'

'I have to,' said Sammy. 'Mrs Grock says I have the makings of a Dragon Knight. Sir Ragnarok says it's my destiny.'

'Oh,' said Andradore, clearly taken aback. 'Well, perhaps I can offer you something else? Anything,' he added, holding his arms wide open. 'Name your price.'

Sammy scratched his head. 'Well,' he said quietly. 'There is one thing.'

'Name it,' said Andradore. 'Name it and it shall be yours.'

'Well, can I, er, may we...'

'Name it boy,' said Andradore clicking his tongue impatiently. 'Anything.'

'May we have the money for Sir Ragnarok to pay the rest of the Shape's ransom,' Sammy ran the words together in one breath.

Andradore gave a curious laugh. 'It's yours.'

Professor Sanchez came up to Sammy and grabbed his shoulders, tears streaming down her usually severe nose. Her eyes were shining and she stared straight at Sammy. 'You will be a fine Dragon Knight,' she whispered. 'A very fine Dragon Knight indeed.'

Andradore clapped Sammy on the back. 'I'll get that money down to Sir Ragnarok right away. Professor Sanchez, would your dwarves Stronghammer and Firebreath assist me.'

Professor Sanchez nodded and checked her watch. 'Go children, re-join the others. Everything will be fine.'

Quiet with the sudden lull in what had proved to be the most exciting day of the year, Sammy was glad to go back with Dixie and Darius to the glass building to take the lift back down to Dragamas.

They rode back with Captain Firebreath, Professor Sanchez and some of the last students to leave the Floating

Circus. Inside the lift were several sacks that Sammy knew held the precious coins Sir Ragnarok would be able to use to pay the ransom and save the school from the Shape.

Captain Firebreath let Sammy and Darius help carry the sacks to a wheelbarrow brought by another flame haired dwarf who could have been a close relative of the flame haired Captain Firebreath.

The dwarf touched his cap. 'Them's all talking about this one,' he growled, pointing at Sammy. 'The lion charmer, heh, heh.'

Dixie laughed too. 'Sammy's a hero.'

Darius nodded, holding up the blood stained sleeve of Sammy's t-shirt. Sammy looked down at his feet.

'Sir Ragnarok will probably want a word with you before you go home,' said Captain Firebreath. 'Us dwarves is grateful to you, keeps us in a job.'

'No one else'd have a family of fifty dwarves,' said Captain Firebreath's twin.

'A family?' asked Sammy.

'Yeah,' said Captain Firebreath's twin. 'Not by blood of course. Otherwise we'd be shy, you know, to be with her.'

'Dr Lithoman,' explained Captain Firebreath. 'She's the black sheep. The dark horse. Never quite know what she's thinking.'

Sammy nodded. 'I know,' he whispered. 'And there's something Sir Ragnarok needs to know too.'

CHAPTER 24

PUT WRONGS TO RIGHT

Sammy left Dixie and Darius to load the wheelbarrows and heave them up to the castle. He ran on ahead, through the grounds and up to the North entrance. He didn't stop running until he got to the Main Hall. He dragged open the knight tapestry and ran, puffing slightly, up the spiral stairs to Sir Ragnarok's office.

Sammy knocked on the door a little harder than he meant to and tried the handle. To his surprise, it opened and he ran up the seven stairs, calling "Sir Ragnarok, Sir Ragnarok".

At the top of the stairs, Sammy stopped in his tracks. Professor Sanchez, Professor Burlay and Dr Lithoman were standing like schoolchildren opposite Sir Ragnarok's desk.

Professor Burlay was frowning. Dr Lithoman, only tall enough to reach Professor Burlay's waist, was shaking and Professor Sanchez was rigid, holding a torn piece of brown paper in her hands. All four looked to the door as Sammy burst in.

Sir Ragnarok stood up, his eyes as dark as ever. 'I have been expecting you,' he said, smiling at Sammy. 'Please, sit down, entertain Lariston a moment. I shan't be long.'

Sammy obeyed and sat on the purple sofa and stroked Sir Ragnarok's smoke grey cat, each as alert at the other as Sir Ragnarok started to speak.

'As I was saying,' said Sir Ragnarok.

'Should the boy be here?' asked Professor Sanchez. 'We are discussing serious matters.'

'On the contrary Simone,' said Sir Ragnarok. 'You and I both know the debt this young man is owed by us all, by Dragamas but above all, by myself.'

On the sofa, Lariston sat up straight and Sammy held his breath as Sir Ragnarok went on.

'Dr Lithoman,' said Sir Ragnarok quietly. 'We both know the evidence brought before me. Professor Burlay saw you enter the lion's cage shortly before Rolaan was taken ill. Professor Sanchez has the package you carried the poison in.'

'I saw her too,' Sammy spoke up from the sofa.

Dr Lithoman spun around and gave him an icy glare.

'Quite,' said Sir Ragnarok calmly. 'Not just any poison either.'

Dr Lithoman shook harder.

'Crushed draconite,' spat Sir Ragnarok. 'Using stones you stole this year from dragons you murdered. A potion mixed with lion's blood to make you immortal and part of your plan to close Dragamas. How you arranged for me to be at the school gates, right when I am needed most in the land above.'

'No sir,' said Dr Lithoman, her bottom lip quivering. 'Those sheep were not my doing.'

'An accomplice perhaps,' spat Sir Ragnarok. 'There are after all, supposed to be five members of the Shape. Rest assured, I shall find you all Dr Lithoman, or, shall we call you by your real name, Eliza Elungwen?'

'No!' wailed Dr Lithoman, clapping her hands to her ears. 'No!'

'Yes,' thundered Sir Ragnarok. 'Had it not been for you, Sammy's life would not have been in danger and five of my dragons would still be alive.'

Dr Lithoman burst into tears. 'It's not me,' she wailed. 'I was forced into it.'

'You have committed acts of high treason,' said Sir Ragnarok in a calm but deadly efficient voice, as if he was reciting an arrest warrant. 'Acts punishable by death alone...'

'No!' Dr Lithoman screamed and ran out of the tower room.

Professor Burlay and Professor Sanchez leapt after her.

'...so justice will be served,' finished Sir Ragnarok.

'So it was Dr Lithoman,' said Sammy, standing up. 'I thought it was, but Professor Burlay said I had to get proof. How will you kill her if she is immortal?'

'A good question Sammy, but you are not yet old enough to know. There are things that go on in the dragon cells that would make my blood run cold just telling you about them. Rest assured, only the guilty will suffer.'

Sir Ragnarok clasped his hands together and smiled. 'You played your part Sammy. This was not possible without you. Your wish "put wrongs to right" on your very first day. You may never know how that meant a call to arms, to stand up to the Shape. To break them down, piece by piece.'

Sir Ragnarok paused and reached behind his desk, pulling out a silver briefcase with a golden dragon on the front. 'A Dragonball set,' he chuckled. 'I trust this will suffice.'

Sammy stared at the briefcase, a huge "thank you" burning in his throat. 'How did you know?'

Sir Ragnarok touched his lips with his forefinger. 'Some things are better left unsaid. Now with Eliza Elungwen gone, I'll need a new Gemology teacher.'

'Gone?' echoed Sammy. 'Eliza Elungwen, Dr Lithoman.'

'Exactly,' said Sir Ragnarok. 'It's a shame when the good go bad, but that's a part of life you'll meet time and again.'

'And she was part of the Shape?' asked Sammy, his mind whirling.

'I believe so.'

'The E?' asked Sammy. 'Eliza Elungwen could be the "E" in Shape?'

Sir Ragnarok looked keenly at Sammy. 'I think you may be on to something there.' He took a swig from a glass of red liquid on his desk. 'Every dwarf has a real name and an assumed name. Dr Lithoman chose hers to reflect her profession, gems, pearls, the other dwarves,' Sir Ragnarok chuckled to himself, 'keep it under your hat, but Captain Duke Stronghammer's real name is Fignus Hubar.'

'I can see why he changed it,' Sammy grinned. 'What will happen to Dr Lithoman, she won't really die, will she?'

'Perhaps a fitting punishment for the dragons she helped murder,' said Sir Ragnarok quietly. 'But no, she will go to the Snorgcadell, what we call the dragon cells, where she will be encouraged to talk to the guards about the Shape. To think they have brought terror in this region for over thirty years and all along she was under my nose.'

'Will she tell you about the others?'

'Who knows,' said Sir Ragnarok. 'Hopefully, but until then please keep your guard up. Validus Aureus Draco.'

Sammy nodded. 'Yes sir.'

'Now,' said Sir Ragnarok, shuffling papers on his desk, 'as you are aware, I have a ransom to pay.'

'But,' started Sammy.

'No buts, Sammy. A promise is a promise. If I break our end of the bargain, why should I expect them to keep theirs.'

'But with Dr Lithoman gone...'

'Small fry,' spat Sir Ragnarok. 'The bottom of the chain, the weak link. There are four others to find and stop and we play fair.'

'We will get them,' asked Sammy, 'won't we.'

'Eventually,' Sir Ragnarok smiled, 'good will prevail. Now, I understand you are staying with Dixie until your parents are back.'

Sammy nodded, following Sir Ragnarok's pointed finger. On one of the large screens monitoring the school, Mrs Deane was helping Dixie hoist five suitcases into the back of her Land Rover. Five dragons, including Kyrillan, were circling above her.

'Go,' said Sir Ragnarok. 'Enjoy the holiday. Give my regards to your parents and above all, be safe and return in September for your second year.'

Sir Ragnarok smiled and offered Sammy one of his sweets from the glass bowl on his desk. Sammy took one of the flavour-cycling purple sweets and said goodbye to Sir Ragnarok. He ran down the castle courtyard and was greeted with a huge hug from Mrs Deane.

Serberon, Mikhael and Jason hoisted him into the back of the Land Rover and they sped off down to the gates. The three large dragons belonging to Dixie's brothers flew protectively around Kyrillan and Dixie's dragon, Kiridor, as they soared higher and higher, following the car.

'Goodbye Dragamas!' yelled Sammy, waving wildly at Darius, Gavin and Toby. 'See you next year!'

Alone in his office, Sir Ragnarok reached across to his bookshelf and withdrew an old leather bound book. Followed by Lariston, he climbed the spiral stairs to his room.

'See you next year,' Sir Ragnarok nodded, closing the door behind him.

The End.

Dragon Talks

The journey writing the Sammy Rambles series has been full of ups and downs. It has been an adventure starting with a pen and a piece of paper, through to publishing and promoting the books around the world.

I've created a series of Dragon Talks and Writing Workshops to share my experiences and help inspire children in their writing. In the sessions everyone is encouraged to create their own story with memorable characters, layers of detail and inventive plots.

Dragon Talks and Writing Workshops are available for schools, libraries and clubs with tailored content suitable for children from Year 1 to Year 6 (KS1, KS2, KS3) either as a full school assembly or class sessions.

Find out more about:

- The inspiration behind Sammy Rambles, the reason for writing.
- Philosophical influences, mythology, love of words, hidden meanings within the stories.
- Writing the stories using pen and paper in every spare minute and very unusual places.
- Editing, proofreading, aiming for 95%.
- Agents, Publishers, Rejection and the route of self-publishing.
- The reason for publishing the books in quick succession.

- Promoting the stories, creating the website and Facebook page.
- Visiting fairs, events, schools, meeting the readers.
- Writing more stories in the future.

In the Dragon Talks, children are encouraged to create their own dragons and their own fabulous stories to share.

These are some of the comments following Dragon Talks in schools, libraries and clubs.

"The Canadian and British Sections were delighted to welcome JT Scott, author of the Sammy Rambles series of novels, to SHAPE International School. Over the course of two days, the children were privileged to experience a series of writing workshops designed and delivered by this celebrated British author. The two sections learned all about the grit and resilience required to get a book published; how to structure and develop a story arc; and how to utilise a rich and powerful vocabulary to engage and enchant the reader. The children were also enthused to learn a plethora of facts about everybody's favourite mythical monster: dragons! The two days were an unqualified success and packed full of exciting writing experiences. It also allowed the British and Canadian Sections the time to start developing the close relationship that will be an incredible boon of their new shared school. This was an amazing learning opportunity, and both Sections would like to extend their gratitude to JT Scott and to Common Services for making this unforgettable two days a possibility." – SHAPE International School.

"The children enjoyed creating their dragons. Some really good ideas." St. Nicholas Church of England School.

"Thanks a lot for coming in yesterday. It was lovely to meet you and thank you so much for coming to talk to the children. I know the children found it really exciting and got loads of great ideas from it." - Pelynt Academy.

"In Jenny's Sammy Rambles Dragon session boys who usually refuse to write anything spent the hour engrossed and they did not stop writing. Thanks for all the work and time you've given us. I will recommend you to our other schools! All my class were motivated and it was great to see their creative ideas." - Looe Primary School.

"Jenny came to visit our vibrant Year 4 class of 37 pupils and had them truly engaged with her stories. It was thoroughly enjoyable to have Jenny share her writing tips and enthrall our students with extracts from the books. The children relished the chance to write their own dragon stories, based on the adventures portrayed in Sammy Rambles and now they can't stop talking about dragons! Thanks Jenny, please come again." - Elmhurst Junior School.

"Thank you so much for coming over, sharing your work and inspiring our children. I know the visit was a huge success from our point of view and both children and staff, from both the British and Canadian Schools, loved the experience." – Acting Head, SHAPE International School.

Dragonball

Dragonball is the sport played by Sammy Rambles and his friends in the Sammy Rambles books.

It's a hybrid of football, netball and rugby where players use their hands or feet to kick, throw and pass the seven Dragonballs to score goals and the team with the most Dragonballs in the opposition goal wins.

Although in the books Dragonball is played whilst riding on a dragon the ethos of Dragonball translates into real life and Dragonball is a tactical game for social and competitive teamwork, fitness and entertainment.

Dragonball is a sport anyone can play. It's for all ages and all abilities. There's no "you're not good enough", "you can't play", "we don't want you on our team".

It's all inclusive and a great way for children and adults to keep active, fit and healthy, to make friends and work together to score goals and win games.

For more information or to book a Dragonball game or tournament, please visit www.dragonball.uk.com.

These are some of the comments from recent Dragonball taster sessions, sports lessons and tournaments.

"We are thrilled to be endorsing, promoting and delivering Dragonball as one of our inclusive sport options in The South West." - Sports Way Management.

"I think it's a really good game. Everyone is running about. It doesn't matter if it's crowded, there's loads of space and everyone's around the balls." – Oliver, Dragonball Player

"Your visit was brilliant, thank you so much for inspiring our pupils. Just to let you know that our KS2 children have all been playing Dragonball this morning courtesy of our Sports Coach! It has been great fun!" - Headteacher, All Saints CE VC Primary School, Dorset.

www.dragonball.uk.com

Dragon Shop

You'll find lots of exciting things in the Sammy Rambles Dragon Shop and also in the Dragonball Shop.

Sammy Rambles Books / Audiobook
Sammy Rambles and the Floating Circus
Sammy Rambles and the Land of the Pharaohs
Sammy Rambles and the Angel of 'El Horidore
Sammy Rambles and the Fires of Karmandor
Sammy Rambles and the Knights of the Stone Cross

Sammy Rambles Kyrillan Soft Toy
Sammy Rambles Fridge Magnet
Sammy Rambles Keyring
Sammy Rambles Standard Mug
Sammy Rambles Colour Changing Mug
Sammy Rambles T-shirt
Sammy Rambles Hoodie

Dragonball Fridge Magnet
Dragonball Keyring
Dragonball Standard Mug
Dragonball Colour Changing Mug
Dragonball Kit
Dragonball T-shirt
Dragonball Polo
Dragonball Hoodie

Dragonball Equipment and Coaching Workpack

www.sammyrambles.com | www.dragonball.uk.com

Sammy Rambles and the Floating Circus

J T SCOTT

Sammy Rambles is given a dragon egg on his first day at his new school. The egg hatches into a dragon called Kyrillan and Sammy learns to look after his new pet.

He makes new friends, a girl with bright green hair called Dixie Deane and Darius Murphy, a boy with unusual parents. Things are going well for Sammy Rambles, until he learns of a dark fate hanging over the school.

An enemy, known only as the Shape, wants to destroy all of the dragons and close the school. It is up to Sammy Rambles and his friends to try and stop this from happening.

www.sammyrambles.com

Sammy Rambles and the Land of the Pharaohs

J T SCOTT

Sammy Rambles is keen to return to the Dragamas School for Dragon Charming for his second year with his friends Dixie Deane and Darius Murphy. There are new lessons, new teachers and new skills to be learnt.

On the school trip to the Land of the Pharaohs, Sammy learns his parents once knew about dragons but cannot see them any more. He finds out about the Stone Cross and discovers the enemy, known only as the Shape is trying to rebuild it.

When the fifth years' dragons are poisoned, Sammy has no choice but to find out more about the Shape and uncover why the Stone Cross is so important.

www.sammyrambles.com

Sammy Rambles and the Angel of 'El Horidore

J T SCOTT

A wedding gift from King Serberon to his future Queen, the Angel of 'El Horidore is an ancient whistle used for calling dragons. With one single blast, the whistle will call all of the dragons in the world together.

The Shape want to find the whistle and use it to kill the dragons, steal their draconite, rebuild the Stone Cross and obtain the powers of immortality and invincibility.

Sir Ragnarok cannot let this happen. He is sure the Angel of 'El Horidore is hidden near Dragamas and sets a task for his students to find it so he can protect it from the Shape. Sammy Rambles and his friends Dixie Deane and Darius Murphy embark on their most serious quest so far.

www.sammyrambles.com

Sammy Rambles and the Fires of Karmandor

J T SCOTT

Tying the past and the present together, Sammy Rambles needs to find his best friend and uncover the link to the ancient Queen Karmandor.

He must use all his skills and attempt a daring rescue, whilst staying on top of his schoolwork. As the legend of Karmandor comes true, it begins the systematic destruction of everything Sammy Rambles cares about in the Dragon World.

He finds himself yet again in the hands of the Shape and almost powerless to do anything about it.

www.sammyrambles.com

Sammy Rambles
and the
Knights of the Stone Cross

J T SCOTT

Bringing everyone together one last time, Sammy's final year at the Dragamas School for Dragon Charming sees him fight his fiercest battle yet.

Can he find the last member of the Shape?

Can he free Karmandor?

Will he escape with his life?

www.sammyrambles.com

40777865R00251

Printed in Poland
by Amazon Fulfillment
Poland Sp. z o.o., Wrocław